Shades of Pemberley

Shades of Pemberley

SHELLY E. POWELL

SWEETWATER BOOKS
An imprint of Cedar Fort, Inc.
Springville, Utah

ISBN 13: 978-1-4621-4308-5

Published by CFI, an imprint of Cedar Fort, Inc.
2373 W. 700 S., Suite 100, Springville, UT 84663
Distributed by Cedar Fort, Inc., www.cedarfort.com

Library of Congress Control Number: 2022941365

Cover design by Shawnda T. Craig
Cover design © 2022 Cedar Fort, Inc.
Substantive by Rachel Hathcock
Edited and typeset by Valene Wood

Printed in the United States of America

10 9 8 7 6 5 4 3 2 1

Printed on acid-free paper

Dedication

Dedicated to mothers and daughters everywhere, but especially to my own mom who, for the record, is and always has been amazing.

Author's Note

It is extremely intimidating to write a book that follows the lives of Jane Austen's beloved characters. I know that my style of writing is obviously different from Jane Austen's, but I would hope she would take it as a compliment that I was intrigued enough by Lydia's character to write this continuation.

I'd also like to make a brief note about Lydia's age. While movies and much of the discussion on the internet lead us to believe that Lydia was married at age 15, the book makes it clear that she was 16 by the time she married George Wickham. In Chapter 49 of *Pride and Prejudice,* Mrs. Bennet exclaims, "She will be married at sixteen!" Several sentences later in the same chapter, Mrs. Bennet declares, "And she was only sixteen last June." So, that is the fact I have stuck with for this book.

I hope readers will recognize my efforts to stay true to the original characters as much as possible, and I earnestly hope that fans of Jane Austen and Regency romance will enjoy what I have created here. Happy reading!

Prologue

The distance is nothing when one has a motive.

Jane Austen, *Pride and Prejudice*

*I*n the still of night, Captain Styles regarded the moon, that tiny almond sliver in the sky that shone on *her* regardless of whether he knew where she was.

They're right to think I'm mad, he thought.

Though he had long since given up hope of ever seeing his wife again, the moon's light had been a small comfort over the years. If he and his beloved did not share the life he had once hoped for, they at least shared the light.

He ran a callused hand across his sweat-dampened brow and mourned for years either lost at sea or hidden here in the outskirts of Pemberley's shadows. No one but Darcy knew he had returned to the little cottage he had once called home. The fewer people aware of his presence, the better.

With a bracing breath, he leaned into the planked wooden door and forced it to slide over the warped sill of the frame. A rush of dank air filled his nostrils, evidence the cottage had sat empty for some time. *Pity,* he thought. It could have been a delightful place for a small

1

family or young couple, especially if the garden was well tended and the roses in bloom, but in the darkness, such charm was lost.

He raised his lantern, its flame quivering, and inched his way in, grateful, at least, that no one would see him cower at the ghosts he called memories. The light cast stark shadows across every angle. A glance around revealed the same sash windows he had gazed through in years past, the same wall to ceiling shelves his books had once rested upon, and the same crooked staircase he had tromped over countless times. Even in the dark, the smallest sight of them brought to mind the day he had carried his bride up those stairs. In the faint whistle of the outside breeze, he could almost hear their laughter and whispered endearments rising from his memories.

No matter how many years passed, he would never forget the day he had kissed his wife goodbye.

He shook his head. Remembering only tugged at a wound still struggling to heal. Why had he come at all if it was so painful?

Pain comes before healing, he reminded himself, *first pain, then healing.*

For one fleeting moment, he was tempted to explore the entire cottage and accept those ghosts of years gone by as his company that night, but he decided against it. He had come with a purpose, and reminiscing was not part of it. There remained a personal treasure tucked beneath stone, and he had come to add to it. His more rational side reminded him the treasure was best left undisturbed, but how could he ignore it? He needed to leave one last evidence of his love as much as his wife needed to find it, if ever she returned.

Yes, they're right to think I'm mad.

Without wasting time further, he knelt by the fireplace and ran his fingers between the same grey hearthstones he and his beloved had once knelt at together, now cool and gritty where there had once been heat.

As expected, the stone on the far left lifted with effort, revealing a space carved from the earth that guarded a cylindrical, metal capsule. Reaching down, he uncapped the cylinder and confirmed its contents. Unfortunately, all was exactly as he'd left it. With one final contribution to make, he pulled a paper from his waistcoat, rolled it tightly enough to fit inside the capsule, and made himself a promise.

This is the last time. Then comes healing.

Chapter 1

*The more I see of the world, the
more am I dissatisfied with it.*

Jane Austen, *Pride and Prejudice*

*K*elsey Wickham slumped onto the chaise by the window of
the bare little cottage of Whitewell and slammed her book
shut. *A rose by any other name . . . Rubbish!* If people suddenly decided
to call a rose a 'Wickham,' she was certain it would be the most
scorned flower in the garden, no matter how sweet its scent.

She flicked a tear from the corner of her eye as quickly as it had
appeared and blinked several times before any more followed. There
wasn't a person she had yet met whose respect for her didn't dimin-
ish after learning she was a Wickham. Everyone had either heard the
rumors about her parents or had observed enough to make their own
conclusions. It was a heavy enough burden for any young lady to bear,
but there was more.

Her mother had insisted on bestowing her with a name both
unique and full of meaning. Kelsey's name was certainly that. Rather
than a simple, dignified name like Emma or Anne, she was given the

name of Kelsey, after the little village in Lincolnshire where her mother had realized she was expecting. Her parents couldn't have been married long. Now, more than eighteen years later, Kelsey wondered what new rumors would arise if her mother remarried.

Her infamously beautiful mother, Lydia Wickham, currently sat behind closed doors with her latest suitor, Mr. Phineas, expecting a proposal that very minute, and Kelsey was fervently hoping against it. The man might have been a gentleman by birth, but he was just as brainless as he was untrustworthy. Why her mother wasn't more bothered by this, Kelsey couldn't understand.

One thing she did know. Scandal was a certainty when one carried the name of Wickham.

Kelsey turned toward her friend, Sarah, who sat on the sofa across from her. "If that man does not make my mother an offer of marriage today, I doubt you and I will be neighbors much longer." She drummed her fingers on the windowsill, ignoring the pang of regret that arose from not having had sufficient time to become better friends with Sarah. "Either way, my life is ruined."

Sarah's eyes flitted to Kelsey's before returning to her needle and thread. Of course, Sarah didn't understand. No one ever did. No one ever expected a widow with two daughters to behave as Mrs. Wickham did. Though Kelsey was all too familiar with her mother's habits, they grew harder to bear with each passing rumor. She was entirely exhausted with the way her life teetered on the point of ruin whenever her mother fluctuated between love and mortification, but what could Kelsey do? It had simply become a fact, a circumstance to live with like the tea stain on the cushion.

When a particularly noisy fly sped past her head, Kelsey shooed it away, tossed her book aside, and pressed her ear to the door.

"Blast! All I hear are muffles."

"Such language, Kelsey."

As Sarah tsked, Kelsey sauntered away as if cursing and listening at the door were innocent pastimes. She returned to the chaise and gazed out the window of the cottage she had called home for the past ten months. The rolling hills, which she fondly called mountains, were the tallest mounds of earth she had ever seen. They were the first feature she had noticed when she and her mother and younger sister, Cecilia —usually shortened to Cissy— had relocated to Whitewell.

Was that after Mr. Bronstone had broken her mother's heart, or after Mr. Dawson had? Kelsey no longer kept track.

For as long as she could remember, her life had been like those hills outside her window, rising and falling with every sort of weed and wildflower hiding in its crevices. Even before her father died, there was never any place to truly call home, but she always maintained hope that her mother's lust for wandering would one day bring them back to Pemberley.

Though nothing was certain yet, Kelsey knew another move was looming. She had already written to her dearest cousin and friend, Lucia Darcy, about it. Kelsey's mother was sure to write to the Darcys to beg for pounds, but what Kelsey wanted most was the chance to be with her cousin again, her one steady friend through all the chaos. Though their times together had been short and spaced through the years, she and Lucia had managed to maintain a consistent correspondence, no matter where Kelsey lived, no matter the distance.

"I wonder where I'll be next month," Kelsey sighed to herself, not daring to utter her hope aloud. If she could somehow be reunited with Lucia, she thought she might find the strength to build a respectable life for herself.

Down a small slope by a tree, she spotted Cissy through the window following a ginger cat that appeared to be stalking some poor creature in the grass. At age thirteen, Cissy straddled the line between girlhood and womanhood, completely innocent, yet too informed for her own good.

Kelsey ran her thumb over the windowpane to remove a smudge of dirt that obstructed her view, but her efforts only spread it. *How can I do it all?* she wondered. *How can I give Cissy the guidance I never had?*

The arched clock on the mantle ticked away the minutes, and still, the door to the small parlor remained closed.

"What do you mean, Kelsey?" Sarah asked. "Why should you wonder where you will be next month?"

Kelsey considered how to explain. "Mr. Phineas has been calling on my mother for the past two months, but I hear he has also been visiting Miss Bowens quite frequently." Kelsey stood to pace. "Mother is convinced Mr. Phineas is in love with her. I, however, am convinced his feelings run no deeper than a potato's."

"Kelsey!" Though Sarah gave a disapproving glare, Kelsey didn't miss the way she bit back a smile.

"As soon as my mother catches the slightest hint that he has no intention of marrying her, she will be instantly offended and unable to abide his presence ever again. She will then make arrangements to relocate our family to some corner of the country where the men are new and the townsfolk are hopefully ignorant of her reputation."

Sarah scrunched her face. "I don't understand. Why would that be reason to leave? I don't mean to pry, but can she reasonably shoulder the expense of moving again?"

"That is a fair question, indeed." Kelsey had a much keener understanding of her mother's expenses than she usually let on, mainly because she was the one who, ever since the death of her father, assumed the responsibility of managing the books and keeping their family from becoming destitute.

Kelsey mindlessly walked to the writing desk in the corner of the room and checked whether there was sufficient ink and paper to compose another letter to Lucia once Kelsey's mother finished talking with Mr. Phineas.

"I can't believe your mother would be so hasty." Sarah carefully rethreaded her needle. "It feels as though you have only just settled into society here. Surely, there will be other men to interest her, and you will stay."

"That is my hope, Sarah. We can certainly hope."

Kelsey circled the room, sat on the chaise, then stood and circled the room again. She would miss Sarah. Despite her overly cautious ways and delicate constitution, Sarah Pendlestone had been one of the few girls in the village willing to befriend Kelsey once the rumors had started circulating about her mother.

Lydia Wickham? That ridiculous woman? The widow who shamelessly flirts? The one who always makes such a spectacle of herself?

Married at sixteen, Lydia had been the first, though youngest, of her sisters to marry, a fact she still discussed with pride, but Kelsey doubted her mother had cause to be so proud. Kelsey had been born a mere eight months later, and no one needed to explain to her why. She had often endured the stories whispered in sitting rooms, around card tables, and at balls, but never had she heard them from her own mother. Truthfully, even if Kelsey had, she wouldn't know who was more credible, her mother or the gossips. So, she preferred not to ask.

"Have you considered," Sarah yanked on her needle, "that you might be able to stay if you made a match of your own? Perhaps if you gave Mr. Jenkins some encouragement?"

Kelsey scoffed. "If that is the cost of staying, it is much too high."

Sarah shrugged and rhythmically pushed and pulled her needle through her fabric once more. Mr. Jenkins had shown interest in Kelsey, but he had also shown interest in every other kind of deplorable behavior, giving him an unfortunate resemblance to her father.

Kelsey's mind went back to six years ago when a message arrived from the constable informing her family that her father had been killed. The constable wasn't entirely certain what had happened, only that Mr. Wickham reeked of liquor and exhibited a severe head injury. Cissy had been too young to understand everything the constable said, but Kelsey remembered the way Cissy had clung to her, sobbing alongside her and their mother as they all held each other.

It was after the funeral, after seeing her mother squander what little money they had left on extravagant mourning dresses of crepe and silk that Kelsey insisted on viewing the bills and notes and began to teach herself how to make sense of it all. If she didn't, who would?

Over the years, Kelsey's understanding of what might have caused her father's death grew, casting shadows over everything she knew about him. As rumors surfaced, she learned to interpret her memories of him in terms of late-night revelries, mounting gambling debts, and offended friends. She had loved her father, but never would she tolerate such reckless habits in a spouse. Never, and since Kelsey remained unconvinced that men without such vices existed, she was certain she would never be enticed to marry.

She wasn't against the idea of her mother remarrying, however, especially if it would add to her happiness, but Kelsey did not want to be bogged down with a fool of a stepfather. Unfortunately, that was precisely the kind of man her mother always attracted. With no money to her name and a shaky reputation that yipped at her heels, what else could she expect? If only her mother waited before entertaining the idea of marrying each dolt that came courting.

The door to the parlor snapped open suddenly, making Kelsey jump as it rattled against the wall.

Her mother stormed through, rosy with anger. "You can show yourself out!" Sweeping past the girls, she exclaimed, "Kelsey, please see that Mr. Phineas makes a swift departure!" Seconds later, a door slammed upstairs and shook the house.

Sarah's eyes grew large as Kelsey pinched the top of her nose and searched within for strength to go through the motions once more. Seeing no reason to delay, she walked into the other room to carry out her mother's request.

Mr. Phineas, hardly meeting her eye, lifted his grey felt hat off the table and put it down again. There was no need to make conversation. Kelsey simply opened the door and waited for him to leave. With mouth agape, he stared at her before finally placing his hat on his head.

"Good day, Mr. Phineas," she said blandly.

He lingered at the door and removed his hat once again. Dusting the top, he spun it around his finger. "I don't know why she's so upset. It's not as though a man can help fancying different women at the same time. Doesn't mean I don't still like your mum."

Kelsey hated this part. It had happened before. The man didn't get the chance to have his final word because her mother stormed out too soon. So, he tried to say his final words to Kelsey. She had long ago given up trying to formulate a cohesive response.

"Good day," she repeated firmly.

"I haven't made any decisions yet. Your mother is pleasant. I may not be in the business of marriage just yet, but I don't see why she and I couldn't still—"

"Good day!" Kelsey nudged him out the door, pushing on his arm. Fortunately, he yielded. With the door secured and bolted, she heaved a sigh that ended in a grumble. Would she never be free of such burdens? She knew it was improper of her to push him out like that, but it was improper for her mother to expect her to deal with him alone.

"What's going on?" Cissy wandered in from the back door with stray bits of grass clinging to her skirts. In looks, she was a miniature version of their mother with blooming cheeks and jaunty brown curls.

Kelsey possessed her mother's well-shaped cheekbones and slim nose, but there was a great deal more of her father in her, his easy smile, his round green eyes, and the sort of hazelnut hair that could trick the beholder into thinking it a rich honey in the sunlight.

"It's time to move again," Kelsey mumbled as she straightened herself and walked to the other room, wondering whether her looks had anything to do with why her mother always preferred Cissy.

Sarah rose from her seat. "Perhaps I had best leave you for the time being." She gathered her needlework and placed it in the dainty basket she had brought. Kelsey had momentarily forgotten Sarah was still there witnessing everything. "Goodbye, Kelsey." Sarah gave a quick glance and small curtsey.

"Goodbye, Sarah." Kelsey returned the curtsey, knowing full well it was their final farewell.

Chapter 2

They were always moving from place to place in quest of a cheap situation, and always spending more than they ought.

Jane Austen, *Pride and Prejudice*

The light rain of the morning was already easing as thin shafts of sunlight cut through the clouds. The faint scent of horses mingled with the sweetness of the wet barley fields outside. Kelsey leaned back in the carriage across from her mother and sister and silently added the expenses of the past three days. Traveling from Whitewell to Lambton had required two nights at crowded inns as well as fees for the carriage and hired men, not to mention the meals they had paid for along the way.

The increasing numbers were giving Kelsey a headache, but at least the Darcys had been kind enough to dispatch one of their own carriages to meet them for this last stretch of the journey.

"It was clever of me to order those extra sheets before we left," Mrs. Wickham commented. "Someone really must talk to the innkeeper about the cleanliness of the rooms. Oh, dear!" She looked out the window, though the inn was already miles behind them, and shook her head. "I do believe I forgot to pack the sheets this morning."

New sheets. Easily purchased and easily lost. Kelsey rubbed her temple and subtracted the cost from their small savings. She did her best not to complain, however, knowing Lucia must have used all her influence to convince her father to allow the perfidious Wickhams a place on their land. Just as it had cost Kelsey's mother all her desperation to accept such a charitable offer, it must have cost Mr. Darcy a fair dose of pride.

Little choice her mother had, though. She had already exhausted the charity of their other relatives. Even Kelsey's grandmother, who was always glad to see them, had nothing to spare since the passing of her husband. For the past two years, she had roamed nearly as much as the Wickhams, alternating her time between her daughters and other relatives.

Cissy squirmed in her seat until she let out an exasperated sigh and folded her arms. "I still can't believe we had to leave Whitewell before Jack Pendlestone's Dalmatian had her puppies. Oh! Wouldn't a tiny Dalmatian be the sweetest thing?"

Kelsey mustered a smile but didn't have the heart to agree. Time and food for a dog was not theirs to spare nor hers to provide.

"I dare say, Caroline Pendlestone was happy to finally be rid of us." Mrs. Wickham smoothed back her hair before shifting in her seat. "She only tolerated us as a favor to your Aunt Jane. Oh, I wish we could have stayed with Jane again."

"You recall what Uncle Bingley said last time we stayed with them." Though it had been three years, Kelsey could still hear the hesitant but unapologetic way her uncle had suggested Mrs. Wickham honor her other relations with her presence for the time being, especially since Jane had recently given birth. Kelsey understood. Her aunt and uncle wanted to enjoy the little miracle that had finally come to their home after fruitless years of hoping to fill their empty nursery. The least Kelsey's mother could have done was leave without putting up a fuss.

"Kelsey, dear, when we arrive, I want your help hiring a servant girl as soon as we can."

Kelsey closed her eyes and took a deep breath. "I've shown you the ledgers. Nothing has changed. There isn't enough." Her mother protested with her eyes, but the fact remained. They would have to complete the household chores themselves.

Sunlight began to flicker through denser clusters of trees now that they had left behind the barley fields, a sign they were getting closer. To pass the final hour before they arrived, Kelsey's mother pulled out a sewing box that smelled faintly of lavender and contained scraps of ribbon, lace, thread, and silk flowers. Before leaving Whitewell, Mrs. Wickham had insisted she needed a new bonnet to wear before the proud folk of Pemberley, but Kelsey had maintained that their funds did not allow for it. Rather than relent completely, Mrs. Wickham brought an old straw bonnet, which she now held, and was using every trick she possessed to make it over. By the end of the carriage ride, Kelsey had to admit, it was a very pretty hat.

"I shouldn't wonder if Lizzy is quite envious when she sees this, even if she does have so many."

"I doubt we will be seeing much of the Darcys," Kelsey mumbled. "Except for Lucia. She'll visit us, I'm certain, but our younger cousins will be receiving the finest education at the hand of the best governess while their parents run their massive estate and entertain families much finer than ours."

Mrs. Wickham showed no signs of hearing Kelsey's speech as she put on her remade bonnet and tested various lengths of ribbon to tie it with. She finished adjusting it just as the carriage turned down a small lane shaded by leafy ash trees on each side. After a short way down the lane, the carriage pulled up the gravel path that led to their new home.

Kelsey stepped out of the carriage first, took one look at the cottage, and promised never to overestimate the generosity of the Darcys again. The walls were a dingy grey, and several roof shingles were missing. The garden was overgrown with weeds, giving the air a bitter scent, and Kelsey could swear the entire left side of the house had sunk several inches lower into the ground than the right side.

"Is this it?" asked Cissy, scrunching her nose as she stepped out and shooed away a bee.

When Mrs. Wickham saw the cottage, she dropped her reticule and lost her smile, making Kelsey fix hers all the more tightly on her lips.

"If you tilt your head and compare it to that ghastly place we stayed at in Bransford, it's really not that dreadful. And imagine how lovely it will look when the roses start blooming." Kelsey pointed to the unruly bushes beneath the windows and hoped she correctly identified them. They held an abundance of green leaves and thorns but not a single bud.

Just as the Wickham ladies were beginning to puzzle over what to do next, an elderly, rather dignified woman came walking from the side of the house.

"Welcome to Barley Cottage. It certainly has been many years, hasn't it?" She dipped into an easy curtsey despite her wealth of years. "As you may recall, Mrs. Wickham, I'm Mrs. Reynolds, the housekeeper at Pemberley. I remember Miss Kelsey when she was a wee thing running rampant with Miss Lucia Darcy, but I don't believe I've ever seen your youngest."

Mrs. Wickham gestured to her daughters. "Well, you see how Kelsey has grown, and this is Cissy."

"Cecilia." Cissy straightened her back before dipping into a quick curtsey.

Mrs. Wickham glanced at the surrounding land. "Pray, where is my sister?"

Mrs. Reynolds's smile slackened. "Mrs. Darcy and her daughter wished me to convey their regrets at not being able to welcome you themselves. Urgent matters arose only days ago that required their hasty departure. I'm afraid I don't know the details of the emergency or how long they'll be gone, but I'm sure they'll pay you a visit as soon as they are able. What with the Darcys' younger boys already visiting their Aunt Georgiana, Pemberley has become rather quiet. I do hope they return soon. Your sister left this note for you, Mrs. Wickham." She handed Kelsey's mother a letter. "And your cousin left this for you, Miss Wickham." She handed Kelsey a similar letter, then took her by the hand. "Why, my dear, you look a great deal like your father. I knew him when he was a boy, you see."

"Yes, thank you." Kelsey wasn't sure whether to be flattered or embarrassed. Her mother had often hinted at the existence of various grudges the Darcys held against her father. Though the exact reasons and details were a mystery to Kelsey, she never doubted her father had done something to warrant their displeasure. Despite Mrs. Reynolds's politeness, Kelsey assumed the grudges at least partly explained why the Darcys were not there to greet them. Surely, the letter from Lucia, dry in Kelsey's hand, would contain a more thorough explanation, but Kelsey would wait for a private moment before reading it.

"My, what a lovely bonnet." Mrs. Reynolds tilted her head as she appraised Mrs. Wickham's handiwork, then pulled a key from her reticule. "The key sticks in the back door, I'm afraid, but a little jiggling should do the trick. Now, if you will follow me, and ah, here we are." She indicated their carriage driver who was trudging up the path with a large trunk balanced in his arms. "We'll let Mr. Hall carry your things inside while I show you around."

Kelsey doubted they would need help finding their way. The cottage looked very small, but as it turned out, they did need Mrs. Reynolds's help. Otherwise, they might never have gotten inside. The key worked perfectly well, but the door itself needed extra pushing and lifting at the handle to guide it over a warped lip of wood in the sill of the door frame.

Stepping inside, however, was like stepping into a daydream. Sunlight bathed the whitewashed walls in the entryway which contrasted with the dark wooden floors like cream against chocolate. Rising before Kelsey was a welcoming staircase of matching wood, and to her right, a sitting room where a blue sofa and two wooden chairs sat before a lit fireplace as if waiting for comfortable conversation. Beside each chair was a small table with a vase of fragrant violets and bluebells that hinted of what the outside garden could produce if well-tended.

After a brief tour, they discovered the house also boasted of a modest dining area, three tiny bedrooms upstairs, and a bare kitchen containing the essentials. It was a far cry from perfect, but Kelsey felt its potential sprouting in her thoughts. Looking around, she was eager to point out anything and everything nice.

"See, Mother, how this sitting room has more shelf space than our cottage at Whitewell? And an extra window. What a lovely carpet in the landing here. I can hardly tell the floor slopes." The promise of home was real, especially knowing Lucia would be nearby. *As soon as she returns*, Kelsey thought with a thickness in her throat. *But never mind that. This will all work wonderfully. At the very least, it must work.*

On their way downstairs, Mrs. Reynolds said, "I've left some baskets of food in the kitchen, just a few cuts of meat and vegetables, and there's two loaves of freshly baked bread. Mr. and Mrs. Darcy have also given permission to send one of our maids once a week to help with the wash."

"Thank you," Kelsey said. "That is very generous." Such help would greatly alleviate her household burdens.

"We're so pleased you've come." Mrs. Reynolds clasped her hands and smiled. "The cottage garden has needed tending for some time."

"Indeed." Mrs. Wickham glanced around.

"Oh, yes, the cottage has been vacant for much too long, which is most unfortunate. It has long been a favorite of Miss Darcy's, you see."

Mrs. Wickham's hum of acknowledgment was barely audible as she plucked off a browning leaf from a flower in one of the vases and spun it between her thumb and forefinger.

Mrs. Reynolds directed them through the kitchen where a large wash basin sat next to a brick inglenook fireplace. Kelsey glanced at copper pots, spoons, ladles, and tongs hanging nearby for easy access. A hint of bread and something savory wafted as she passed the baskets on the table and followed Mrs. Reynolds out the back door.

Except for a partially crumbled stone wall at the farthest end, the garden was fenced off with rough wood that might have once been painted white but was grey with peeling paint. Weeds and overgrown grass were everywhere, and a thin trail of morning glory wound its way up the clothing lines that hung between two large birch trees.

Kelsey, her mother, and Cissy followed Mrs. Reynolds down an overgrown path. "Mind your step. There are loose pebbles everywhere."

They passed a stone well that provided water, then made their way through grass and more morning glory to a leaning shed built into the corner of the fence where the wood met stone.

"Inside you'll find all the tools you'll need, but do let me or Mr. Hall know if there is anything else you require. I'll give you a chance to settle in now." With that, the old housekeeper dipped her head and walked around the side of the cottage toward the Pemberley carriage they had arrived in.

Mrs. Wickham stared as if she had just been slapped. "Excuse me," she called, chasing after Mrs. Reynolds. "Did you say tools?"

Mrs. Reynolds turned around. "Why, yes. You'll need them to tend the garden unless you brought your own."

Both ladies now looked at one another with varying degrees of confusion. Mrs. Reynolds shook her head and laughed. "Forgive me! I fear I'm becoming forgetful in my old age. Of course, you'll need this." She pulled out another key and placed it in Mrs. Wickham's hand. "To open the shed. I imagine the first thing you'll want to do is clear the weeds around the paths and vegetable beds. It's a bit late in the season for planting, but there should be a reserve of seeds somewhere in that shed, and I do believe there might be some onions and potatoes growing under all this overgrowth. Of course, there is no need to rush. The garden can wait a few more days while you settle in. Good day to you."

Mrs. Wickham continued to stare blankly as Mrs. Reynolds climbed into the carriage. "Weeds?" she mumbled, turning the key over in her hand. "Kelsey, you said nothing about tending the gardens."

Kelsey looked away from the enormous thistles thriving beneath one of the cottage windows. "Lucia mentioned it in her letter. It was one of the conditions of our being permitted to stay here without paying."

"I don't recall it."

"She clearly included it, so please don't look at me like that. I can't help it if you choose to ignore inconvenient details."

"I don't know how to tend a garden!" Her mother crinkled her nose in disgust. "I should hate to be caught kneeling in dirt."

Cissy bounced on her heels. "I don't mind. I'll help. I want to plant a mango tree like the one in my book. Do mangos grow in England? No, never mind. Maybe we'll find something valuable buried back here. Didn't you say the Darcys have money pouring out their ears? Perhaps some of it fell under those weeds," she giggled.

"Oh, hush." Mrs. Wickham pinched her lips and shook her head. "That Mr. Darcy! I should have known he might expect us to work like servants. Spiteful man. Always was jealous of your father." She glanced at her fingernails before a mischievous smile rose to her lips. "Of course, there will still be balls and dinners to attend soon with new men to meet. We can make this work." She danced back to the cottage door and, after a bit of pushing to get it open, went inside, leaving the door ajar.

"Do you think there will be many young men my age?" Cissy tugged on Kelsey's arm, her eyes full of eagerness. "Or perhaps a bit older." She winked before picking one of many dandelions along the path.

Kelsey opened her mouth, but no response left her lips. Cissy was careening into womanhood at a steady gallop and was sounding more like their mother every day.

"Kelsey!" Their mother's voice echoed from inside the cottage. "Can you help me search these trunks for my cream-colored ball gown? I want to be ready the moment we get an invitation!"

"I'll go help her," Cissy said. "I want to find my gowns too." After picking one more dandelion, she skipped inside.

Alone in the garden, Kelsey took several slow breaths. *Mother is only looking for her ball gown. No harm in that, nothing scandalous or improper.* Yet, Kelsey felt the hollowness of her attempts to reassure herself. Why deny the truth? Her mother was preparing to spring into her usual attempts to flirt and find a man at the first opportunity.

I must make this work anyway! This must work!

She picked a dandelion with an especially tall stem and spun it in her fingers. *Dent de lion,* she thought. Lion's Tooth. *A fearsome name for a tiny flower.* Though usually regarded as a weed, Kelsey knew its worth. Every bit of that flower was edible, down to its very root, and she would make use of it all. True, she would want to keep them out of the vegetable beds and off the path, but that tiny flower would help feed her family and attract bees to pollinate the garden.

There is good to be found, even among weeds.

A faint, cheerful whistling interrupted her thoughts. She recognized a popular tune often played in ballrooms. Turning toward the road where the sound was coming from, she saw a tall, young gentleman in a fine grey coat strolling along with a leather satchel slung over his shoulder. He paused near the juncture that, should he turn right, would lead him up the path to Barley Cottage. Reaching into his satchel, he pulled out a bright red apple. Kelsey watched him rub it on his sleeve, then turn it around as if inspecting it.

She hadn't meant to stare. She had seen plenty of men move with a similar confidence, but there was something about him she didn't understand, something in his face or stance that held her attention even when her rational mind told her to look away.

A bird above her trilled, and a twig snapped under foot, making her jump. The gentleman turned toward the sound and instantly found her eye. In that moment, the world around her held its breath. Or had only she stopped breathing? Something deep within Kelsey awakened and stretched like a foal on new legs. She couldn't explain what it was, only that nothing so pleasant, yet terrifying, had ever shaken her insides like that before. Even from a distance, as the wave subsided, she could see a smile widen across his lips, and her cheeks flared.

He glanced between her and the apple still in his hand. Did he guess they were her favorite? He tossed it straight up, easily caught it, and with a wink at Kelsey, placed it on the fence post. He tipped his hat at her and continued on his way, whistling an even livelier tune.

Kelsey turned away and held her cheeks, willing them to cool. What was she thinking, staring like that? As soon as she had perceived the slightest hint he was aware of her, she should have walked away. It's what she normally would have done. Any man who looked that satisfied with himself was not to be trusted.

Trustworthy or not, however, he had left a perfectly good apple, and Kelsey was not one to waste food. Once he was out of sight, she walked down the path to the fence and took the fruit. Upon closer inspection, she saw shades of yellow merging into red, creating the impression of a gentle glow. She gave the apple a toss just as the gentleman had done and brought it to her lips. As her teeth broke the smooth skin, the crisp flesh released a stream of juice in her mouth made all the sweeter for its time in the sun.

How unfortunate, she thought, *that men are not as innocent as apples.*

Returning to the cottage, Kelsey breathed deeply and looked around the garden. Everything was a mess, to be sure, but somewhere under all those brambles were flowers waiting to bloom and a green, earthy smell that dared her to make a home of it all.

Chapter 3

You must learn some of my philosophy. Think only
of the past as its remembrance gives you pleasure.

Jane Austen, *Pride and Prejudice*

*K*elsey spread out on the quilted bed, thrilled to have a room
to herself for the first time in ages. No matter that it was the
size of a closet. The skinny wooden chair was more comfortable and
the pint-sized chest of drawers a perfect fit simply because they were
hers. Even her complexion gleamed brighter in the speckled, worn
looking glass because she didn't have to squeeze behind someone to
steal a glimpse. The cup full of bluebells taken from downstairs gave
her room the final touch of color and cheer.

She would have been quite content if only Lucia had not made
such a hasty departure for Nottinghamshire to stay with the Bingleys.
Lucia's note had simply stated she was terribly disappointed to leave,
that it was not her choice, and she didn't know how long she was to
be away. The letter from Aunt Elizabeth had conveyed similar regrets,
the only difference being that her and her husband's destination was
London. Though they were family, Kelsey couldn't help but wonder

whether the Darcys had left on account of her mother, familiar as they were with her habits.

A brisk knock on the cottage door echoed up to her room. After the wooden door below scraped open, Kelsey heard her mother greeting two ladies. Just as Kelsey emerged from her room to join them, Cissy bounded past her, nearly knocking her down the stairs.

"Sorry, Kelsey!" she called before their mother shooed her outside to amuse herself.

When Kelsey reached the sitting room, her stomach clenched. There above the fireplace hung a painting she had fervently wished lost or damaged on their journey from Whitewell. It was an amateur portrait of her parents commissioned just after they were married. Kelsey vehemently disliked the way the artist had warped their facial expressions to make them appear more in love than she could ever believe they were, with exaggerated smiles and desperate eyes shaded in such a way as to make them look slightly inhuman. Staring at the painting, Kelsey felt she could see the scandal of their elopement displayed like a family secret against the clean, white walls of the Darcys' cottage. The hollow space atop the crackling logs would have been a much more fitting place for the ghastly painting, but Kelsey's mother protected it like a mother hawk.

"Kelsey, this is Miss Chatham and Mrs. Winters, the rector's wife. Kelsey?"

She finally tore her eyes away from the painting and curtsied to the ladies before her, first taking in the polite smile and curious eyes of Miss Chatham's symmetrical, youthful face. The middle-aged woman's eyes were more assessing while her frizzy hair burst from a large lacy bonnet that might have been the fashion when she was younger. She had a lean figure and smooth face, but the sternness behind her eyes stole a portion of her youth away.

"Kelsey? Usually a surname, is it not?" Mrs. Winters's blue eyes were so light, they were almost colorless.

Kelsey flushed as she recited the smallest explanation she could give. "I was named after a village."

"A village?" Miss Chatham asked. "I suspect there is a story behind your name, then."

Kelsey cleared her throat, readying a vague explanation, when her eyes inadvertently wandered back up to the painting of her parents.

Following her gaze, Mrs. Winters gasped. "Goodness. I heard rumors, but are you related to Mr. George Wickham?"

"How rude of me not to introduce myself!" exclaimed Mrs. Wickham. "Come, have a seat. Yes, he was my late husband, bless his soul." Looking down as if in remembrance of him, she spoke a little too solemnly. "Did you know him?"

Mrs. Winters hesitated but followed Miss Chatham onto the blue sofa. "It was a long time ago. My husband was given the parsonage in Kympton, the same parsonage Mr. Darcy's father initially offered Mr. Wickham all those years ago."

Mrs. Wickham looked at Mrs. Winters with new understanding. "Is that so?"

"Yes. Though, we both know your husband had other plans."

Mrs. Wickham only arched her brow in response. Kelsey had heard the story. The late Mr. Darcy had loved Mr. Wickham like a son and bequeathed the parsonage to him. Kelsey wasn't sure why her father had never been given the living, but she knew her mother still thought it a great injustice, however ill-suited her father would have been for such a position.

"I see you are not in mourning. Does that mean your husband died some time ago?"

"My, what a question." Mrs. Wickham put a hand to her chest. "And us having only just met. Yes, I'm afraid he died over six years ago."

"I see." Mrs. Winters's eyes strayed to the painting.

Several seconds passed in silence.

"I almost forgot. I was to deliver an invitation." Miss Chatham reached into her reticule and pulled out a folded note. On the outside, it simply said *Barley Cottage*. "My sister, Alice Salaway, and I would like to invite you to dinner next week. Her husband is the constable. They're both very amiable. Not as wealthy as the Darcys, but they do hold their fair share of parties. I've been living with her for the past six months. She regrets not being able to join me today to deliver the invitation herself, but she has several tasks to see to at the moment. She does hope you will come."

"Pity, the Darcys won't be there," Mrs. Winters added. "What with Mr. and Mrs. Darcy gone off to London, and their daughter rushed off to Nottinghamshire while the younger ones stay with yet another aunt. It's all rather sudden, isn't it, Miss Chatham? We're all wondering what the trouble is. No one seems to know when we can expect them back."

Miss Chatham shifted to the edge of her seat. "You will, no doubt, be interested to know that Mr. Worth will be attending dinner with us."

Mrs. Wickham leaned forward. "Who is Mr. Worth?"

"He is a naval officer recently resigned from his duties at sea." Mrs. Winters lengthened her words as if pleased to hear herself talk. "Apparently, he's come to manage business on behalf of his former captain. His recent arrival has the village ladies in quite the uproar."

Miss Chatham bit her lip. "He and I have already spoken on many occasions. Naturally, many ladies will set their caps at him, but never fear. My brother will also be at dinner, and he is very eligible. Perhaps you should focus on catching his eye, Miss Wickham."

Not wishing to show the least bit of interest in catching the eye of Miss Chatham's brother or any other man, Kelsey remained silent.

Mrs. Wickham, however, took in every word. "Who is Mr. Worth's former captain?"

"That is a name you will hear often," Mrs. Winters explained, "though most people hardly know a thing about him. I, myself, know more than most. His name is Captain Styles. He owns Thistledown Hall, the manor a few miles west of this cottage, just a short way from Pemberley. It's small but has the potential to become a respectable estate. Unfortunately, it's sat fallow for some time. The captain is said to be most eccentric, and he rarely visits these parts."

"That isn't surprising, considering his duties," replied Mrs. Wickham.

Mrs. Winters shrugged. "I suppose not, but he hates the talk. You see, the few of us who are old enough still recall the scandal." She lowered her voice. "Shortly after his marriage, when duty called him away, his wife ran off with another man, and we never heard of her again."

"The poor captain."

"Yes. Most unfortunate. Unless my memory fails me, he and his wife lived in this very cottage." Mrs. Winters looked around as if she expected to catch a glimpse of them walking by.

"Did they, really?" Mrs. Wickham also surveyed the room with curious eyes.

"Indeed. That was before the captain became wealthy enough to purchase Thistledown Hall. His ship must have had great successes to bring him a bounty large enough to purchase the estate."

"I should think so."

"Oh, yes. I don't know who the previous owners were, but before the captain owned Thistledown Hall, it was always being let. I suspect it was a profitable property in that regard."

"It was foolish of the captain not to do more with the estate," Miss Chatham added with a tinge of bitterness that Kelsey thought curious. "But all that is about to change. Everyone suspects Captain Styles has appointed Mr. Worth his heir. I, for one, am quite looking forward to seeing Mr. Worth transform Thistledown Hall into a respectable estate again. No doubt, he'll be searching for a bride to help him."

"How old is Mr. Worth?" Mrs. Wickham asked.

Kelsey rolled her eyes. Must her mother ask such direct questions?

Mrs. Winters guffawed. "Much too young for you, dear. I'd say five or six and twenty."

"Hmm." Mrs. Wickham tapped her chin, neither agreeing nor disagreeing. "And how old is Captain Styles?"

"I've never taken note of his exact age, but I'm certain he is old enough to be Mr. Worth's father."

Mrs. Wickham's lips curled mischievously. "Are either of them rumored to be very handsome?"

Just as Miss Chatham leaned forward to answer, Mrs. Winters's eyes filled with pity. "Such gossip falls beneath the notice of a married woman such as myself."

Obviously, Kelsey thought, silently chuckling to herself.

"I see." Mrs. Wickham stiffened and rose from her seat. "Well, you will forgive me then, if I inform you that a poor widowed woman such as myself has a great deal to do to keep a household even as small as this one properly running. Thank you for your visit."

Mrs. Winters didn't look at all disappointed to receive such a hint. "Of course. We must be going, mustn't we, Miss Chatham? It's been a pleasure."

As the ladies rose and curtsied to one another, Miss Chatham reached for Kelsey's hand. "We must all become friends. I hope to see you at dinner next week."

Mrs. Wickham spoke with emphasis. "You certainly shall."

Chapter 4

Perhaps she is full young to be much in company.

Jane Austen, *Pride and Prejudice*

Kelsey didn't need to look beyond the shadow spreading across the pages of her book to confirm that her mother stood behind her.

"I sometimes wonder, Kelsey, how it is possible that you are my offspring. Now, put down your book and go upstairs this instant to dress."

Holding in a retort, Kelsey finished the last few lines on the page and inserted a worn silk ribbon to keep her place. It was nearly the time she would have gone to dress for the Salaways' dinner anyway. She stood and stretched and returned the tattered copy of *The Tempest* to the shelf. She had been happy to discover that the cottage had come supplied with a handful of books, and she was determined to savor them.

In her room, Kelsey pulled on her favorite gown, a light rust colored muslin that showed off her green eyes and heightened her confidence to endure an evening of tedious conversation. A simple twist with her hair and a few rearranging of curls to frame her face completed her preparations.

The carriage, which the Salaways were kind enough to send, announced its arrival a short while later with rattling wheels and nickering horses heard all the way from the path to her window. Even before Kelsey had finished descending the stairs, she could feel her mother's disapproving glare sweep over her.

"Kelsey, that gown is worn to its last threads. I thought we left it in the poor box in Whitewell."

Kelsey shrugged. "I may have rescued it before our donation was made. We don't have money to spare on new dresses right now."

"One would think you hardly cared what impression you made tonight."

"Suppose I don't. Suppose I only want to be as comfortable as I can amidst a new group of gossips who I am not likely to know for more than a few months. Not even Lucia will be there."

"Don't be so dramatic." Her mother ran upstairs and returned a minute later with a thin white ribbon strung with amber beads. "At least wear this." She came behind Kelsey and fastened it around her neck. "It adds a much wanted touch of elegance, and I can't stand how bare your neck looks without it."

Kelsey didn't protest. She patted the beads, surprised by the way her eyes welled up at the gesture. Her father had given it to her mother for some special occasion that Kelsey couldn't remember. He had patted Kelsey on the head as he walked by and promised to buy her a set of beads when she was old enough to wear them. Without any warning, her father didn't come home once during the five days that followed. To console herself, Kelsey had snuck into her mother's room and caressed the beads, evidence for her little heart that her father loved his family. When he finally returned, he collapsed on the sofa in a drunken stupor and ignored them all. Mrs. Wickham hadn't worn the beads in years, but Kelsey still sometimes looked at them when she was able to steal a private moment, just to see if they were still there.

"Thank you," she said quickly, swallowing back the memory before her voice betrayed her.

"Cissy! Are you ready?" her mother called out.

Cissy skipped down the stairs and spun around, showing off a deep red gown that looked much too grown up for her and emphasized more of her budding figure than Kelsey thought appropriate. While their mother cradled Cissy's face with her hands and cooed at what a lovely daughter she had, Kelsey pinched her eyes and shook her head.

"Cissy, is that Mother's old gown? Don't you think your pale yellow would serve better for tonight?" *It has a much higher neckline,* she thought.

"Nonsense!" their mother exclaimed. "Cissy looks breathtaking. She is sure to turn heads tonight."

"Precisely what I'm afraid of." Did their mother not see the imprudence or danger of allowing Cissy to edge her way into society so early? Of course not. It was merely one act of imprudence among many. Why should one more matter? *Because Cissy is still a child,* Kelsey argued within. *But no one ever heeds my advice.*

She patted the beads around her neck a second time and followed her mother and sister to the Salaways' carriage. The warm air outside hinted of coming rain and carried the sweetness of the far-off barley fields.

"What a fine carriage the Salaways have sent for us. I hope they know many prosperous gentlemen." Once they were all comfortably situated inside, Mrs. Wickham gave Kelsey's knee a brisk pat. "Kelsey, please pay attention. I am very much hoping to meet this former naval officer tonight, and it is entirely likely he will bring a friend or two with him. If I understand these officers as well as I think I do—"

"Which is entirely debatable."

"Oh, hush!" Her mother lightly slapped her fan against Kelsey's leg. "I do, and they will be paying very close attention to every single lady here tonight, so—"

"Mother, haven't we had this conversation before? You want me to smile frequently, laugh at their jokes, and otherwise remain quiet. Do I have that right?"

"And pinch your cheeks!" taunted Cissy, earning a tired glare from Kelsey.

"All I ask," said Mrs. Wickham, "is that you do not ruin this opportunity for me. You have no idea how difficult life is for a woman my age in my position."

Though Kelsey had never been in her mother's position, she had listened to her complaints for eighteen years. "Mother, you underestimate my understanding."

"If any gentleman is going to seriously consider me worth courting, he will be examining my daughters as well. Cissy, I can rely on, but you?" Her disappointed sigh coupled with the swaying of the carriage made Kelsey's stomach roll. "Please be kind tonight. We don't need another scene like the one you caused at the Renfords' dinner."

Kelsey bit back a smirk as she remembered the dinner her mother referred to. Kelsey had placed a large slice of butter on the chair of the man her mother had been flirting with at the time. The way he squirmed in his seat was enough to make Kelsey grin, but when he stood to dance, revealing an oily stain in a most unfortunate place, Kelsey couldn't remember a time she had ever laughed so heartily.

"I wish I had been old enough to attend that dinner," Cissy giggled.

"You're still not old enough." Kelsey gave Cissy a teasing nudge. "Even if we do happen to meet our future husbands tonight, there's no need to single them out so quickly."

"Oh, Kelsey." Her mother looked wistfully out the window. "If only you knew how these things worked. When you find the right one, nothing else matters. Love doesn't take long. Why, your father and I . . ." Her mother looked down and pulled out a handkerchief. "I knew almost instantly that he and I—" She patted her eyes and swallowed. "Please behave, Kelsey. That's all I ask."

"Of course." Kelsey looked out the window again and fingered the ribbon with the amber beads weighing coolly on her skin. If the love her mother and father had fallen into happened quickly... *True love,* she thought, *must take a very long time.*

Chapter 5

Have you seen any pleasant men?
Have you had any flirting?

Jane Austen, *Pride and Prejudice*

The first thing Kelsey noticed when she was shown into the Salaways' sitting room was not the green and gold walls aglow with the light of several candelabras. She didn't notice the finely carved mantle above the welcoming fire or the hushed whispers of those that watched her enter. All she noticed was the same intriguing gentleman who had left her the apple.

In closer proximity, she saw he was tall and broad chested with dark blond hair, smoky eyes, and the cockiest smile she had ever seen. When strange, new sensations began to stretch inside her just as they had the first time she had seen him, she rallied her strength and hastily quelled them into submission. She understood this man's sort, and she knew his swagger, having seen it in her own father on many occasions. There was no doubt in her mind. This gentleman had all the tell-tale signs of trouble.

And he was relentlessly following her with his eyes.

As Kelsey adjusted to the flickers of light glinting off gilded furniture, she tried to concentrate on the other guests, but her eyes kept wandering to that distinctive gentleman, who she was beginning to suspect was the famed Mr. Worth. How could she think clearly with him staring at her like that? They hadn't even been introduced yet.

It must have been one of his tricks. Raise her curiosity from across the room with smolders and devilish grins, as if they already shared a secret. Well, it wouldn't work. Not on Kelsey. An apple and a smile weren't enough to gain her favor.

Like her father, he probably took pride in being able to conjure a blush from any fair cheek whenever he wanted, but this time, he would be disappointed. Kelsey had spent her entire childhood building an immunity to such charms. Her father had provided her with ample opportunities to observe the fickle falsity of such flirtations. For, no sooner would he flatter and simper than the next moment, he would curse and betray. No matter how much she loved her father, she never wanted a man who was anything like him. Never. She was all too familiar with what happened once the charm wore off.

She patted the beads around her neck and couldn't think of a single memory of him, no matter how fond, that was not somehow coupled with unsavory circumstances. She had gleaned what lessons she could from him, deciding that, if she had to live with such discordant memories, at least the pain of them would not go to waste.

Mrs. Salaway approached with the flustered air of a hostess anxious to please. With a deep curtsey, she welcomed Mrs. Wickham, Kelsey, and Cissy to her home. Kelsey in turn curtsied and followed Mrs. Salaway to meet the other guests. They were briefly introduced to Mr. Winters, a man who looked every part the respectable clergyman Kelsey's father never could have been. Next, she met Mr. Salaway, a tall balding man who looked eager to return to the conversation he had been having with Mr. Winters.

When Mrs. Salaway presented Mr. Worth, Kelsey held her breath and suppressed any show of recognition.

"It's a pleasure to meet you, Miss Wickham." Mr. Worth's voice was everything it ought to be, rich and caressing like the warmth of a fire, but his confidence, along with that knowing look in his eye, only put Kelsey more fiercely on her guard.

She breathed easily once again when they came to Mrs. Winters and Miss Chatham.

"You know my half-sister, Beatrice Chatham." Mrs. Salaway continued the introductions. "And this strapping young man who has just arrived is my half-brother, William Chatham." A tall fellow who had the same round eyes as Mrs. Salaway bowed before them, exchanged a few polite words, and joined the men on the other side of the room. Mrs. Salaway leaned close enough for Kelsey to catch whiffs of the lady's vinaigrette. "Beatrice and William are staying with me indefinitely. Ever since their father died a year and a half ago, they are poorer than church mice."

"How unfortunate." Kelsey regarded Miss Chatham with more sympathy than she had the first time they'd met. Had Miss Chatham's experiences been similar to her own, always moving about with no place to call home? Were Miss Chatham's smiles just as practiced as Kelsey's?

With introductions complete, the ladies took their seats by the fire while the men conversed by the bookshelves.

Mrs. Wickham glanced at the men several times. "My, how the women outnumber the men tonight."

Miss Chatham followed her gaze. "You're quick to count, Mrs. Wickham."

"Oh, I do apologize." Mrs. Salaway placed a hand on her cheek. "I always feel it my duty as hostess to make the numbers equal, but Mr. Worth had no idea when the captain's ship was due to arrive. Mr. Salaway believes inviting the captain is a fruitless endeavor, but it never hurts to extend the invitation, does it? At least we have the pleasure of Mr. Worth's company tonight." She looked up and tapped her lip. "The Darcys aren't here, of course, but I did hope that—"

Mrs. Salaway was interrupted by the butler announcing the arrival of a Mr. Baxter. From a distance, it was difficult to guess his exact age.

"Our prospects improve," Mrs. Wickham whispered under her breath. "Kelsey, do you think he's single?"

"You know nothing about him," she snapped back.

"Hush!"

When Mrs. Salaway introduced him, Kelsey observed him in greater detail. Dressed in a dark brown, rumpled jacket and waistcoat that covered his slightly rounding belly, he bowed to the ladies, revealing wispy blonde hair that was thinning on top.

"Surely, I can't be the only sane man in this room," he said in exaggerated tones. "Those gentlemen must be suffering a peculiar ailment to willfully place themselves so far from heaven." He simpered at each lady but let his gaze linger on Mrs. Wickham.

Kelsey rolled her eyes as her mother giggled, and with that, Mr. Baxter placed himself next to her in the empty space on the sofa. Cissy met Kelsey's eye, and the two shared a knowing look. It was Whitewell and Mr. Phineas all over again.

"Pray, dear angel," Mr. Baxter asked Mrs. Wickham, "tell me your name once more."

As they fell into conversation, Mrs. Salaway remarked, "We are fortunate to have so many new neighbors. I'm sure we will all become friends in no time."

"I'm sure you're right," Mrs. Winters agreed with hardly a trace of feeling.

"Oh!" Mrs. Salaway face lit with an idea, and she began to talk with her hands. "Have you all heard? There is talk of Mr. Darcy receiving a title."

"In truth?" asked Miss Chatham. "Why, even from my little hometown of Beltham, the Darcys are famous for their wealth, but I never heard talk of him receiving a title. Are you certain?"

"Well, I don't know." Mrs. Salaway sat up taller. "But everyone in these parts knows he assisted the crown with some debts incurred during the war. It may be nothing but rumor. People at Pemberley have always thought him deserving of a title, but perhaps it explains why he left so suddenly."

Mrs. Winters pinched her lips. "Yes, but why would they send Miss Darcy and the children away while he and Mrs. Darcy ran off in another direction? Such haste!"

"With money like theirs, one has no need to plan ahead," Miss Chatham smirked.

"Don't misunderstand me. I do hope it's true. No one deserves such an honor more than he." Mrs. Winters nodded. "He's been very good to my husband and me. All these years he's seen to my husband's needs as the rector, and I've always said he's an excellent judge of character."

Kelsey didn't miss the way Mrs. Winters's critical eye landed on her mother.

"What do you think?" Miss Chatham now looked at Kelsey. "I hope your uncle is knighted, but whether or not he is, I will always consider your aunt quite the lady, Kelsey."

Kelsey had to bite her tongue. Perhaps she could forgive Miss Chatham for her familiarity, but Kelsey was in no mood to imagine her excessively rich relatives being further favored by providence, not when they had not favored her with a kind welcome.

"It's all very exciting, indeed, but if you will excuse me." Kelsey stood as knots tightened in her shoulders. "I am suddenly in need of air." She knew it was not the most polite way to leave the conversation, but Miss Chatham had asked a question she unexpectedly couldn't answer. What did Kelsey think? She *couldn't* think about it. Not when Lucia hadn't even visited her yet. With heat creeping through her skin, she spun around the corner of the sofa too quickly and bumped into *him*.

"Pardon me, Lady Kelsey," Mr. Worth said, dipping his head slightly. "Allow me to accompany you to the terrace."

Kelsey blinked, taking in his audacious use of her Christian name coupled with a mock title. "That's not necessary." She tried to wave him away, but he kept stride with her as she walked.

"I'm sorry you're not feeling well," he persisted, "but it gives me an excuse to step away from whatever conversation this lively group will think up next."

He smiled expectantly, but there was no laughter for Kelsey to spare him. "I'm sure you are most adept at using others to your advantage." She kept walking without feeling an ounce sorry for her harsh words.

Mr. Worth missed a step but soon made up for it.

"It allows me the opportunity to offer you my assistance, Lady Kelsey." The smile he offered, Kelsey had to admit, did rank among the handsomest she had ever seen, but she made the observation as easily as if she were noting it looked like rain.

Or so she told herself.

When her feet hit the terrace stones, cool under her thin slippers, the fresh air rushed at her with the minty tang of pine and grass. The darkness of the evening was softened by the waxing moon and light glowing from the sitting room windows.

She looked into Mr. Worth's dark eyes and bit her lips, realizing she had stepped outside with a man she had only just been introduced to. It was precisely the sort of thing a Wickham would do. "Why do you call me Lady Kelsey?"

A glance at the partially open door reminded her they were only a few steps away from the sitting room and could still see the people within, a small comfort.

"It's what I heard Miss Chatham call you."

"Were you eavesdropping?" Kelsey tried to sound offended, but it had no effect on him.

He shrugged. "Would you like me to call you something else?"

"Miss Wickham will do."

"I like Lady Kelsey better." He took a step closer. "It suits you."

"But I'm not a Lady."

He raised his brow, leaned closer with a laugh, and whispered, "I wouldn't toss that statement around lightly if I were you."

"Aren't you clever," she frowned.

"No, I'm Nathaniel Worth."

"Oh, goodness!"

"Thank you," he grinned.

"That wasn't a compliment, Mr. Worth."

"I'd prefer Nathaniel." He kept his grin the whole time he spoke.

"I may not be a *Lady*, but I'm still a lady, *Mr. Worth*." She enunciated each word.

He snapped his fingers. "I knew it. Lady Kelsey it is! If it makes you feel more comfortable, you may call me Sir Nathaniel."

The leaves in the trees shook in the wind as if laughing in response. The pine in the air was much easier on Kelsey's lungs than the stuffy sitting room air.

"Sir Nathaniel?"

"Has a satisfying ring to it, don't you think?"

He looks much too pleased with himself. But through some small gap in her focus, she met his eyes again and became caught there. They were deep brown, almost black, and the little glints of light that swam in them sparkled like stars. It had been a long time since Kelsey had even paid attention to such details that she momentarily lost track of her intent to rebuff him.

She closed her eyes and shook her head. "A true gentleman has no need to pretend anything." Feeling robbed of a private moment outside, she forced out the words, "Now, please let me be!"

Was it Kelsey's imagination or did Mr. Worth's expression drop? Looking straight ahead, he spoke softly. "Such a temper, Lady Kelsey. Whatever have I done to provoke it?"

"As I said before, it's Miss Wickham." She knew it was the proper thing to say, but there was less force behind her words this time.

The truth was, she did have a temper, and she wasn't entirely sure what he had done to provoke it. He was too attentive? Too cheerful? Too interested in her? Or perhaps he was too free with her, too confident, and too eager. Any kindness or appealing quality from this man who flirted like her father and treated her with uncurbed familiarity had to be a ruse, a strategy she could never believe in.

Her feet grew colder as the stone pressed into her soles, and Mr. Worth tugged at a button on his coat. Leaves continued to whisper and shake. Though Kelsey's irritation dwindled, any possible apology stuck in her throat, and her face burned.

The tiny stars in Mr. Worth's eyes dulled when he looked at her again. "Forgive me. Clearly, I've offended you, and you were already not feeling well." With a slight bow, he added, "I am still at your service should you think of anything I can do for you this evening. Please don't foreclose the possibility that I may still be a gentleman. Excuse me."

Without waiting for a reply, he turned away, leaving Kelsey to listen to his boots retreat across the terrace.

She breathed deeply, trying to savor a minute alone, but the pine in the air grew sharp and the wind made her shiver. What had just happened with Nathaniel Worth? He seemed every bit the kind of man she had taught herself to be wary of. She should consider herself fortunate for giving him the set-down so quickly, and yet, she felt as though she had just been scolded. *I've done nothing wrong,* she reminded herself. *He was the one being improper.* More than likely, she had saved herself from further unwanted attentions.

When the breeze grew too harsh on her arms and neck, she returned to the sitting room just as Mr. and Mrs. Salaway invited everyone to the dining room. Mrs. Wickham took the arm of Mr. Baxter while Miss Chatham tossed a smile to Kelsey and took Mr. Worth's. Cissy soon hung on the arm of Mr. Chatham.

Rather than feeling slighted, all Kelsey could think was, *When had the child grown so tall?*

Once seated, Kelsey enjoyed as much of the shamelessly rich food as she could without drawing attention to herself, a feat made easy by the way Mr. Chatham ate his weight in roasted pork. Why Cissy continued to smile at him so coquettishly, Kelsey could not comprehend. That she even knew how to make such a smile was just as vexing. As Kelsey wished she were close enough to pinch Cissy, a teasing voice sang from across the table.

"Oh, Mr. Baxter! You shouldn't say such things!" Kelsey's mother tilted her head back and laughed before slapping Mr. Baxter's arm with her fan.

Kelsey almost choked on her meat, and for the first time since the terrace, Mr. Worth was regarding her.

Mrs. Wickham and Mr. Baxter continued to gaze at one another and laugh so much that Mrs. Salaway took notice. "My, you two look comfortable. Are you already acquainted with one another?"

Mr. Baxter straightened his cravat but did nothing about the ridiculous grin on his face. "If only. If I had been acquainted with Mrs. Wickham sooner, I doubt I would be sitting before you an old bachelor."

Mr. Salaway and Mr. Winters exchanged dubious looks before returning their focus to their meat and potatoes.

Mrs. Wickham giggled like a child. "We were just laughing at how amusing it is that we were both in Bath at the same time but were never introduced."

"Yes," Mr. Baxter agreed, his voice swelling with enthusiasm. "How ironic is it that we should so often be in the same places but never acquainted with the same people until now?"

"Oh. Yes. I see. Very amusing." Mrs. Salaway nodded politely. "I find the waters there very restorative. Did you visit for your health or for holiday?"

Clearing his throat and tugging at his lapels, Mr. Baxter answered, "I wasn't there for long. It was really for a friend. We were making a few . . ." He looked up as if searching for the words. "Business ventures. Didn't succeed as I'd hoped, I'm afraid, but had I met this lovely creature in Bath, I would have spent my time quite differently, I assure you."

Kelsey pressed her knife viciously into her roast and hoped Mr. Baxter would find his way back to Bath or anywhere else, for that matter, soon.

Sometime after dinner when the ladies were discussing entertainment, Mr. Chatham suggested cards, but Mrs. Wickham and Mr. Baxter were the only ones eager to play.

"Won't you play with us, Miss Wickham?" Mr. Chatham asked. "Your sister is already occupied, it would seem."

Across the room, Cissy held a small Pomeranian on her lap. Mrs. Salaway and Mrs. Winters were taking turns cooing at it and scratching its ears. Cissy would never choose cards over an adorable bundle of fur.

"You must excuse me. I do not play frequently enough to remember the rules. Why not ask your sister?" Kelsey never played if she could help it.

Mr. Chatham shook his head. "Oh, no. I refuse to play with Beatrice. She has an uncanny ability to discern the strength of my hand merely by how high I arch my brows."

Miss Chatham was rifling through sheets of music as if deciding whether she might play something on the pianoforte. Mr. Worth was sitting by the fire conversing with Mr. Salaway and Mr. Winters and had just said something that made the men burst out in deep chuckles.

"Please, Miss Wickham?" Mr. Chatham persisted.

"No, really, I hardly ever play."

Fortunately, Mrs. Salaway stood up. "I am happy to sit in for a round or two, Mr. Chatham, but perhaps we may use that time to acquaint Miss Wickham with the rules. I say, Mr. Worth!" She gestured at him from across the room. "Would you be so kind as to take Miss Wickham to the other table and explain the rules to her so she will be capable of replacing me when I tire of the game?"

Mr. Worth smiled instantly. "With pleasure." When a disgruntled looking Mr. Chatham walked off with Mrs. Salaway to a table at the other end of the room, Mr. Worth offered his hand to Kelsey. "Shall we?"

She stared his hand as if it might be a trap waiting to spring, but she then saw her mother snugly situated at Mr. Baxter's side. If Kelsey learned the rules well enough to play, she could at least keep a closer eye on them. "Very well." She took Mr. Worth's hand and followed.

The way his touch radiated up her arm and tightened inside her chest made her think the trap had sprung after all. The light pressure of his fingers pressed against hers.

"Don't worry. I'm an excellent teacher."

"And a modest one, at that," she added. "How fortunate."

He smiled but his eyes turned thoughtful. "Are you still not feeling well?"

Remembering her harsh words from earlier, she wavered between rebuffing him anew or apologizing. "I'm not one for parties. It's not your fault." It was the best she was willing to give.

He gestured toward a fashionably carved wooden chair at a small table and took the seat across from her. Pulling a stack of cards from his pocket, he deftly shuffled and distributed their hands.

"Have you never played Speculation before?"

"Not recently enough to remember the rules or strategy," she admitted.

"Then you have just broken the first rule."

Kelsey tilted her head innocently. "Never agree to play cards in the first place?"

He laughed again and leaned forward. "Never let your opponent see your weakness."

"Why don't we adhere to the official rules?" She began sifting through her cards, memorizing which ones she held as he did the same with his.

"But the implied ones are the most entertaining. Either way, it's an idea worth adopting." He explained the rules to Kelsey, which she found rather straightforward. She appreciated his clear and easy manner and the soothing depths of his voice, but she wouldn't give herself permission to admire such qualities. Admiring was for ladies who were looking for a man to attract, which she certainly was not.

"Now to test you." He shuffled the cards once more and laid down the first.

Their game ensued.

The first moves were obvious. Kelsey knew what she was doing, though it took her a few seconds longer than Mr. Worth to decide which card to lay down.

He looked at her much more than he looked at his cards. "Did you enjoy the apple?"

His question sprang to her thoughts like a kitten to her lap, sending her back to the moment she'd first spied him on the path. "Yes, I did, though it seems a bit early for apples."

He gave a quick wink. "I know a man who grows a special variety." He laid down another card and glanced over his shoulder where the others were sitting. "Pardon my asking, but I can't help but notice you seem concerned for your sister."

"Oh, I . . ." Kelsey hadn't realized she had been watching Cissy who now stood at Mr. Chatham's side with the Pomeranian in her arms. What were they laughing at? "Is it not natural that I should be concerned for my sister?"

Mr. Worth laid his next card. "Of course, it's natural. I think it demonstrates a certain care and perceptiveness."

"You do?" Was he teasing her again? Suddenly, none of her cards seemed worth playing.

"Having a younger sister myself, I can easily imagine what you must feel when you see her next to Mr. Chatham."

Kelsey hastily laid down her next card. She would not be fooled into thinking he understood her.

"Lady Kelsey," he tested the name again. "What would you say if I informed you I would be interested in calling on you in the near future?" He laid down a rather high card.

Kelsey met his eye briefly before examining her cards. Was it true her previous rebuffs hadn't sufficiently deterred him? She pulled out a card that overruled his. "I would say you'd have more success with the other ladies you've been courting." She drew a new card. "I have no patience for callers."

Mr. Worth's eyes sharpened. "Other ladies?" He shook his head. "You have revealed another weakness, my lady." He laid down another card that matched Kelsey's.

"I don't think so, Mr. Worth." Her next card was not a very good one, but it was all she could play. "I merely speak the truth."

"How can you know the truth," he asked, laying down a better card, "when you cannot see my hand?" He gave his cards a little shake, keeping their faces hidden.

"I may not know your hand, but I certainly know what kind of player you are." At last, she had another card worth playing.

"Again, you reveal yourself." He played his next card as swiftly as if he had anticipated her last. "You could take a chance admitting me. I might be different from what you expect."

Kelsey now had two cards to choose between. One was a riskier move but might win her the game. The other was a safer card to play but could still lead to victory in only a few more moves. "I'm not one to take chances, Mr. Worth."

"Well then," he sighed, "I had best not try my luck any further tonight." He laid down a low card and admitted defeat. Before she could answer, he bowed and left the table.

Curious, Kelsey picked up Mr. Worth's remaining card, the one he hadn't played. She sucked in a quick breath and looked where he now stood across the room. It was the highest card possible. He had let her win.

Chapter 6

*I thank you for my share of the favour . . . but I do
not particularly like your way of getting husbands.*

Jane Austen, *Pride and Prejudice*

K̶elsey stared at Mr. Baxter, who sat on their tiny sitting room
sofa like a lump of unevenly cooked bread. The morning sunlight, unhindered by clouds, enhanced several pale patches of whiskers across his rounded jaw while the wrinkles in his brown jacket and
waistcoat followed his belly like cracks in the crust.

Cissy was observing him too but kept springing from her seat to
gaze out the window or retrieve something from a shelf. "Why aren't
you already married, Mr. Baxter?"

His jaw dropped, and Kelsey smirked. Sometimes having a younger, uninhibited sister was particularly useful.

"How long did you say your mother would be?" Mr. Baxter tugged
at his cravat.

"She'll be down in a few minutes." Though Kelsey's response was
practiced, the weariness in her voice was not. She didn't know how
many more times she could play hostess to her mother's suitors and

maintain her sanity. Or dignity. Still, if her mother insisted on taking extra time to ready herself, Kelsey would make the most of it. "Forgive me if you already mentioned it, Mr. Baxter, but would you remind me what your livelihood is?"

Again, he tugged at his cravat. "I don't recall mentioning it. Usually, those details bore young ladies."

"Are you a farmer?" she pressed.

"Well . . ." He scratched his cheek and looked around. "Not exactly, but I suppose you could say . . . Yes, I'm a farmer, a gentleman farmer. For the time being, at least. It is a respectable living. Yes." He nodded as if he had just convinced himself of the fact.

"As respectable as being an officer?" Cissy asked. "Our father was an officer, you know. He once shot a hole right through the center of a man's cap."

Cissy pointed to her forehead, and Mr. Baxter nodded without blinking. Kelsey bit her lips together to keep from laughing. What Mr. Baxter wouldn't have gathered from Cissy's retelling was that their father had accidentally shot his own hat from across the room when he was inebriated. It wasn't a particularly impressive story, but Mr. Baxter's face was almost enough to make Kelsey pity his ignorance.

"Do you own the land you work, sir?"

"Aren't you a curious girl," he laughed nervously.

"I've been told that before. But what really interests me—"

"Thank you, Kelsey. Cissy." Mrs. Wickham scuttled down the staircase with smiles for Mr. Baxter and a stern eye for Kelsey. "Thank you for entertaining Mr. Baxter while he waited for me."

He heaved a sigh and jumped from his seat as if he had just been unchained. "Mrs. Wickham, what a beautiful vision of youth and bloom, you are."

"An old widow like me?" she lilted, managing a blush.

"I never would have guessed it."

Cissy made a face of disgust that only Kelsey saw and tip-toed out of the room. Kelsey was about to join her, but as her eyes drifted above the fireplace, she was struck with an idea. She flashed her mother a merciless grin.

"You are correct, Mr. Baxter. My mother is a vision of youth and beauty. Why, just look at this painting." She pointed to the horrendous portrait of her parents. "She hardly looks a day older now than when she was a young bride, does she not?"

Now that Kelsey had forced his attention, Mr. Baxter stared at the painting with wide eyes.

"That's your mother, is it?" he stuttered, then turned to Mrs. Wickham. "That is . . . you, my dear? Well, the slant of your eyes is a bit different, and I suppose any artist would have difficulty capturing your precise complexion. Really, any discrepancies are due to the artist's interpretation . . ."

Kelsey pinched herself to maintain her composure.

"I suppose," continued Mr. Baxter, "it would not be fair of me to be jealous seeing you hanging on that gentleman's arm in so . . . intimate a fashion. You were married, after all, were you not?"

The uncertain tremble in his voice made Kelsey suspect he had heard the rumors.

"Yes, well, shall we leave for our walk, Mr. Baxter?" Mrs. Wickham went straight for the door, giving him no choice but to follow.

"You certainly were . . . devoted to your late husband, it would seem." Even over his shoulder, his eyes strayed to the painting.

Kelsey scoffed. *Devoted* was a generous word. *Obsessed* was more accurate, and Kelsey was certain Mr. Baxter had seen it.

Kelsey called after them. "Would you like me to act as chaperone for you, Mother? Shall I fetch my bonnet?"

"We shall be quite all right, I assure you." Even from halfway down the path, her mother's scowl could be felt as well as seen.

"Is he finally gone?" Cissy returned from her hiding place. "Kelsey, would you please arrange my hair in that lovely style Miss Chatham wore the other night?"

She presented Kelsey with a comb, hairpins, and a lavender ribbon and looked at her with such pleading eyes that, after a little more begging, Kelsey relented. The hairstyle wasn't difficult, but it did require a fair amount of time to make several smaller plaits that were to be pulled up and woven throughout Cissy's curls. Once Cissy had examined her hair in the glass and pronounced Kelsey's attempt a success, she lowered her eyes.

"Why do you think Mr. Chatham hasn't come to call on me, Kelsey?"

Kelsey stopped gathering the extra hairpins she'd dropped. Was Cissy already thinking of such things? "You've never had a gentleman call on you before. Why should you start with him?"

"Do you think it wrong of me to hope he will call?" Were Cissy's cheeks growing pink?

Kelsey's mind spun as she formulated a response that would not discourage Cissy from confiding in her. "Did he say anything that gave you the impression he might call?"

"Well, no . . ."

Kelsey suppressed a sigh of relief.

"But after dinner with the Salaways, Mother said she would not be surprised if he did. So, I began to think on it, and he is handsome." Cissy inspected her hair again in the glass, tilting her face from side to side. "Mother was young, you know, when she married. Hardly older than I am, so I might as well prepare."

Now Kelsey understood. Cissy had taken their mother's ramblings too much to heart. "Do you like Mr. Chatham so very much that you want him to visit?"

Cissy shrugged. "I don't know. He is a bit old for me, isn't he?" She smiled sadly. "I actually miss Jack Pendlestone much more than I like Mr. Chatham, and Jack's only three years older than I am."

"I know, Cissy. I miss Sarah and our friends at Whitewell too." Kelsey put her arm around her. "Don't worry about gentlemen callers yet. They'll come in time, and who knows? Perhaps you and Jack will cross paths again one day."

Cissy's eyes brightened. "Do you really think so?"

Kelsey never had the chance to answer.

Mrs. Wickham could be heard struggling to get the door over the warped lip. Once successful, she marched in without removing her bonnet. "Kelsey Wickham, how could you? How could you embarrass me in front of Mr. Baxter like that?"

"I beg your pardon?"

Her mother folded her arms. "You were flaunting my past at him."

From the corner of her eye, Kelsey saw Cissy collect her comb, pins, and extra ribbon and escape up the stairs.

"Flaunting?" Kelsey was in no mood to argue. "Isn't it obvious that you were once a married woman? Or is Mr. Baxter denser than I realized?"

"That is not fair, Kelsey. I would have expected more delicacy from you."

"Let me understand you," Kelsey glared. "When Mrs. Winters and the other ladies come calling, it is perfectly acceptable to draw their attention to that horrific painting—"

"Kelsey!"

"But it is not all right to draw Mr. Baxter's attention to it? I thought you were proud of that painting. I thought you wanted me to be proud of it too." Kelsey folded her arms, mirroring her mother as their breaths audibly flowed in and out.

"Fine," her mother clipped. "I'll move the painting. That's what you want, isn't it?"

Kelsey could hardly believe her luck, but as she was about to tell her mother, *yes, that's exactly what I want,* different words came out. "What I want is for you to pace yourself with Mr. Baxter. Or any other gentleman you happen to meet. Please consider the consequences before you run away again."

Mrs. Wickham's features knotted with offense but softened the next moment. "Is that what's worrying you? You're afraid I'll run off with Mr. Baxter and leave you? That will never happen, my darling."

"No." Kelsey shook her head. "I'm worried you'll make me and Cissy run off with the both of you or some other man I despise. This time, please, for Cissy and me, would you show a little more prudence and take your time?"

Her mother slowly removed her bonnet and hung it on a hook by the door. "Words easily spoken, Kelsey, but you have no idea what kind of uncertainty I feel every day. For me and you girls. I worry about our future. I worry about being left without income, without any way to support you. Your father's pension, what's left of it, won't last long, and my inheritance is a pitiful amount. It isn't enough. It was never enough. I don't want to be a beggar all my life." Mrs. Wickham took a shaky breath. "And I don't want to be alone anymore. I want us all to be happy."

A whirlwind of questions and complaints fought their way to Kelsey's tongue as her muscles flooded with frustration. "Do you truly think this is the way to be happy? Connecting yourself with a man you hardly know? A man who I suspect has his secrets and vices just like the rest of them. Please, we don't have to continue this way. I could apply to be a lady's maid to a respectable family, or—"

"Kelsey, stop." Her mother rubbed her brow. "I am a gentleman's daughter, and you are my daughter, so there's no need for that. All I ask is that you give Mr. Baxter a chance. He has many amiable qualities, and it would mean a great deal to me if you didn't immediately discount him."

Kelsey looked away, the strength to argue draining from her like water from a pitcher. Contending with her mother was accomplishing nothing. Through the window, she could see grasping branches from the neglected garden tapping on the panes, reminding her of the mess they still lived in. "The garden is full of weeds. One of these days we must actually tend to it."

Mrs. Wickham nodded and dabbed her eye with a corner of lace. "Before I forget, I must tell you that your Aunt Kitty and her husband have sent an invitation."

Blood rushed to Kelsey's head. They couldn't leave Barley Cottage yet, not when she still hadn't seen Lucia. "No! Mother, we can't leave yet. I—"

Her mother shook her head. "You misunderstand. Your aunt has written to invite *Cissy* to stay in Warlingham for a while."

"Cissy? That is kind of our aunt, but why?"

Mrs. Wickham shrugged. "I suspect Kitty felt guilty for not helping us earlier. This is her way of offering a compromise." With a twinge of bitterness, she added, "She is able to be generous without directly assisting me."

"How is it to be arranged? Cissy is too young to travel alone, and we can't afford to deliver her there ourselves."

Mrs. Wickham waved her piece of lace in the air. "It will be no trouble at all. Caroline Pendlestone will be traveling through these parts next week."

"Next week?" Kelsey breathed out. "So soon?"

"She, along with Sarah and Jack will collect Cissy and convey her to Warlingham."

The idea was simple enough, but Kelsey remembered that her mother's elopement had come about when she had been permitted to travel away from her family. Cissy was in no danger of eloping, but if she was on the precipice of entertaining male callers . . .

"Cissy is too young, Mother. How can she be trusted to behave herself?"

"I was afraid you would be jealous, Kelsey, but I can't spare you. I need you here. Don't you wish to stay and see Lucia when she returns?"

"I am not jealous, and yes, of course, but—"

"I'm going to miss Cissy too. It's terrible to part with one's daughter, but this cottage is so small. With expenses being what they are . . . Don't look at me like that, Kelsey. I may not know the accounting details as thoroughly as you, but I am fully aware we could use the help. Cissy will have greater opportunities with your aunt and uncle and will be well taken care of. She will spend time with respectable people, and if she is fortunate, she might make a favorable connection."

"She is thirteen!"

"I know!" In a calmer voice, her mother said, "I know. I'm merely looking to the future. Now that I've told you, I'm going to talk it over with Cissy."

As her mother retreated upstairs, all Kelsey could think was, *Cissy gone in one week's time.* First Lucia, and now Cissy. Gone.

No fire crackled in the hearth that morning, the summer warmth making it unnecessary, but as Kelsey paced around the small sitting room, a chill found its way to her neck and arms. Who would she talk to when her heart was heavy? Who would she laugh with when no one else understood her jests? Who would she smile with to alleviate life's ever-mounting burdens?

Herself. All she had was herself. Kelsey would turn within and focus her mind and efforts on things she could rely on and things she could control.

The garden was still full of possibilities. With no one else willing to tend it, she knew it needed her. A garden wouldn't leave her. A garden would respond to her efforts. Yes, Kelsey would apply her skill and strength to the plants outside and improve her circumstances. All she had to do was pull the weeds.

Chapter 7

I could easily forgive his pride,
if he had not mortified mine.

Jane Austen, *Pride and Prejudice*

As Kelsey stepped into the garden, she felt the pressure around her shift and lighten. The expanse of the sky swallowed her turmoil and spread it so thin, it misted off her shoulders and into the clouds. If only she could lift herself higher and touch that stretch of perfect blue.

She eyed the garden warily. How was it possible the weeds had doubled in size since the day she'd arrived? She had never done much gardening before. A little here and a little there but nothing that could have prepared her for the chaos before her. The sheer volume of growth was overwhelming as it reached for her like claws with each step she took. The very idea of facing so many weeds was like going into battle without a strategy. She hadn't the least idea where to begin.

"I can help with this garden if you would permit me."

Kelsey spun around and saw Nathaniel Worth casually leaning against a tall peach tree just beyond the splintering fence. How long had he been standing there? He plucked a piece of fruit that still looked a bit green and hopped the fence, offering the peach to Kelsey.

"Who said I was in want of help, sir?" Ignoring the fruit, she stooped down and took hold of an especially large, spiny plant that clearly didn't belong. "Ow!" Her hand instantly retracted as it erupted with piercing prickles.

"No one need tell me what I can see with my own eyes." Tossing the peach aside, he reached for her hand and examined her palm.

Stunned by his boldness, Kelsey didn't resist as he removed two thin prickles.

"That was merely a mistake." She pulled her hand back, uncertain whether the sting from the weed or the heat from his skin was more uncomfortable.

"One you're likely to make again unless you're wearing gloves."

"Gloves..." Kelsey looked around her. The spiny weeds were everywhere. Of course, she should have considered gloves, but his presence had distracted her.

Mr. Worth nodded. "Gloves. Thick, heavy gloves. Nothing like those silky white ones you ladies are so fond of."

"Always presuming, aren't you, Mr. Worth?" Kelsey lifted her chin. "I, for one, do not care for things like silk gloves."

"Do you prefer another fabric? Or do you still insist you are not a lady?"

Kelsey was through with his taunts. "Are you on your way somewhere, sir?"

He gestured toward the road. "I'm on my way to Lambton. Couldn't ask for finer weather. I don't suppose you would like to accompany me. If your mother or sister care to join us, we can make a proper outing of the day."

Kelsey didn't answer because, at that moment, Mrs. Wickham burst through the cottage door, uttering a string of unladylike curses at the warped lip of the door frame.

"Oh! Good day, Mr. Worth!" Quickly composing herself, she rushed to Kelsey's side and took her arm. "Did I hear you're on your way to the village?"

Kelsey hoped the bright sunlight did something to disguise the heat spreading on her cheeks.

Mr. Worth's dark eyes sparkled. "That's right, Mrs. Wickham. How can I be of service to you?"

"It so happens there is a new straw bonnet waiting for me at the milliners. It is already paid for. I would be so grateful if you would collect it for me."

"Of course, madam."

Kelsey closed her eyes. Her mother had purchased a new bonnet without consulting her?

"I don't think I'm equal to the task of such a walk today, but I'm sure Kelsey would be delighted to accompany you." Mrs. Wickham gave her a nudge. "I was just thinking you could use a bit of exercise, Kelsey dear."

Kelsey pinched her lips in a tight smile. Did her mother not care about them going off together unchaperoned? Of course, she didn't. It simply wasn't her mother's way. "Thank you, Mother, but I've just declined Mr. Worth's offer. You forget I've promised to tend to this . . ." She considered calling it a mess but reluctantly finished with, "garden."

"Well, then." Mr. Worth gave a gracious bow. "I mustn't keep you from your promises. Another time, perhaps." He returned to the path, whistling the same lighthearted tune Kelsey had heard from his lips earlier.

Kelsey wasted no time removing her arm from her mother's and striding to the shed to look for gloves. A moment later, her mother was again at her side.

"That was a rather stupid thing to do."

"What are you talking about?" Kelsey searched the various tools but saw no gloves.

"He is as handsome as they come, my dear daughter! Why on earth did you decline to walk with him?"

"Was that your revenge, Mother? Embarrassing me in front of Mr. Worth after I embarrassed you in front of Mr. Baxter?" She searched through shelves containing old clay pots and rusted spades. Still no gloves.

"Embarrassing you? A mother only wants what is best for her daughter."

"You have much to learn about what is best for me." Most tools in the shed Kelsey didn't dare touch for fear their rusty tips would puncture her skin. "If you'd like, Mother, you can choose a spade and help me in the garden."

Keeping her eyes on the tools, she heard the soft swish of her mother's skirts followed by fading footsteps over gravel. The peace of being alone returned. Kelsey settled on a single spade that had minimal rust and might spare her hands from the weeds' prickles if she was careful. At the very least, it was a tool she understood.

Stepping out of the shed, she surveyed the garden. Thistles bloomed in great purple buds while rose bushes remained green and dry. Bright dandelions and spindly plants like the one she had tried to pull speckled the grass, while dried brambles suffocated what might have once been vegetable beds. Dead vines and thriving morning glory covered half the stone well. Overgrown grasses of green, brown, and yellow spread across the grounds like unraveling thread. A bitter, green scent wafted up as her feet crushed the leaves and grass. What would Lucia think if the cottage garden were still in such a state when she returned?

Kelsey bent down and decided the dandelions were the first weeds to tackle. They wouldn't bite her like the prickly variety, which could wait until she acquired gloves at the market. Dandelion after dandelion came up with the help of her spade, but even after what felt like hours, her work had hardly made a difference.

When an especially large dandelion came up by the leaves while the roots remained in the ground, Kelsey grumbled, "You'll be pestering me again with new growth, won't you?"

Through trial and error, and more blisters than she had expected, she eventually learned to sink her spade deep enough into the ground to leverage her strength against the roots to remove the bulk of those as well. After one last dandelion, she swelled with satisfaction to see the hefty mound that had finally accumulated. The greens would make an excellent addition to her family's meals. The blossoms she would use for tea, and the roots she would save for medicinal purposes.

When Kelsey noticed the sun sinking behind the trees, she eyed a particularly large dandelion and proclaimed it to be her last victim of the evening. She pushed her spade into the ground, but it clanked against something hard. Assuming it to be a rock, she continued to apply her spade. As the dandelion released its hold in the earth, Kelsey saw a gold guinea resting in its place. *What luck!* Wiping it off, she flicked it in the air and slipped it in her boot for later. Perhaps gardening had its benefits.

In case there were more, Kelsey sunk her spade again with renewed vigor and was rewarded with another clink. This time, she found three guineas. A little more digging and another dandelion pulled, and she found five more guineas. *This is more than luck,* she thought, tying the coins up in her underskirt.

Had someone lost them? Did anyone miss them? The ground appeared to have been undisturbed for some time, and surely, no one would hide them there on purpose. Suddenly, the garden held more possibilities than ever.

Despite the darkening sky and her promise to finish, she was about to start on another dandelion when the faint sound of whistling met her ears. Nathaniel Worth, small in the distance, was returning with a hat box and a parcel tucked under his arm.

Kelsey didn't know whether he had noticed her yet, but she was determined to avoid another conversation with him. Springing off the ground, she raced out of his view to the back of the house where she could access the shed. She ran to return the spade, dusted off her hands, and shook out her skirts. Smatterings of dirt and vivid grass stains were abundant. Her hem was stained brown as were her knuckles and fingernails. Grains of dirt stuck to her arms and face. Kelsey Wickham was not a vain girl, but she cringed to think Mr. Worth might see her so disheveled.

Knowing her time to retreat was nearly spent, she raced to the well and splashed water from the bucket onto her face. Cupping her hands, she tried to wash the dirt off her arms. However, in her haste, her elbow bumped the bucket, spilling water onto the fresh earth she had loosened with her work.

"Oh, blast!" Somehow, while reaching to right the bucket, its rope slunk under her foot like a snake and sent her slipping forward with hands outstretched.

Mud squished between her fingers, on her neck, and down the front of her dress, chilling her from head to toe. In an attempt to stand, she slipped again, then a third time, rolling onto her side so she was entirely covered in muck. Finally standing on her next attempt, she flicked a worm off her arm and, with nothing to use but her fingers, she brushed off as much mud as she could, which wasn't much at all.

Mr. Worth's whistling was growing louder.

There was no time for washing. She dashed inside through the back door, leaving an unavoidable trail she would worry about later. Cutting through the kitchen, she grabbed a pile of rags reserved for cleaning and ran to her room. She scrubbed her hands and arms with the rags as best she could, but new trails of mud clung to her skin as she struggled to pull off her dress.

Damp and cold like a newly caught fish, she stood shaking in the middle of her room in nothing but her soggy chemise. Where to put her filth-laden dress? Kelsey's insides squelched like the mud behind her ears when next she heard her mother opening the cottage door and thanking Mr. Worth for delivering her bonnet. Soon, his voice carried throughout the house and his boots clomped on the floorboards below. Holding as still as she could, despite the chills rushing over her in unrelenting waves, Kelsey earnestly wished him gone.

"Kelsey?" her mother called, her footsteps creaking up the stairs. "What on earth? Where did this trail of mud come from?"

Oh, no. Kelsey looked around, still holding her muddied dress, still puzzling over what to do when her mother knocked, then knocked again. Finally, she threw open the door.

Dropping her ruined dress, Kelsey yelped, and her mother screamed, slamming the door the next instant. Seconds later, Cissy's head popped in.

"What's all the screaming about? Kelsey, can I borrow your—" Cissy's eyes went wide. "Kelsey . . .?"

The humiliation was too much. Kelsey pushed Cissy out and closed the door with no explanation. Oh, why couldn't her door have a lock? No longer caring about the mud, Kelsey kicked her dress to the corner, leaned against the door, and sank to the floor. No doubt, Mr. Worth had heard everything.

Hot tears began to stream down her face, carrying the finer grains of dirt down her cheeks and the salty taste to her lips. She wasn't listening closely enough to hear any of the words spoken below, but she heard the regret in Mr. Worth's voice and the apologies in her mother's. At last, Mr. Worth stomped away, and the front door scraped into the ill-fitting frame.

Before long, her mother was outside her door once again. "Kelsey!" She pounded repeatedly on the wood. "Do you care to explain yourself? What sort of prank is this?"

Kelsey couldn't speak, her words as thick as the mud on her dress.

"Are you all right?" Several seconds passed in silence. "Kelsey, if you don't answer, I'll force this door open and hear all about it."

Kelsey swallowed forcefully, feeling the grit on her teeth and lips and wished for a glass of water. "I fell in the mud. Nothing more. Please let me be!"

Her mother's breath rasped with frustration. "Very well. I trust you're capable of cleaning yourself. Surely, you heard Mr. Worth downstairs. He delivered my new bonnet, but he also left a parcel for you. I wonder what it is . . ."

Kelsey heard paper crumpling just outside the door. "Are you opening it?"

"I only want a glimpse!" her mother called back. "Oh, the string is too tight. Here. I'm leaving it outside your door. I hope your sanity returns before he calls again. If ever he dares."

When her mother's footsteps retreated, Kelsey opened the door and collected the parcel. Wrapped in plain, brown paper, it was tied with twine with a small note stuck under the knot.

To a lady whose hands I should not like to see pricked by thorns again.

Kelsey snipped away the twine with scissors from her sewing box and unwrapped the paper. A great ripple of laughter pushed its way through the mud in her throat and burst from her lips like a butterfly when she saw the gift. It was a pair of thick, brown work gloves. Catching hints of new leather and soap, she held them up to the remaining glow of light that seeped through her window and put them on. As they warmed her hands, Kelsey wiggled her fingers and wondered whether Mr. Worth had tried them on. They were too big for her, but she didn't care. She would put them to good use.

Even she couldn't deny that Mr. Worth rose a trifle in her estimation for giving her something so practical. She laughed again, feeling the grains of dirt clearing from her lungs, and laid them back in the brown paper. Where to put them?

Searching her room, she stopped suddenly. In her distraction and filth, she must not have seen it. There, on the wall above her chest of drawers, in all its colorfully distorted glory, was the painting of her mother and father.

She dropped the gloves on the floor by her bed, crumpled the brown parcel paper, and flung it as hard as she could at the painting.

Chapter 8

"I often think," said she, "that there is nothing so bad as parting
with one's friends. One seems so forlorn without them."

Jane Austen, *Pride and Prejudice*

The next week was spent fussing over Cissy and her impending trip. When Mrs. Wickham wasn't spending time with Mr. Baxter, she was making lists of things to purchase, giving advice of varying quality, and crying over losing her daughter for such a long time.

"Oh, my dear Cissy! I begin to feel as if my nerves won't be able to handle you leaving!"

"I'll miss you too, Mama."

Such was the exchange Kelsey observed each day leading up to Cissy's departure.

When the Pendlestones finally arrived to convey Cissy to Warlingham, Kelsey was stunned by the amount of things Cissy was bringing with her. Beyond her usual wardrobe, her portmanteau held three new gowns, a new pair of calf-skin boots, new dance slippers, new gloves, two new bonnets, and a fine wool pelisse. If her mother had somehow convinced herself that having Cissy stay with relatives would help her and Kelsey economize, she was completely addled. Any amount of money they might have saved in Cissy's absence would be negated by this influx in spending. How had their mother managed to purchase so many things without Kelsey noticing?

Out of Cissy's hearing, Kelsey confronted her mother. "I thought we agreed on one new dress and one pair of boots."

"I won't have my daughter looking like a pauper among her rich relatives." Mrs. Wickham carefully laid the last of Cissy's things at the top of her portmanteau.

"Certainly not, but you'll make paupers out of *us* nonetheless." If Mrs. Wickham said anything after that, Kelsey ignored it. She much preferred her last moments with Cissy to be spent laughing and smiling rather than arguing with their mother.

A brief tea was laid out for Sarah and Jack Pendlestone and their mother before they continued on their journey. Mrs. Pendlestone spoke but a few civil words. Sarah was her usual reserved and proper self but kindly enquired about the cottage and whether Kelsey was enjoying herself. Jack was quiet but watched Cissy with obvious interest, and Cissy's smile was always brighter when it was directed at him.

Oh, please let Cissy behave herself!

After the Pendlestones returned to their carriage and it was time for Cissy to join them, Kelsey pulled her close. "I wish you didn't have to go, but I'm sure you'll have a marvelous time. I'll miss you, Cissybear." It was her old pet name, the same their father had liked to call her when he was sober.

"Oh, Kelsey!"

Surprised to see tears in her eyes, Kelsey wrapped her into another hug. "We'll see each other again soon." She took Cissy's hand and placed in it five of the nine guineas she had discovered in the garden, neatly bundled in a plain, white handkerchief. She didn't want Cissy to be away from home with empty pockets, even if those pockets were lined with silk.

Cissy's jaw dropped when she realized what she had been given, but Kelsey quickly closed Cissy's fingers around them, not wanting to draw their mother's attention to the gift. "For a rainy day. Into your reticule. Quickly." Their mother was pulling out a fresh handkerchief and hadn't noticed the exchange. "I'm already eager for your return, but I'm glad you have this opportunity. My only fear is that you won't want to return."

Cissy laughed through a choked sob. "Little chance of that. I'll have to return eventually, won't I? Who else will be your bridesmaid?"

Kelsey released Cissy's hand and looked her in the eye. "What nonsense are you referring to?"

"I'm talking about Mr. Worth. He likes you." Cissy poked her in the side, her tears already drying. "And I think you like him."

Kelsey gave Cissy a playful push. "Oh, you do? Well, I think it's time for you to go."

Cissy giggled, and Kelsey was able to blink back her own tears. It felt good to end their goodbyes on a jest.

Cissy hugged their mother again and stepped into the carriage. "I'll write to you!" she called from the window.

"Goodbye, my darling!"

Kelsey and Mrs. Wickham ran down the path and waved until the carriage was out of sight. The dust hadn't yet settled when Kelsey and her mother looked curiously at one another. Were they thinking the same thing? *Alone with you for several weeks.*

"I'll be working in the garden today," Kelsey said. "I could use your help clearing the vegetable beds."

Her mother took a sudden interest in the pebbles at her feet. "I was planning on calling on Mrs. Salaway and Miss Chatham today. I wouldn't mind if you wanted to accompany me."

But Kelsey headed for the vegetable beds while her mother went strolling down the road.

The next few days were long and lonely for Kelsey as she and her mother fell into a routine. They breakfasted together, exchanged a few words, then parted for much of the day. Whenever they passed one another in those in-between moments, Mrs. Wickham was often carrying a handful of ribbons or an extra bonnet. Kelsey always watched for the bills that would reveal her mother's spending, but she never found any.

Besides cleaning, cooking, and keeping the books, Kelsey spent her time in the garden or, on the rarest occasions, by a window reading. Once, she saw Mr. Worth from her window walking along on the road, then a second time while she attempted to clear more weeds. She held her breath each time, wondering whether he would approach, but he only sauntered on in that swaggering way of his. *Good,* she thought. *Very good. I don't want him visiting me at all.*

A letter came from Cissy stating she had arrived safely, and all was lovely at Warlingham, especially the pond where eight ducklings lived. Hardly a week had passed, and already Kelsey missed the way Cissy would bound down the stairs with stale bits of food in her hands for hungry creatures. Kelsey hadn't realized until now how often Cissy had lightened their home with her simple chatter and bridged the conversations between Kelsey and their mother that otherwise faded like the sun each night.

Time alone in her room was hardly a reprieve. The painting of her parents still hung there to mock her with the possibility of a future she never wanted for herself. Why didn't her mother ever ask about it, she wondered? And why did Kelsey not feel entitled to remove it herself? All she understood was that she was determined never to raise the topic with her mother, no matter how sorely she was tempted to hurl the painting out the window or toss it in the fireplace.

One night, Kelsey took her shawl and draped it over the painting, but when she retired to bed, she could not forget her parents' faces, giggling and kissing behind the fabric.

"I know I'm being ridiculous," she said to the painting as she rose from her bed and tore down the shawl, "but covering you has accomplished nothing."

A fortnight after Cissy's departure, news began spreading that the Salaways were organizing their annual summer ball. When an invitation arrived, Mrs. Wickham was in ecstasies.

"There are sure to be any number of eligible men there for both you and I!"

On the day of the ball, Kelsey decided she had more important things to do than fuss over her dress and hair. She dusted every corner of the cottage, wiped the kitchen shelves, cleaned the cutlery, and churned the cream Mrs. Reynolds had given them into butter. Her final task to firmly impress on her mother that she wanted nothing to do with the ball was a final sweep of the sitting room.

With broom in hand, Kelsey made her way around the furniture, careful to reach under each chair. The hearthstones around the fireplace needed extra attention due to their several cracks and grooves for dirt to hide in.

"Kelsey!" her mother called from upstairs. "Don't be too long down there. I need your help with my hair."

Kelsey spun around too quickly to respond and knocked a vase off the side table and onto the floor. Ceramic shards of various sizes scattered among the hearthstones she had swept seconds earlier.

"Confound it!"

Bending down to gather the shards, she noticed something tightly tucked in the crack beneath the windowsill and the wall, a paper perhaps. Why would a paper be tucked into the crack? Careful not to tear it, she used her fingernail to urge it free.

The paper was slightly damp and emitted an earthy smell that reminded Kelsey of old books. The inside was faded, but even so, the slanted strokes and speckled ink splotches were clear enough to make out.

The sky is a canopy we share no matter the distance that separates us. I will think of you always, my darling wife, the brightness of whose cheeks would shame the stars.

Kelsey recognized the words adapted from Shakespeare in the final line. Could the note have been written by Captain Styles? Hadn't Mrs. Winters said he once lived in the cottage? The sitting room took on a new feeling as Kelsey imagined his lonely wife finding the tender note during one of his absences. But if it was still tucked beneath the windowsill, had his wife ever found it? Bringing the note to her heart and releasing a sigh, Kelsey realized for the first time in her life that she might have a sentimental side after all.

"Kelsey!" Her mother's call shook her from her daydreams. "Could you help me now?"

Kelsey hastily folded the note and wedged it back within the crack as best she could. If the captain's wife had never discovered the note, Kelsey didn't want to disturb it. After taking care to discard the shards of the broken vase, she went to her mother's room and found her sitting before the glass. Kelsey picked up a comb and silently went to work on the thick, wavy strands that had not a single grey hair yet among them.

"Have you heard, Kelsey? Mr. Baxter has been talking about me."

Kelsey methodically twisted and pinned her mother's hair, still thinking of the words of the note . . . *the brightness of whose cheeks would shame the stars.*

"Apparently, he commented to Mrs. Salaway that he is looking forward to seeing me at the ball tonight, and I will admit, I'm looking forward to seeing him as well." She clapped her hands together when Kelsey finished. "Perfect! My, you are a wonder with hair." Standing up and twirling around the room, she stopped abruptly. "I have a surprise. This came for you earlier today while you were cleaning the kitchen." Reaching down beside her bed, she produced a large package wrapped in brown paper. "Someone from Pemberley delivered it."

From Pemberley? Kelsey took the package and tested its weight. Not a single idea came to mind as to what it could be. Sometimes Mrs. Reynolds or one of the maids brought fresh fruit or eggs, but nothing specially wrapped. Sitting on the bed, Kelsey tore off two layers of paper to reveal a white box with a violet ribbon wrapped neatly around it. Kelsey ran her hand over the smooth surface and slid the ribbon between her fingers.

"Goodness, Kelsey. Just open it!"

"All right." Kelsey brushed a stray curl from her eyes and pulled the ribbon, undoing the small symmetric bow that felt like a gift in itself. She gently lifted the lid. Inside was a white, satin ball gown that shone in the light like an iridescent pearl. Thin strips of delicate lace resembling snowflakes traced the neckline and waist while the sleeves made Kelsey think of frosted tulips.

"Oh my!" both Kelsey and her mother breathed out.

Kelsey gingerly lifted it from the box and let wonder give way to excitement. Was this gown really meant for her? Never had she owned anything so fine. In a very uncharacteristic manner, she held the gown against herself and spun around the room with it.

"Have you ever seen anything so lovely?" Mrs. Wickham sighed. "Is there a card inside?"

Kelsey sat back on the bed and laid the gown across her lap. A note rested at the bottom of the box.

Dearest Kelsey,

I know the Salaways always hold their summer ball this time of year, and I couldn't imagine this dress on anyone else. If you and I are still of similar size, the fit should be close enough. I hope you will accept it as both a gift and an apology. I'm sorry I was not at Pemberley to welcome you, and I'm sorry to keep this letter so brief. All my news will be best told in person, but I assure you, Barley Cottage will be the first place I visit when I return.

Your cousin,
Lucia

"That dress almost makes me able to forgive that girl for tricking us into tending the garden."

Kelsey laughed, too delighted to point out that her mother never tended the garden. Never had Kelsey cared for gowns or fashion of any sort, but she instantly loved that dress. It was a gift from Lucia, and it was unimaginably breathtaking.

The gift would have been perfect if only Lucia's note had contained some news, any news that might have explained how Lucia fared and why she was away. To be so close to Pemberley and still separated from her was supremely frustrating. Why did Lucia not account for her absence? It left a hole in Kelsey's middle as empty as a dried up well, and all Kelsey could do was fill it with suspicions that the Darcys had left because she and her family were Wickhams.

At least, she knew Lucia was thinking of her.

"You must wear it to the ball this evening." Her mother spoke softly, brushing her hand over Kelsey's curls before running her fingers along the detailed lace.

Kelsey looked up at her mother and smiled. For once, she completely agreed.

Chapter 9

*Lydia was Lydia still; untamed,
unabashed, wild, noisy, and fearless.*

Jane Austen, *Pride and Prejudice*

Candlelight and crystal glittered in every corner of the ballroom, but Kelsey stepped in feeling like she had a special star illuminating her, a result of the pearlescent dress from Lucia. Her mother had skipped ahead, already lost among those dancing, and for the first time in her life, Kelsey was not trapped in her mother's shadow. She was shining, bright, clear, and lovely. Her confidence drove her through the crowds of finely dressed people. Gentleman smiled at her. Ladies enviously eyed her gown, and she smiled in return with a grace she didn't know she possessed.

At first, she didn't care whether she danced or spent the whole evening watching others be merry. All she cared about was being able to interact with others exactly as she wanted without the reputation of her mother dragging her along.

Mr. Chatham was the first to find her. "Good evening, Miss Wickham. I'm surprised to see you alone. Why are you not dancing?"

Kelsey regarded his brown hair, firm brow, and lean figure. Cissy had called him handsome. She supposed it was true. "Good evening, Mr. Chatham. I've only recently arrived, but I find just as much pleasure in being among friends as I do in dancing."

Mr. Chatham scoffed. "I can't believe that. All young ladies prefer to dance. There is much more opportunity for us to enjoy one another's company while dancing." He leaned closer and pointed toward the musicians. "They're about to start again. Shall we?"

Why not? Kelsey took his hand and followed him to the dance floor. From the corner of her eye, she saw her mother joining the couples on the arm of a gentleman with particularly thick side whiskers. Kelsey's skirts caught the candlelight in its sheen, and she held her head high, determined not to worry about her mother.

A cheery tune began to skip, and their feet soon followed. After weaving through the couples and rejoining one another, Mr. Chatham took her hand and looked her over. "I have been puzzling over something, Miss Wickham, and perhaps I am a fool not to ask your opinion."

"My opinion of what, sir?"

"Of what I might do or say to bring a smile to those rosy lips of yours. I can't bear the thought of finishing this dance with you wearing that sullen expression on your face."

Kelsey didn't think her expression could be sullen, not when she had felt the evening's light surrounding her, but at the unmistakable sound of her mother's shrill laughter, a tightness crept into her face which she immediately forced away with an easier expression.

"That's a start." He winked. "Though I don't feel I've earned it. You are quite the mystery to me."

Kelsey narrowed her eyes. What did Mr. Chatham want? "Well, becoming acquainted usually begins with civil questions."

Mr. Chatham chuckled as if she had said something dreadfully amusing. "I won't waste precious time on *civil* questions. Like most ladies, I'm sure you either draw, sing, or embroider." He spoke as if completely confident in his assessment.

"Embroider?" Kelsey had never embroidered anything. She only patched up tears in clothing when it was strictly necessary. She didn't sing or draw either.

Another reel of laughter recognizable only as her mother's stretched the air, making Kelsey grimace.

"Your mother is certainly very . . . spirited." Mr. Chatham's amused tones were unmistakable. "Unfortunately, such spirits don't seem to run in the family." His critical brow arched up as a provoking grin twisted his lips. "Or do they, Miss Wickham?"

"I beg your pardon?" She instantly regretted responding to his bait.

"I never hear you laugh the way your mother does."

Kelsey scoffed. "I should hope not."

"Ah, I see. You wish to be unique, but I don't hear you laugh at all."

Kelsey stiffened, then stumbled. Dancing down the line of couples had brought them to a shadowed corner where the candles were nearly spent. His words hit her like a jab to her side, but he was right. She didn't laugh as much as her mother, not nearly as much. Since Cissy's departure, Kelsey couldn't remember the last time she had laughed at all. What could she do to remedy that? She determined to think on it, but not with Mr. Chatham smugly observing her.

"Perhaps you ought to ask my mother to dance if you wish to hear more laughter."

"I don't think so. Nothing you've said convinces me you're as pure as that gown. You and I just need more time."

Anger prickled through her skin. The last thing she wanted was more time with Mr. Chatham.

On the next spin, she noticed Mr. Worth a few couples down dancing with a pretty girl whose ginger curls bounced with each step. Both were smiling.

Very good, she thought. *I'm glad he's enjoying himself. I don't care to dance with him at all.*

When the dance ended, Mr. Chatham kept at Kelsey's heels as she tried to retreat. What had she done to embolden him?

"What kind of escort would I be if I left you unattended?" he asked as he followed her. "Are you searching for your mother? You'd be welcome to join my sister and me. Ah! There's Beatrice now." He pointed to Miss Chatham who stood a few paces off with Mr. and Mrs. Salaway. "She makes eyes at every gentleman, but there is only one she is genuinely interested in."

At that moment, Miss Chatham's gaze wandered to where Nathaniel stood, still talking with the young lady with ginger curls.

"Mr. Chatham, you must excuse me. I intend to find my mother." Kelsey didn't really want to return to her mother, but she didn't want to join Mr. Chatham, not after the way his eyes grazed her while dancing. Kelsey strategically maneuvered between two large groups of people so he would have difficulty following.

It didn't take Kelsey long to locate her mother. She merely listened for the continuous giggling that was more befitting of a young schoolgirl. On the outskirts of the ballroom where the guests were thin stood her mother with Mr. Baxter by a set of open doors that led outside. His hand rested on the slope of her mother's neck, and he was leaning, whispering something. Kelsey's jaw clenched and her fists tightened with the urge to tear Mr. Baxter away. She nearly thought she had the strength to do it. When her mother smiled and crimsoned in response to his whispers, Kelsey knew she had to act.

"Mother!" she cried out, but either her mother hadn't heard or was choosing to ignore her. "Mother!" Kelsey called louder, navigating around wandering couples to get closer.

Her mother turned only to whip an impatient glare at Kelsey before giggling with Mr. Baxter again. Kelsey's fingers and toes went numb as her mother wrapped her arms snugly in his and pulled him through the double doors toward the heavily shaded gardens beyond.

Suddenly aware of several pairs of eyes that might be watching, Kelsey wished to dim the sheen of her dress that she was beginning to fear was too fine for a Wickham like her. The thought felt like a betrayal to Lucia, but for the first time since moving to Barley Cottage, she was glad no one from Pemberley was there who might witness her humiliation. Rumors were sure to follow, and she hadn't yet had even a sliver of an opportunity to demonstrate to the Darcys that she wanted to be respectable. Oh, why did this always happen? Why did her mother rush into every possibility of a relationship in the most improper way, never pausing to think?

Kelsey leaned against the wall and tried to quell the wave of nausea that rose in her stomach. She had to do something to end the pattern.

Mrs. Winters and three other matronly ladies appeared from the crowds, pausing only a small distance from where Kelsey still leaned against the wall. They hadn't yet noticed her, too enthralled by their whispering and snickering.

"The captain was here, I tell you! I'm certain I saw him."

"Of course, you didn't, Matilda. One hardly ever sees him even when he is here."

"The only way he'd attend a ball is in a mask. Though, I do wonder..."

"There was a gentleman here earlier who looked like him. I'm certain."

Mrs. Winters shushed the ladies and pointed toward the garden doors. Mrs. Wickham and Mr. Baxter could just barely be seen near the trees before slipping further into shadow. "Looks like the Wickham legacy lives on," she sang.

Like a flock of birds, the ladies turned in unison to see.

"It's astonishing how George Wickham managed to find someone exactly like himself."

"Just look at how she carries on as if she cared nothing for her late husband. Although, I'm not sure anything would be different if he were still alive."

A new round of giggles broke out. It was the same no matter where Kelsey went, but the sting of such words always spread like venom. All Kelsey could do was bite her lips and fight nausea with anger.

"I, for one, am anxious to see what scandal the daughters will raise up. With parents like theirs, it's only a matter of time."

"Oh, to be sure!"

"Once a Wickham, always a Wickham."

As they turned away from the garden doors, they saw Kelsey. For a moment, they all stood staring with mouths agape. A conflict of emotions skidded across their faces, but none looked apologetic.

Kelsey lengthened her spine and endured their stares. *Never mind them*, she thought. They hadn't said anything new. She, on the other hand, could think of several original remarks to make, but just as she was mustering the energy, the words soured in her mouth. The last thing she wanted to do was provide those women fodder for their fire. All she would give was a dark glare, the depths of which she had perfected over the years in similar moments.

Eventually, the ladies moved along, tilting their noses and fluttering their fans like hens with ruffled feathers. Kelsey followed them with her eyes as long as she could, hoping to appear as if they hadn't wounded her, but as soon as she lost sight of them, she leaned against the garden door and stared into the darkness. All the confidence Kelsey had radiated earlier faded to nothing as two fat tears slid down her cheeks.

A gentle touch on her shoulder startled her breathing. Mr. Worth stood next to her with that smile of his that always looked ready for a jest. She might have walked away without a word had his face not swiftly shifted to concern when he took in her troubled expression.

"Dare I say it?" The corners of his lips lowered. "You look unwell yet again, Miss Wickham."

Kelsey wiped the wetness off her cheeks as casually as she could. "Do not call me Miss Wickham!" she spat. If there were any way to change her name in that moment, she wouldn't have hesitated.

Mr. Worth shook his head. "I cannot do right with you, can I, miss? That temper is going to get you in trouble one day."

When he turned to walk away, Kelsey felt a tug in her center. "No, wait! Please. I . . . I'm sorry. I spoke without thinking. You're right about my temper, but I'm not angry with you."

He stopped and tilted his head. "An apology is nice. I would ask you to dance, but you look as though you wish to avoid the crowds for the time being. Would you like to talk outside in the gardens?" He gestured toward the path her mother had just taken with Mr. Baxter. "We'll stay on the terrace where it's well lit, of course."

Kelsey's first instinct was to refuse, but she didn't want to leave the ball having made enemies of everyone. Something inside her refused to risk another offense to Mr. Worth. "Let's go to the east gardens."

Those appeared brighter with more torches and faced the largest of the ballroom windows, making them, at least in Kelsey's mind, the more respectable option.

Mr. Worth followed as she led the way.

A smiling moon with violet-grey clouds greeted them outside. The breezes blowing through the trees' leaves made Kelsey think of rushing water, a sound that always calmed her. As the music and the chatter of the crowds grew fainter, her chest lightened, and she had room to breathe freely again. Mr. Worth alternated between straightening his lapels and examining the buttons on his coat. Was it possible he was nervous? Kelsey smiled to see him suddenly self-conscious and found herself wanting to offer him an explanation.

"I must apologize again, Mr. Worth, for my behavior. I have not been myself these past few . . ." How long had it been since she had last felt like herself? Weeks? Years? The gift from Lucia had given Kelsey a taste of her own light, but the flavor had dissolved on her tongue and left her craving more.

Mr. Worth stopped fidgeting, and his eyes softened. "It's all right. A gentleman should forgive."

Kelsey nodded, remembering the hasty comment she'd made at the Salaways' dinner implying he was not a gentleman. "Yes, thank you." She looked beyond the terrace to where the glistening of a pond was barely visible in the moonlight. "And thank you for the gloves."

His expression brightened. "I hope they suit you."

"Quite well, yes." She felt a smile spring to her lips, but at the thought of her mother's behavior and the insults from the gossips, it faded away.

Mr. Worth drew his brows together. "But they are not the sort of gift you would have preferred?"

"Oh, no! I adore the gloves." She bit the inside of her cheek. Was it wise to sound so pleased with his gift?

"But there is something troubling you, is there not?"

She didn't know what overcame her. Perhaps it was his sincerity. Perhaps it was the novelty of having someone interested in her woes, but with no thought for the consequences, she told him. "Yes, there is. You have no doubt noticed my mother. Everyone notices her."

He nodded like he understood.

"My mother has a knack for attracting two things, scandalous gossip and scandalous men. I don't think she ever intends to be imprudent, but regardless of her intentions, the past follows us, and scandal holds on for dear life. It is the same wherever we go. I can't help but be frustrated." When she looked up and realized Mr. Worth was listening to her every word, she felt like a broken fountain spouting everywhere. "Forgive me for telling you this. I know it is improper."

A single tear slid down her cheek. She didn't realize she had shut her eyes until the touch of Mr. Worth's hand on her shoulder jolted them open again. If his features had conveyed anything beyond understanding and sympathy, she would have pulled away, but the longer his hand was there, the more her muscles felt a softness overcoming them like candle wax melting in the heat.

"Think nothing of it," he breathed out, dropping his hand. Staring toward the light on the pond, he added, "Would that I could help you."

She blinked out yet another tear. She couldn't remember the last time anyone other than Lucia had wanted to help her, and Lucia was miles away.

"Thank you." Kelsey was suddenly brimming with a desire to release the thoughts that had been building for so long without any sympathetic ear to hear them. She tried to swallow down the memories, the past humiliations as well as the looming ones, but one thought overpowered her. "My mother must be stopped." The truth of those words reverberated through her chest like a ringing bell until it sunk to her core and echoed in her toes.

"Stopped?"

"Yes, I am certain of it. My mother must be stopped." Her conviction grew each time she said it. "She is ruining us. She doesn't realize it, of course, but she doesn't know any other way."

"Any other way to what?"

"To catch a husband," Kelsey intoned as if it were the most sinister of plots. "She wants to remarry."

"What's the matter with that? Your mother is a pleasant woman. I don't see why that should cause you trouble."

Kelsey rubbed her arm as she considered how to explain. "I don't blame her for not wanting to be alone, but all the respectable men are put off by her flippancy and the way she embraces any show of attention, even when it is from the village idiot."

"Mr. Baxter?" Nathaniel smiled knowingly.

"The worst part is once she realizes the village idiot either lacks the means or the intention to marry, she displaces our family."

"Displaces?" Mr. Worth's gentle attentiveness grew into concern.

"It is the reason we are here. My mother left Whitewell once she realized her last beau was not the knight in shining armor she had been hoping for. When I see her and Mr. Baxter together . . ." She shuddered. "Well, I would hate to leave Barley Cottage before I finish unpacking."

Mr. Worth stared into the distance as if seeing the possibilities, then turned to her. "I want to help."

The tiny pinpoints of stars sparkled in his eyes, and she released a wistful sigh. "Thank you. If only."

"No, I really want to help. I don't want you to . . . Well, you've only just arrived. It would be a shame to lose you so quickly."

"I don't want to leave, but what can I do? I don't know if my mother can be stopped."

"Perhaps not, but might there be some way to distract her?"

"Distract her . . ." Kelsey repeated, delighted by the sound of the words. "I don't know. Men have always been her distraction in life, and nothing distracts her from men. Not even gowns and jewelry."

"It's simple, then. We have to distract her from Mr. Baxter with another man."

Kelsey frowned. "I don't see how that will solve anything."

"It might not, but it can give Mr. Baxter some healthy competition."

"Competition," Kelsey mused. Something about Nathaniel's idea held promise, but how could she arrange it? "I don't know who or how or . . . I don't suppose you know anyone respectable. Or are you volunteering?"

"I am not volunteering," he said emphatically, "but perhaps I can think of someone for you." He folded his hands behind his back and looked up in thought.

"Even if you do," Kelsey considered, "there is no way to guarantee he would court my mother. Or that she would behave herself."

"I suppose not, but perhaps we could—"

"We'll make him up!" Kelsey was seized by the idea. "You're brilliant!"

"That's not exactly what I said," he chuckled, "but I won't argue with your belief in my brilliance."

"It's perfect!" Kelsey ignored his jest. "She doesn't need an actual man to distract her from Mr. Baxter, just the idea of one, the promise of someone more compatible to help her see Mr. Baxter's flaws and realize her own errors of judgment."

"You're not serious, are you?" Mr. Worth leaned closer and met her excited look with a dubious one.

Mr. Worth's sudden proximity made Kelsey's mind leap. A made up man? What had she been saying? And to a man she hardly knew! "Oh, my! Forgive me, Mr. Worth! We shouldn't be talking this way. Once again, I've said too much." She turned away with her hands to her cheeks, hoping to hide their color and calm her spinning mind.

Mrs. Winters's voice echoed through her thoughts. *I, for one, am anxious to see what scandal the daughters will raise up.*

The heat in her face would not go away. Kelsey couldn't help it. She was making a fool of herself. She was revealing feelings on matters much too sensitive to disclose to a mere acquaintance. She was acting like a Wickham.

"Wait." Mr. Worth put his hand on her shoulder again, and she turned to face him. "All you've done is honor me with your confidence. I promise I'll be worthy of it. You can trust me."

He dropped his hand, and Kelsey searched the openness in his eyes, looking for the laugh or the lie. She wasn't sure she trusted him, but she had no one else to turn to. She was desperate.

As if sensing her wariness, he added, "We'll solve your dilemma. I really want to help you, Miss—" He stopped abruptly. "Well, there is one problem."

"Only one?" Kelsey tittered. "What is that?"

"I need to know how to address you without raising that temper of yours."

Her cheeks burned deeper under his stare despite the soft breezes that kept coming. He really was offering his help. She didn't know what sort of scheme he had in mind or what she had in hers, for that matter, but his was the only offer of help she had ever received to stop her mother's destructive ways. Mr. Worth would still be under her scrutiny. He was still a swaggering man who held his own secrets, but what choice did she have? She would make a friend out of him, and she decided right then and there that she never wanted him to think of her as one of *those Wickhams*.

"You may call me Kelsey."

"Well, then, Lady Kelsey." He took her hand and brushed a quick kiss on her knuckles. "I am at your service."

Chapter 10

It is very often nothing but our own vanity that deceives us.

Jane Austen, *Pride and Prejudice*

When the sun cast its earliest light, Kelsey rose from bed to initiate her plan. She could hardly sleep with ideas and schemes bouncing through her thoughts like wild rabbits. Such schemes would require deception, a point which nipped at Kelsey's conscience, but she reminded herself that the well-being of her entire family was at stake.

The more Kelsey thought the matter over, the more she realized her idea was genius. As long as she could convince her mother that she had another admirer – never mind that he wasn't real – her mother would keep their family at Barley Cottage even after Mr. Baxter disappointed her. Kelsey's mother only needed to remember she had options to choose from. Perhaps, in time, she would find a match worth waiting for.

While her mother still slept, Kelsey ran to the fields just beyond the cottage where the forest began and collected a rainbow of wildflowers. Early morning mist drifted around her ankles like a nuzzling cat while a robin hopped from the grass to the trees. When her bouquet was large and varied enough to satisfy her, she took a yellow ribbon and tied it together with a note she had prepared the night before that said, *To Lydia Wickham, the brightness of whose cheeks would shame the stars.*

Kelsey was quite proud of her note. She had no idea what kind of romantic line would catch her mother's attention, so she drew inspiration from the message lying tucked between the wall and windowsill. She also attempted to pattern her own handwriting after the note's to disguise her own. When she was finished, Kelsey laid the flowers at the cottage door and returned inside to wait for her mother to discover them.

Unfortunately, patience wasn't a virtue Kelsey possessed in abundance. To distract her thoughts, she stoked the kitchen fire and began to prepare some dandelion tea. She gathered all her clothes that needed laundering and threw them in the large wash basin, then swept the kitchen floor. With those chores underway and her mother still in bed, she settled on writing letters to Cissy and Lucia. What were they doing just then? Cissy was most likely chasing a puppy or kitten, but Lucia was sure to be practicing the pianoforte if one was within her reach. How Kelsey missed them!

When her patience could hold no longer, she started devising ways to get her mother to discover the flowers, but a knock on the door saved her the trouble. Mrs. Wickham strolled down the stairs, inserting the last of her hairpins, and answered the door.

Mrs. Winters stood expressionless with the flowers in hand. "Good morning, Mrs. Wickham. It would appear you have flowers. Ah!"

She sneezed as a bee emerged from the bouquet and circled her head, making her drop the flowers and wave frantically until the bee flew off toward the fields. "Oh, dear! Forgive me. I've been afraid of bees ever since stumbling into a nest as a child."

"How lovely!" Oblivious to Mrs. Winters's outburst, Mrs. Wickham took the flowers and pressed the petals to her nose. "Oh, my!" she whispered as she opened the note and silently read its contents. She smelled the flowers again, then looked at Mrs. Winters as if noticing her for the first time. "Good morning, Mrs. Winters. Do come in."

Mrs. Winters sneezed twice more and stepped inside. "I assume you know the flowers are not from me."

Mrs. Wickham giggled. "Of course, not. Please, have a seat while I put these in water."

She bustled past Kelsey to the kitchen, leaving her alone to greet Mrs. Winters with a stiff curtsey. The memory of her backbiting words at the ball still stung in Kelsey's thoughts.

"I do hope you enjoyed yourself at the ball last night." Mrs. Winters dipped into a solemn curtsey.

Kelsey did her best to pull up a smile, refusing to give Mrs. Winters the satisfaction of seeing her upset. "I did, despite a few unpleasant words I overheard. Thank you."

Mrs. Winters's eye made a slight twitch. "I'm surprised you're not still resting after such late festivities. I, myself, left at half past ten. That's my rule. I always leave by half past ten, no matter how late a ball begins. As the rector's wife, it is essential I set a good example."

"Of course," Kelsey responded lightly. "I don't know what I would have done last night without your example."

Mrs. Winters's nostrils flared as she opened her mouth, but before she could say anything, Mrs. Wickham returned, humming a dancing tune. In her hands was a vase full of the wildflowers, which she set on the table next to the sofa. A light, floral scent drifted through the room.

"To what do we owe the pleasure of your company on such a beautiful day, Mrs. Winters?" She gestured to the sofa and eased into her chair as gracefully as a duchess.

Mrs. Winters glared at the vase of flowers as she took her seat. "I merely thought I owed it to you to see that everything . . . that you . . ." She seemed to struggle for the right words. "I do hope you are all right after last night."

Kelsey prepared her arguments as her mother spoke easily. "Of course. Why wouldn't I be?"

Mrs. Winters frowned, revealing lines around her mouth and chin. "Because of all the talk." Her eyes momentarily shifted to Kelsey.

"After the compromising circumstances in which you were seen last night with a certain gentleman, you must be feeling troubled this morning."

"Compromising?" Mrs. Wickham smiled as if Mrs. Winters might be jesting. "I hardly think strolling among open gardens at a private ball is compromising. I assure you, a widowed woman such as I can certainly fend for herself in a garden." She leaned forward and pressed Mrs. Winters's hand. "I trust you know better than to listen to silly rumors."

Kelsey had to cough to cover a small, involuntary laugh as Mrs. Winters's eyes widened.

"Very well." Mrs. Winters rose from her seat, shaking her head. "I see I shouldn't have taken the trouble to care as I do. The burden of a rector's wife is never light, and not all are fit for it."

"Oh, but it's very kind of you to care."

Mrs. Wickham stood, still aglow with the delight of receiving flowers. Kelsey could clearly see that gossip, at least in this instance, was harming the gossiper more than the one being gossiped about.

"I'll leave you to it." Mrs. Winters made for the door. "Only, I must warn you. Other ladies in the vicinity will not be as generous in their assessments as I am. Good day." After a brisk curtsey, she saw herself out.

"How odd," Mrs. Wickham mumbled. "Oh, but never mind! Kelsey, did you see those beautiful flowers?"

Kelsey shook off Mrs. Winters's sourness and made herself cheerful. "I wonder who they're from."

"I have a suspicion." A teasing look stole into Mrs. Wickham's eyes.

Oh no. "Mother, you cannot think these are from Mr. Baxter." Kelsey cursed her lack of foresight. Of course, her mother would leap to that conclusion.

"It is just the sort of gesture a romantic gentleman like him would make. I knew coming to Derbyshire was a good idea."

"The note is quoting *Romeo and Juliet.*" Kelsey started to sweat. "Does Mr. Baxter strike you as the sort of man who would quote Shakespeare?"

Mrs. Wickham pressed a finger to her lips as she examined the flowers. "I don't know. I haven't heard him mention Shakespeare, but that doesn't mean he couldn't quote him."

Kelsey also regarded the flowers. The yellow, violet, and pink blossoms, so vibrant an hour ago, were now wilting around the edges.

"I suppose not, but you shouldn't take it for granted. There were many men at the ball last night who could have given those to you."

Mrs. Wickham turned a keen eye on Kelsey, and for a moment, Kelsey wondered whether her mother saw through the charade.

"You are absolutely right." Her mother leaned in and smelled the flowers again. "Did you hear all the talk last night about the captain? Several people said they saw him at the ball. I wonder . . ." She tilted her head and moved a few petals around as if searching through them. "I won't say a word about the flowers to Mr. Baxter. If he gave them to me, he'll surely give me some sort of sign. It's entirely possible I have another admirer."

"Absolutely." Kelsey agreed.

Chapter 11

*It is particularly incumbent on those who never change
their opinion, to be secure of judging properly at first.*

Jane Austen, *Pride and Prejudice*

*K*elsey sat on her bed reviewing the letters that had recently
arrived. A few were requests for payment of purchases her
mother had made in the village, one of which was for a new gown.
Kelsey groaned. The village shopkeepers didn't yet know better than
to trust her mother's credit. The last letter in the pile pushed away her
dismay and made her insides bubble with delight. It was from Lucia.
All other letters were dropped on the bed as Kelsey broke the seal and
read.

Dear Kelsey,

*How are you and your mother getting on at Barley Cottage?
Isn't it a dear little place? I hope the garden is not too much trouble for you. When the blackberries on the south side ripen, you
will see that tending them was worth the effort. I hope you wore*

the white silk gown to the Salaways' ball. I am sure you were the most beautiful lady in attendance that night. I truly regret not being there with you.

I still do not know how long I am to remain away, as much depends on when my father finishes this mysterious business of his in London, but know that I miss you. There are many enjoyable paths around Pemberley that I long to show you. All in good time, I suppose.

Until then, I'm afraid I have a message that will seem strange to you. I recently met a man by the name of Woodcox here in Nottinghamshire who expressed an interest in visiting Pemberley and the surrounding parts. I have reason to suspect his motives are less than worthy. I don't feel equal to the task of writing those reasons in a letter, but there is something about his speech and manner I do not trust. I don't wish to discredit him, only to put you on your guard should you encounter him.

Unfortunately, I must also hint that Mr. Chatham has not particularly impressed me with his ideals of honor. I'm afraid I have a much stronger basis for my warning in this instance. And, dear me! What a terrible letter I have written to you! Forgive me if I have alarmed you. I dare not say more until we speak together in person. Until then, take care to be safe.

Lucia

As Kelsey finished reading, her eyes strayed to the window where she had a perfect view of the garden. Though she had been tending it, the weeds seemed to grow faster than she could clear them, and much remained to be done. She didn't even know blackberries were growing amidst all that bramble. But more than berries and weeds, Kelsey wondered at Lucia's warnings. Kelsey didn't know anyone by the name of Woodcox. Why would Lucia make such an ominous mention of the man but explain nothing? They had always confided their secrets to one another. The only part that made sense was the warning about Mr. Chatham, but such a warning was not necessary. Kelsey already knew what that man was.

A creak and groan of the door below indicated her mother's return. Kelsey pushed the letters aside, even the one from Lucia, and went downstairs to confront her mother about the new dress.

"Mother," she said, waving the note in the air, "I have just received a bill from the seamstress—"

Her mother spun around with a glazed, far-off look in her eye.

"Kelsey, I'm absolutely certain the flowers were from Mr. Baxter!" She danced around the room holding a single white daisy. "You see?" She held the flower out for Kelsey to observe.

Kelsey stared at the wilting flower. "No, I do not see."

"There's no need to be so dismal." Her mother tapped Kelsey's nose with the flower before bringing it back to her own. "Mr. Baxter handed me the flower and said, 'You are as pretty as a daisy.' He invited me to go riding in his carriage today. He'll be returning any minute."

Kelsey rubbed her forehead, still clenching the bill. "That sounds nothing like the note that came with the flowers. Surely, those were from a different man."

Mrs. Wickham placed a hand on her hip. "Unless another man appears who is ready to court me, I'll give Mr. Baxter the credit."

Kelsey fought the sudden urge to pluck off every petal of the pitiful daisy to expose its feeble center. She would have to do something more drastic to draw her mother's attention away from Mr. Baxter. Tightening her fist, she remembered the bill.

"Mother, I just received a bill from the seamstress. You bought a new gown?"

Her mother's arms dropped to her side. "I had to get something more fitting to wear for next time there's a ball. Now that you have that lovely gown from Lucia, all my gowns look dreadfully medieval."

"How do you propose we eat this month after trading that much money for a bundle of fabric? We're still recovering from the gaping hole in our accounts that resulted from Cissy's new wardrobe." Kelsey clenched the bill so hard that it was now a crumpled ball in her hand.

"Kelsey, I understand why you are worried, but it really isn't as bad as that. Why, only the other day, Mrs. Reynolds gave us a dozen eggs, what with all those Pemberley chickens—"

Images of feathered fowl strutting elegantly across manicured grounds flickered through Kelsey's thoughts. Even chickens were refined when coupled with the grand name of Pemberley.

"—and we can always eat what's growing in the garden."

Kelsey scoffed. Her mother had hardly spent five minutes in the weed-infested garden. How would she know what grew there? Even Kelsey hadn't known about the blackberries until minutes ago.

In a timid voice, her mother added, "I also believe Mr. Baxter is going to invite us to dinner soon. I really don't think we need worry, not yet anyway."

A thousand rebuttals rivaled their way to Kelsey's tongue, but not a single one freed itself. Though her mother lacked restraint, Kelsey was determined to exercise hers.

Needing a quiet moment to walk and think, she grabbed her bonnet and shawl, and left to settle her mother's account with the seamstress. The last thing Kelsey needed was the stress of debt, and the first thing she wanted was a long walk in the open air.

The road between Barley Cottage and the village of Lambton cut through a mix of field and forest. To Kelsey's right, a gradually inclining hill showed off a green patchwork of trees, grass, and flowering shrubs that eventually thickened into forest. To her left, a shabby fence lined with thistles and dandelions guarded a field of maturing barley whose plaited tips dipped as if bowing to the breeze. Further down the road, another fence contained a dozen grazing sheep, their soft bleating blending with the rustle of the grain. After rambling down the road for some time, cottages and stables as well as a smoky blacksmith's shop and the ringing of his hammer indicated she was nearing the Lambton marketplace.

The closer she drew to the high street, the more the road swelled with people. A mother with two small children carrying baskets of vegetables nodded to her. An older gentleman tipped his hat at her while balancing parcels under his arm. Men on horses cantered along, and a few elderly women stood in the shade waving fans and talking.

A sudden squawking rose above the general stream of noise. A greying man came trotting past Kelsey with several chickens tucked inside his faded brown work coat.

"Good day, miss!" he said cheerfully, tilting his cap as casually as if the chickens wriggling and pecking him were an everyday occurrence.

Kelsey nodded in reply, too amazed to laugh or speak. A short distance further brought her to the heart of the market. People of all stations bustled in and out of the shops and booths lining the road on either side. A butcher with fresh cuts hanging in the open air called out prices to passers-by, while another blacksmith clanked his hammer. People manning carts of various sizes sold fruit, vegetables, milk, and eggs. The man with the chickens stood by a cart holding a pail of eggs, but Kelsey couldn't tell whether he was buying or selling them. As she continued on, she passed a jewelry shop, an inn, a shop displaying baubles and trinkets in its window, and finally, the seamstress's shop that had sent the bill.

If Kelsey was fortunate, the owner would not scoff at her request to pay a relatively small amount in even smaller portions. With her hand on the door handle, she took one long breath. How many times would she be forced to clean her mother's messes and endure the embarrassment? *At least once more,* she thought, determining right then to do something more drastic than send her mother flowers.

A little bell chimed as Kelsey stepped in, and a young girl with a round face came out from a curtain in the back and curtseyed to Kelsey.

"Good day, miss. How can I help you? No, let me guess. A new gown, right? I know all the popular fashions in London right now."

"Thank you, but no." Kelsey hurried to show the girl the bill. "I merely came to settle the debt my mother recently incurred. See."

The young girl took the bill and looked over its numbers. "I'll take this to my mother. One moment."

As the girl swept behind the curtain, Kelsey looked around. Various fabrics hung along the walls, many of which she could only dream of ever affording, canary yellow silks, forget-me-not blue muslins, and rosette lace as fine as baby's breath. After a few minutes, an older woman came from the back room, holding the bill and smiling at Kelsey.

"Good day, Miss Wickham," she said. "Was your mother unhappy with her gown? I can make alterations if it wasn't to her liking."

"That's very kind of you, but no." Kelsey pulled her reticule off her wrist, grateful she had saved some of the guineas from the garden for just such an emergency. "I came to settle my mother's account with you. I must beg you, please do not take her on credit in the future."

The woman stared blankly at first, then shook her head. "There must be a misunderstanding. Your mother already paid for her gown."

"She did?"

The woman nodded. "Indeed. I must have sent this bill to her right before she came in with the money. I'm sorry for the confusion. Are you certain I can't help you with a new gown? The pink silk would look lovely on you."

"Another time, perhaps. Thank you."

When Kelsey stepped outside, she could hardly think. Had her mother once again taken money they could not spare without consulting her? Kelsey rubbed her temple, suddenly finding the day rather hot.

"Miss Wickham!"

Kelsey turned to see Miss Chatham waving to her from across the road. Her brother stepped out of a milliner's shop carrying several finely wrapped parcels precariously balanced in his arms. How could they afford all those parcels if they were, as Mrs. Salaway had said, poorer than church mice?

Kelsey waved and walked over, hopping out of the way of a passing phaeton. "Hello, Miss Chatham. Mr. Chatham. How are you?"

Mr. Chatham smiled appreciatively from the top of his pile of parcels. "We are quite well, especially Beatrice, to be sure." He flashed an impish grin at his sister, whose cheeks were reddening, then tilted his head toward Kelsey. "She has received a most improper letter from one of her beaus today, haven't you, sister?"

"William!" She wacked him on the arm, making him lose one of the parcels.

When Miss Chatham ignored it, Kelsey bent down and retrieved it herself.

"Look what you made Miss Wickham do. How ungentlemanly of you."

"It's no trouble—"

"Besides, Miss Wickham doesn't want to know about my boring letters. Even if she did want to know all about my beau and how terribly devoted he is to me —always promising me every kind of comfort if only I will accept him— I couldn't tell her." Her eyes grew sly and her cheeks rosier. "I simply wanted to say hello, Miss Wickham, and see how you were faring after that dreadful scene your mother made at the ball, or at least the one we all suspect she made in the gardens." Innocence may have graced Miss Chatham's brow, but her lips tilted up just enough to be provoking.

"I am doing quite well," Kelsey said sweetly. "But remember the words of Shakespeare, Miss Chatham. *Suspicion haunts the guilty mind.*"

Laughter sputtered from Mr. Chatham's lips, sending him swaying to keep the tower of parcels balanced.

Miss Chatham's face quickly crimsoned. "Well, we must be on our way, mustn't we, William? I'd show you my new lace, Miss Wickham, but people will talk if we linger too long in the streets like this. Good day."

Miss Chatham marched off without her brother. He stood by Kelsey, watching his sister go, and chuckled. "I've embarrassed her, you see, so she reacted by embarrassing you. Spiteful thing, my sister is, but you rebuffed her beautifully. That letter from her beau will make her forget her anger, though. Nothing makes a young woman so giddy as a love letter. At least, nothing I've seen yet." He regarded Kelsey and dropped his voice. "Which would you prefer, Miss Wickham? A love letter, or do you share your mother's preference for moonlit walks in heavily shaded gardens? I, of course, prefer the latter."

Kelsey shook her head. This was always the way. Her mother gained a reputation, and the men assumed Kelsey would follow suit. "Neither option appeals to me, Mr. Chatham."

"Come now. I saw you walk off with Mr. Worth at the ball."

"Exactly. You *saw* me. We remained close to the doors in the public's view the entire time."

"I do hope you will consider allowing *me* to show you the gardens next time." He managed a slight bow, despite the awkwardness of the parcels in his hands, and followed after his sister.

Kelsey watched him go, wondering at his impertinence, but mostly she thought of his comment about love letters. He had said a love letter always makes a girl giddy. Perhaps that was what her mother needed, a love letter to distract her from Mr. Baxter. The flowers hadn't been enough. But how to accomplish a love letter? Letters were harder to forge than flowers, but if she could manage one simple letter to her mother . . .

"I said GET OUT OF HERE!"

Kelsey spun around to see a shopkeeper yelling at a shabbily dressed man. It was difficult to guess his age because much of his face was covered by an unkempt beard, and the skin that was visible was in need of a good wash. The shopkeeper had the man firmly by the ear and gave him a final push into the road. The poor man stumbled to his hands and knees and coughed several times before righting himself. Kelsey took in his thin, grey shirt that might have once been white. It had tears in the sleeves and one long gash spreading diagonally in the back. His trousers weren't in much better condition, fraying above boots with holes in them, and even from a distance, Kelsey thought she saw a toe poking out of the left one.

Once he regained his balance, he ran his fingers through his hair, a pointless effort with that matted mess, and started down the street. He progressed slowly, lingering before a fruit stand until the owner shooed him along. When the smell of freshly baked bread filled the streets, the man clenched his stomach and stepped unsteadily.

Kelsey reached in her reticule for a few coins to give the man, but she was beaten to it. Nathaniel Worth exited a shop with an awkwardly wrapped brown parcel and immediately noticed the beggar. Balancing his parcel under his arm, he drew a few coins from his pocket and dropped them in the man's hand. It appeared to be the end of their exchange, but then Mr. Worth placed a hand on the beggar's shoulder and began to speak with him. All Kelsey could discern as she watched from across the road was that their conversation grew more intent, and the concern in Mr. Worth's face deepened. Mr. Worth handed the beggar his parcel, then bought him a loaf of bread, a wedge of cheese, and a large bag of nuts from one of the vendors.

Soon, Mr. Worth and the half-starved beggar were laughing and pointing toward the road. Was Mr. Worth acquainted with the beggar? When they parted ways, Kelsey realized she was staring rather openly. What was it about Mr. Worth that always drew her gaze?

He started to look about, and she panicked. Hoping to escape his notice, she hopped to the side of a nearby cart selling fruits and vegetables and pretended to be interested in the apples.

"Lady Kelsey, is that you?"

She sighed. Even though they had come to an understanding at the ball, she wondered whether she had made a mistake by giving him leave to use her Christian name. Still, the sound of it was easier on her ears than Miss Wickham.

"Hello Mr. Worth."

"No, no no," he said lightly. "You must call me Nathaniel. It's only fair, don't you think?"

She smoothed back a stray hair, keeping her eyes on the apples. "I'm afraid I was a bit rash the last time we discussed the matter."

"I see. Would you prefer I call you Miss Wickham, then? Simply say the word, and I will obey."

That was considerate. She had worried he was the kind of man who might take any liberty he could with a young lady. She wasn't entirely convinced he wasn't that sort, in some measure, but the truth was, it was refreshing to have someone other than her mother know her as Kelsey. Though she shouldn't have allowed it, hearing Mr. Worth call her Kelsey made her feel more like herself and not a deplorable agent of scandal.

"No. I still prefer Kelsey."

"Very well." He grinned. "Then please, call me Nathaniel. It will make me feel better, putting us on equal footing."

"If you insist . . . Nathaniel." She smiled timidly and lowered her eyes. His name held a surprisingly sweet tang on her lips, but she still had the presence of mind to remember it was only one of his flirtatious tactics.

"Well, good day, Mr. . . . Nathaniel." Kelsey walked toward the road but looked back in time to see him purchasing two apples. A minute later, he was at her side.

"Do you always go to the market unaccompanied?" He offered her a golden apple with pink blushes on the side.

She hesitated, but the apple looked too ripe to turn down. "Does it concern you whether I go to the market unaccompanied?"

"Perhaps it does," he answered before biting into his fruit.

Kelsey rubbed her apple on her skirt, then took a bite. Its warm, sweet juice quenched the thirst that had been building from so much walking.

"These roads to the market," he gestured before them, "are not always frequented by the most savory characters."

Just then, a chicken scurried past, clucking wildly and frantically flapping its wings. The man who Kelsey had seen earlier with the chickens in his coat came racing after it, pushing his way between Nathaniel and Kelsey.

"Beg your pardon!" he yelled without looking back. "Clementine!" The chicken man raced after the poor creature while the other chickens in his coat scratched the air with their squawks and cackles. How the man managed to keep any of the chickens contained in his coat, Kelsey had no idea.

Her laughter rose instantly as the chicken ran through the wild grasses and into the trees beyond, quickly lost to sight. *There now!* she thought. *I still laugh.*

Nathaniel tilted his head in the direction the man and his chicken had just run in and snickered. "A prime example."

"I see your point," Kelsey laughed again. "But he seems harmless, mostly." She took another bite of apple, catching its sweet, almost floral scent. "I can't help it though. There is no one to accompany me."

"Ahem," Nathaniel put a hand on his chest as if she had just wounded him.

"You are not a fit companion."

He leaned closer. "Yet, here we are." He took one last bite of apple and threw the core into the fields for the sheep. "And I beg to differ. You have yet to discover just how fit of a companion I can be."

"How am I to discover that?" She took her time savoring the last bites of her apple.

"By doing what we are doing. Spending time together."

At the bend in the road, they left the fields behind and fell into the shade of the trees that grew denser the farther along they walked.

"We are not spending time together," she insisted. "We simply happened to be walking the same way today."

"Ah, I can see how it might appear that way, but what if I told you that once I saw you in the market, I abandoned all other plans so I might walk with you?"

It's one of his tactics, she reminded herself. *It means nothing to him.* Though, she had to admit, his flirtations did not make her squirm the way Mr. Chatham's did. "Are you trying to be charming?"

"Surely you've noticed by now that I don't need to try."

He swung his arms a little more cavalierly as Kelsey rolled her eyes. "Surely you've noticed by now that I am not affected by such speeches." She really wasn't, she told herself. She merely had a weakness for apples.

He chuckled under his breath and said nothing more. As the trees ahead thickened, the road grew narrower and curved to their left. Kelsey might have been able to resist such speeches, but her mother certainly couldn't. Again, Kelsey considered writing a love letter for her mother, supposedly from the same man who had given the flowers. A letter full of flirtatious compliments could be just the thing to draw her mother away from Mr. Baxter.

Kelsey had no idea how to write such a letter, but she had a feeling she was walking next to someone who did. She stole a glance at Nathaniel from the corner of her eye. Hadn't he already offered to help her?

"Mr. Worth, or rather, Nathaniel," she began, only partially aware of the thunderous racket that was gaining volume on the road behind them. "Do you suppose—"

He looked behind them, and his eyes grew large. "Kelsey move! MOVE!"

She couldn't have moved even if she'd had the presence of mind to. Nathaniel had barely shouted the warning when his arms circled tightly around her, and he tackled her to the ground, sending them rolling into a ditch. Her breath disappeared, and her heart rattled in her chest, scaring her more than anything else. She didn't realize she was clinging to Nathaniel's lapels until they stopped moving and she opened her eyes.

Finding air again, she gasped and pushed his arm away. "Get off of me!"

She looked at the sky, which seemed to swim before her, then at Nathaniel who was staring straight up with wide eyes and his hand on his chest. She tried to stand, but her muscles shook like custard. Nathaniel reached out as if he wanted to catch her, but she slipped past his arm and hit the grass a second time. He must have been dizzy too. On the road, Kelsey saw a great cloud of dust trailing behind a speeding carriage. A loud peal of suspiciously familiar laughter pierced through the hammering of horses' hooves.

Submitting to the need to rest and breathe, she closed her eyes. "I suppose you just saved me from being flattened in the road, didn't you?" She peeked one eye open at Nathaniel, then shut it again.

"I suppose I did." His breathing was heavy. "Are you hurt? I wasn't aiming for the ditch, you know."

"With half a second to spare, I'd say your aim was quite good." Kelsey opened her eyes, and slowly pushed herself up to sitting. Her head was throbbing as wildly as the horses running away with the carriage. "I'm well enough, all things considered. And you? Are you hurt?"

He sat up and rubbed his head. "A little shaken, but I'm well. Was that your mother in the carriage? I only had the briefest glance before grabbing you."

"I sincerely hope not. Oh, ow!"

She retracted her hand from the ground, feeling as if she had just been bitten, and clasped it in her lap. Whatever the culprit was, it had set her skin on fire.

"Let me see your hand." Nathaniel reached out.

Kelsey clasped it closer. "I'm all right. Really."

He frowned. "I saw the nettle, Kelsey. I know your hand is burning right now." He looked around and plucked a leaf from another weed. "I know what to do. Here. Give me your hand." He held his palm open and waited.

Reluctantly, she placed her hand in his, palm up, and winced. The mere movement sent the burning deeper into her muscles. Red bumps were already rising on her otherwise lightly tanned skin.

Nathaniel gingerly secured her hand in his like a bird in its nest, and her mind emptied. The only thing she was aware of was how the warmth of his touch completely overshadowed the nettle's sting. With his other hand, he took the leaf he had plucked, crushed it slightly, and, taking his time, carefully rubbed it over the patches of red on her hand. As his fingers worked the leaf, his thumb caressed her palm, sending nervous waves up her arm and into her heartbeat. At first, the leaf, rough and dry, only agitated the bumps, but a moment later, her skin began to cool, and the sting from the nettle lessened.

"Oh," Kelsey breathed, surprised Nathaniel's remedy worked, surprised he kept her hand.

"Dock weed," he said. "Had to use it a few times myself. Is your hand much improved yet?"

Kelsey didn't know how to answer. Was it an improvement to have her thoughts so muddled?

When she didn't say anything, he turned her hand over and traced a finger along her knuckles. "I could check for more red bumps if you'd like."

"Yes, thank you. I mean, no." She pulled out of his grasp and stared at her hand as if his touch had made it something new. The redness was still there, but she couldn't tell whether the heat now dissipating from her skin was from Nathaniel or the nettles.

He stood up and brushed the grass off his trousers. Kelsey took the hand he offered to help her stand and felt the same rush of heat.

"Oh dear." She bit her lip. "You're covered in the stuff." Without considering her actions, she brushed the grass off his shoulders in several brisk movements. When she was done, she blushed to see him watching her.

"I don't think I should help you in the same manner, but you do have a bit of grass right there I can get." He reached out and plucked several pieces from her hair, his thumb barely touching her cheek with the last one.

"Thank you," she said, hoping her voice was calmer than she felt. Brushing off her skirt as best she could, she straightened her spine and looked to the road. "I had best be on my way now. Good day."

She hurried up the slope to the road, needing the use of her hands to lean forward and climb out of the ditch. Nathaniel followed closely.

"Kelsey, you can't go on by yourself now."

"And why not?"

"That," he said, gesturing in the direction the racing carriage had gone, "is proof you need me."

"Pardon me? Proof I *need* you? I'll admit your actions were well timed in this instance, but who's to say the carriage wouldn't have swerved out of the way at the last minute? Or that I wouldn't have jumped out on my own?"

"For one thing, the road was too narrow, and second—" He stopped, then shook his head, fixing his mouth into his usual smile. "Let's not argue. I'm still shaking from such a close call. My reflexes haven't been tested like that since the hurricane my ship endured last summer."

She took a good look at him. His face was flushed. His gait was shaky, and his breath came out in shallow, quick bursts. Reaching out, she hesitated but put a hand on his arm. "Thank you, Nathaniel. I'm very grateful."

His breath released slowly, calming at her touch. "My dear Lady Kelsey, *the very instant that I saw you, did my heart fly to your service.*"

She instantly recognized the line from *The Tempest* and, for a moment, felt as though she might fly. If Nathaniel had made the statement just then about himself being charming, she wouldn't have had the presence of mind to disagree with him. Instead, she asked for his help with a letter.

Chapter 12

My ideas flow so rapidly that I have not time to express them—by which means my letters sometimes convey no ideas at all to my correspondents.

Jane Austen, *Pride and Prejudice*

*A*s Kelsey and Nathaniel approached the cottage, her conscience grappled with the idea that he should help her write a letter to her mother. Kelsey had already spent the walk convincing herself that her mother needed more than flowers to distract her from an imprudent match, but accepting Nathaniel's help would require Kelsey to abandon her sense of propriety and honesty.

Not abandon, she countered. *They'll simply be tucked away for a while for the greater good.*

But was she willing to tuck them away long enough to tell Nathaniel her secrets and let herself be alone with him?

Cissy was already approaching womanhood with no prospects and no clearer path to follow than the one their mother had paved. Kelsey shivered and thought, *yes, I must take the risk.* Her own reputation was already shaded with her mother's, but if she could spare Cissy the same hardships, it would be worth it.

Something had to change. She needed Nathaniel's help.

She had disguised her handwriting for one brief line when she had prepared the flowers, but she could never manage it through an entire letter. Not only did she need his hand, but she needed the inspiration of a flirtatious mind. Whether she wanted to admit it or not, she also needed a confidant.

When they turned the bend in the road that brought the cottage in sight, they had a clear view of the carriage that had raced past them earlier. Mr. Baxter sat on the perch holding the reins while Mrs. Wickham skipped out of the cottage door with a basket swinging in her arms.

"Oh, hello, Kelsey! Mr. Worth!" her mother called, waving to them as Mr. Baxter nodded a greeting. "We've just had the most delightful carriage ride! We're now going on a picnic. Would you care to join us?"

"Not at all. I mean, thank you, Mother, but no. I was hoping to invite Mr. Worth inside for a few minutes."

"Ah, I see. Well, the maid from Pemberley who did the washing this morning left some biscuits in the kitchen. Please help yourself, Mr. Worth."

"Thank you." Nathaniel helped her step into the perch next to Mr. Baxter. Once Mrs. Wickham was situated, Mr. Baxter shook the reins and set the carriage racing.

"If that isn't the final straw!" With a hand on her hip, Kelsey shook her head.

"Pardon?" asked Nathaniel.

"Well," Kelsey huffed, "besides going off with that man alone, I can't believe she makes it so easy."

"Makes what so easy?"

Was he teasing her? Did he not see the imprudence of the situation? "So easy for us to be alone together. She didn't care at all." Before Kelsey could have second thoughts about inviting Nathaniel in, she marched up the gravel path, leaving him to follow. "I shouldn't wonder at it," she grumbled. "Chaperones are for ladies with money and scruples, neither of which the Wickhams possess in abundance."

As she pushed open the cottage door, the emptiness of the sitting room pressed upon her, heightening her awareness of Nathaniel's every breath and movement. She had never been alone in her own home with a man before, let alone one who confused her as much as Nathaniel did.

He leaned against the threshold, looking rather pleased with himself but unsure how far to enter. His dark eyes, captivating smile, and fine, tall form made Kelsey's palms sweat and her knees wobble.

"Are you certain you want my help?" Just as he stepped forward, rippling his fingers through his hair like water, she put a halting hand on his chest.

"Before you enter, let us be clear. You have come to help me, and I have agreed to . . . be civil with you. We have an arrangement, not to be confused with anything more. Are we agreed?"

His hand covered hers, keeping it on his chest. "I understand you perfectly, my lady. I was hoping my charm had gotten to you at last, but I am your humble servant and promise to be the perfect gentleman."

If she hadn't just witnessed his kindness to a beggar and been saved from severe injury by him less than an hour ago, she might not have been so trusting. He released her hand, and she waved him to follow. He stepped in and left the door open at her request, a feeble attempt to make the situation the tiniest bit more proper, but it was the best she could think of in the moment. Nathaniel's eyes passed over the empty space above the fireplace, and for the first and only time, Kelsey was grateful the horrid painting of her parents hung in her room.

"This is a charming cottage." He smiled and stood waiting. "How shall we begin?"

Kelsey paced, finding strength in her knees again. "As I explained, I thought we should write a letter."

"You're certain?"

The tender note hidden beneath the windowsill was proof enough that love letters held a bewildering capacity to sway the heart. "I am." She met Nathaniel's eye, daring him to disagree.

"And you believe this will . . ."

"Distract my mother from Mr. Baxter." When he looked un-impressed, she added, "Which will stop her from making a terrible match. Or it will stop her from depleting our income further by forc-ing us to move our family again."

"And you're certain this is the best way?"

Her eyes suddenly swelled. "I hate to deceive her, but she'll ruin us if I don't do something. She is already careless with her reputation, and I don't want to see her with a man who disappoints her. And what is to become of Cissy if that is her lot in life? To always follow the trail of scandal and embarrassment with no connections and no prospects. All I want is peace, but I can hardly . . ."

When her voice broke, Nathaniel inhaled deeply and looked as if he might embrace her. "Very well, Kelsey. What can I do?"

At first, she stared at his arms and realized she already knew their strength, having felt them pull her out of danger. If she didn't act quickly, she was certain she would soon find herself in an entirely different sort of danger. In one swift stride, she slid behind the writing desk and ran her fingers along the grains of wood. When she sensed Nathaniel's warmth at her side, she became aware of every hair tickling her neck, every breath he took, and every beat her heart attempted. Did he have to stand so close? She scooted her chair closer to the desk and gave her thoughts a shake.

"Tell me how I should start." She unstopped the ink and anchored herself to her reason once again.

Nathaniel leaned over her shoulder as if inspecting her paper, his grey jacket brushing her arm.

"We need to capture your mother's attention." He finally stepped back, allowing Kelsey room to breathe again. "We need to immedi-ately make her feel like a queen."

"Oh, goodness," Kelsey groaned. "I can't do this."

Nathaniel chuckled. "Then I suppose you'll want to reconcile yourself to calling Mr. Baxter, *Father.*"

Kelsey glared over her shoulder at him. "You're horrible!"

"You are a vision of loveliness."

"You can leave right now if you try to flatter me." She hated the way her cheeks betrayed her just then.

"There's that temper again, Lady Kelsey. I wasn't talking about you. I was starting the letter."

"Oh." Kelsey looked back at the blank parchment sitting before her and could hear Nathaniel softly laughing. If she weren't absolutely desperate, she would have thrown him out.

"We should start it with something like, *If you hold this letter, I have finally mustered the bravery to express my admiration for you. Though I am not yet brave enough to reveal myself, I am convinced I must do something. I must write what I feel until I find courage to speak it. Though this letter is an incomplete introduction, I cannot ignore what my heart discovered when I saw you.*"

"Have you done this before?" Kelsey lifted her brow.

Nathaniel leaned on the desk, bringing his face very close to hers. "Does the thought inspire jealousy?"

She cleared her throat and shooed him back. "Tell me what to write next."

Nathaniel paced behind her. "Let's see . . . *Had I not felt the ground beneath my feet, I would have thought myself taken up to heaven.*"

"I feel ill," Kelsey mumbled as she etched the words onto the paper, then immediately crossed them out. "No, not that last line. The letter is already becoming a sentimental mess, but it cannot be so trite. This letter cannot sound like Mr. Baxter."

Nathaniel hummed his understanding and resumed pacing. When his eyes settled on Kelsey, he nodded as if making a decision and took a large breath. "*Do not censure me, my lady, for wanting your attention. I find I must try for it. I must attempt to gain your favor, though odds combine against me. Forgive my boldness, but I could not sleep peacefully without expressing myself.*"

Kelsey ignored her accelerating heart and frantically scribbled away, feeling Nathaniel's expectant gaze on her. "It's an improvement," she conceded. "Now, we need to end it in a way that will leave her desiring more. And it must be anonymous."

"Let's sign it . . . *your mortal admirer.*"

"What is that supposed to mean?"

"It means she's an angel and her admirer is but a mortal man."

"That's stupid."

"That's hurtful," he said lightly, placing a hand on his heart. He came very close and spoke low. "*Your devoted admirer?*"

His breath tickled her face with an alluring scent of sage and mint, but she forced herself to concentrate on the task before her. "Why not?" she shrugged. "I haven't time to be picky." She scrawled the lines, then stopped. "I almost forgot. I'll need you to copy this onto a separate sheet of paper. My mother will recognize my handwriting."

Nathaniel stared at her. "You would have me write this?"

Kelsey bit her lip. "It puts you in a terrible position, doesn't it? I promise I'll take full responsibility."

Still, he hesitated.

"Never mind. I understand." She looked down at her lap, aware that she was asking too much. He was right to hesitate. She started to put away her writing things when he heaved a sigh.

"No, leave it. I really do want to help you." His fingers brushed hers as he took the pen. "If you weren't absolutely certain . . . I wouldn't do this for anyone else." It only took him a minute to copy the lines. He waved the paper in the air to allow the ink to dry, then folded it and tucked it in his waistcoat.

Kelsey couldn't believe she was putting so much trust in this man. He may have acted nobly that day, but what did she know of his past? Still, she wasn't one to withhold her thanks. "It's very good of you to help me, Nathaniel."

He flashed a devilish grin. "I don't claim to do it out of goodness, Kelsey. You must know that."

"Must I? I haven't a clue what you could mean."

He leaned in. "Not a single clue?"

Her face flared so quickly it hurt.

"I'll send this through the post tomorrow. Good day, Lady Kelsey."

As he rushed out the door, she ran to her room and watched him walk briskly along the path to the main road. Oh, what was she doing? What was she thinking? It was too late to change tactics. The letter was in his hands, but worse than that, she was allowing this man, this probable rake, into her confidences.

But she would not allow him any closer.

Chapter 13

*To find a man agreeable whom one is determined
to hate! Do not wish me such an evil.*

Jane Austen, *Pride and Prejudice*

$\mathcal{K}$elsey collected the post early that morning. She recognized Nathaniel's handwriting at the top of the stack of letters. It wasn't too late to hide the letter and forget such nonsense, but she didn't hesitate for long. All her past attempts to help her mother had been too reasonable, too easily ignored. It was time for something unreasonable. Before she could waver any longer, she placed the letter at the bottom of the stack and dropped the letters in the middle of the table where her mother would see them.

"Good morning, Kelsey," her mother yawned, drowsily entering the kitchen and settling herself at the table. "Oh! Peaches."

Kelsey had already placed a few slices on her plate, though she hardly touched them.

Her mother took several bites and pointed her fork at Kelsey. "See. I told you we would have enough from the garden. I could eat peaches every day. Ah, is that the post?"

Choosing not to argue about their need to economize regardless of the peaches, Kelsey scooped up the letters and offered them to her mother. "Why don't you have a look. I've only glanced at them." She took a bite of bread, trying to behave naturally.

Mrs. Wickham tsked at the first letter. A bill, most likely. The second was from Aunt Jane, who sent a small sum of money and her love. "Of course, Lucia Darcy may visit, but they cannot have us," Mrs. Wickham mumbled. "Oh, this one's from Cissy."

Kelsey looked up from her plate. She must have passed over Cissy's letter in her anxiousness over the other letter. Mrs. Wickham tossed the letter to Kelsey when she finished reading. Only a few lines were scrawled out. Cissy was impressed with Aunt Kitty's wardrobe and her uncle's kindness. She got on well with her younger cousins, favored the cook's way of preparing fish, and enjoyed feeding the ducks that roamed the lake on the Warlingham estate. A few lines were hastily added at the bottom about Jack Pendlestone coming to tea.

"Odd," her mother said, turning over another letter. "I don't recognize this seal. It looks like a clover blossom."

Kelsey's teacup clattered onto her saucer. It wasn't a clover blossom. It was a thistle blossom for Thistledown Hall, Nathaniel's home.

Mrs. Wickham gasped, turned pink, and covered a grin with her hand.

"What is it, Mother?"

"It's . . . a letter."

"Only a letter?" Kelsey used the same teasing voice her mother liked to use.

"I don't know what else to call it. It's very flattering." Her smile widened. "Mr. Baxter . . ." Her voice momentarily wavered. "Yes, it must be Mr. Baxter. He is remarkable."

"What!" Kelsey stood and snatched the paper out of her mother's hand to verify it was the letter she had composed with Nathaniel. "This hasn't a name signed to it."

"I know, but doesn't that make it all the more romantic?"

A far-off look overtook her mother's eyes, and a wave of nausea rippled in Kelsey's stomach. "You cannot think Mr. Baxter would send a note like this. These words are beautiful! *If you hold this letter, I have finally mustered the bravery to express my admiration for you.* That doesn't sound like Mr. Baxter at all!"

Mrs. Wickham snatched back her letter. "I don't know how you would know. Perhaps Mr. Baxter is more romantic than you realized."

"The man in this letter says he isn't yet brave enough to reveal himself. All Mr. Baxter does is reveal his supposed admiration."

Mrs. Wickham tapped her lip. "True. Mr. Baxter is not at all shy in that regard, but I don't know who else it could be. I suppose he is simply being poetic."

Kelsey helplessly watched her mother waltz from the room with the letter held against her chest, more in love with Mr. Baxter than when she had entered.

What had Kelsey done?

She dropped her head to the table and cursed her awful luck.

"Oh, I almost forgot to tell you!"

Kelsey sat with a start as her mother skipped back to the table.

"Mr. Baxter has invited us to dine with him tonight. It is to be quite the formal affair. Are you feeling all right, Kelsey? Perhaps you ought to lie down." Mrs. Wickham didn't wait for a reply before turning around and heading up the stairs.

"Mother!" Kelsey followed after her. She was in no mood to dine with Mr. Baxter, not after her letter had failed. She needed time to think and fix the mess she had created. Once again, she would need Nathaniel's help. "Mother, I don't know if I will return in time. You see . . ." She had never been to Nathaniel's home, but he had described to her its location, just two miles away, and how to find it. He had invited her to visit whenever she had the notion, which she had doubted she would ever have, but in light of the morning's events, she was experiencing a change of heart. "I am going to Thistledown Hall for the afternoon, and I don't know when I'll return."

Mrs. Wickham smiled. "Thistledown Hall? That charming manor only a few miles away that Mr. Worth resides in? The one Captain Styles has given to him?"

Kelsey gulped. "I don't know whether Captain Styles has *given* it to him. It will only be a cordial visit, the sort often shared between neighbors, so there is no reason for you to get that excited gleam in your eye."

"Of course."

Kelsey hated the way her mother winked, no doubt making all kinds of assumptions.

"Go and enjoy yourself, my darling. I'll simply have Mr. Baxter send his carriage over to fetch you. Wear something nicer than that old thing." She gestured to Kelsey's gown, then lowered her voice. "Give my regards to Mr. Worth." Humming softly to herself, Mrs. Wickham strolled to her room.

Kelsey looked at her faded yellow gown. "This dress is more than adequate."

An evening at Mr. Baxter's could be informative, even if it wasn't Kelsey's preferred way to pass the time. One of her mother's past suitors had led them to believe he was extremely rich, but when he finally invited them to his home, they saw an unkempt house that was falling apart. Kelsey never knew what her mother thought of him and his lies after that because later that night, he was carried off to debtor's prison.

Kelsey shuddered at the memory and ran out the door. The two miles to Thistledown Hall seemed to stretch the more she hurried. Had she set off in the wrong direction? The trees lining the road looked the same no matter which way she walked. Just when she considered turning back, she saw the crumbled stone remains of a small medieval fort, the landmark Nathaniel had told her to watch for. Beyond that, in the distance, was another edifice.

Thistledown Hall. But the closer she drew, the more she wondered whether it was another abandoned building. Though still intact, portions of the west wall and one of its chimneys were crumbling. The east side had the charred markings left by a fire, and the grounds were as brambly and thorny as Kelsey's own cottage garden with ivy covering half the windows.

Little wonder Nathaniel understands weeds so well. But she had not come to enquire about weeds.

She ran to the main doors, but at the sight of the splintering wood and tarnished brass knockers, all the determination that had driven her there in the first place fled. What would her Uncle Darcy think if he saw her standing on the doorstep of a single gentleman's derelict home unaccompanied? Of course, her conscience chose that precise moment to remind her how much she wanted the approval of her ever-proper relatives and how what she was doing was quite the opposite of proper.

Was she even more of a Wickham than she realized? It was a sobering thought, but she couldn't turn back now. Pressing her lips together, she pounded one of the knockers against the door. Several minutes passed without a response. Perhaps the house was abandoned after all.

"Lady Kelsey? Is that you?" Nathaniel emerged from a small, cobbled path that cut through the trees, then hurried toward her. "This is unexpected."

"Nathaniel." Her heart fluttered and her mind emptied. Why did she feel like she had been caught?

As he drew closer, she could see concern growing in those rich, dark eyes. "You need to sit, I think." Taking her arm, he led her to a small stone bench under an aged birch tree.

The cool stone had a steadying effect as she recovered from the long walk and gathered her thoughts. Until he sat in the small space next to her, his arm brushing against hers.

"Are you all right?" he asked. "Has something happened?"

"My mother—" Kelsey swallowed, urging her mind to function. If she was risking the imprudence of such a visit, she had to make it worth the effort.

"Did she read the letter?" Nathaniel pressed. "Did she discover us?"

"She read it and loved it, and no, she did not discover us."

"That's fortunate, isn't it? All according to plan."

Kelsey met his eye and frowned. "She concluded it was from Mr. Baxter."

"Oh. I see." Nathaniel pinched his lips and drew his brows together. Was it possible he was sympathetic to her pain? She thought so until he covered his eyes with his hand and began to shake.

"Are you . . ." She stood up and watched him until he couldn't contain his laughter. "This isn't amusing, Nathaniel!"

"I'm sorry, Kelsey." He sputtered, not sounding sorry at all. "She thought it was from Mr. Baxter?"

"Yes."

"That's awful!"

When he continued to tremble, she whacked his arm. "This is serious! What are we going to do about it?"

"We? You want me to interfere further?"

Kelsey paced in front of him. "I need your help. I can't do nothing. At this rate, my mother will become Mrs. Baxter in less than a fortnight, and I'll have to live with the fact that it was expedited by my own meddling!"

Nathaniel's face was now as red as a berry. "At least you won't have to leave Barley Cottage."

Kelsey wished she could inflict punishment with her gaze. "It was foolish of me to come here. The whole thing is admittedly ridiculous, and I never should have asked you to take part in my schemes. Forgive me, Nathaniel. Mr. Worth. Good day." She meant every word as she turned and walked away.

"Kelsey, wait!"

She could hear his boots on the cobbled path behind her.

"Kelsey!" His hand reached her arm, barely brushing her skin.

"I'll sort this out myself, Nathaniel. It's all right. Really."

"I apologize for laughing. You know I'm still willing to help you, but I'm not sure what to do. Please walk with me."

She kept her brisk pace, assuming he would follow, but when she turned to look, he was still several paces back. His eyes were focused on her, but he stepped no closer. The road to the cottage was lonely and shaded while the sun's rays settled upon Thistledown Hall. When the wind weaved up her arms, urging her back to Nathaniel, she returned to his side.

"Of course, I want your help, Nathaniel. If you're certain you're willing to risk being so very imprudent with me."

"Aw, yes, you remind me. That is something we should discuss."

"Being imprudent?"

"Well, yes." He led her back to the bench. "But I'm specifically referring to the risk you ask me to take by involving myself."

Oh, no. Kelsey knew it. She had made a mistake by letting herself become indebted to him. "What do you want, Nathaniel?"

"Truly to be your friend. I see the worry in your eyes, so allow me to reassure you. I help you of my own will and do not hold you in my debt. I only want to acknowledge that our actions are what others would call imprudent. There will be talk. I've seen too much real danger in my time to be scared off by mere words, but the risk is there. Do we agree on that point?"

"Yes." Kelsey waited for the rest of his argument.

"If you are willing, there is something you could help me with, something I would very much consider myself in your debt for accomplishing."

"And that is?"

His eyes grew bashful as he reached down to pluck an especially long piece of grass, which he twiddled in his fingers, avoiding her gaze. Kelsey waited, unwilling to ask for details.

After a long breath, he said, "My sister is coming for a visit." He plucked another piece of grass and tore it to pieces.

"I'm happy to befriend her, if that is what you are asking."

"Yes, thank you, but there is more. She is my half-sister on my mother's side. Until recently, I had not seen her since our mother's passing fourteen years ago, which was not long before I enlisted. My sister and I have exchanged a few letters over the years, but that is all. After my last ship returned, I visited her in London before coming to Thistledown Hall. She has quite the fortune from her father, so she feels she owns the world and everyone in it. Unfortunately, she believes it to be her responsibility to settle my entire future." He paused as if recalling something terrifying. "She is travelling from London to West Yorkshire and plans to spend the night here at Thistledown Hall. She is expected by her friends, but I'm quite certain she will consider staying longer."

Kelsey nodded, searching his words for the meaning behind them. "Go on."

He looked at the clouds, thin and feathery, then at his boots, solid and worn. "She can be quite difficult at times. Most of my childhood memories involve her bossing me about, and it would seem she feels at liberty to do so again. Her letters come more frequently than ever, and each contains descriptions of ladies she would like me to choose from." He looked straight into Kelsey's eyes. "She has become unusually keen on seeing me married." He finished with a large exhale and waited.

What he waited for, Kelsey had no idea. "Surely, this is not your idea of a proposal, Nathaniel. I could never speak to you so candidly if I thought it were one."

His cheeks crimsoned, making Kelsey instantly regret her words. "No, of course not." His voice grew hesitant. "But as I am not currently married, my sister now threatens to live here to put my affairs in order until I am. So, you see . . ."

Kelsey folded her arms. "No, I do not see."

"She is coming to determine whether, after she completes her visit in West Yorkshire, she should retire here for a time."

"As I said, I will be happy to befriend her."

He shook his head. "No, Kelsey, you do not understand. She can't live here. When you meet her, you'll see why. Thistledown Hall is not yet mine, but even if it were, and if it weren't in such a dreadful state, I would go mad living under the same roof as her. If she's determined, though, I'm not sure how I can prevent her."

"Nathaniel Worth." Kelsey put a hand on her hip. "Are you informing me that you are afraid of your sister? Do you want me to tell her she can't stay? I don't know why she would listen to me."

"I'm admittedly terrified of her, but no, that is not what I'm asking."

"Well, then? I'm tired of guessing."

"Would you . . ." He spoke slowly, then finished his sentence all at once. "Allow her to believe you are my wife? Only for the day she visits. We could make her think we eloped."

At the weight of his words, Kelsey's jaw dropped, then snapped shut. "I can't do that!" Her heart rolled against her chest like a barrel in a moving wagon while the sun's heat threatened to smother her. Was he trying to ensnare her? Surely, such a scheme would end in scandal. How foolish she had been to think for a moment that Nathaniel might not be as terrible as other men!

"Why not?" he asked quietly.

Her stomach clenched. "What would my mother say?" It was the first argument that came to mind, but as she considered it, she felt certain her mother would think it the best kind of lark. "I simply can't. I don't know how to be a wife. Oh, and the gossip! Suppose others found out. What would my uncle say? My reputation already hangs by a thread simply for being a Wickham. But of course, you already know that, don't you? You probably think—"

"I promise, I don't." He looked down and shook his head. "Say no more, Kelsey. It was a foolish whim. Forgive me." Bending low, he plucked another piece of grass. "Allow me to accompany you back to the cottage, and we'll discuss what to do about Mr. Baxter and your mother."

His eyes had dulled, and the downward tilt of his mouth communicated a sincerity Kelsey was unprepared to see. She hardly knew what overcame her, but as he stood waiting for her, she found herself considering his request.

"Is your sister truly so terrifying?"

"Clarice Wimpleton," he chuckled, "said to be the most headstrong, imposing young lady this side of the Thames."

"Tell me about her." Kelsey didn't know why she wanted to know, but she did.

"Well," Nathaniel looked up in thought, "she goes anywhere she wants, speaks to whomever she wants, and buys whatever she wants. She is completely accustomed to having her way. Imagine growing up alongside such a person." Despite the picture he was painting of his sister, a smile spread across his face. "As children, she always chose what games we would play. She would make up rules to favor her, and she always convinced her father to align with her whims. Oh, and the tantrums! I remember her once throwing the most frightful tantrum because I wouldn't wear the breeches she had selected for me. I won't even tell you how many times she's pinched me for disagreeing with her. You wouldn't believe it, but she's three years younger than I am."

"That's horrible." Kelsey found herself laughing. "How did an older brother allow his sister such power?"

He scratched his cheek. "I was taught to be kind and respectful to women, and that included my sister."

Kelsey's heart leapt at his words. Did he mean them? Though she had often questioned his intentions and habits, she couldn't think of a time when he hadn't been respectful. "Surely, now that you are older, such squabbles are in the past."

He shrugged. "I would hope so, but I wouldn't be surprised if she's made more enemies than friends in London."

"And you think my presence, the idea of our being . . . married," Kelsey gulped, "would stop her from placing herself at Thistledown Hall indefinitely?"

His eyes grew hopeful. "If there is anything my sister cannot abide, it's the presence of another female, especially one who has greater claim on the domain."

Tiny hairs tickled the back of her neck. If she agreed to pretend to be Nathaniel's wife, she would be giving her uncle very clear grounds to dismiss her and her mother from Barley Cottage. In the worst case, she could be forced to marry Nathaniel. She had to say no, but she could not forget that without his help, she would be entirely on her own. Perhaps, they could be discreet enough to keep the affair a secret.

What a habit of dishonesty I am falling into!

How could she even consider it? She couldn't be his wife. There was too much at stake. No. She really couldn't do it. But as she looked at Nathaniel with his dark blond hair tousled on the breeze and his expressive eyes cast down, something in her softened, and the idea of a compromise came to her.

"What if your sister thought us engaged instead? Would that satisfy her?"

His face instantly lifted. "I suppose it would. If she believes we are engaged, she would be at ease about my future, and she would feel free to make a lengthy stay in West Yorkshire. If all goes well, she'll be there for a few months, at least."

"And you're certain she is only staying at Thistledown Hall for the night?"

"One night is all she indicated in her letter."

"No one else will be involved in the visit?"

"No one other than a few servants, only those necessary to make the place comfortable for my sister."

"What will she do when she hears of our becoming unengaged? Won't she try to stay again?"

Nathaniel grimaced. "That is a risk, but it still gives me time. Her as well. I don't think she would stay, for example, if she made a match of her own, which I am certain she is out to accomplish. If given the choice, I'm sure she would prefer to run her own household rather than mine."

"If word spreads that we are engaged, don't you think it would be easier to manage than if rumors implicate us acting as a wedded couple?"

Nathaniel looked at her with wide eyes. "That is a very convincing argument. Stupid of me not to consider . . ."

She tapped a finger on her cheek, her conscience still stalling. "Can you think of any other way for me to help you without lying to my mother? I already feel guilty about the letter."

"As a matter of fact . . ." A playful grin stole over his face, and he dropped to one knee. "Let's make it official. Kelsey Wickham, will you make me the happiest of men by engaging yourself to me in three weeks' time?"

"To repulse your sister?" She smirked to keep the flutters at bay. As long as she could make a jest of the facade, she would manage her way through it.

"Precisely."

She couldn't help but laugh. "All right. I accept. I'll be engaged to you for a day."

He stood up and took her hand in both of his. "I don't suppose you'd be willing to seal our engagement with a kiss?"

She pulled her hand back and placed it on her stomach. "We're not engaged today!"

He dipped his head in submission, but his impish grin remained. "Very well. I'll ask again in three weeks."

Chapter 14

May I ask whether these pleasing attentions proceed from the impulse of the moment, or are the result of previous study?

Jane Austen, *Pride and Prejudice*

hy must Nathaniel stand so close? Kelsey thought as the groaning of carriage wheels awakened her mind and jerked her heart from the conflicting moment.

"Mr. Baxter is here for me."

"What?" Nathaniel followed her gaze.

"My mother told him to send a carriage for me. He has invited us to dine with him tonight. I don't suppose he invited you?"

Nathaniel shook his head. "He didn't, I'm afraid. I don't envy you having the pleasure of his company tonight, but I do envy him having the pleasure of yours."

Nathaniel and his flirtations! Kelsey should have been accustomed to them by now, but it continued to surprise her how quickly they could flush her skin, quicken her breath, or make her forget what she intended to say. When had she stopped wanting to roll her eyes at such remarks?

"I'd prefer not to go, but I think it best to meet my fate head on this time."

Nathaniel chuckled. "I'll escort you to the carriage, my brave lady."

The same carriage that had nearly run them over the other day was waiting by the front of the house. The driver, dressed as a farmhand, clumsily descended from his high-perched seat, barely saving himself from a nasty fall.

Nathaniel mumbled something under his breath and took Kelsey's arm. "I'm coming."

"What? Why?" She didn't know whether to pull away or not.

"You can't go alone with that man."

"I agree to be engaged to you for one day, and already you are jealous?"

"Kelsey, I'm serious. I've seen him in Lambton. It isn't safe for you to ride with him by yourself. I'm coming for your own protection."

She shrugged. The man had a rough look about him, but so did many working men. Was that reason enough for Nathaniel to fear for her safety? Fending for herself had always been her way, but the truth was, she didn't mind him coming along. Having someone express concern for her was an unexpected gift that pleasantly tickled from the inside out.

"Evening, miss." The driver tilted his cap and displayed a toothy grin. "Oliver Billows at your service. Mr. Baxter sent me to transport you to Calder Glen."

"His home, I presume?"

Mr. Billows shrugged. "I reckon so. Mr. Baxter didn't exactly include me in his plans. I've only been hired for the evening."

"I see. Well, thank you." Kelsey waited as he opened the carriage door.

"Yes, thank you," Nathaniel said, stepping forward, still with Kelsey's arm in his.

The driver looked Nathaniel up and down and shrugged. "I was only told to collect the lady, but I suppose I get paid if you come too."

Nathaniel's grip on her relaxed as he helped her inside where she caught whiffs of sweat and oiled canvas. Once Nathaniel climbed in, he positioned himself next to her though the seat across the way was empty. The carriage tilted, pushing Kelsey into Nathaniel as Mr. Billows clambered up to his perch outside, and the carriage lurched ahead.

Pushing against Nathaniel's arm, Kelsey righted herself and smoothed her skirts. "It's kind of you to be so concerned for me, Nathaniel, but if I had gone alone, it would have been no different from how I've lived for the past several years."

"That is what upsets me, Kelsey. You've been fortunate to meet with kind people, and I value your independent spirit, but I've seen too much in my travels to take your safety for granted. You're worth protecting."

A timid smile crossed her lips as she looked the other way. She could not let him know how his words were affecting her. She shouldn't let herself be so affected in the first place! Steeling herself against scoundrels had always been a necessity, but Nathaniel presented a different sort of challenge. He was more focused, more persistent, and dare she hope? Much more sincere.

But was there any way of knowing his true intentions? They were playing a dangerous game with their plans and schemes which were encouraging a proximity to passions that had no place in Kelsey's life. Hadn't her father behaved that way with her mother? Smiling at all the right moments and tossing compliments like bread crumbs for a hungry bird. Was that how he convinced her mother to banish all sense of propriety for the chance to escape with him? Kelsey was willing to claim Nathaniel as a friend, but she promised herself anew not to let his charms sway her any further from her convictions.

Once Kelsey felt securely anchored in her commitment again, she asked Nathaniel if he would write another letter to her mother. He listened attentively as she explained her ideas, reasons, and worries, all while his arm occasionally brushed hers.

"Will another letter make you happy, Kelsey?"

Though the carriage rambled on, everything inside her stopped. His question stole all words from her. Perhaps it was the way he asked it or the way he looked at her, but it was a question she had never considered. Sending anonymous letters to her mother was never meant to lead to Kelsey's happiness. It was a drastic step intended to thwart her mother and hopefully lead to greater insight, but if the plan worked, would that not also make Kelsey happy?

Finding her voice again, she folded her arms. "Yes. It will."

He frowned and cocked a brow.

"Yes, Nathaniel. It will make my mother happy. It will save her from a terrible choice, which will make me happy."

The silence that reigned for the remainder of the ride was blaring. Nothing but Nathaniel's question and his arm against hers held her attention. Why did it matter whether another letter to her mother made her happy? Why did Nathaniel care? And what could she do to shake off his incessant attentions?

Soon, they were stepping out in front of Mr. Baxter's house, which, to Kelsey's disappointment, was rather normal looking. True, it was no manor or great hall, nothing compared to Pemberley, but it was larger than the cottage and looked adequately kempt.

Mr. Baxter himself came out with his arms held wide.

"There she is, the daughter of the belle of the ball!"

Only half a minute into the visit, and already Kelsey was losing her patience.

"Oh, and hello Mr. Worth. I was not expecting you this evening."

Nathaniel gave Kelsey a quick glance. "I'm not staying. I only came to see Miss Wickham safely delivered. Now that I know she is with friends, I wish you all a good evening."

As he bowed and turned toward the road, Mr. Baxter twisted his hands together, looking at the house, then at Nathaniel. "Mr. Worth!" he called out. "Come back, Mr. Worth! You are welcome to stay."

Nathaniel returned a few steps. "Are you certain? I don't wish to impose."

"Well . . . yes, I'm certain." Mr. Baxter didn't sound certain, but he waved Nathaniel forward. "It will make our numbers a bit uneven, but I don't think Miss Wickham will object."

"I should hope not." Nathaniel winked at Kelsey, who told herself she didn't care whether he stayed, and together, they followed Mr. Baxter through the doors.

With wall mounted candelabras lighting their way, Mr. Baxter ushered them through a small vestibule into a brown sitting room with a small fire swaying on the grate. The curtains were drawn despite the remaining daylight, and the air hung with dust and mildew. Nearly everything was made from the same dark wood or was faded in color, including the paintings on the walls. Kelsey could think of no word to describe the room beyond brown. Still, Kelsey had to admit, it was tidy.

"Our party is complete!" Mr. Baxter announced.

Kelsey could see the back of her mother's head, adorned in her signature ring of plaits and curls.

"Kelsey, there you are, darling!"

As her mother turned and rose from her chair, a painful jolt shot through Kelsey and escaped in a sharp gasp. Her mother, smiling innocently, stood painfully beautiful against the dark backdrop of the brown room, blazing in the luminescent glory of the dress from Lucia. She was ravishing, undeniably so, but the dress was insanely extravagant for the affair. Not even Mr. Baxter was dressed so formally.

A swirl of anger boiled in Kelsey's stomach, and for an instant, she did not think she could suppress it. As her mother glided over like a pearl in the mud, Kelsey stood transfixed to the spot, breathing through her nose.

"How could you?" she hissed as her mother kissed her cheek.

"Don't embarrass me," her mother whispered back before giving Kelsey's plain yellow dress a critical glare.

Mr. Baxter cleared his throat. "I'm happy to announce that Mr. Worth will be joining us this evening." Nathaniel bowed. "Miss Wickham, Mr. Worth, allow me to introduce Mr. Edgar Woodcox, recently arrived from Nottinghamshire."

A tall figure emerged from behind the glow of her mother.

"It's a pleasure to meet you." Mr. Woodcox reached up to tilt a hat that wasn't there and dropped his hand with a sheepish grin.

In a dark blue tailcoat, yellow silk waistcoat, and neatly tied cravat, he had all the looks of a man of quality, but Kelsey remembered Lucia's warning to be on her guard around Mr. Woodcox, should she ever meet him. Lucia already knew that Kelsey distrusted men in any circumstance. So, why the warning?

Coming to her side, Nathaniel whispered, "Kelsey, are you all right?"

She forced a smile, and soon, they were all entering a chilly dining room, more cream-colored than brown, where a long, polished table was spread with plates, candles, cutlery, and a few wilting flowers. Mr. Baxter sat at the head with Mrs. Wickham and Kelsey to his right and Nathaniel and Mr. Woodcox across from them.

With an exaggerated flourish, Mr. Baxter gestured for all to be seated, and a nearby servant filled everyone's glasses.

Mr. Baxter gazed fondly at Mrs. Wickham. "I do hope you enjoy the trout. Freshly caught from Mr. Darcy's very own stream."

"With his permission, I gather?" Kelsey asked innocently.

"Of course." He scratched his cheek and mumbled, "At least, I'm sure he would have given it had I asked."

Kelsey smirked behind her glass as she took a sip. Whether Mr. Baxter was correct hardly mattered. Any mention of Mr. Darcy's belongings, acquired with permission or not, was the wrong way to garner favor from her mother.

In a small voice, Mrs. Wickham said, "That is lovely, Mr. Baxter, but I believe I mentioned to you only yesterday how very much I dislike trout."

"No, no. You distinctly said you dislike venison."

"I'm certain I said the opposite." Mrs. Wickham ran her finger along the handle of her fork. "I quite enjoy venison. It is trout I dislike. And parsnips," she added. "There are few foods less enjoyable than parsnips."

The servant behind her paused at these words. He glanced at Mr. Baxter, then slowly lowered a bowl for Mrs. Wickham and proceeded to serve the other guests. Kelsey looked at the bowl laid before her. No trout yet, only a creamy looking soup. One sip, and she had to bite back a laugh. Parsnip soup.

Mr. Baxter began fiddling with his spoon. "Yes, I remember now. Of course. You did tell me that, didn't you, which is why the rest of us are having trout while something special is being prepared for you, my dear. Meanwhile, I do hope you will enjoy the soup."

Mrs. Wickham dipped her spoon and lifted it to her mouth. "Parsnip soup?"

Mr. Baxter tugged at his collar and frantically motioned to his servant. The two whispered for a moment before the servant left the room.

"Tell us, Mr. Baxter," Kelsey said, eager to see how the evening would develop, "how long have you lived here? Do you have any family nearby?"

He nervously scratched his cheek. "I've lived here for almost a year, ever since my brother returned to London."

"Your brother?"

"Yes. He lived here before I did." Mr. Baxter stirred his soup and took a bite.

Mrs. Wickham's face lightened. "You never mentioned a brother. Does he visit often?"

"On occasion. He comes to observe the state of Calder Glen and make improvements from time to time. I don't know why he doesn't trust me . . ."

"It's a charming house," Nathaniel commented. "Does he have a particular interest in it or is he simply helping you with such improvements?"

Mr. Baxter waved his hand and stumbled over his words. "I suppose it is because, well, he owns it."

No one seemed bothered by this news except Mrs. Wickham. "I thought you said you own it." She frowned and pushed a loose curl out of her eye.

"No, no. I said I would like to own it. I would have purchased it from him had I not made some unfortunate business wagers last year."

"Business wagers?" Mrs. Wickham said the words as if they tasted like parsnip soup. "Do you mean gambling? Speculating?"

"Well," Mr. Baxter tugged on his lapels and twiddled his spoon. "Much of what we do in life is a gamble. At the time, I didn't think there was much risk. I really didn't expect to lose as much as I . . . Well, Mr. Woodcox here has a much more promising venture this time, so enough about me. I'm eager for you all to know Mr. Woodcox. He is my special guest this evening. No need to keep all the attention to myself."

Mrs. Wickham stirred her soup. "You said I was your special guest this evening."

When Kelsey finished her soup, which was rather flavorful, if a bit oversalted, she said, "Tell us about this new venture, Mr. Baxter. I'm rather interested to hear the details."

Mr. Baxter looked at Mr. Woodcox, who was indulging in a long drought from his glass. "It's nothing, really, a small matter, having to do with some racehorses in Ashby. I don't know why I even mentioned it. Nothing may come of it. Mr. Woodcox and I are merely . . . researching right now."

Mr. Woodcox finally spoke. "Mr. Baxter is correct. There isn't much to say about it. I simply saw an opportunity and wanted to share the good fortune with my friend." He looked around as if waiting for someone else to speak. "Surely, the ladies would like to discuss something besides investments and wagers. Tell me, Miss Wickham, how do you like Barley Cottage? I hear you've only recently arrived in these parts."

Kelsey noticed Nathaniel watching her as she answered. "Yes, that is so. We find the cottage quite comfortable."

"What brings you here to Derbyshire?"

Kelsey gave her usual explanation. "It was simply time for a change. Or at least, my mother thought so." She didn't mean to add that last sentence, but she hadn't bit her tongue in time. "I'm grateful my uncle permits us to stay at the cottage."

"Your uncle? Your uncle is Mr. Darcy?"

Mrs. Wickham looked up from her soup, ignoring Mr. Woodcox's last question. "It *was* time for a change, and I'm quite happy we came. We never would have made such lovely friends otherwise."

Nathaniel grinned at Kelsey. "I couldn't agree more."

Everyone had nearly finished their soup except for Mrs. Wickham who had hardly touched hers.

Mr. Woodcox scraped his spoon against the sides of his bowl, capturing every last drop. "I've heard an old sea captain used to live in Barley Cottage. You haven't found any of his buried treasure, have you?" He finished with a laugh, but Kelsey didn't miss the eagerness in his eyes.

Her mind went to the guineas she had found in the garden and the note hidden under the windowsill. The guineas weren't much compared to riches of wealthier folks, and the few sentimental lines in the note could hardly be considered treasure to anyone besides the owner. But they held a charm that Kelsey felt worth protecting.

"Buried treasure?" Mrs. Wickham leaned forward. "What a delightful notion."

"Indeed," Mr. Woodcox chuckled. "Of course, that would have been before the captain tried to acquire Thistledown Hall."

Nathaniel put his spoon down. "Tried, sir?"

"The captain never lived there." Mr. Woodcox only spared Nathaniel a cursory glance.

"No, but I believe he successfully acquired the estate."

"I doubt that." Mr. Woodcox met Kelsey's eye and smirked.

Mrs. Wickham said, "Our friend, Mr. Worth would know, sir. He now lives there with the captain's leave. We're all very excited to see what improvements he makes on the estate."

"Is that so?" Mr. Woodcox narrowed his eyes, giving Nathaniel his full attention.

Before anything else was said, the same servant who had served the soup returned with dinner plates to distribute.

Mr. Baxter leaned toward Mrs. Wickham. "I hope you like pork, my dear Lydia. I'm afraid it's the only other suitable option available tonight."

Never mind the pork, thought Kelsey. He just called her mother *Lydia*. Had her mother given him permission, or had Mr. Baxter merely taken the liberty? The expression on her mother's face suggested it was the latter.

Squirming like a worm in a bird's beak, Mr. Baxter reached for his handkerchief and patted his glistening forehead. "I had better see how our dessert is coming along."

The wooden chair released a scraping rasp as he stood abruptly and collided with his servant who held a long silver tray. The servant wobbled and swayed like a reed in the wind, trying to maintain the oversized tray, but anyone could see what was coming.

"Careful, Clyde! Careful!" Mr. Baxter cried.

Just when it looked as if the man might regain his balance, he stumbled right into Mrs. Wickham's chair. The tray crashed halfway on the table before falling into her lap, sending pieces of pork, potatoes, and gravy all over the gleaming dress from Lucia.

Never noticing the tiny splashes of gravy that flicked on her arm, Kelsey's hands shot to her mouth to cover her horrified gasp. Her dress, her beautiful, fairy tale dress was ruined. Her mother would wash and recover, but the dress never would. Kelsey closed her eyes in a moment of silence amidst the commotion and wished herself anywhere else.

It must have taken at least half an hour to clean the mess and convince Mrs. Wickham to stay, despite the grease stains on her gown. Kelsey could hardly believe her mother agreed to stay at all, but Mr. Baxter was exceptionally pressing about it, expressing his desire for her to taste the dessert and share his company a little longer. With the use of a fresh serviette, Mrs. Wickham wiped a final smudge of gravy off a lock of hair and relented, but it was clear she was through trying to enjoy herself.

Perhaps Kelsey wouldn't need to send her mother another anonymous letter after all.

The dessert was a large almond cake with a custard drizzle on top, and though everyone agreed that compliments were due to Mr. Baxter's cook, no one said much otherwise.

Kelsey was in the middle of her final bite when she noticed Nathaniel and Mr. Woodcox both watching her and casting quick, critical glances at one another. When plates were swept away, and Mr. Baxter invited everyone into the sitting room, Nathaniel went straight to Kelsey's side.

"What are you doing?" she whispered.

"Sending that dolt a message."

"Is that so?" She glanced at Mr. Woodcox who was mindlessly scratching his ear. "Nathaniel, there is no need to be jealous."

"Of course, there is. You and I are engaged to be engaged soon."

Kelsey shushed him as everyone took their seats. Eyes met, but no one spoke.

Finally, Mr. Baxter clapped his hands and looked around expectantly. "A game, perhaps?"

The fire snapping over the logs was the only answer he received.

"We could always have a rematch at cards," Nathaniel whispered to Kelsey.

"Don't you dare suggest that now." She poked his side with her elbow.

"Charades?" Mr. Baxter persisted. "Whist? Spillikins?"

"Thank you, Mr. Baxter." Mrs. Wickham rose from her seat. "I'm sure you would be willing to entertain us all evening if we let you, but I cannot take advantage of your kindness any longer. We really must take our leave now."

It took persuading, but Mr. Baxter soon had the carriage brought around. As Mrs. Wickham and Mr. Baxter spoke their farewells, Kelsey overheard Nathaniel asking the carriage driver to convey her and her mother home first.

"What?" Mr. Billows grumbled. "And take twice as long doubling back like that to your house?"

"Yes," Nathaniel answered firmly. "The inconvenience of the task is why I'm offering you extra pay to do it."

Kelsey could hardly believe it. Yet again, Nathaniel remembered her. He was taking care to ensure her safety, and he was doing it at his own expense without any expectation. Every new insight into his character tugged at beliefs she thought she had understood.

During the carriage ride, Mrs. Wickham dabbed at the gravy stains on the skirts of the dress from Lucia with her handkerchief. Each time Kelsey's eyes strayed to one of the stains, she renewed her wish for the ride to end so she could curl up in her blankets and fall into the merciful forgetfulness of sleep. Finally, the cottage came into view with its flimsy fence and slanted walls.

Nathaniel waved for Mr. Billows to remain where he was while Nathaniel helped Mrs. Wickham step out of the carriage himself. When next he took Kelsey's hand, he pressed it with the careful affection he might give to something precious, sending familiar tremors through her that she was beginning to savor as much as fear. As much as she didn't want to fall prey to his charms, she worried she was succumbing.

Before she could pull away, he met her eyes briefly and brushed a kiss on her knuckles. "Good night, Lady Kelsey."

"Good night." Her voice came out thin and wispy as she tried to convince herself there was nothing in his look, nothing in his touch that had meant anything to her.

But she could no longer lie to herself.

The instinct to guard and protect her heart throbbed against the effort to comprehend the possibilities Nathaniel was awakening her to. As she watched the carriage ramble out of sight, she asked herself, was this why her mother had been unable to resist her father? Was the pull to be loved always so strong? It was only a tug, she told herself, a hunger she hadn't realized she would ever feel, but now that she had? There had to be a better way. It was a hunger she could temper, a pull she could resist. There had to be a safeguard against the same wiles her father had ensnared her mother with, a safeguard against the life of heartache that would follow if she gave in.

Yet, her thoughts were as clouded as the starless sky.

Her mother cleared her throat, reminding Kelsey where she was.

"Finally, home," Kelsey sang, pretending she hadn't been at all affected by Nathaniel. She scurried past her mother, to the cottage door, eager to be by herself again. "I've never been so happy to see this snug, little place."

Her mother followed closely with a far-off, dreamlike expression. "Wasn't it a lovely dinner, Kelsey?"

Kelsey fumbled in her reticule for the key. "You cannot be serious." Her mother's words were an efficient antidote to the flush she had felt only moments ago.

"But I'm quite serious."

Kelsey rolled her eyes. "Admit it. Even you did not enjoy yourself tonight."

Mrs. Wickham shook her head. "I'll admit no such thing. Mr. Baxter was extremely attentive."

"Oh, really? So attentive that he ordered a dinner of trout and parsnip soup?"

"Anyone could forget a person's food preferences."

"And I assume you were frowning at his sparkling conversation out of politeness? Or perhaps it was his talk of betting on racehorses that charmed you."

"We don't know what kind of investments he and Mr. Woodcox meant by that."

"It's gambling. No other way to say it." Kelsey would not relent on that point. She and her mother both knew what kind of toll gambling could take on a family, her own father having indulged in the habit his whole life. "And look at your gown, Mother. My gown! I can't believe you would take it like that."

"Oh, Kelsey, I'm so—"

"Stop. Please. That dress was a gift from Lucia, and you ruined it."

Her mother's eyes widened. "No one could have predicted that spill, but I cannot believe you would talk to your mother like this."

"I hardly believe it myself! I am the child. You are the mother! Why am I forced to be the responsible one? Why do you steal my things like a jealous sister? Not even Cissy would take a dress I adored without first asking permission." The hollow space in her chest grew cold as she thought of Cissy. She would have understood the treachery in their mother's choice of dress. "And why do you swoon over a man who you, yourself, think is ridiculous?"

Without waiting for an answer, Kelsey shoved the key into the door's keyhole and stomped inside. Her mother's footsteps were right behind her.

"I do not think Mr. Baxter is ridiculous." She stopped in their small sitting room and sighed. "But I am sorry about your dress."

Kelsey gave her ruined dress one last contemptuous look and ran all the way to her room.

Chapter 15

*I wish I might take this for a compliment; but to
be so easily seen through I am afraid is pitiful.*

Jane Austen, *Pride and Prejudice*

Kelsey sat by the sash window in the sitting room with *The
Tempest* in her lap while her mother adjusted the newly
added silk roses to one of her bonnets.

"How many times must I say it?" Mrs. Wickham asked quietly.
"I'm sorry."

Kelsey turned the page. "I know."

Her mother picked a stray ribbon from the table and twisted it
around her finger. "If you'd like, I thought I might help you in the
garden today."

Kelsey gave her mother a quick glance. "You're welcome to pull
weeds any time you like, but I have the notion to read today." She
turned another page. On any other day, she would have held her
mother to her word, but today, Kelsey could hardly speak without
remembering the awful image of thick, dark gravy dripping down her
gleaming, silk dress. Kelsey knew dresses would come and go, but that

one in particular was her one reminder that Lucia was thinking of her. Its clean, white brilliance had instilled a hope in Kelsey that she could begin a new life for herself, but like everything the Wickhams touched, the gown became tainted. Kelsey would forgive her mother, but she needed time.

From the corner of her eye, she saw her mother pick up a handful of papers from the table. Letters, perhaps? Kelsey didn't know whether Nathaniel had finished the latest letter to her mother, but moments later, a small gasp confirmed that he had.

"Another letter?" her mother said.

Mrs. Wickham broke the seal and drank its contents, never lifting her eyes. As a steady glow lit her features, a small satisfaction nestled inside Kelsey.

"What does it say, Mother?"

When her mother finally looked up, Kelsey was struck with what a truly beautiful woman she was.

"*My dear lady,*" she read, "*I have done nothing to earn the privilege of calling you Lydia, so I will continue to call you my lady . . .*"

Kelsey wondered if Nathaniel had been inspired by his own playful name for her.

"*. . . which, to me, sounds similar enough. Still, I cannot remove your name from my thoughts. You may very well wonder at my boldness in writing again. The only way I can account for it is to explain that duties have called me away when I otherwise would have called on you. All I can do is beg your forgiveness and patience. When I return, I will not hesitate to arrange a proper introduction and make my regard for you known. Truly, I wish circumstances had not necessitated my leaving. Yet, even in the absence of your smile, I hold the memory of it close. Sincerely, your devoted admirer.*" Mrs. Wickham finished the letter out of breath and covered her mouth.

"Whoever he is, he sounds very taken with you." Kelsey knew her mother would like to hear such a confirmation.

"I can hardly believe it."

Closing *The Tempest,* Kelsey placed it on the shelf and went to her mother's side. "You cannot possibly still believe this man to be

Mr. Baxter." She had been very clear to Nathaniel that this next letter needed to remove all such doubt.

Mrs. Wickham turned the letter over and frowned. "No, I suppose not." She tapped her chin and whispered, "But who could it be?"

The flustered blush on her mother's cheek was enough to make Kelsey's anger lose its sting. "This is an incredibly romantic letter, Mother. Rather than torment yourself with guessing, you should simply enjoy it."

Mrs. Wickham stared at the words a moment longer. Her smile came slowly but once released, grew to its full width. "You're right. Isn't it flattering the way he regrets being away from me?" She softly giggled. "It's the most romantic letter I've ever received."

Mrs. Wickham retrieved her bonnet along with a few stray silk flowers and walked off smiling, never aware of how Kelsey smiled too.

Over the next few days, Kelsey observed her mother carefully. Mr. Baxter didn't come calling, and Mrs. Wickham never uttered a complaint about it. Rather than contriving a way to see him, she remained occupied with her ribbons and bonnets. Sometimes, when Kelsey saw her adorning them with new trimmings, she caught her pausing to pull out the letter, which she always seemed to have on hand, and read it before returning to her work, quietly humming to herself.

Kelsey was rather fascinated to see how often her mother fussed over her bonnets when her time wasn't devoured by half-witted gentlemen. Even if it was another frivolous pursuit, to Kelsey it was a welcome change.

After three days of this, Mrs. Wickham slumped down to breakfast with the same letter in hand. "Perhaps I should not be too pleased with this note."

Kelsey's stomach dropped. Had her mother discovered the truth? "What do you mean, Mother?"

"It is too improper for a gentleman to write to a lady he is unacquainted with."

Kelsey exhaled. At least her mother did not suspect her. "I thought you decided to enjoy the letter."

"What if he isn't trustworthy? Mr. Baxter, at least, treats me with respect. Mostly."

Not Mr. Baxter again, and whatever did her mother mean by *mostly?*

Kelsey swallowed. "I would guess he's trustworthy. What is so improper about a man expressing his feelings for you, especially if he had to leave before he could call on you? He was probably too captivated by you to worry about silly rules of etiquette."

Her mother patted the letter against her palm. "Do you really think so, Kelsey?"

"Absolutely. And since when have you been so concerned about propriety?"

Kelsey waited for her mother to respond with an "Oh, hush!" but her mother only stared at the letter.

"I care about propriety." Yet, her tone was unconvincing. "And since when have you been so trusting of unfamiliar gentlemen?"

Heat immediately swept Kelsey's neck and face. "What? I'm not! I—"

"It's Mr. Worth's doing, isn't it? I see the effect he's having on you."

"No. There's no effect. I—" Kelsey looked up, searching the ceiling for a defense, but all she saw were cobwebs.

Her mother laughed and took Kelsey's hand. "It's all right, my darling. I understand these things much better than you realize."

After fleeting smiles passed between them, they headed to the garden and finally pulled weeds together. Despite her mother's complaints of dirt and thorns, the day became one of the most pleasant Kelsey had spent with her since Cissy had left for Aunt Kitty's. Together, they cleaned the cottage, picked peaches, wrote Cissy a letter, and found several things to laugh about. After sharing a dinner they each took part in preparing, Mrs. Wickham trimmed bonnets while Kelsey read, and not once was Mr. Baxter's name mentioned. Or Nathaniel's.

Chapter 16

It seems likely to rain; and then you must stay all night.

Jane Austen, *Pride and Prejudice*

The next day brought a letter from Cissy. The ducklings were growing. Aunt Kitty and her little cousins were delightful company. Warlingham Manor had eight chimneys and three dogs, and couldn't they please get a dog when she returned home? Although all was lovely, Cissy did have one complaint. She had been terribly disappointed to remain with the younger children in the nursery while the rest of the family attended a ball. The sting, she mentioned, was especially sharp knowing Jack Pendlestone was permitted to attend. Mrs. Wickham thought it a great shame, but Kelsey inwardly applauded Aunt Kitty's good sense.

When Mrs. Wickham finished reading Cissy's letter, she tossed it on the chair and let her arms fall. "When will my admirer write again, do you suppose?"

Kelsey coughed on her tea. "Does he need to write often to please you?"

"I suppose not, but why does he not reveal his name? Or where he is? Perhaps he remains anonymous because he is actually quite repugnant." Gripping the arms of her chair, she leaned forward. "He could be that eccentric man we see on the road sometimes, the one who carries all those chickens in his coat. The other day when I was in Lambton, I counted at least four in front and another writhing underneath on his back." Mrs. Wickham shuddered.

Kelsey put her cup down and laughed. "Would a man like that write something so beautiful?" When her mother hesitated, Kelsey exclaimed, "Of course he wouldn't! Besides, didn't your admirer say that duty had called him away?"

"Yes he did, but still, I'm rather upset with him."

"What? How can you be upset with someone you've never met before?"

"I'm upset because he keeps his distance. It's vexing to have a man express feelings for me without revealing himself. Flattering words are lovely, but what then? I can't become acquainted with someone who remains anonymous."

Before Kelsey could respond, her mother went upstairs and returned wearing her shawl and bonnet. "I need some air. I might walk to the village or perhaps near the pastures by Calder Glen. I'll return for dinner." With a distracted fog in her eyes, she passed through the doorway as easily as a breeze.

Kelsey groaned. Her mother was walking toward Mr. Baxter's home in hopes of seeing him. If she did, she was likely to get caught up with him and forget the hour, so Kelsey wasn't convinced her mother would return in time for dinner.

Alone in the cottage, Kelsey threw herself onto the sofa and ran her fist into the nearest pillow. Why? Why had the letters not had a longer effect? Her mother had clearly been flattered, but Kelsey had forgotten to account for her mother's impatience. Unless Kelsey wanted to inadvertently promote Mr. Baxter again, she would have to convince her mother that her anonymous admirer was reputable and intended to return.

How long would Kelsey keep up the charade, she wondered. She had never intended to write letters to her mother indefinitely. Two was already more than she had ever wanted to send, but she couldn't cease yet either. The stability and happiness of her mother and sister rested on Kelsey finding a solution to their troubles, and though she was willing to sacrifice much to do so, she could not write letters forever.

I must end this, she scolded herself, *but not until Mother is no longer tempted to accept Mr. Baxter's advances.* Her plan had to work at least to that extent. What Kelsey would do after that, she hadn't a clue.

The need to be moving pulled her from the sofa and propelled her to the garden where she could pull and prune and stomp out her frustrations as much as she liked. The damp air and darkening sky told her to retreat, but she met the distant echoes of thunder with a warning of her own.

"I'll stay out here as long as I desire!" She glared at the ashen clouds. "The sun may disappear, but I'm tired of retreating!"

She marched to the slanting shed, thrust open the door, and pulled out the gloves from Nathaniel. Snatching up the spade and shears, she promised to create the largest pile of weeds yet. Restless furor led her to the thorny brambles by the well, which she began punishing soundly. Snip, snip, and snip again. The branches hit the ground like the rain that was starting to fall.

She would not yield.

She wouldn't leave things to chance any longer. She would not let the weeds choke the garden, and she would not let her opportunity to create a home for herself and her family be ruined, not when she still hadn't seen Lucia.

When Kelsey noticed a cluster of thistles by the well, she promptly claimed them as her next victims, refusing to admit they made her think of Thistledown Hall and its handsome occupant. When her shears had done their work and nothing was left but the pale, stubborn root, she knelt without a thought for her sky-blue dress. What did it matter when her favorite had already been ruined?

The root's hold in the ground was stronger than she had realized and its depths greater than she had expected.

"I'm glad to see you're protecting your hands this time."

Kelsey whirled around on her knees. Nathaniel stood only a few feet away, heedless of fresh raindrops hitting his shoulders and wetting his brow.

"Though nothing is protecting you from the rain, I see."

"What are you doing here?" she glowered. "Must you always catch me unawares? I wish you wouldn't."

"Such a temper, Lady Kelsey. Fortunately, I am well enough acquainted with you to no longer be put off by such rash words."

She sat back on her knees and sighed. The rain was gaining momentum, and she knew she looked a mess. "You're right. I am upset. It's my—"

"No, no. Let me guess." Nathaniel snapped his fingers. "Your new bonnet. It doesn't fit properly."

She flashed him a scathing glare.

"Teasing, teasing. I know. It's your mother. The second letter didn't work, did it?" Without concern for his fine grey coat and trousers, he knelt on the ground next to her and gestured for the spade.

"It did at first," she said, handing it to him, "but now she thinks her admirer is being improper by writing to her."

Nathaniel nodded. "Well, he is." He took a turn with the weed. After a bit of digging and tugging, he pulled up a rope-like root speckled with mud.

"Then she said she was angry at him for staying away."

"Aw, I see." Nathaniel tossed the root onto Kelsey's soggy pile of weeds.

"What do you see?"

He inched closer to reach another weed. "Your mother needs to feel important. She wants to feel special to this man, to know he would do anything for her."

As she leaned against the well, the stones pressed into her back and sent streams of icy water trickling down her spine. Nathaniel finished with a large thistle and leaned next to her, stretching his muddied legs out before him.

He eyed the large pile of weeds next to Kelsey. "Did you pull all these yourself?"

She nodded vaguely. "What would he do for her, I wonder?"

"Oh, no," he said. "I can see the inner workings of your mind cooking up the next layer of schemes. Kelsey, don't you think we had better leave off? Let your mother work things out for herself?"

His words only blended in with the raindrops she was already ignoring. "He needs to let her know he's coming for her."

"I'm sure he would. If he existed."

Raindrops plopped and echoed from the bottom of the well and danced across her arms while Nathaniel sat with her, untroubled by the drips running down his face.

"I only want to give my mother a taste of how a real gentleman might treat her. This anonymous man can't hurt her any more than any of her real suitors, can he? Oh, this is a disaster! I don't know what to do." Kelsey shook her head.

"Well, I do. We must get you inside. Come." Nathaniel stood and offered his hand.

She stared at it, debating whether to take it and risk the flutterings his touch always created in her, but she wanted the help. As expected, the flutterings came when she accepted his sturdy hand and let him pull her up.

With puddles forming around her and rain loosening her hold, she slipped on the gravel and teetered backward toward the well. In an instant, his hand reached around her waist, and the flutters inside her turned to great tremors, impossible to fight when he had just prevented a much worse fall.

"You're very charming when wet, Lady Kelsey."

Even in the rain, she could see his eyes intent with those familiar bits of light that sometimes looked like stars. Oh, why did they have to look like stars at that precise moment when she was in his arms? She didn't know what to say. She was soaked all over, and though he played the part of expert flirt regardless of the circumstances, she didn't feel the least bit charming.

The rain gathered speed and cooled her cheeks. Pushing wet hairs out of her face, she straightened herself and stepped out of his hold.

"You've just smudged a bit of dirt there. No, that's not it. Here. Allow me." Nathaniel brushed her cheek with his thumb, and again, his warmth simmered against the chilled drops that continued to fall.

"Please—" She stepped back.

A terrible clap of thunder cracked the sky and sent a torrent of rain cascading down. Without thinking, Kelsey took Nathaniel's hand and ran for the cottage. She had to skip over a shovel she had left on the path earlier, but he must not have seen it. His hand slipped from hers as he tumbled over the shovel and landed forcefully in the mud.

"Nathaniel!" She dropped beside him and placed a hand on his shoulder. He had rolled to his side and was clutching his knee, grimacing.

"I'm all right." He steeled his expression and pulled himself up. "Let's hurry."

Reaching the cottage's back door, Kelsey hopped inside, thinking Nathaniel would follow, but when she turned around, he was lingering at the threshold.

"Why do you hesitate? You're a mess, and you're hurt. Come in before I have to pull you inside!" She held the door open and waited.

He limped in grunting and looked at the puddles he was leaving on the floor.

"Never mind those," Kelsey said, reaching for a cloth to dry her face. "I've already made several. Is your knee terribly hurt?" She handed him his own clean cloth.

He grimaced again and dried his face. "Unfortunately, I twisted it when I fell. It struck against a stone in the path. I've injured this knee before, so the old ache will flare up for a few days, I'm afraid, but don't worry. I'm sure it won't take long to improve, and I can still walk on it."

Seeing him take a limping step, she worried he wasn't telling her just how much it hurt. "Go sit by the fire. Or . . . oh dear."

With the recent downpour and no one inside to tend the fires, the kitchen flames had extinguished entirely.

"Don't fret. I'll start it up again." Dripping wet, Nathaniel found the tinderbox on the mantle and set to work until tiny sparks took to the logs with flames that grew and radiated heat throughout the room. "There. Now, let's see to the fire in the sitting room. Once I get that blazing as well, you'll be quite warm."

She followed him into the sitting room and watched him work. Though he moved quickly and his hands were deft, Kelsey could tell he was avoiding putting weight on his hurt knee.

"Thank you, Nathaniel, but I wish you would sit and rest your knee. I'm going to dry off, but I'll be back with some blankets for you."

As she rushed upstairs, she was reminded of the day she had slipped in the mud while trying to avoid Nathaniel. She laughed bitterly at the puddles she was leaving and felt as though fate were trying to prove a point.

She replaced her wet dress and chemise as quickly as she could with a worn but warm forest-green dress, fully aware she was not much more presentable in her current dry state than she had been in her wet one. Still, she was dry. Next, she found two thickly woven blankets.

Without making her presence known, she paused at the top of the staircase to silently observe Nathaniel. He had removed his jacket and hung it on the corner of the mantle. He awkwardly stood before the flames in his white shirt and grey trousers, pausing occasionally to take his shirt by the hem and shake it out. Because of the wetness, however, the fabric clung to his skin, revealing more shape and muscle than Kelsey had ever been accustomed to seeing.

She turned away, blushing furiously. How could she allow herself to be alone with him in such a state? What would happen when her mother returned? Or if her uncle ever found out? She shuddered at the thought, but the rain was pouring incessantly. The sky was darkening, and Nathaniel was injured. He would have to stay.

"Kelsey! Kelsey, can you hear me?" he called.

"Yes." She only dared descend a few steps to where she could see him more clearly.

"I'm obliged to you for letting me warm myself by the fire, but I do not wish to make you uncomfortable. Considering the circumstances, I think it best if I leave."

"But your knee!" she cried, nearly tripping down the rest of the stairs. "You can't walk on it, not in this rain. You'll catch pneumonia if you attempt it." Already, he was putting on his wet, grey jacket. "Nathaniel, please." Her conscience couldn't let him leave.

He tugged at his lapels and adjusted his sleeves, but he stopped when his eyes met hers. "Can this be true? Do you really care?"

She took a step closer, hugging the blankets tightly. The answer lodged in her throat, so close to the truth but never fully forming. The cottage door then burst open to admit Mrs. Wickham, completely soaked herself but not looking an ounce sorry for it.

"Kelsey, I just had the most divine afternoon with— Oh, my!" Mrs. Wickham almost collided into Nathaniel, avoiding him by mere inches. "Mr. Worth! What a surprise!"

Nathaniel's words trembled like Kelsey's shaking hands. "Good evening, Mrs. Wickham. Forgive, me. I—"

They had been caught. Would her mother assume the worst? Kelsey felt her cheeks glowing brighter than the embers in the hearth.

"We were outside in the garden when it started to rain. Mr. Worth hurt his knee, so I insisted he warm himself by the fire and rest." She clumsily placed the blankets on a chair and clasped her hands together to contain her shivers.

"Yes," Nathaniel agreed, his voice cracking slightly, "and I beg your pardon for the trouble I've caused you. I must be leaving now. Excuse me." He dipped his head and, with fingers fumbling, buttoned his jacket.

"Leaving?" Mrs. Wickham looked between him and Kelsey with a mix of elation and suspicion, and for a moment, Kelsey was certain she had great reason to fear. "I won't allow it. Not in this weather. Now that I'm here, you shall stay the night, and we will make a very pleasant party!" She clapped her hands, then pointed to the fire. "You stay right here where it's warm, Mr. Worth, and make yourself at home while Kelsey and I make ourselves presentable."

Kelsey followed her mother, expecting to hear the argument that she and Nathaniel must marry after being caught alone like this, but at least she knew he wouldn't catch his death or lose his way trying to hobble home in the cold, dark rain. At the top of the stairs, still dripping like a fountain, Mrs. Wickham took Kelsey's hand and pulled her into her room.

"Mother, I know this looks dreadful, but I promise, nothing happened."

"Kelsey, this is perfect!" her mother whispered, oblivious to Kelsey's fears. "This reminds me of how my mother got Charles Bingley to fall in love with your Aunt Jane. I never knew you had it in you!"

"Whatever you think is in me, Mother, isn't. He walked by the cottage, and we spoke for a moment. Then the rain started pouring. That is all."

"Of course, that is all, but what a stroke of luck! I came home at just the right time. At this rate, you'll be married before the leaves change colors!"

There was the mention of marriage Kelsey had been waiting for. "I am not trying to ensnare Mr. Worth, and I don't want to be married before the leaves change colors."

"Oh, hush!" She put a finger to her lips. "He'll hear you. Now come with me. We need to fix your hair. Hurry!"

After her mother changed into dry clothes, Kelsey humbly submitted to her efforts to sweep up Kelsey's damp hair in an admittedly flattering knot. Though there was no more talk of marriage, Kelsey was filled with a new worry. What would they eat? She didn't think they had much of anything worth sharing with company.

Mrs. Wickham, however, insisted she would take care of everything. "Don't worry about a thing. I'll have the tea ready first and a lovely dinner laid out in no time."

"But Mother—"

"Pinch your cheeks, Kelsey." She pulled her into the hallway and placed a stack of pillows and blankets in her hand. "You can give these to Mr. Worth."

"Mother, people will think it very improper for him to spend the night. Consider the consequences if Mrs. Winters learns of this. Or if my uncle—"

"Nonsense," her mother said. "I don't care a wit for Mrs. Winters's judgments, and your uncle isn't here. Besides, I'm a perfectly acceptable chaperone."

"But—"

"I just remembered something. Wait here!" She hurried off, leaving Kelsey with the blankets and pillows and a head that was beginning to ache with the tightness of more hairpins than she would have chosen for herself.

Her mother returned with what looked like another blanket or two, or . . . Kelsey sucked in a breath. It couldn't be.

"Here." Her mother gingerly laid a folded white shirt and a pair of men's trousers on top of the blankets Kelsey held. "Mr. Worth can wear these."

Kelsey swallowed hard and blinked back the threat of tears. "Are those . . .?"

"Your father's," Mrs. Wickham nodded. "I know it was silly and sentimental of me to save them, but I wanted . . ." Her mother's voice grew thick. "I just wanted to hold onto something he had worn, so I could put them with my things."

"You saved these all these years?" Kelsey stared at the clothes and didn't know what to think. "Are you certain you now wish to . . ."

Her mother slowly ran her hand along them. "Mr. Worth can have them. It's time I let them go. They're only clothes after all."

"But Mother—" Kelsey wasn't sure she wanted to see Nathaniel in her father's clothes.

"Not another word about it. Our guest is waiting." And with that, she gave Kelsey a nudge toward the stairs.

Kelsey took a measured breath with each step, wondering whether she could justifiably be upset with anyone other than herself. What a mess the evening was turning into!

In the small sitting room, Nathaniel was pacing before the fire. He stopped abruptly and straightened his back when he noticed her. "Welcome back, Kelsey. You look lovely."

Her spirits lifted a touch to see him calm and cheerful despite being wet. "Thank you. I'm afraid we don't have much to offer you, but I can give you these." She placed the blankets and her father's clothes on the chair next to him. "The clothes were my father's. I'm not certain they will fit." She had the strange notion, however, that they would.

"Not to worry," he said. "I've spent many nights at sea soaked to the bone. Even if these don't fit, my own clothes will be dry soon enough with the help of the fire." His expression softened. "Please tell your mother how much I appreciate it." He truly seemed grateful.

"However, I really can't stay." Nathaniel shook his jacket before the fire. "I'll be off as soon as the rain eases up."

Another crack of thunder shook the cottage, and the rain poured relentlessly against its walls and roof. A drip of water landed on Kelsey's arm as a spot of moisture grew on the ceiling. Another drop landed on her head.

"Even if your knee wasn't hurt, Nathaniel, it would not be safe at this late hour. The road wouldn't be visible, and by now, it is nothing but mud." She reached out and caught the next drop.

Nathaniel gave the ceiling a scrutinizing look. "I can fix that leaky roof for you when the rain ceases. But for now . . ." In a minute's time, despite a little clumsiness from his knee, he positioned a small table under the drip along with an empty vase to catch it.

"Thank you." Kelsey appreciated his quickness.

He stepped close to her. "Will it trouble you if I do stay the night?"

His question sent a thousand feelings flooding through her. She couldn't deny she liked him in her home, tending the fire, showing concern for her, and sharing his smiles. With him there, she no longer minded the smallness of the room. If all her worries could dissolve, she might have admitted to deeper feelings taking root, but those feelings were strange to her and unpredictable. She had promised herself she would not be taken in by the same tricks of charm her own father had used, eventually bringing her family to such a disreputable standing in life, but she was no longer certain she knew the difference between a trick and a truth.

What did it mean for Nathaniel to make her insides swirl and simmer? Surely, such thrills were not a trustworthy foundation. How could she trust her heart when it was betraying her?

"Of course, it will trouble me, Nathaniel. Mother or no, this is not appropriate."

"Your honor is safe with me," he said solemnly. "You have my word."

Kelsey bit her lip. "I want to believe you. I honestly do, but this is not the test of honor I had hoped for."

He scratched the back of his head, and his lip titled up. "Were you hoping to test it? Is there a better way?"

She knew he was teasing, simply catching her in her words, but the blush rose to her cheeks all the same.

"I'm sorry," he sighed and looked at the floor. "I see what a vulnerable position this has put you in. I suspected it might rain today. I came because I wanted to see you, but I never intended this."

Kelsey walked to the mantle and leaned against it, soothed by the warmth of the fire but unable to ignore the drip, drip, drip that was pinging in the vase. "We need to consider the situation. No one who knows my mother would consider her an acceptable chaperone, and I can't decide when it would be best for you to leave. If someone saw you exiting the cottage at dawn, the onlooker would conclude the worst, and knowing my luck, it would be my uncle returning. We cannot allow that to happen. If, however, someone saw you leave in the middle of the day, they would only assume you were paying a visit. So . . ."

He leaned opposite her against the mantle. "You want me to stay until tomorrow afternoon?"

Kelsey frowned. Why did he sound so delighted? "I suppose that is what I'm asking, but it's not what I want. There is a difference."

She could see the firelight frolicking in his eyes.

"Then I hope to make up the difference."

Chapter 17

I hope, my dear . . . that you have ordered a
good dinner today, because I have reason to
expect an addition to our family party.

Jane Austen, *Pride and Prejudice*

*R*ain continued to slap the windowpanes, alternating between
gentle waves and enormous torrents. Though the current lull
promised peace, Kelsey found sleep impossible, knowing Nathaniel
was downstairs on her sofa. If she sat very still and held her breath, she
could swear she heard his breathing through the floorboards despite
the rain.

She had to give her mother credit for achieving a remarkably successful dinner under the circumstances that night. Cold cuts from
the market, fluffy bread, roasted potatoes covered in herbs, dandelion greens, and fresh peaches appeared at the table faster than Kelsey
thought possible. She had never known her mother capable of such
domestic skill, and though it was not the grandest of meals, Nathaniel
had paid every compliment possible.

During dinner, he had regaled them with stories of his most memorable voyages, describing whipping sea winds, smothering rains, and the oddities of life on a ship. Kelsey shuddered to imagine him suffering hunger and cold while braving the elements and performing his duties.

After Mrs. Wickham had collected the plates, she asked Nathaniel how he came to be Captain Styles's heir.

During a particularly terrible storm, Nathaniel explained, he had seen the captain ascend the deck to issue orders. Nathaniel had become aware of a faction of men who had recently been disciplined for going against orders and blamed the captain for being caught in the storm. When Nathaniel chanced to see one of those officers stealthily following the captain, Nathaniel's instinct was also to follow.

He described the deck as wet and precarious. The curtains of rain obscured his visibility, but when he caught sight of the man raising a knife to the captain's back, Nathaniel rushed forward and delivered a blow that knocked the treasonous man to the ground unconscious. That was the night Captain Styles claimed Nathaniel as his heir and promised to make it official as soon as he could. Nathaniel had been given leave through the captain's written consent to inhabit Thistledown Hall and manage the estate until the captain retired.

As Kelsey listened to the rain and stared into the darkness, she thought of Nathaniel being tossed on the waves in such a storm. She shuddered and pulled her blankets to her chin. What did she truly feel for Nathaniel? She kept thinking of his eyes and the way his lips parted when he smiled, but mostly she thought of the moment he had asked if she cared about him. What might she have said had her mother not returned in that moment?

What were feelings but fleeting notions and inner stirrings that passed like clouds and sometimes like storms? As far as she could tell, there were few that lasted. The anonymous letters she had written for her mother had only exerted a temporary effect. Even the passions between her parents that paraded as love had dwindled to strange insecurities. Wouldn't the effect Nathaniel had on Kelsey also be temporary? What did it matter if he was different from other men? What did it signify if she was destined to move away again anyway?

She shivered beneath the blankets, still aware of the steady stream of rain, when the floorboards creaked below. *Only Nathaniel,* she reminded herself. She couldn't blame him for having trouble sleeping on the small, lumpy sofa that was too small for his tall frame. At the sound of another creak, longer and more whining this time, she looked around her room in consideration of what item she could use as a weapon if she needed to defend herself. Her best idea was an old parasol with a rip in it.

Another floorboard made a rickety groan. She wished Nathaniel would be still, but the sounds continued, only slightly masked by the rain. When Kelsey sensed the creaks moving from the sitting room to the dining room, she got out of bed and threw on her robe. What was he doing? Guest or not, he had no business wandering through their home, rifling through their belongings.

She quietly opened her door. All she wanted was to steal a peek of him without being observed herself, just to see what he was doing. As an extra precaution, she brought her parasol.

At the top of the stairs, she could see Nathaniel's boots on the hearthstones by the fire, but she didn't see Nathaniel. The sofa was empty. A draft wrapped around her ankles and across her neck, sending shivers all through her. She crept further down the stairs and still didn't see him.

"Nathaniel?" she whispered, no longer caring about going unobserved. "Nathaniel!"

From the dining room, he stepped slowly into view still in her father's clothes with his shirt untucked. Kelsey blushed to see his bare feet and calves.

He raised a finger to his lips. "There's someone outside."

She stared as she comprehended his words. Who was outside? Who would possibly be out in the middle of the night in this weather? She tightened her grip on her parasol and didn't know whether to return to her room or wait where she was.

Just as the rain's patter on the roof eased into softer blankets, a clap of thunder shook the walls, and Kelsey, driven by instinct, dropped her parasol and ran straight into Nathaniel's arms. Her hands went around his waist, and everything inside her stilled. The steady rhythm of his heartbeat drowned out all other sounds as she shut her eyes and attuned herself to the warmth of his arm wrapping protectively around her.

When she opened her eyes and saw his chest, the reality of where she was struck her full force. "Forgive me!" She jumped back and raised her hands to her cheeks, mortified she had done something so completely hazardous to her reputation. That's when she noticed he carried the fire iron in his other arm. "What are you doing?" she whispered.

"Nothing, for now. I'm only preparing to defend you, if necessary."

Thunder sounded again, and the rain gained speed. She remained close to Nathaniel, careful not to touch him this time, no matter how strong the pull, as he raised a finger to his lips and looked intently around. Kelsey didn't hear anything, but Nathaniel walked back to the sitting room, and listened again. He went to the window, then finally braced himself by the main door. Kelsey followed closely, hearing only the rain and her own footsteps. Was Nathaniel imagining things? Perhaps all those months at sea had made him easily frightened at night.

Then she heard it, an irregular shuffle against stone and gravel that didn't come from the rain. Someone was right outside the door. The lock began to rattle. Kelsey covered her mouth and looked at Nathaniel, suddenly willing to put all her trust in him.

He took her hand and gently pressed it. "Step back and hide."

She hopped across the room as quietly as she could to the fireplace where she grabbed the iron shovel, then retreated behind the sofa. Kneeling on the cold floorboards, she peeked from the corner to see what happened next.

Nathaniel took a wide stance with the fire iron raised behind him. Kelsey bolstered her courage and promised to fly to his aid at the first sign of danger, so long as her feet kept up with her racing heart.

The lock clicked, and the wooden door scraped against the warped frame. The sound of rain grew louder. With the shovel in her hands, Kelsey clamped her lips shut to smother the scream she felt inside. An intruder was grunting as he pushed against the door.

A man in a heavy wool coat stepped halfway inside. His wet hat hung limply as water streamed off it, obscuring his face in darkness and rain. He had a pistol in his gloved hand. Nathaniel stepped from the cover of the door and, as fast as lightning, struck the hot iron against the intruder's hand, making him drop the weapon. The man released a groan of surprise mingled with pain. The next instant, Nathaniel swung the fire iron against the man's right arm. The man grunted and pulled his arm protectively to his chest as he stumbled back. Just as Nathaniel reared back to swing the iron again, the intruder escaped into the stormy darkness.

Kelsey held her breath, viewing the incident as if it were a scene in a book she was imagining, but there was Nathaniel standing in the doorway, blocking the entrance as he gazed outside. Kelsey could hear the rain sizzling off the fire iron in his hand.

"Nathaniel?" When she had waited behind the sofa as long as she could tolerate, she ran over, picked up the pistol, and placed it in his free hand. There was no sign of the intruder, and Nathaniel was getting wet all over again.

"Is he gone?" Trembling, she took his arm and urged him inside.

"I think so." Nathaniel submitted to her pull. "He ran off, I think, but I can't be sure."

"Shut the door. Please!" Kelsey could barely control the tremor in her voice.

Nathaniel carefully shut the door and secured the lock.

"I don't understand," she whispered. "We have nothing worth stealing. Nothing. Why would an intruder come here? Do you think he intended to harm us?"

"I don't know." Nathaniel returned the fire iron to its place on the hearthstones and hid the pistol in his jacket, which still hung on the mantle.

A glance at the fire iron and then at Nathaniel, and the tears finally came. "Oh, Nathaniel! What would we have done if you hadn't been here?"

He took a clumsy step closer and wrapped Kelsey's hands firmly in his. She let her tears drip on his already wet hands, afraid of what might have happened, afraid of how much she wanted to stay there with him and fall to the safety of his arms again.

His shoulders eased with the fervent sigh of, "Kelsey!"

She met his eyes, deep and captivating, and saw everything there, every hope, every desire. She could feel him effortlessly pulling the knowledge of her heart from her eyes. All he wanted to know, every feeling she had wanted to hide but couldn't was there. In one brief look, there were no secrets between them.

She had to get away.

"I . . . Nathaniel, I . . ." She could feel herself slipping, closer than she had ever been before to the same mistakes her mother had made. "I must return to my room."

His thumb ran over her knuckles, his grip loosening. "Yes," he whispered.

Without looking back, she retreated upstairs, and for the rest of the night, she listened to his footsteps below.

Chapter 18

This was a lucky idea of mine, indeed!

Jane Austen, *Pride and Prejudice*

No sooner had Kelsey drifted to a restless sleep than she felt her mother shaking her awake.

"Come, my darling. I've prepared breakfast, and I must say, your guest is quite handsome even in his sleep."

Kelsey groaned and rolled over, pulling the pillow over her head, but her mother yanked it away and tossed it on the floor before mercilessly pulling back the curtains to let the light spill over her face. With nowhere to hide, Kelsey stretched her arms and rubbed her eyes. Had her mother nothing to say about the intruder from last night? Or had Kelsey dreamed the whole thing?

One look from Nathaniel as she met him at the breakfast table confirmed it had not been a dream. He now wore his own clothes, wrinkled and dirty, and a pleasant smile, but Kelsey could see the shadows under his eyes and the worry behind them. Like her, he couldn't have slept much.

Kelsey's mother again proved more resourceful in the kitchen than she usually was, providing a simple breakfast of eggs, toast, and tea.

She chatted easily about how pleasant the morning air was after a good rainstorm, how she was sad Cissy wasn't there to enjoy breakfast with them, and how fortunate it was she had saved some eggs yesterday.

"It's rather amusing," she said in her ramblings, "but I think I slept particularly well last night knowing our good friend, Mr. Worth, was here to keep our little home safe."

Mrs. Wickham gave Nathaniel a maternal smile and went on talking about the contents of Cissy's recent letter, never noticing the tension that arose between Kelsey and Nathaniel as she spoke. They seemed to have an unspoken agreement not to mention the intruder. It was exactly the sort of catastrophe that would send Mrs. Wickham into a nervous panic. She might insist they move again, and Kelsey didn't know which she feared more, the intruder returning or leaving Derbyshire before she had seen Lucia. Or before she understood her feelings for Nathaniel.

For much of breakfast, Kelsey could scarcely meet his eyes, lest she betray herself and reveal the tumult of emotions from the previous night. Though images of the shadowed stranger raised the hairs on her neck, thoughts of nestling into Nathaniel's arms hushed those fears and spoke of new ones. She hardly knew how she managed to eat and drink that morning without completely spilling her tea.

Once breakfast was finished, they went to the sitting room to while away the morning. Kelsey attempted to read but had trouble finding something that would hold her attention. When Nathaniel settled into the chair across from her, she smiled to see him reading *The Tempest*.

Mrs. Wickham restlessly switched between her own needlework and gazing out the window. Was she expecting someone? Kelsey didn't think she could face callers that morning, especially if those callers were Mrs. Winters or Miss Chatham. There was so much Kelsey wanted to say to Nathaniel and so much she didn't want to say to her mother, that time spent doing nothing was its own sort of torment.

Finally, Mrs. Wickham suggested tea again and asked for Kelsey's help.

One step into the kitchen, and her mother's forceful whispering began. "What are you doing, Kelsey? I'm trying my best to help you along, but you aren't making any effort at all."

Kelsey pinched her eyes together. "I didn't sleep well last night. That's all."

Her mother's eyes grew stern as she pulled the tea tray from a shelf and dropped it on the table with a clatter. "What is Mr. Worth to think of your silence this morning?"

"He knows we didn't plan for him to stay the night. I doubt he expects us to entertain him every minute." Kelsey kept her hands busy adding teacups and spoons to the tray. Her mother had no notion of how Kelsey's insides twisted like a rope with every reprimand.

"Well, try to put a little more effort into this visit, if you please. If I were that man," she pointed toward the sitting room, "I wouldn't plan on returning here any time soon after the coldness you've shown."

Kelsey tried to keep her voice steady. "I promise I'm not being cold. I merely have much to think about. Mr. Worth will understand."

"Will he, now?" her mother lilted. "Have you two grown so close that you speak without words?"

Kelsey turned away to hide her flushing face. A rasp on the main door spared her from having to give a response.

"Thank goodness!" her mother breathed out, taking the steaming kettle from the fire. "At least now, we'll have another person to turn to for conversation."

Her mother bustled into the sitting room with the tea tray, and before long, Mr. Baxter's voice filled the cottage. Judging from the clanking of teacups, he was joining them for tea. Kelsey waited in the kitchen, finding pots to clean and saucers to rearrange until, finally, her mother returned and beckoned her to join them. Bracing herself, Kelsey stepped into the sitting room.

"Kelsey! Wonderful news!" A full grin spread across her mother's face, all signs of her previous frustration gone. "Mr. Worth has had the most pleasant idea. He suggested we all walk to Thistledown Hall together this afternoon."

Nathaniel scratched his cheek and reddened. "There isn't much to see yet, but there are some interesting paintings in the gallery, and I'm eager for any opinion on how I might improve the grounds."

"What do you think, Kelsey? Shall we not say yes and leave at once?"

All three awaited her answer. If she declined, she was certain her mother would wander off with Mr. Baxter anyway, and Nathaniel would leave. Scenes from the previous night reminded Kelsey that she did not want to be in the cottage alone just then. She would agree, even if it meant enduring Mr. Baxter's company.

"I . . . think that sounds lovely."

"Wonderful!" Her mother clapped her hands. "You fetch your bonnet and meet us on the path."

It didn't take Kelsey long to fetch her bonnet and shawl, but when she stepped out, her mother and Mr. Baxter were already nearly to the road. Where was Nathaniel?

"Not having second thoughts about our walk, are you, Lady Kelsey?"

He seemed to step out of nowhere, and before she could think, she slapped his arm with her reticule. "How dare you startle me! Especially after last night. I told you to stop doing that. Fortunately for you, I'm not carrying my parasol. Otherwise, you'd be nursing a new bruise right now."

He chuckled. "I'm sorry. I didn't mean to frighten you. I decided to wait for you here rather than follow your mother and Mr. Baxter."

On the arm of Mr. Baxter, her mother looked back and waved.

"I can't blame you for that."

"I hope you don't mind my suggestion to walk to Thistledown Hall. I've been eager to talk with you all morning, but when Mr. Baxter arrived, I thought I'd never have the chance. My instincts told me you would want fresh air, and I'm very much hoping that a little distance from those two will give us a moment. I hope you're not disappointed." His tone hinted at guilt, but she saw the promise of his plan. And he was right. She wanted fresh air and a chance to talk with him.

She was reminded of what her mother had said about them not needing words, and she placed a steadying hand on her stomach. "I'm not disappointed. Thank you, Nathaniel. You know how I detest anything that brings those two together, but I think my desire to talk about what happened overrules even those feelings. Last night was so terrifying!"

"I know," he said solemnly. When they approached Mrs. Wickham and Mr. Baxter, Nathaniel adjusted to his usual, charming smile. "All ready, then. Shall we?"

Kelsey recognized the familiar, scheming glint in her mother's eye. "Won't you lead the way, Mr. Worth? You know the road best. Mr. Baxter and I will follow."

Kelsey didn't appreciate the greedy way Mr. Baxter's eyes fell on her mother just then.

"Yes, of course." Nathaniel dipped his head and offered his arm to Kelsey.

She hesitated but took it, unable to deny the comfort of his touch, and comfortably fell into step with him. At first, Mr. Baxter offered his observations of the weather and how beautiful the land surrounding Pemberley was, but eventually his conversation with Mrs. Wickham separated from Nathaniel and Kelsey's. Before they had travelled a quarter mile, Mr. Baxter and Mrs. Wickham were lagging far behind, despite the easy pace Nathaniel and Kelsey were keeping.

Then Kelsey remembered.

"Nathaniel, your knee! I can't believe I didn't ask earlier how it was feeling this morning."

He laughed. "It's understandable, given all that has happened."

"Yes, but . . ." She observed his stride and noticed a slight limp. "How have you managed to walk this far? Does it hurt?"

He winced slightly. "It's sore but I can walk easily enough."

She guessed he wasn't telling her how much it really hurt, but he was maintaining a steady pace. "It was careless of me to leave that shovel on the path, and I must take the blame for your injury."

"I expect you to do no such thing, but I'll gladly accept your sympathy." He glanced over his shoulder at Mrs. Wickham and Mr. Baxter, then focused on the road ahead. "Kelsey, I've been thinking the matter over. You can't remain at the cottage any longer."

She bit her lip and inwardly agreed with him. The very idea of the intruder roaming free would keep her from ever sleeping peacefully in her bed again, but she couldn't think of a feasible alternative.

"I doubt the intruder will return, not after you scared him off."

"Kelsey—"

"My mother and I have nowhere else to go." The words fell from her lips like a terrible confession.

Nathaniel cleared his throat. "Would you consider staying at Thistledown Hall? At least until you find another suitable place?"

Panic swelled in her chest. One night under the same roof had already tampered with her grasp on propriety. She needed time to understand why she had fled to his arms when the thunder struck. Why had she felt safer there than anywhere else, even when it was the most compromising situation she could place herself in? Why had she allowed it? Those were feelings she could not trust, and spending time with him in his home would only create more opportunities to fall prey to scandal.

When she still didn't say anything, Nathaniel added, "I only assume it will be easier to protect you in my own home, but if you're opposed to the idea, I must hope it rains again tonight when I walk by." He looked at the sky, completely clear of clouds, and smiled at Kelsey.

Perhaps she was right to still be wary of him if he could so easily jest about the situation, but the best response, the kind that would not give too much away, had always been a playful one. "You might not find such a ready welcome the second time now that I know what you're up to. Besides, I can wield a fire iron just as well as you can." She hoped she sounded casual enough, despite the fear she had expressed only moments ago. "I will need your help with another letter, though." Back to their plans. That was the surest way to maintain her balance with Nathaniel.

He glanced over his shoulder again. "I hope you know what you're doing with these letters. I strongly suspect Mr. Baxter has his secrets."

"As do I, which is why the most I can hope for is for my mother to gain insight into what she is doing. I know you must think I'm a fool for this charade—"

"I don't."

"Well, sometimes I do." Her throat unexpectedly tightened.

"You're not." He paused long enough to pierce her with his eyes. "I think honesty is best, but I know you care a great deal for your family. The night we met, I could see how much you love your sister. I see how diligently you work to keep your household in order. You cook and clean and pull the weeds. You never stop listening and observing, and I see how unselfishly you lay aside your own interests when others need your help. You experience your emotions very keenly even if you don't always know what to do with them. I don't think you're a fool, Kelsey. I only think life hasn't loved you enough."

For several steps, Kelsey hardly managed to breathe. Did he really see that much goodness in her? Was he really so forgiving of her shortcomings?

"I've said too much, haven't I?" He picked a leaf off a low hanging branch and twirled it between his thumb and forefinger. "Well, I don't know how we will manage a letter with your mother and Mr. Baxter in tow, but I suppose we can try. If you won't be my guest for the next month, Lady Kelsey, I am still pleased you will be my guest for the afternoon."

"Sir Nathaniel," Kelsey tested the title, trying to find her voice again through jesting, "how you persist in getting me to Thistledown Hall."

His broad smile made her hope they were past the temptation to talk further of serious feelings.

"You forget, my lady, that we are engaged to be engaged in only a few weeks' time, and I must sufficiently acquaint you with the place."

Kelsey frowned. She had forgotten her promise to help him deter his sister, but after last night, she didn't know how she could manage it. After what she had felt in his arms . . . How was she supposed to sort through the perplexities of genuine feelings for this man while pretending to be in love with him?

"Kelsey?" He looked at her. "Are you all right?"

She released his arm and rubbed hers, trying to brush off his warmth, though it seeped to her bones. A loose pebble lodged in her shoe, and the sudden breeze stripped away her efforts to fortify her heart.

When the tip of the ruins that marked the Thistledown estate became visible over the trees, Kelsey grasped at the chance to change topics.

"Tell me about those ruins."

"Truthfully, I don't know much about them," he shrugged. "Perhaps Captain Styles can enlighten us when he arrives."

"Then tell me more about the captain. The entire village is fascinated with him. From what little you've told me, he is a great mystery."

"So he is. I only know what he chooses to reveal to me."

"Which is more than anyone else knows of him. Does he have any family?"

"No, he doesn't." Nathaniel's voice grew subdued. "He once mentioned a wife and son who were lost to him."

"I'm sorry to hear that." She thought of the note beneath the windowsill. Had the captain hidden it before losing his wife and son?

"There was a scandal, but whatever you hear, I know it couldn't have been the captain's fault."

"You put that much trust in him?"

He met her eye. "I do."

"What of your parents, Nathaniel?" Beyond him having a sister, she realized she knew very little about his family.

"You don't want to hear about my parents." He waved the thought away, but his words were heavy.

"But I do. If you would like to tell me."

He looked down and shook his head. "My father died shortly after I was born. My mother never spoke of him. I still don't know how he died."

"I'm so sorry, Nathaniel." She thought of her own father and wondered whether it would have been better to be ignorant of the details of his death. "And your mother?"

"She quickly remarried and gave birth to my half-sister. My stepfather is respectable and wealthy. When I was young, we lived well, and he saw to my education for a while. My mother died giving birth to her third child. The baby only lived a day longer than she did. I was eleven years old."

"I'm so sorry." She didn't know what else to say.

"Except for a few holidays, most of my time was spent at school. When I was thirteen, what I had suspected all along was confirmed to me. My stepfather did not care for me. Though he was wealthy enough to support me, he had me enlisted. I had no say in the matter. Between then and now, I've spent just as many days at sea as on land."

"Nathaniel . . ." Kelsey couldn't hide the sympathy from her voice.

"I suppose I am grateful to Clarice for maintaining a connection with me these many years. It's why you must not think ill of her when you meet her. She's the only family I have, and she's the only one who cares." The old manor was before them, the main doors a short walk away.

"But your stepfather—"

"Wants nothing to do with me."

Kelsey searched his face, devoid of expression, but when he caught her examining him, his features softened. "I've had time to come to terms with it, Kelsey, so you mustn't feel too badly for me. Captain Styles has been more of a father to me than my stepfather ever was. I have nothing to complain of."

She knew he meant it, but she also recognized words spoken from the hollow place where his father should have been. It was the same sort of hollowness that existed in her. "I know, Nathaniel, but I'm still sorry for the pain it has caused you."

"Thank you." He choked on the words and cleared them from his throat. "Now, shall we go inside? I'm eager to give you a proper tour of the house this time." He paused with his hand on the door, then looked at the empty path as if remembering something. "Where are your mother and Mr. Baxter? I fear we've lost them. How much longer do you suppose they'll be?"

Kelsey knew exactly what her mother had done. She had left Kelsey alone with Nathaniel on purpose while she and Mr. Baxter wandered off on some other path.

"I never know with my mother."

"Would you prefer we wait for them?"

"No, but I . . ." She considered walking back to the cottage, but thoughts of the intruder made her willing to stay and risk a little more imprudence. "Let's go inside. They know where to find us."

Nathaniel parted the splintering wooden doors, which groaned on their hinges. Inside the large, square entrance hall, Kelsey felt the shadows of years gone by nestling in the dusty corners and cobwebs, but despite the tickle that grew in her nose, the house held promise. Sunlight pouring from windows reflected the silver veins in the marble tiled floor. A wide staircase to the right boasted strength with its wide, molded balusters despite years of neglect. A little polish, and they would gleam anew.

A man Kelsey assumed to be the butler scrambled over, his boots clicking on the marble like raindrops.

"Good day, sir. Miss." Wearing a wide grin, he bowed deeply before each of them. Kelsey didn't know much about the training of butlers, but the man, dressed in a plain, blue coat, lacked the formal posture and attire she might have expected.

"Good day, Joseph," Nathaniel dipped his head a little too stiffly in return, making Kelsey suspect they usually dispensed with such formalities. "Kelsey, this is Aaron Joseph. Joseph, this is Miss—"

"Oh, ho! Don't tell me, don't tell me! This is the lovely Miss Wickham whose praises I've been hearing sung so often. Yes, she is very lovely. I'll agree with you on that, Worth." Speaking from the corner of his mouth, he elbowed Nathaniel in the side. "It's a pleasure to finally meet you, Miss Wickham, a real pleasure." The man bowed even lower.

Kelsey managed a small curtsey, no longer certain this man was the butler. The understanding looks exchanged between him and Nathaniel went beyond master and servant, and she became aware of something familiar about Joseph's features. Perhaps if his hair had been longer and his clothes less tidy . . .

"If I may add—" Joseph began, but Nathaniel cleared his throat and gave a slight head shake.

"Joseph, would you please see that tea is ready on the terrace in approximately an hour? I will be giving Miss Wickham a brief tour of the main rooms and gardens in the meantime."

"Certainly, sir!" He sunk into another low bow, nearly folding himself in half as they passed.

Once Joseph trotted off to fulfill his master's request, Nathaniel looked guiltily at Kelsey. "He might not fit the usual mold of butler, but he's loyal and trustworthy."

Images of Nathaniel talking to a disheveled man in Lambton filled her mind, and recognition hit. "He's the beggar from the marketplace!"

Was it possible Nathaniel was turning pink?

"I didn't expect to be caught, but yes."

"That is kind of you, but why?"

Nathaniel gestured for her to follow him as he led her further into the house. "Joseph was once a naval officer like me. We served together at sea. It was only one brief voyage, but it was long enough to tell he was an honest sort. Joseph even once stepped in and took a blow for me from another officer I had offended. I was young and impulsive then. We also have common acquaintances, including the captain. When I saw Joseph in the marketplace, he explained to me that on his last voyage, he broke his arm and received an awful blow to his head during a storm. He grew severely ill for a time. He was forced to take leave, but it became clear his eyesight had suffered and wasn't recovering. He lost his position and had nothing to return to, no home, no family. The navy wouldn't accept him again. No one would, so he has been begging from town to town for the past two years. I barely recognized him, but when I did, I couldn't simply say hello and move on, not when I've gained so much in the time that he's lost everything."

Nathaniel finished the story as modestly as he'd begun it, but Kelsey stared in awe. She couldn't deny her trust in him had grown, but he now held the honor of being the most kind-hearted man she had ever met. Before meeting Nathaniel, she didn't think such kindness existed in a man. Yet, here he was, the evidence impossible to deny.

Her chest tightened and twisted like a weed being pulled from the earth. Why could she not let herself enjoy his attentions? Why must she fight to maintain the defenses around her heart if the very ideas they were built upon were crumbling before her?

She had an inkling, a horrible suspicion as to why she fought so stubbornly, and it was already smothering the possibility of hope. In the brief moment the idea had occurred to her, it was already burrowing into her insecurities and doubts. Perhaps, the problem was not Nathaniel after all . . .

It doesn't matter, she told herself. *It was never meant to be, anyway. I'm a Wickham.* With these sobering thoughts tangling inside, she followed him down a long, bare passageway into a dim sitting room. Pale, sea-green curtains hung from floor-to-ceiling windows, but a layer of dust shifted their natural hue toward a dingy grey. The walls were a similar color, and paint was chipping around various edges of dull, white molding.

The furniture, however, looked much more cheerful. A lengthy sofa the color of bright daffodils waited as if with outstretched arms before a stone fireplace nearly as tall as Kelsey. Two mahogany chairs with matching blue cushions stood ready to make guests comfortable. A large silvery-grey carpet patterned with green leaves was spread between the sofa and chairs, uniting them like a family in a room full of troubles.

"What do you think?" Nathaniel turned with his arms held wide. "Can you help me get Thistledown Hall ready for my sister?"

"I can try, but the first thing you need is fresh air." Kelsey went to the window, coughing up dust that flew into her lungs when she disturbed the curtains, and fought against a rusty latch to push it open. "How much time did you say we have before your sister arrives?"

Nathaniel laughed. "Only two and a half weeks now, I'm afraid."

"And you want my help?"

Kelsey had never taken on such an ambitious project before. All her previous efforts to brighten the homes she had previously dwelt in were small compared to the work needed here. She had no idea where to begin.

"Am I asking too much? You need only give your opinion. Joseph and I will handle the rest."

"I'll do my best," she said, but even she could hear the uncertainty in her voice.

Nathaniel showed her a gallery sparse of paintings but full of moth balls, a library with just as much must and mildew as books, a dining hall with a table that needed polishing, and a room that was to be eventually converted into a study. Though all the rooms were severely in need of dusting, and more than half could benefit from new curtains, the only other improvements Kelsey suggested were things like the rearranging of furniture or swapping paintings in certain rooms where the colors would be more complementary. The rest of the work would have to be done when there was more time.

"I don't know how you'll ever do it all. Is Joseph the only help you have?"

"Three times a week, I hire a woman and her daughter from Lambton to help with cooking and cleaning. I know I'll need more help eventually when the estate is brought to life again, but you'd be surprised at the amount of work Joseph and I can accomplish together. We're both accustomed to fending for ourselves."

"Well, you must start by cleaning everything and clearing the chimneys. And you must have good linens for Miss Wimpleton's bed and a vase of fresh flowers in her room when she arrives." Kelsey trailed off, trying to think of anything else as Nathaniel guided her to the doors that led to the back gardens.

Nathaniel nodded attentively. "I really should be writing this down. We may need to go through everything once more."

Kelsey looked at him suspiciously. Was he trying to secure more time with her? "These are minor things," she said. "I doubt your sister will care much to notice the placement of tables and chairs."

Nathaniel vigorously shook his head. "Oh, no. Do not underestimate the usefulness of your suggestions. I have no eye for such things. Clarice, however, will notice everything. *Everything.* Besides," he looked around and scratched the back of his head, "I want these rooms to be agreeable to you too."

Kelsey looked away as the warmth rose to her cheeks. *He can talk all he likes,* she thought. *It will all come to naught.*

"On to the gardens." They had just passed through a tarnished ballroom to a pair of double doors that lead to the back gardens. Nathaniel held the door open for Kelsey as she passed through.

"Good heavens!" she exclaimed, stumbling on a root that poked through the pavement. "Is this your garden or have we magically transported ourselves to the Amazon? This is worse than the cottage." It was worse than the front of the house as well as the side paths she had seen before.

Tangles of weeds and dandelions grew in every crack of stone throughout the spacious terrace. Just beyond, where she might have expected to see a manicured lawn or a line of finely pruned trees and shrubbery were jumbled curtains of vines and branches. Kelsey avoided the portico to her left lest she become ensnared in its dripping ivy. The most promising feature, a rectangular fountain at the right edge of the terrace, was devoid of water and covered in bird droppings. The place where a small stream might feed it was blockaded by rocks and rotting wood.

"What do you suggest?" Nathaniel asked hesitantly.

Kelsey rubbed her brow. "Don't let your sister leave the house." As she walked around, daring to examine things up close, she couldn't help but pluck at the dandelions.

"The captain was never concerned about the upkeep of the gardens. Truthfully, I'm not sure he had money to spare on such a project, especially one he thought he might never see the fruits of. I only came to reside here a few weeks before you moved into the cottage, so—"

"It's all right, Nathaniel." Kelsey hopped around a large, out of place rock. "I don't judge you for the state of things. You've seen the cottage garden. I'm no stranger to weeds. I'm sure this will all look lovely once it's had a sound lashing. I mean pruning." After sharing a laugh, Kelsey asked, "How did the captain come to acquire the estate?"

Nathaniel pulled at a particularly tall weed that was budding with small yellow flowers. "He didn't share many details with me, but I know it belonged to a gentleman who was in a significant amount of debt. The man was desperate for money, and the captain used his years of saved wages and rewards from captured ships to purchase the place for a significantly reduced amount."

"Why has he never come to live here, then?"

"I don't know," he shrugged. "I think he didn't know how to leave the sea. He used to jest about saltwater flowing through his veins. When he offered to make me his heir, he said he didn't want this place rotting empty and going to waste." Nathaniel tugged at an overgrown vine and pulled it up by the roots. "I think the captain would still like to live here eventually, but his timing is never predictable. During our last voyage together, he insisted I not wait any longer to enjoy a more settled life."

Kelsey settled on the edge of the fountain where there were fewer bird droppings. "And are you enjoying a more settled life?"

"I am." Nathaniel sat by her and reached out as if he might take her hand but stopped short. "Part of me will always love the sea. There's nothing quite like traversing from continent to continent with the ocean as your highway, but a lowly officer is lacking in privilege. The sea taunts us with a freedom that is never truly ours, not while we wear the uniform and bear the title of officer." He glanced at her fingers again.

Kelsey felt as small as a pebble when she considered his years of experience. "After all you've seen in the world, my troubles must seem insignificant to you."

"Not so, not when your happiness is at stake. That makes them quite significant."

How did Nathaniel always know what to say? She tried to hide a smile as she met his eyes. "Then, you don't mind writing another letter for me?"

"It's difficult to say anything but yes when you look at me like that, you know." His eyes drifted to her lips, and he moved closer. "When nights at sea were especially long, I would imagine myself retiring and starting a family. You'd laugh to know how sentimental I became at times. The moon, for example, was always a comfort because I knew its light shined on both me and the lady I would one day choose."

A quivering breath filled her lungs. "Th-the moon?" But she knew Nathaniel was not talking about the moon.

"These letters, Kelsey . . . Are you still certain this is the best way?"

The best way . . . Kelsey felt his breath on her cheek, and she lost track of what he was asking. The best way to what? Protect her heart? To keep herself from becoming like her mother? Sitting with him, letting him draw closer, however, was not the best way.

"I . . . I must go!" She jumped from her seat. "I've stayed too long. I really must find my mother."

"But the tea . . . the letter . . ."

"Would you write it? Please. I don't think my mother is coming. I had best go."

He didn't speak for several seconds. "If you're certain."

"Yes." Kelsey began walking. "This is best this way."

Chapter 19

*As I must therefore conclude that you are not serious
in your rejection of me, I shall choose to attribute it
to your wish of increasing my love by suspense,
according to the usual practice of elegant females.*

Jane Austen, *Pride and Prejudice*

*B*efore a dwindling fire in the small sitting room of Barley
Cottage, Kelsey sat on the sofa with her feet curled under
her and a book on her lap that served as a temporary writing desk.
Satisfied with the lines she had written, she signed her name at the
bottom of letters to Lucia and Cissy. She had considered writing
about the trick her mother had recently played on her by leaving her
alone with Nathaniel and wandering off with Mr. Baxter, but Kelsey
couldn't bring herself to do it. Her desire to relieve her embarrassment
didn't outweigh her distaste of burdening her sister or her cousin with
her complaints. Under no circumstances did she want either to imagine that something existed between her and Nathaniel.

If only Lucia would return! The relief of discussing everything in
person would be great, indeed. As she folded her letters and sealed

each with a wafer, her mother glided into the room with the post in hand.

"Kelsey, I'm glad you're home. My admirer has written again." Her mother discarded a stack of unopened letters on the table and waved a single creased sheet in the air. "*My dearest lady,*" she giggled, "*It feels an eternity since I first laid eyes on you, but still, I find myself frequently wondering— Are you well? Are you happy? Do you think about me or wonder where I am? At times, the distance feels like nothing, like I could cross a continent and be home in a day. Sometimes the only comfort I find on lonely nights at sea is the knowledge that the moon shines on both of us, lighting your face as it does mine. It is a gift we share, a light we can both look to no matter where we are. I don't know when I will return, but my hope is that your heart will still be free when I do.*" Pressing the letter to her heart, Mrs. Wickham fell back onto the cushions and sighed heavily. "This man is a poet."

Impressive, thought Kelsey. "That is quite the letter." She replaced the stopper on her ink and folded her letters into her book to send out later.

"I know. It makes me want . . . It makes me hope . . ." Mrs. Wickham paused just when Kelsey most wished to know her thoughts. "I believe Mr. Baxter will be calling on me this morning, but after this," she lifted the letter, "I don't think I can receive his attentions anymore."

Kelsey dared not move or say anything, lest her mother change her mind.

"I . . ." Her mother swallowed. "I think it's time I let Mr. Baxter know that, after due consideration, I no longer think we will suit."

Kelsey knotted her fingers tightly in her lap. "Really?"

"Yes, I'm quite sure. Now that I know who writes, I cannot in good conscience continue to encourage Mr. Baxter, not when I now doubt I could ever honestly accept him."

Kelsey froze. "You know who writes? How?" Had she heard her mother correctly?

"It's only speculation, of course, but there are clues." Her mother's eyes danced as she spoke. "He must be a man of mystery, someone who has come and gone with no one noticing. He is someone who has seen me but now faces lonely nights at sea. Such beautiful words! Isn't it obvious, Kelsey? The only mysterious person who is absent from this neighborhood because he is at sea right now is Captain Styles."

If Mrs. Wickham had sat with Kelsey a minute longer, Kelsey feared she would have had to explain the stunned look on her face, but a knock on the door interrupted the silence. Mrs. Wickham placed a hand on Kelsey's and gave it a squeeze. "I expect that's Mr. Baxter. Upstairs, if you don't mind. He and I will need a private moment."

Kelsey nodded solemnly though her insides skipped and jumped. Her letters had finally served their purpose, but what was Nathaniel thinking, referencing lonely nights at sea? What would happen when Captain Styles did return? How could her mother meet him without facing utter embarrassment? What would Kelsey do then? A shudder ran through her as she sat herself at the top of the staircase, hidden from view, and listened.

Mr. Baxter's footsteps thudded on the floor as his voice echoed through the house. "How lovely you look today, my darling Lydia."

"Please have a seat Mr. Baxter."

At least her mother didn't match his familiarity. Kelsey listened to their shuffling and assumed they were sitting.

"Mr. Baxter, there is something I must tell you. I—"

"No, please!" he interrupted. "Allow me. I know what you want to say, but it is a gentleman's duty to proclaim his love first."

The silence that reached the top of the stairs nearly smothered Kelsey.

Finally, her mother spoke. "Mr. Baxter, you presume too much. We have spent a great deal of time together, and for a while I thought—"

"That I might not be in earnest?" he interjected. "I don't blame you in the slightest. I know how eager such beautiful ladies are to secure their futures, and perhaps you have been wondering whether I am put off by the rumors, but—"

"Mr. Baxter, please let me finish."

Kelsey silently applauded her mother's assertiveness.

"Mr. Baxter, the truth is, I . . ."

Kelsey held her breath.

"I no longer believe we will suit."

Ha! There, she said it!

"No longer suit?" The disbelief in his voice was clear. "I told you I was dreadfully sorry for the gravy spill at dinner the other night. I told Clyde if he ever—"

"No, it has nothing to do with that."

"It doesn't? Is it because I like parsnips? Because I drove the carriage too quickly? Or perhaps you know how large a bet I placed—"

"No, Mr. Baxter."

"And I've already told you the butcher's daughter means nothing to me."

"Mr. Baxter, please stop."

"Well, then, is there . . ." He stuttered out his next question. "Is there . . . another gentleman?"

Kelsey knew that even Mr. Baxter was intelligent enough to interpret the silence that followed as a confirmation.

"I see," he said softly. "Perhaps I should have known, given your reputation."

"Mr. Baxter." It came out like a warning.

Kelsey waited and listened, expecting to hear his footsteps carrying him out the door, but instead she heard a thud on the wooden floor and a gasp from her mother. Kelsey sincerely hoped Mr. Baxter was not stupid enough to drop to one knee.

"Lydia, my dear."

Oh, no.

"I'm sorry. I've never been the kind of man who gives up easily. I'm not ready to lose you, my little rosebud."

It wasn't until Kelsey heard that horrible endearment that she truly questioned whether she should be eavesdropping. *Too late now.*

"Ma . . . marry me?"

His question dropped on Kelsey's ears like a pile of bricks. She waited, waited a few seconds more, and then groaned. Why was her mother not speaking? Why wasn't she firmly refusing and insisting he leave?

"I . . ."

Kelsey held her breath again, straining to hear the wispy voice of her mother.

"I will consider your proposal, Mr. Baxter, but please leave me. I must have time to think."

It was not the response Kelsey had hoped for, but she could tell from her mother's tone that she was no longer under the spell of having Mr. Baxter as a suitor.

"You will consider my proposal?" he exclaimed. "Blessed news!"

"Yes, but I must ask that you leave me now."

"Of course, my dear. Of course, especially if it means you will consider my offer."

Kelsey heard a puckering sound, which she hoped was merely a kiss on the hand. At last, Mr. Baxter exited the cottage.

Kelsey waited on the top step, but her mother never came up. Eventually, Kelsey tiptoed downstairs. Her mother was sitting in the chair closest to the window with her arms wrapped around herself, gazing steadily out as if she saw something beyond the road and trees.

"Why didn't you refuse him?" Kelsey didn't know whether she was upset or confused. "I thought you were going to wait for Captain Styles." Her conscience pecked at her words. Was it taking the charade too far to promote the idea of the captain to her mother?

"As I'm sure you heard me say to Mr. Baxter, I need time to think, Kelsey. I don't want to be alone for the rest of my life. Right now, Captain Styles is nothing more than a possibility. I would very much prefer having time with him before I make any hasty decisions, but I can't grow old with a dream no matter how lovely it is."

"But you would grow old with Mr. Baxter? You admitted less than an hour ago that you do not suit each other." The first glint of a tear appeared on her mother's cheek. "Mother, I . . . Of course, you need time to think. I'll be upstairs if you need me." Treading lightly, she kissed her mother's cheek and climbed the stairs. She didn't understand everything her mother was feeling, but she had the distinct impression that her mother missed her late husband.

Entering her room, Kelsey took in the image of her parents, painted in their exaggerated embrace, and for a moment, she allowed herself to miss her father too. He had been unpredictable and reckless at times, but he could also be pleasant and kind. Perhaps if he were still alive, if Kelsey still had her father in her life, she would understand what her feelings for Nathaniel really meant.

Without making a sound, she gingerly lifted the painting off its nail in the wall and crept inside her mother's room. There wasn't anywhere to hang the painting, but she stood it on top of the chest of drawers and leaned it against the wall. *Mother needs this more than I do.*

Before leaving, Kelsey saw her white dress splayed across her mother's bed like a sleeping angel. A pang of emotion swelled in her chest. She hadn't seen her dress or even asked about it since the fiasco at Mr. Baxter's dinner, but it was obvious that work had gone into cleaning the stains. The dress was still pearlescent and lovely, and though it was much improved, the stains on the skirts remained.

Chapter 20

*Of the lady's sensations, they remained a little in
doubt; but that the gentleman was overflowing
with admiration was evident enough.*

Jane Austen, *Pride and Prejudice*

$\mathcal{K}$elsey spent the next two weeks in a fragile state, alternating
her time between helping Nathaniel prepare Thistledown
Hall to receive his sister and waiting for her mother to declare her
acceptance of Mr. Baxter. Kelsey didn't have the heart to write additional letters to her, and her mother had noticed the lack of news from
her mysterious admirer.

"He must still be at sea," she would sometimes sigh while gazing
out the window.

Whenever the guilt of the charade grew too heavy for Kelsey, she
wandered to Thistledown Hall to pull weeds with Nathaniel or dust
the furniture or finalize the menu for the night of his sister's visit. She
no longer worried about the propriety of these visits, having already
spent hours alone with Nathaniel. Even when Miss Chatham encountered her on the road or gave her an insinuating look, Kelsey smiled in

return with all the grace of one who was learning not to care. Joseph was with her and Nathaniel on most occasions anyway, and when he wasn't, the ladies Nathaniel employed from Lambton were usually there cleaning.

Mrs. Smitt, who had taken on the role of Nathaniel's housekeeper, was a cousin of Mrs. Reynolds and bore a fair resemblance to her. The daughter, Hannah Smitt, couldn't have been older than Cissy, but she was much more shy. Kelsey saw her flush whenever Nathaniel spoke to her, but Hannah was attentive to her tasks and was sometimes coaxed into a smile when Kelsey gave her a compliment.

That morning, as Kelsey made her way up the hill toward the estate, she hummed a light tune and let the exercise ease the tension from her shoulders. The sight of the ruins always improved her spirits. Though crumbled and worn, the remaining stones stood with a firmness that attested to their right to be there. Nature had grown around them and accepted them as part of the landscape. If ever she found the strength to be like those ruins, she was certain she would also be able to weather the strains of life.

Her pace slowed when she noticed Nathaniel leaning against an open archway in the stone wall with his head bent down and his back toward her. A magpie hopped not far from his feet, and a cool breeze ruffled his hair before making its way to Kelsey's neck. She considered continuing on without disturbing him, but he turned as if sensing her eyes on him.

"Kelsey." His lips rose, but the levity that so often played on his brow was mixed with pensiveness.

"Hello, Nathaniel," she said, slightly winded from walking. "Why are you out here?"

His eyes scanned the surroundings with unmistakable fondness. "I come here to think sometimes. Would you like to come inside? There's something I'd like to show you."

Kelsey stepped through the archway and felt the air around her become wild with the concentrated scents of earth and stone and greenery. Many walls firmly remained intact, but the roof was missing entirely, giving Kelsey a clear view of sky and cloud. The breeze continued to weave around her arms and whistle through gaps between stones where morning glory pushed its way through. Several stones had sunk in the ground and several more jutted out at odd angles with grass growing around them to form a precarious path.

Carefully choosing her steps, Kelsey followed Nathaniel through the remains of a corridor until he stopped before a wall of ivy. With a wink, he parted it like a curtain, and the corridor opened into a spacious, circular stone room with thin rectangular windows cut regularly around the top. Tendrils of bright green ivy hung from the walls, some with tiny flowers budding on them. Dandelions and tiny purple wildflowers grew between fallen stones and in the grass. In the middle of all the stone and wild growth was a large cherry tree whose leafy canopy stretched the length of the room like a green ceiling speckled with blue sky.

"Oh!" Kelsey sighed.

"Do you like it?" Nathaniel stepped close and looked earnestly at her.

"I've never seen such a lovely place! How did a cherry tree come to grow here?"

"I have no idea, but I love it too." He picked a few cherries and handed one to her.

Kelsey's lips puckered when she bit into it. "Oh! You picked them too early, Nathaniel. They're not yet ripe."

He examined his cherry and tossed it over his shoulder. "Forgive me, my lady. I am always trying to rush things. Waiting for the right time is difficult."

The way he looked at her made her suspect he was talking about more than cherries. "Are you planning on showing this place to your sister when she arrives?"

Nathaniel shook his head. "Never. She would want to domesticate it. With a proper bench here and some curtains there. Oh, and we mustn't forget a few cushions and a table for tea."

Kelsey laughed at the way he gestured around as if he could see the curtains and cushions before him. "Oh, no! That would never do."

"Not at all. I prefer it wild. Clarice Wimpleton must never see this place. I claim it as my own." He spread his arms wide.

Kelsey examined a cluster of ripening cherries. "But you have let me see it."

"Yes, I have." He was at her side in an instant. "I knew you'd appreciate it just as it is, and I wanted to share it with you. It is your secret place now too."

She ran her hand along the rough tree bark as her throat thickened. "Thank you, Nathaniel." Her heart began to gallop, and her breathing grew shallow. The desire to draw close to him hit her suddenly, powerfully, irrationally. Perhaps he was not the gambling rake she had once imagined. Perhaps he was kind and thoughtful, charming and respectful, and so much more, but whatever her feelings were, whatever they could be if she let them free . . . Did any of it matter when she was a Wickham? No matter how good Nathaniel was, she feared her own heart was selfish and cold. She would never escape the shame of her family and the unsteadiness she had inherited from her parents. What did trusting Nathaniel matter when she couldn't trust herself?

"Lady Kelsey?" He laid his hand next to hers on the tree bark, softly bringing their fingertips together.

Her insides began to swelter. He knew what he was doing. She hadn't a doubt, and she feared he could already see the feelings she was still determined to hide, if not for her own benefit, then for his. If Kelsey could not trust herself, he shouldn't either.

When his fingers traced their way along her hand, she spun around and covered her burning cheeks, but it wasn't enough. She needed to get away and back to the open path where the way was clear, where she wouldn't again be on the brink of behaving like her mother.

"We shouldn't be here alone together." Skipping over loose stones, Kelsey stumbled and tripped her way through the ivy curtain and down the crumbling corridor.

"Kelsey!" Nathaniel ran after her.

Almost to the threshold, she stumbled over a stone hidden by grass. She would have fallen had Nathaniel not reached out to steady her in time, but she shrugged off his hand, still under threat of an impulse to draw closer.

"What's wrong? Are you all right?"

Once she stood on the open road, she could breathe again.

"I'm all right. Thank you. I don't know what came over me. I . . . I think I merely needed room." She started up the final stretch to Thistledown Hall, keeping a brisk pace whether he kept up with her or not. Once they were at the splintering doors and Kelsey could look him in the eye again, she knew the moment had passed. "What is on the list for today?" She was eager for tasks that would keep her occupied.

Nathaniel's eyes dulled, but she couldn't fret over it. She couldn't let him know what had truly overcome her inside the ruins.

"Two paintings have arrived from London. I need your help deciding which to place above the sitting room fireplace and which to place in Clarice's room."

He led her into the drawing room while Hannah laid out tea and biscuits. Joseph could be seen through the windows trimming plants in the back garden, which was slowly being reclaimed from the wild overgrowth. Next to the fireplace, two large paintings leaned against the wall. Kelsey examined each one. From what she could tell, they were well done, though she wondered how Nathaniel could afford them. She did, indeed, like them both.

One was of a girl from behind as she walked through a rose garden. The sky looked on the verge of rain, except for one beam of sunlight breaking through in front of her. Kelsey loved how the girl walked toward the sunbeam with the light ready to embrace her.

The other painting was of a girl walking on a bridge with a man tipping his hat to her. The girl's face revealed no reaction except for the tiniest upward curve of her lips, and there was something in the man's style of dress and manner that reminded Kelsey of Nathaniel.

"This one," she said, pointing to the painting of the couple, "should go above the fireplace here. The painting of the girl should go in your sister's room, I think."

Nathaniel nodded. "It makes sense as soon as you say it, but I was truly unsure."

Kelsey sipped her tea and nibbled at biscuits as Joseph came inside carrying a ladder and helped Nathaniel mount the painting above the fireplace. As the two of them worked, Kelsey noticed how similar their heights and builds were, especially now that Joseph had gained more weight. There were several moments when Kelsey was sure either the painting, Joseph, or Nathaniel would fall, but the two of them eventually managed to get the painting leveled in just the right position.

Nathaniel climbed down the ladder and assessed their work. "That certainly brings the room together, doesn't it?"

Joseph moved the ladder out of the way. "I've no eye for art, but it's a pretty painting if ever I saw one."

Kelsey was happy with the sitting room's transformation. The furniture was dusted. Blue and white damask cushions accented the sofa and chairs. The shelves no longer sat empty but were filled with books. Crystal vases holding roses and violets were placed around the room, making the air light and fragrant. More could have been done if time had allowed for it, but Kelsey couldn't think of a more inviting room.

A thunderous pounding on the main door echoed in the corridor.

"I'll see to that." Joseph hurried out. Moments later, he announced, "Mr. Woodcox here to see you, sir."

Mr. Woodcox stepped in, his face flushed. "Mr. Worth?" He dipped his head and removed his hat.

"Yes. How can I help you, Mr. Woodcox?"

Kelsey had never heard Nathaniel speak in such a reserved, formal tone before. Had he been practicing?

Mr. Woodcox's gaze landed on her briefly. "Might I have a word in private, Mr. Worth?"

Nathaniel turned to Kelsey. "Would you excuse us for a moment, Miss Wickham?"

"Certainly." She was grateful he thought to address her formally in front of Mr. Woodcox. As they retreated down the hall and through a door on the left, she mumbled, "What is that man about?"

"Ahem." Joseph appeared at her side. "I was asking myself the exact same question." He lowered his voice. "It isn't common knowledge, but if you walk over to that bookcase," he pointed across the way, "and have a look at *Canterbury Tales*, you might be able to hear some of the conversation happening on the other side." He finished with a wink and walked off with the ladder.

Kelsey couldn't hide her grin. Joseph was certainly no ordinary butler. She went to the shelf he had indicated and found a worn copy of *Canterbury Tales*. How would looking at a book help her overhear Nathaniel and Mr. Woodcox? Still, she picked it up. In the space where the book had sat, she found a small grate covering a narrow conduit in the wall. Leaning close to it, she could hear voices.

"That is quite the claim, Mr. Woodcox. What proof do you have?"

"Calm down, Mr. Worth. There's no need to get upset. I've merely come to talk with you. There's time for proof later if it comes to that."

"Which it will." Nathaniel's voice was firm.

"When was the last time you actually spoke with the captain?"

"That is none of your concern."

Kelsey had to strain to make out Mr. Woodcox's words. "I believe it is, Mr. Worth, but if it is proof that interests you, I must ask what proof you possess that the final installment was paid."

"What grounds do you have for assuming it wasn't? If your claims are true, you must still possess the bundle of deeds showing transfer of ownership over the years."

"Naturally, you want to see my proof. I'll provide it in good time, of course, but until then, I think it best if I took up residence here while we—"

There was a brisk scraping of chairs. "Until you can provide an inkling of evidence for any of the claims you are making, you are not welcome here. You will leave immediately, and I must ask that you not attempt to come here again until the matter is settled." Kelsey had never heard Nathaniel sound so adamant.

"Mr. Worth." Mr. Woodcox mumbled an appeal to reason, but Nathaniel was already calling for Joseph.

When Kelsey heard the door creak open, she tip-toed back to the sofa by the fireplace and pretended to be engrossed in *Canterbury Tales*. She didn't even glance back as Joseph and Nathaniel led Mr. Woodcox forcefully, by the sounds of it, out the door. After several minutes, Nathaniel slumped onto the sofa next to her.

"Ah, *Canterbury Tales*. I take it Joseph showed you where to listen?"

She nodded, unsure whether to be embarrassed, but he didn't appear upset. "I only caught a bit of what was said."

Nathaniel rubbed his brow. "Mr. Woodcox says that Captain Styles purchased Thistledown Hall from his brother who recently died. I have no idea whether that is true or not, but what concerns me is that he is claiming that Captain Styles is delinquent on his final payment."

"Oh, dear. Well, surely, the captain can remedy that."

Nathaniel let out a nervous laugh. "If only that were all. Mr. Woodcox claims he has been trying to contact Captain Styles for weeks without success. He is certain that if no word is soon received from him, he will be presumed dead or missing and in default of payment. Due to the particulars of the purchasing agreement, Mr. Woodcox ultimately claims he still owns Thistledown Hall as his rightful inheritance."

"What?" Kelsey covered her mouth in disbelief. "He must be mistaken."

Nathaniel nodded. "I think he must be, but I am not certain."

After weeks of working alongside Nathaniel to improve Thistledown Hall and observing how proud Nathaniel was to call it home, Kelsey could hardly imagine the pain he must have felt to have it all threatened so suddenly.

"You can write to the captain about this, can you not?"

The dismay in his eyes twisted her stomach. "I haven't heard from him for the past six weeks."

Chapter 21

I am only resolved to act in that manner, which will, in my own opinion, constitute my happiness, without reference to you, or to any person so wholly unconnected with me.

Jane Austen, *Pride and Prejudice*

Kelsey stood in the bright afternoon sunlight holding Nathaniel's arm as a gleaming black carriage with gold accents pulled up the path. The air around her buzzed with expectancy as if it knew something Kelsey didn't.

Nathaniel patted her hand. "Ready to be engaged for the day, my lady?"

"Not at all, but here I am." She willed her breath to steady as she watched the carriage driver pull the horses' reins. "Nathaniel, are you certain you still want to do this? What with all the trouble Mr. Woodcox is causing you, I would think you might not have the same enthusiasm for this."

If Nathaniel wanted to retain the estate, he would need to track down solicitors, find proofs of payment, and reckon the accountings, among other legal hurdles. Kelsey wouldn't have faulted him if he had changed his mind about their agreement.

"Are you joking?" An unmistakable grin rose on his lips. "This is the one thing I've been looking forward to these past few weeks. Mr. Woodcox has done nothing to alter that." With a wink, he added, "If my days at Thistledown are numbered, I want as many of them as possible to be with you."

Without thinking, Kelsey gave his arm a squeeze. "What will you do if Mr. Woodcox's claims are true?"

A cloud passed overhead, darkening Nathaniel's brow. He gazed ahead as if searching for something beyond the road. "I will return to service. I have nowhere else to go." When his eyes returned to hers, they pierced like a needle. "But I would find a way to stay if I had the right reason."

Kelsey inhaled slowly to steady her heart and tried to imagine life with Nathaniel gone. What would it be like to live at Barley Cottage knowing he would no longer surprise her with his visits? All her walks, all her afternoons would be spent alone. *Which is how it should be,* she tried to convince herself, as she unwillingly remembered his promise to ask for a kiss when the day of their temporary engagement arrived.

"Surely, you won't have to reenlist. Mr. Woodcox's threats are nonsense, and you will find a way to keep Thistledown Hall."

"I hope so, Kelsey."

Two towering footmen in matching light grey suits hopped off the carriage and set about their work unloading trunks of various size, which Kelsey eyed ominously.

"Are you certain your sister only plans to stay the night?"

"I never know what she is really planning." Nathaniel's face paled as three, four, then five trunks were added to the pile in quick succession. "Which is exactly why I have enlisted your help today." He placed a quick kiss on her hand.

Like a practiced dance, the footmen finished their work and took their positions with exact posture and opened the carriage door with all the pomp that a princess or duchess might expect. Kelsey felt Nathaniel's arm stiffen as they waited.

From the shadows within, a delicately gloved hand emerged, taking the outstretched hand of the closest footman. Intricately laced calf-skin boots took to the steps with the lightness of a bird, revealing a tall, slim figure in a midnight blue pelisse. With lace and pearls peeking out at her neckline and sleeves, Kelsey wondered how Miss Wimpleton dressed when she wasn't traveling. Though her face held a feminine resemblance to Nathaniel's with her lips fixed in the same amused upward tilt, she held a beauty the likes of which Kelsey had never seen before. An ivory complexion and well-defined cheeks were complimented with a brow both commanding and elegant that suggested she was ready to take charge at any moment should the situation require it.

Miss Wimpleton dipped into a fluid curtsey, took one appraising look at the house, then regarded Nathaniel and Kelsey. No one breathed. When all the birds hushed, and even the breeze paused to await her approval, she smiled.

"Nathaniel, dear brother, it has been far too long!" Miss Wimpleton took him by the shoulders and pulled him into an eager hug, making Kelsey lose her grip on his arm.

"Hello, Clarice. It's a pleasure to see you again."

She tilted her head and gave her cheek a double tap, a signal for Nathaniel to place a kiss there. No sooner had he done so than she moved him aside. "And this lovely young lady must be the dear Miss Wickham I've heard about."

Kelsey remembered saying something along the lines of *pleasure to meet you*, but Miss Wimpleton was already gushing words like an overflowing river.

"Of course, I was surprised when Nathaniel wrote to me about your engagement. Seems to have happened rather fast, but these things are unpredictable, aren't they? One only needs enough time to realize they've found the person they want to be with forever. After that, what greater confirmation does one need? That's what I say, though there are people like my aunt who believe in lengthier courtships. Never mind about her though. I hope I have half your good fortune when I circulate among West Yorkshire's society. I long to settle away from all the fuss and fatigue of London life and begin a family of my own with lots and lots of babies. Do you like babies? I'm sure you and Nathaniel will have the most darling children, what with his smile and your lovely eyes, and— Listen to me go on! Of course, I want to hear all the details of how Nathaniel won your heart, Kelsey. Do you mind if I call you Kelsey? We are to be sisters, you and I, so I shall call you Kelsey right off, and you must call me Clarice, and we shall be the best of friends. Oh, don't look at me like that Nathaniel! I must be myself. She must know me so she knows what she is getting into. Shall we go inside?"

When she was finally finished, Nathaniel looked at Kelsey with such a blank expression that she suspected his mind had been talked into a corner. Well, Kelsey knew how to handle a stream of chatter, having heard her fair share from her mother and sister over the years.

She put a welcoming hand on Clarice's arm. "Yes. I'm sure you'll want to be shown to your room and have your things brought in. Nathaniel has arranged for his maid, Hannah, to assist you for the night, and he can show your footmen where to stable your horses. I'm still learning my way around Thistledown Hall, but I believe I can show you the way to your room if you would like to follow me."

"So very kind and convenient too since my poor maid fell ill right before the journey."

"How unfortunate. Hannah is a dear. You should be quite happy with her, but I am also here to help in any way I can."

The gratitude in Nathaniel's eyes was evident as Kelsey led the way inside. Clarice took her arm as if they were old friends. She was at least five or six inches taller than Kelsey, which was almost as tall as Nathaniel, and carried herself with a calm confidence that told any onlooker she knew exactly who she was and what she wanted.

Everything Nathaniel had told Kelsey about Clarice Wimpleton had prepared her to meet a very imposing lady, which Clarice Wimpleton certainly was, but she was not the least bit unlikable. Nathaniel had painted a picture of someone cold and prideful, but the woman at Kelsey's side conversed easily, smiled frequently, and listened eagerly to everything Kelsey had to say.

"I can see why Nathaniel admires you," Clarice leaned in to say. "And I'm grateful he has you. I know I don't know anything about you beyond what he has shared, but you must be a quality lady or he wouldn't like you. You see, despite what he has told you of me, I have quite a favorable opinion of him. You are a very fortunate woman, indeed, to have caught his eye. His heart, once gained, is frightfully loyal. Oh, I know he's terrified of me and has likely told you so, but I intend to make you my friend immediately."

"Thank you," Kelsey answered. "I would like that very much." *Pity it won't be for long,* she thought. She really would like Clarice for a friend.

"Good," Clarice declared as they arrived at her room. "Because you will be most grateful for my help when we make all the arrangements for your wedding."

Kelsey had no response to that. She merely curtsied and left Miss Wimpleton alone with Hannah, who stood waiting to help her dress for dinner.

⁊⁊

Clarice, Nathaniel, and Kelsey settled themselves at the end of the long dining room table where the aromas of seasoned venison, roasted potatoes, fresh bread, and butter hung heavily enough to taste before the food ever passed their lips. Kelsey was guaranteed a satisfied belly by the end of the meal, but whether she could enjoy herself under the attentive gaze and special smile of Clarice was yet to be seen.

"Nathaniel, you and Kelsey must have an autumn wedding before the snow sets in." She spoke as if the matter were settled simply by her saying so.

"We haven't made any definite plans yet," Nathaniel said as if he had rehearsed his reply.

"Well, there's no point in waiting. Kelsey's complexion will work wonderfully with fall colors. Oh, I can hardly wait to tell Father and all my friends in town. Won't Miss Parkley be jealous! She admired my brother quite a bit, you see, but he was never interested." She paused for a bite and chewed quickly. "You know, I already feel as if we are family. I've always wanted a sister. Kelsey, you must come visit me in West Yorkshire. I'm sure the Clavenports won't mind. We can all spend Christmas together. Can't you see it? The three of us in some lovely little out of the way location? And you must let me help you select your wedding gown. Why, I know the perfect modiste, and we can . . ."

Kelsey rubbed her temple while Clarice went on about different styles and fabrics. Her lungs grew heavy as she struggled for air, and the hairs on the back of her neck began to stick with sweat.

"My guess is that you will have no trouble conceiving, so you must prepare your nursery right away—"

"Stop! Please." Kelsey's chair groaned against the recently polished floor as she stood. "Miss Wimpleton, thank you for your thoughtfulness. You really are so kind, but Nathaniel . . . Mr. Worth and I . . ."

"Kelsey, please." Nathaniel reached for her arm.

"I'm sorry, but I can't do this." There was so much more she might have said, but all she could do was hope he would understand as she turned to Clarice. "We're not engaged. Not really."

The disappointment in Nathaniel's eyes was just as unbearable as the pity in Clarice's. Before anything more could be spoken, Kelsey rushed out. She intended to head straight for the main doors and run all the way to Barley Cottage, but the sound of softly padded slippers behind her made her pause.

"Miss Wickham! Kelsey! Wait, please!" Clarice soon had a hand on her arm. "Don't leave yet, Kelsey. Please. Come sit with me." Clarice led Kelsey to the daffodil-colored sofa. "There, now. Isn't this nice? My father always says sitting before a cheerful fire can ease any sadness."

Kelsey liked Clarice much more than she had expected, which only made her confession worse. "I'm sorry, Miss Wimpleton. I can't imagine what you must think of me."

Clarice waved her hand in the air like it was nothing. "I know you didn't mean it."

"I beg your pardon?" Had Kelsey not been clear enough?

"Kelsey, when you've lived in London as long as I have, you see an inordinate number of couples become engaged, and all of them experience any number of challenges. The words you spoke, well, I've heard those exact words shouted from ladies who meant it and from those who didn't, and *you* didn't mean it. You were merely upset. Believe me, I've seen enough lovers' quarrels in my time to know the difference. You and my brother are having a disagreement of some sort, aren't you?"

Kelsey flicked away a tear. "We both have a great deal weighing on our minds at the moment, but—"

"But nothing. You need not explain the details for me to understand."

"Miss Wimpleton, I must tell you the truth. We really are not—"

"Engaged? Yes, I heard you. And it's Clarice." She scooted closer and rubbed Kelsey's back. "You're upset right now, and you want to break it off with my brother. Believe me, no one besides myself knows how difficult he can be sometimes." Her light laughter drew a smile out of Kelsey. "If you truly do not love him, I won't say another word." She looked expectantly at Kelsey, then nodded as if her suspicions were confirmed. "I know love when I see it. I've seen him around dozens of lovely, eligible girls, and he never looked at any of them the way he looks at you."

"Really?" Kelsey hiccupped.

"Absolutely!" Clarice answered. "Why, just a few months ago, when he was staying with me in London, I told him I was determined to see him married now that he is transforming into quite the eligible gentleman. I put every unattached lady I could find in his path, but he never responded to any of them, though quite a few liked him." She wrapped her arm around Kelsey's shoulder. "I also see the way you look at him. Now, I want you to go back in with me and finish dinner with my brother. He's obviously trying to impress you." She gestured around the newly made-over sitting room. "And I'm not leaving this house until I see that you are two happily engaged love birds once more."

"No really, please—"

"Kelsey, I'm certain that whatever has caused this rift between you was only worsened with the stresses of preparing for my visit. No doubt, you argued over some silly matter like the best color of paper for the walls or which vase should be on display. I cannot have my brother's future happiness on my head like that. You must allow me the chance to see your futures neatly tied together before I leave.

Whatever quarrels you have after that, it will be up to you to mend. So, you see? I am quite reasonable about it all. Are we agreed?"

"Ahem." Nathaniel stood with his hand on the door frame, looking in as if he were afraid to proceed further.

"It's all right, Nathaniel." Clarice rushed over, took his hand, and pulled him to Kelsey. "I have explained to your bride that I am fully aware of how difficult I can be sometimes, and I won't have your engagement broken on account of my visit. The rest is up to you." Clarice folded her arms and waited. "Don't stand there like a half-wit, Nathaniel." She gave him quite the nudge. "You must apologize and kiss your bride while I inform the staff we will be continuing with our meal shortly."

Clarice's footsteps pattered away, leaving Kelsey and Nathaniel alone.

Nathaniel scratched the back of his neck and risked a glance at Kelsey. "Is it really so difficult being engaged to me?" His tone was jovial, but his voice was barely audible above the crackle of the fire.

"Nathaniel, your sister was planning our wedding. She was talking about babies! Did you see how animated she became?"

"I certainly did."

"Even after I tried to tell her, she insisted on believing we're a couple."

Nathaniel ran his fingers through his hair and took a deep breath. "How would you like to proceed?"

Kelsey sat down. "Your sister thinks we are reconciling right now."

Taking her hand, Nathaniel sat next to her. "Then, why don't we reconcile?"

"But I'm not really upset with you." Kelsey thought the lines around his eyes relaxed just a bit. "I merely spoke the truth. I suppose we should go back in, and if she won't hear us, then..."

Her words thinned into air when he entwined his fingers with hers.

"Kelsey, I meant what I said the other day when I asked you to be engaged to me. No pretending tonight. No lying. I asked, and you accepted. I still want to be engaged to you tonight, completely, wholeheartedly engaged to you, Lady Kelsey."

"Nathaniel, please stop toying with me." She pulled her hand away and gave him her best *you-know-better* look.

He drew very close. "I'm in earnest!"

"What does it mean to be engaged for a day? What of tomorrow? What then?"

He stood abruptly and paced. "What then indeed?" When he stopped in front of her, he took both her hands and pulled her to standing. "If you will give me the opportunity to be your betrothed tonight, in the very sincerest meaning of the word, we will see what your feelings are tomorrow. Let us envision what it could be like if we stay on this path. We can return to the dining room an engaged couple without any plans for the future. All I ask is for this opportunity tonight."

Kelsey held still as her mind screamed a warning. *This is madness! Pure folly!* How could she say yes to such a scheme? His handsome, earnest eyes had already lured her into situations she never should have allowed. There had to be a trick hidden in his words, a deception somewhere whether he knew it or not.

But if not?

Though swaggering and charming, he had protected her and risked his own reputation to help her, and he had done it with great self-control, especially when they had stood together alone in the still of night. She had no reason to doubt his honor, but she had no intention of being convinced of anything, not when she had lost all trust in herself.

"Are you two kissing yet?" Clarice's voice echoed from the other room. "The venison is getting cold!"

"All right," Kelsey breathed out before she could stop herself. "Let's go back in." She had no idea what it meant to be truly engaged for a day. It was absurd. How could it accomplish anything other than confusing her further?

"Wait." Nathaniel stayed by the fireplace keeping her hands in his. "My sister told me to kiss you."

Their eyes met and the only sound above the snapping fire was her heartbeat.

"Do you do everything your sister tells you to do?" She needed to get Nathaniel back to jesting. She didn't know what to do with this serious side of him.

"Only when I agree with her." He brushed a loose hair behind Kelsey's ears, sending cool ripples down her neck and arms as his fingers found her jaw. "I did tell you I would ask for a kiss, didn't I?"

She stood completely still, knowing she had waited for a ridiculously inconvenient moment to decide whether she would let him kiss her. His thumb slid to her cheek and tested the feel of her skin, as if he too were deciding.

"You're not pulling away," he whispered.

"And you're leaning in."

His breath warmed her face like a sunbeam wrapped in a breeze, and she closed her eyes, hoping her kissing abilities weren't lacking. Despite all the rumors to the contrary, Kelsey had never so much as kissed a man, but never before had she been so tempted. Never had any man sent her blood coursing like a river. Never had any man persisted past her stubbornness to find the part of her that wanted to be held. Never, until Nathaniel.

Now, as she stood with her eyes closed, and the passing seconds lost meaning against her racing heart, she gave up deciding and only waited. Just when she expected to discover what his lips felt like on hers, she opened her eyes. His lips were a hair's breadth away, but rather than close the distance, his stubbled cheek nestled against hers and filled her with the scent of sage and mint. His hands traced their way along her arms, awakening every nerve inside her, but rather than indulge in the fullness of a kiss, the corner of his lips only met the corner of hers.

"I won't kiss you the way I'd like to unless you truly want me to." His breath tickled her ear as she tried to comprehend him.

The moment he moved away, disappointment sunk inside her like a stone. Her face was hot, and she didn't know how to interpret the look in his eyes. Something intimate had passed between them, but only in that he had understood a feeling she could not articulate.

She had to blink back her confusion as he laced his fingers with hers and led her into the dining room. Kelsey didn't know what to say or how to explain anything to Clarice, but Nathaniel took care of it all.

"Not a word about this to anyone, Clarice. I'm quite serious. Kelsey and I have only agreed to give our relationship due consideration. In the meantime, you must not consider anything as official. Are we clear?"

Clarice stood up and clapped her hands. "You reconciled!"

Chapter 22

*But how little of permanent happiness could belong
to a couple who were only brought together because
their passions were stronger than their virtue . . .*

Jane Austen, *Pride and Prejudice*

The moon shone like a pearl nestled in a silken sky as Nathaniel led Kelsey outside to wait for Clarice's carriage to convey Kelsey home. Whispers of summer winds ripe with the scent of blossoms encircled her and Nathaniel as if urging them together. But she knew the winds would die, and the ride home would be short. Still, the day had passed entirely too quickly.

When Clarice had bid Kelsey good night only moments earlier, she had made Kelsey promise to write to her once she and Nathaniel had chosen a date for the wedding. Kelsey had no trouble agreeing since it was unlikely a date for their imagined wedding would ever be chosen. Clarice had kissed her cheek and waved as Nathaniel wrapped his arm around Kelsey and walked with her outside.

With his warmth keeping the evening chill at bay, Kelsey thought of other gestures Nathaniel had shared with her throughout the day, an endearment spoken, a touch of the hand, and of course, the kiss on her cheek that had both tempted and disappointed her. It was regrettable that those small freedoms allowed to engaged couples would have to be promptly given up.

Only, Nathaniel didn't remove his arm once they were alone.

Kelsey cleared her throat. "It was a pleasure being engaged to you, Nathaniel." She smiled and gently pulled away.

He quickly took her hand. "The day's not over yet, Kelsey."

"What do you mean?" She was suddenly short of breath. *Why must he make this so difficult?*

"This doesn't have to end, Kelsey. You accepted my proposal to be engaged today, but I never said anything about it ending."

"Nathaniel," She didn't need to pretend to sound disappointed. She didn't want him playing with her affections like a kitten with string. "That isn't what you meant."

Under the dim night sky, she could see his jaw flex with emotion. "It's what I mean now. Or, at least, it's what I hope for. Kelsey, I've loved you from the beginning. Surely, you knew. I thought I could handle it today, having you near, calling you my intended. I thought I could continue to be your friend and wait until I saw the evidence of your feelings, which I have earnestly hoped for, but Kelsey, this day, this beautiful, magnificent day, has been blissful torture! Everything I want is so clearly before me in this small sample of joy, but all the uncertainty remains. Please help me understand what I saw tonight. I am certain I saw something in you, something more in your look and manner toward me . . . But if I was mistaken . . . If you truly cannot return my feelings, it is you who must end our engagement. I cannot bear to. Darling Kelsey, I will hold you while I can."

He did nothing more than press her hand against his cheek, caressing it with his thumb, and she very nearly thought she could remain his intended. But as she looked around at the flowers they had recently planted and the poplars softly swishing in the night breeze like waves at sea, she knew it was just a spell, probably akin to the one her parents had succumbed to when they ran off to elope. It was nothing more than a generous dose of moonlight so deftly misapplied.

No words came to mind which sufficiently captured her web of feelings. She shook her head. "I . . ." Still no words. "I need a moment to think. I . . . forgot my shawl inside."

"Allow me." He turned away, his shoulders drooping.

She stood watching him as he returned through the main doors of the shabby manor. It was old and neglected, but with proper care and love, she could see it reviving to a truly charming estate. Yet, how would she feel about it once the charm wore off? Once the spell had been broken?

Nathaniel returned and wrapped the shawl around her shoulders. Why did it hurt so much to meet his eyes? It was frightening to see the smile completely gone from them.

A moment later, the carriage came around with Clarice's driver at the reins. In silence, they climbed in and headed down the path to the main road that would lead them past the ruins and back to the cottage. Kelsey could hear Nathaniel breathing as he sat beside her, never once touching her arm or hand.

She owed him an answer. She had to say something, anything that would explain why she couldn't accept him.

Her voice nearly failed her, but she finally managed to speak. "I don't think you really want to marry me, Nathaniel."

"Oh, no? And pray tell how you have become the expert of my heart."

His words pierced her sharply, but she had to continue.

"Because I think you are more in love with an idea than you are with me. Tonight was lovely, a glimpse into a perfect picture of a home and a marriage. But it wasn't real. You were pretending. You simply got caught in your emotions. Let's not spoil our friendship. Please."

His chest rose with each breath. "Your words hurt more deeply than you know, but that is the problem. You don't know how I care. You refuse to see it. You're so worried about getting hurt that you convince yourself my feelings are false. You have done such a remarkable job building a fortress around your heart that you never have to worry about getting hurt. You never let anyone in."

The steady, unwavering manner in which he spoke made Kelsey wonder how long he had since come to such a conclusion. It wasn't fair.

"You'd understand if you really knew who I was, what my upbringing has been."

"Then tell me, Kelsey. Tell me everything. I want to know it all."

He took her hands as the carriage rambled on.

"Oh, Nathaniel!" she choked. "I would be such a shameful connection for you. My mother and father eloped. I was born eight months later. Scandal and gossip follow our family the way spring follows winter."

"And who am I, but an orphaned sailor that another poor sailor took pity on? I have the tenuous promise of a home, but even that is being contested. I care nothing for rumors and inherited reputations. I only care about you."

"But I've inherited more than a reputation. I've inherited doubt and skepticism. I don't know what it means to love someone the way you'd want me to. I've had no one to turn to, no one to trust. Everyone I've learned to care about either leaves me or I'm forced to leave them. Even Lucia, who I love like a sister, has fled away. Everyone here knows what it means to be a Wickham. You've been my friend, Nathaniel. That isn't easy for me to say, and I do care, but nothing in my life lasts. I can't trust that what we felt tonight was real. All I can do is avoid the same fate my mother suffered. I must help her get what she wants without ruining our family completely."

Nathaniel's face momentarily constricted. "Do you hear yourself, how calloused that sounds? Can you not see that your fortress is preventing you from knowing your own feelings? I hear a great deal from you about what your mother wants, but what about you, Kelsey? What do you want?"

His question knocked the air out of her lungs, and she staggered. Her heart was so divided, full of sectioned off portions reserved for managing problems or protecting feelings that were never meant to escape.

"I don't know," she whispered. "I simply don't know." Her eyes filled with tears.

"We could be so happy, you and I. Leave your mother to work out her future for herself. Right now, this is about you and me. Say yes, and I promise I'll make you happy every day of your life."

In the brilliance of a second, Kelsey saw herself and Nathaniel together, hand in hand, and it was beautiful. But in the next second, she imagined her father convincing her mother to run away with him. Scenes of heartache and broken promises, disguised with declarations of love, passed through Kelsey's mind in the space of a heartbeat, and she could no longer see herself and Nathaniel without also seeing her mother and father within.

And she knew Nathaniel was right. She didn't let anyone in, not even her mother or sister. She wasn't even sure she knew how to. If she said yes to him right then, she would somehow eventually pull away, too scared to love, too scared to be loved. No matter how much she wanted to believe it was possible, she couldn't accept him.

Chapter 23

Angry people are not always wise.

Jane Austen, *Pride and Prejudice*

*K*elsey looked around the cottage garden. Things were finally in order. The brambles were gone. The dandelions were few, and there were pink buds promising roses on the bushes beneath the windows. The peach tree no longer had vines scrambling around its trunk, and the pathway that curved around the back was finally clear of roots and weedy invaders. She had even found the supposed blackberry bush along with two more gold guineas.

All proof Kelsey had too much time on her hands.

Nathaniel hadn't come by for an entire week, and she lacked the courage to visit him and admit that maybe he had been right. Maybe she was calloused. Maybe she didn't know her own feelings. Maybe she didn't know how to truly love, but in the week spent without him she had developed a fervent desire to learn.

Until she knew how to approach him again, working in the garden was at least productive. It brought peace to her surroundings and fresh food to her table. She had a garden full of plants that didn't judge her for her inconsistencies or blame her for heartaches. All they did was provide opportunities to work, prune, and harvest.

And ignore the problems she still faced with her mother who had not yet given Mr. Baxter her final answer.

Under the midday sun, Kelsey rested on the edge of the well and wondered whether her mother was currently out with him or simply on one of her walks. *It doesn't matter*, she sighed to herself. She had done what she could to stop her, and it had not been enough.

What was Lucia doing right then, she wondered, besides being adored by her relatives and being blessed with the jewels of fortune? And was Cissy learning better habits from Aunt Kitty and her cousins? Was she gaining an understanding of how proper people behaved? Kelsey sincerely hoped Cissy would not return to the prospect of having Mr. Baxter for a stepfather.

"Good day, Miss Wickham!"

Kelsey stood up, not having heard anyone approaching, and looked for who called her. On the path just beyond the garden was Mr. Woodcox tipping his hat. He looked the picture of a perfect gentleman, but Kelsey remembered the way he had tried to argue his way into Thistledown Hall. *Full of lies like all men,* she thought bitterly. *Well, most men.* Ever since Nathaniel, she found herself willing to acknowledge the exceptions.

"Hello, Mr. Woodcox. What brings you this way? Are you on your way to the market?"

"Yes, the market. Are you alone, Miss Wickham?" The gate rang out a metallic whine as he stepped into the garden.

There wasn't anything obviously distressing about his presence, but Kelsey's stomach tightened at his direct question. "My mother isn't far." At least, she sincerely hoped she wasn't. "But I'm afraid the cottage isn't in a state to receive visitors at the moment." She clasped her hands in front of her and searched the road beyond for any other soul walking along. She couldn't tell whether Mr. Woodcox was satisfied with her answer.

"Very well. I'll be brief." He looked around just as she had done. "Could you tell me exactly how long you've lived in this cottage?"

Kelsey scratched her arm. Why did he want to know? "My mother and I moved in at the beginning of summer."

"I see, and during that time, have you found anything that belonged to previous tenants, anything they might have left behind, perhaps?"

She thought of the guineas she had found as well as the note, which was a trifle, valuable only to its writer and recipient. And to her. She cared about it even if she did not know its history, and she wanted to protect it from outside tampering. "Mr. Woodcox, I don't understand the purpose of your question."

He shrugged. "I suppose it doesn't matter. I was acquainted with a man who lived here before you. I ask merely for sentimental reasons."

"I see." Would he have cared about the note? Surely, a few guineas weren't of much consequence when one had other means of income.

The distant sound of carriage wheels echoed from the road. Even Mr. Baxter would be a welcome sight if it meant not being alone with Mr. Woodcox.

"Perhaps you could help me another way, Miss Wickham." Mr. Woodcox began pacing.

"Help you with what, sir?" She hadn't agreed to help him with anything.

"How long have you known Mr. Worth?"

Kelsey considered how to answer. Why did Mr. Woodcox's questions feel like snakes hiding in the grass? "As long as I've lived here."

At this, he snickered and glanced down his nose at her. "Quite a short period to be allowing the man to spend the night, don't you think? Then again, you are a Wickham, aren't you?"

Kelsey froze from the inside out, and gooseflesh rose on her skin. She looked at his arm, remembering how Nathaniel had struck the intruder's right arm with the fire iron. Was Mr. Woodcox holding his right arm a bit more stiffly than his left? Or was she simply imagining it? She swallowed forcefully and tried to spur her mind to action.

"What a strange comment, sir. Do you make it your business to know where neighboring gentlemen spend each night?" When a rumbling chuckle rose from his belly, Kelsey decided her best defense would be to ask her own questions. "How long have you been acquainted with Mr. Worth?"

"I met him at Mr. Baxter's dinner, the same evening you and I were introduced."

Her suspicions, which she desperately hoped were wrong, were unavoidably taking shape. "You've been interested in the neighborhood longer than that, though, haven't you, Mr. Woodcox?"

He met her eyes with a question in his, but he did not look away.

Kelsey didn't know why he was talking to her, but she would not pretend ignorance. "My intuition tells me you are the kind of man who enjoys late night walks." His eyes hardened, and Kelsey steeled herself. "Middle of the night walks, in fact, though I can't fathom why you would choose to be out in the pouring rain. Perhaps it served to better conceal you."

His fists tightened and her stomach clenched. What had she done? There was no one around to defend her. How many steps would it take to run inside and fetch the same fire iron that had injured his arm?

When he finally spoke, his voice came out low and raspy. All pretense was gone. "Careful, Miss Wickham. There is much more at stake here than you realize."

"I could say the same to you, Mr. Woodcox." As he stepped closer, Kelsey stepped back. "A man who breaks the law would have a difficult time convincing authorities that his claims on Thistledown Hall are just, don't you think?" If she had no tangible weapon to wield, she could at the very least speak boldly.

His nostrils flared. "The same way a ruined woman would have a hard time convincing anyone to listen to her at all."

Kelsey's breathing grew heavy with anger, but her insides trembled. If she ran, which she was sorely tempted to do, it would only strengthen her sudden apprehension of Mr. Woodcox. She needed him to know she had no reason to keep his secret, nothing to be ashamed of, even if every muscle inside her now quaked. "My mother was there to chaperone the entire time. Mr. Worth's word would be believed over yours." She glanced around the yard for a spade or shovel, but there was nothing.

He leaned very close and sneered in her face. "Are you interested in testing these theories, miss?"

They stood face to face breathing heavily. Kelsey didn't dare move for fear she would forget how to use her legs. Mr. Woodcox clamped a hand around her upper arm when a voice echoed from the other side of the house.

"Kelsey! Kelsey!" came a girl's voice. "Kelsey!"

The sound shook Kelsey's mind awake, but Mr. Woodcox hadn't budged. Did he not hear the girl calling?

"Kelsey!" This time, the call came from a man, stern in his exclamation, which only increased Kelsey's trembling.

Now standing before them was Lucia Darcy, in a very fine burgundy traveling dress, and her uncle, Mr. Fitzwilliam Darcy of Pemberley, tall and stately in his trim black jacket and waistcoat. Finally, Mr. Woodcox seemed to remember himself and stepped away.

"Mr. Woodcox?" Lucia hesitated, dipped into a curtsey, then ran and threw her arms around Kelsey's neck. "Kelsey!"

Kelsey returned the embrace, but her heart was wildly beating, and her face was reddening. "Oh, Lucia! I was beginning to think you'd never return!"

Mr. Darcy watched Mr. Woodcox, who only endured a second under his scrutiny. Without any explanation or word of farewell, Mr. Woodcox exited the garden and strode down the path at a fierce pace.

Lucia took Kelsey's hand and smiled as naturally as ever.

Mr. Darcy's brows knit together as he regarded Kelsey. "Is everything all right, Kelsey?"

"I . . . I'm so glad to see you." Her voice escaped like a scratch or a whisper.

"It's a pleasure to see you again. My, how you've grown." His tones traveled the space between civility and indifference, though Kelsey wasn't certain she knew him well enough to truly know.

She rubbed her arm where Mr. Woodcox had tightened his hold and tried to muster a smile, but her eyes kept darting to the road where his figure was growing ever smaller. Lucia followed Kelsey's gaze, and her smile wilted.

Mr. Darcy cleared his throat. "Pray, who was that man?"

What to say? How to explain? Did his question require a full explanation or a simple one? "Mr. Woodcox. Merely an acquaintance."

Mr. Darcy lifted a brow. "And you also know him, Lucia?" An awkward silence settled on them. Lucia gave a timid nod. "I see. Is your mother inside, Kelsey? I'd like to greet her as well."

Kelsey looked around the garden, shaking her head, and all words failed her.

"Were you alone with that man? Truly, you do not seem well, Kelsey."

Her heart sickened and her stomach grew queasy. "Please," she said. "I know what you must be imagining, but he came upon me unprepared. I wanted him gone. Nothing happened. I . . ."

"Naturally, I expect upright behavior, but I wouldn't do you the dishonor of forming a rash judgment."

"Thank you, Uncle." Kelsey considered telling them all she knew about Mr. Woodcox, but her suspicions were new and tenuous, and she still feared her uncle's censure if he learned about all the times she and Nathaniel had been alone together.

"I must say," said Mr. Darcy, "the garden is much improved."

"Yes, you've done wonderfully." Lucia gave her arm another squeeze. "We are only now returning home, but I insisted we stop here first. I was so eager to come and see you today."

"Indeed," Mr. Darcy agreed, though he still regarded Kelsey with a keen eye. "How do you find the cottage?"

With a steadying breath, she began to recover. "It's very comfortable, thank you."

"And your mother is well?"

"Yes, as is my sister who has gone to stay with our Aunt Kitty in Warlingham."

"Yes, I'm aware." He nodded, and for the first time, Kelsey detected his approbation. "When do you expect your mother to return?"

"Later tonight, perhaps? I don't really know."

Mr. Darcy frowned. "I see. We must be going in any event, but we would like you and your mother to dine with us tomorrow. My wife sends her greetings. She has been delayed an extra day but will return with a surprise for you all. Send word to Pemberley if you need anything in the meantime. And please do not hesitate to come to me if that man continues to bother you. Come, Lucia. Good day, Kelsey."

Lucia took her father's arm and waved to Kelsey over her shoulder.

Once their carriage was out of sight, every muscle in Kelsey unraveled and her emotions spilled from her like an overturned pot. She hardly knew what made sense and what didn't. All she knew was that she was a mess, and Lucia, whom she loved, and Mr. Darcy, whom she feared, had been there to witness it. She couldn't deny their arrival had spared her of trouble, but it was precisely her luck that they should first see her alone with a man.

The way of the Wickham, she sniffled.

Chapter 24

Her heart did whisper that he had done it for her.

Jane Austen, *Pride and Prejudice*

*K*elsey closed *The Tempest*, which she had been too distracted to focus on anyway, and closed her eyes. The scene in the garden from the previous hour kept spinning through her thoughts. No matter how intently she tried make sense of events, all she saw was Mr. Woodcox leering over her right when her uncle and Lucia stumbled upon them.

She was rising from the sofa when her mother burst through the cottage door out of breath with her face glowing like a fresh peach.

"He's coming, Kelsey! He's coming!"

"Yes, I know," she groaned, placing her book on the shelf. Kelsey never would have imagined her mother would be so excited to see Mr. Darcy again.

"Kelsey, did you hear me? The captain is coming!"

"What?" Kelsey fumbled at the news, knocking two books over. "What do you mean the captain is coming?" She looked out the window as if he might walk up the path that very moment, but all she saw were trees rustling against the blushing backdrop of the setting sun.

Her mother covered her mouth and giggled. "What I mean is that Mrs. Salaway and Mrs. Winters both heard rumors that the captain is returning! Miss Chatham refused to believe it, but I ignored her."

Kelsey picked up the fallen books. What news that would be for Nathaniel! The captain must have finally received Nathaniel's letters and was coming to settle the dispute Mr. Woodcox had laid against him.

But as Kelsey looked into her mother's eyes, sparkling with hope and wishes, her heart seized. How could Kelsey let her mother meet the captain thinking he was her admirer? How foolish her mother would appear! What embarrassment she would feel! Her heart would break when she learned the letters were not from him.

"When? Are you certain?" Kelsey asked. "Perhaps the rumors resulted because of the Darcys' return. My uncle and Lucia called a short while ago. They've just arrived."

"Well, that is something. The Darcys finally acknowledging us." Her mother rolled her eyes. "But that isn't what the excitement is about. All the ladies are talking about Captain Styles. No one knows exactly when he is to arrive, but we'll all know soon. Everyone is saying that Mr. Worth, your Mr. Worth," she added, nudging Kelsey with her shoulder, "is planning to hold a ball in his honor. Isn't it exciting?"

Kelsey managed a smile, but it hung like a loose thread. With only Joseph and the Smitt ladies, she couldn't imagine Nathaniel managing a ball, but if it was true, her friendship with Nathaniel was over, it would seem. He hadn't confided anything to her about the captain or a ball.

"To think I was starting to despair over whether he would ever come at all! I very nearly accepted Mr. Baxter yesterday, but my intuition told me to wait a little longer. So, you see? I shall be the happiest woman to finally meet my admirer!"

"Mother," Kelsey groaned again. "You mustn't rush into anything. You can't be certain the captain is the one who wrote those letters. We must wait and see."

"Perhaps, but how I shall laugh when all the ladies in the village see me on the arm of my dear captain!"

Already, he was her *dear captain*?

Kelsey rubbed her temple. Should she risk another letter to convince her mother that her admirer was not the captain? Even if Nathaniel was still willing to help her, the thought of continuing the deception made her ill. The very idea of another letter was a thunderous cloud threatening torrents of trouble, but how else could she bring the charade to an end, especially if she still needed to keep her mother from accepting Mr. Baxter's proposal? She had no idea.

Her mother began mumbling about what they would wear to the ball, but Kelsey's nerves prickled at the shuffling sound of footsteps outside. Had Mr. Woodcox returned? When an urgent pounding resounded on the door, she leapt off the sofa and went straight for the fire iron.

Her mother grabbed the nearest bonnet and swatted Kelsey's arm. "Heaven help me, but you startled me, Kelsey! Whatever has gotten into you?"

"Don't answer it, Mother, please!" she whispered, too exhausted to face Mr. Woodcox again and too humiliated to face another Darcy or any other neighbor, but her mother was already opening the door.

"Mr. Worth. What a pleasure it is to see you."

Nathaniel! Kelsey laid the fire iron aside and dusted a thin layer of soot from her hands. Her courage to face him after hurting him so terribly felt as solid as a pastry.

"Won't you come in?" Mrs. Wickham stepped aside with the door open wide. "It's late enough that I'll expect you to stay and dine with us."

"That is kind of you, Mrs. Wickham, but I'm afraid I can't."

When he finally spared Kelsey a glance, a painful tightening in her chest made breathing difficult.

He dipped into a shallow bow. "Good evening, Miss Wickham."

Miss Wickham. Her name had often been a source of shame, but never quite like this. "Good evening, Mr. Worth." What a moment to realize how much she appreciated the openness they had previously shared.

"Forgive me for intruding at this late hour."

"Nonsense, the sun is only just setting." Mrs. Wickham gestured to the sitting room. "We are quite ready to entertain, are we not, Kelsey?"

She wanted to agree but her voice buried itself in her stomach.

"Thank you, madam," Nathaniel said, "but I come with a rather awkward invitation. You see, there is talk of . . . well, how to say this? I have reason to believe there is an intruder in the vicinity. I've heard of at least one cottage that was already broken into." His eyes flickered at Kelsey. "And I could not rest easy thinking of you here without protection."

"Oh, my!" Mrs. Wickham softly exclaimed. "An intruder? Here? Are you certain?"

"It is difficult to be certain of anything, but I should not like you to take the risk without precautions."

"What do you recommend?" Mrs. Wickham wrapped her arms around herself.

Nathaniel let his gaze drift to Kelsey again, but his face flushed and his eyes would hardly meet hers. "I would like to offer you an invitation to Thistledown Hall tonight. I've hired a carriage to be ready should you accept." He gestured toward the door. Kelsey could hear the faint sounds of horses nickering. "It is merely a precaution, but I would be obliged if you would alleviate my worries over you."

"Do you mean it?" Kelsey finally spoke. "You want us to come?" *You want me to come?*

"Yes." There was no hesitation.

"But we have nothing here worth stealing," Mrs. Wickham said. "Do you really think the threat is serious?"

"I believe it is. I do not wish to alarm you, but I have seen with my own eyes the figure of a strange man lurking within the portion of forest between here and Calder Glen. I speculate of course, but his gait struck me as menacing."

A shiver raced up Kelsey's spine. Did Nathaniel know about Mr. Woodcox?

"I see the wisdom in your recommendation, Mr. Worth. Kelsey, what do you say? You agree we should accept Mr. Worth's offer, do you not?"

Kelsey wouldn't have disagreed for anything. "Yes. I believe we should accept."

Mrs. Wickham clapped her hands, shifting from troubled to delighted. "Wonderful. I'll collect my things right away. I should very much like to see Thistledown Hall. Tomorrow, I shall write to Cissy and tell her all about it. She will be so sad she missed it. What a lark this will be!"

Her mother rushed upstairs, leaving Kelsey and Nathaniel alone together for the first time since he had expressed his desire to make their engagement real.

"Leave it to my mother to turn this into an adventure," she laughed weakly. "Thank you for thinking of us . . ." She trailed off, debating what to call him. "Mr. Worth." She mustered a brief smile before heading to the stairs.

"Kelsey?"

"Yes?" She spun around, fully aware that her name on his lips again was music.

"I'm glad you're coming."

"So am I. It's good to see you again, Nathaniel. I'm glad you invited us."

His shoulders relaxed as he took a step closer. "As I said before, it will be easier to protect you in my own home." He gave her the faintest smile. "You're worth protecting."

Her stomach shook with the usual flutters his proximity inspired, but the tides of guilt pulled away their delight. "I don't deserve you. Surely, you've concluded that by now."

He tugged on his lapels, a bit of his playfulness returning. "I never said anyone did, but I could be persuaded by the right young lady to overlook the fact."

She bit the inside of her cheek. How Nathaniel could manage to contrive one of his flirtations in such a moment was shocking, but never had she been so happy to hear one.

A rare moment of bravery surged through her veins. "I'm so sorry I disappointed you the other night. This week without you has made me consider everything anew. I really don't know how to talk about such things, not seriously anyway, not when it concerns my own feelings. I don't know if I'm ready. I don't know how to . . . I'm not sure I understand what I must . . ." The words thinned into a sigh, and she shook her head.

"You don't have to say anything, Kelsey. Right now, I'm content keeping you safe."

Oh, Nathaniel. If only she were brave enough to say more. "Thank you. I . . . I'll collect my things now."

A faint sparkle returned to his eyes. "I shall wait as long as it takes."

⚘

The ride to Thistledown was short as the silence between Nathaniel and Kelsey filled with chatter from Mrs. Wickham, who, to Kelsey's dismay, sat awkwardly clutching the painting of her and George Wickham, refusing to let anyone help her with it. Of course, Kelsey's mother would think to guard that awful thing. Kelsey could see Nathaniel's perplexity as he watched Mrs. Wickham carry it into the carriage, but he didn't object. While Mrs. Wickham constantly shifted to balance it and adjust her grip, she peppered him with questions about Thistledown Hall, which he kindly answered.

Once they arrived, Joseph bowed low to Mrs. Wickham and was very gracious in his attentions. Nathaniel had even asked Hannah and Mrs. Smitt to stay and assist Kelsey and her mother, further evidence he had prepared to receive them. Kelsey was delighted to see that she and her mother were to share the same room Clarice had stayed in.

"I'm sorry, that in a house this large, I can't offer you each your own room," Nathaniel apologized. "I have yet to properly furnish the other rooms and clean all the chimneys, and this was the only acceptable guest room ready to receive you on such short notice."

"No need to apologize, Mr. Worth." Mrs. Wickham huffed as she clumsily leaned the painting against the wall on top of a wide chest of drawers. "I'm delighted to be here. Why, it must be two or three years since the last time we were guests at such a large house."

"It's lovely," Kelsey assured him. "Really, Nathaniel."

After settling in with their things, Nathaniel took Kelsey and Mrs. Wickham on a tour of the house, mostly for Mrs. Wickham's sake. Kelsey was already familiar with the place, but the warmth that met her at every turn caught her off guard. Each room they visited reminded her of conversations with Nathaniel, jests they had shared, and times they had worked together to make improvements on the house. How was it possible that Thistledown Hall held so many memories?

Sitting down to dinner was no exception. The last time she had sat at that table, she had admitted to Clarice that she and Nathaniel were not engaged. Inevitably, Kelsey thought about the moment he had almost kissed her. How confusing it was not to have wanted the kiss but to have felt the loss when it didn't come.

When dinner was over, the three gathered before the fireplace in the sitting room, where reminders continued to course through Kelsey's mind in quick succession.

We're not engaged . . .

We could be so happy . . .

After several unsuccessful attempts to draw Kelsey and Nathaniel into conversation, Mrs. Wickham stood.

"Well, I'm exhausted. I hope you don't mind if I retire for the night. My intuition tells me that either you two have argued, or you have matters you'd rather discuss without me. I hate to be in your way, so I'll let the maid and butler be your chaperones. Good night."

Though neither Joseph nor either of the Smitt ladies were anywhere in sight, Mrs. Wickham walked away yawning. Kelsey looked at Nathaniel and couldn't tell whether the tension between them eased or thickened with her mother's departure. Several minutes were spent listening to the fire snap.

Finally, Kelsey broke the silence. "I can hardly believe it has only been a week since I was last here. It feels much longer since I have seen you."

Was it hope that glimmered in his eyes or merely the fire's reflection?

"I wasn't sure you wanted to see me. I thought if you needed another letter or some such favor, you would come."

The sting of his statement hurt worse than the nettles she had fallen into when he'd pushed her out of the way of Mr. Baxter's speeding carriage. "Surely, you know I value our friendship regardless of the letters."

The fire made a particularly loud pop.

"I am not sure of anything anymore."

As Kelsey watched his chest rise and fall in quick succession, her fingers twisted in her lap like the flames above the logs. "Nathaniel, I must tell you something. Mr. Woodcox approached me today at the cottage. He knew you had stayed the night there. I think he was the intruder, and he knows that I know."

Nathaniel nodded. "I wondered. I've noticed him carrying his right arm more stiffly."

"Yes, exactly. I wondered whether I had only imagined it. I don't understand why he would have attempted to break in while we were home."

"I don't think he feared two sleeping women. Perhaps he expected the rain to disguise his noise. I believe it was my presence that caught him off guard."

Kelsey was reminded of how she had run into Nathaniel's arms that night when the thunder struck. "I'm still reeling from it all."

"As am I. Earlier today, I was debating whether I should call on you when I saw him ahead of me. He entered the garden before I could, never noticing me. My distrust of that man has been increasing, so I lingered near the trees by the path should you need me." Nathaniel's hand clenched into a fist. "Mr. Woodcox is fortunate Mr. Darcy interrupted before I did. I would have inflicted more harm than I did with the fire iron if he had tried to hurt you." He grimaced. "Once I saw him leave, I came back here to make arrangements for you and your mother. I wish I could do something to protect your home, but at least you are safe here. I don't know what else to do."

"Nathaniel, I don't know how I will ever be able to return the kindness you've shown."

He shifted in his seat. "Thank you, but there is actually another reason I wanted to bring you here tonight."

"Oh?" Her heart flew to a gallop. Would he renew his proposal? Would she be brave enough to accept this time?

"Yes. You see, I need your help planning a masquerade."

"Ah, yes." Her heart puttered and began to slow. "My mother told me. News that you are throwing a ball is already circulating in the neighborhood. Does that mean Captain Styles is returning? You have heard from him?"

"I'm afraid not." Nathaniel shook his head.

"Then why on earth would you want to throw a masquerade?"

"Would you be satisfied if I said it was so I could dance with you?"

"Of course not. A dance is not sufficient justification for such trouble and expense." When the fire seemed to tsk at her reply, she cleared her throat and tried again. "Though I would accept if you asked."

"I do want to dance with you, Lady Kelsey," he said in that musical way, reminding her how much she enjoyed hearing him call her that. "But there is another reason. Joseph has been helping me spread rumors that the captain is returning. I need to counter Mr. Woodcox's claims. He has been telling people the captain is dead."

"Oh dear." Kelsey placed a hand to her heart. "Then you should know my mother believes the captain to be her admirer."

"What?" Nathaniel lifted his head. "What reason has she for thinking that?"

"Nathaniel, you wrote something in the most recent letter about being at sea."

"Oh." He stared at the fire and released an audible breath. "Yet another problem to add to the list."

"Exactly. So, why would you want to hold a masquerade while the list is growing?"

He leaned forward. "I suspect Mr. Woodcox would not be lingering in the neighborhood if the captain were present. He's trying to take advantage of my position here and the fact that I'm alone. A few days ago, he made another attempt to invite himself to stay here while I was in Lambton, but there is no need to worry about that happening." Nathaniel chuckled. "Joseph was more than up to the task of seeing Mr. Woodcox off the premises."

"I should have liked to see that." Kelsey chuckled too. "But will rumors be enough to help you? I doubt gossip is ever the key to improving a situation." Her ears had been filled over the years with more rumors than she would have thought possible to tolerate.

"It is my intention to attempt it nonetheless. There are always rumors about the captain, and I want to observe Mr. Woodcox when he has reason to believe Captain Styles has returned. I won't confirm or deny the captain's presence. I merely want to provide everyone with enough grounds to suspect it, which is the reason for making the ball a masquerade. Everyone will assume it is to humor the captain's preference for anonymity."

"But a masquerade? As a means to spy? Consider the preparations, the expense. You'll need to hire a fleet of servants and prepare wagons of food."

"I have enough to bear the costs. You may not realize it, but I have been working to make the estate profitable again. I also have a few modest investments from gains I earned at sea, and I'll need to hire more servants eventually anyway. It's important to me that I'm capable of supporting a family here when the time comes."

Kelsey thought she saw hurt mingled with hope in his eyes. Worry that he would not renew his proposal wiggled inside her. "What if Mr. Woodcox insists on seeing the captain? What if you gain nothing at all for your troubles?"

"I do not believe Mr. Woodcox would want to confront the captain at a ball. If he does wish to speak with him, I'll suggest Mr. Woodcox make an appointment. Joseph has volunteered to keep a close watch on him. He'll warn me should anything odd transpire."

Kelsey still didn't see the logic in his plan. "Why not go to the captain's solicitor instead of all this trouble?"

Nathaniel rubbed his brow. "Because I do not know who the captain's solicitor is. He was planning on introducing me when he returned to town. No one knows this Kelsey..." He leaned close enough for her to see the lines on his lips. "But all I have is a hastily prepared document signed by the captain granting me permission to live here and act in his name. I saw him sign it himself when last we met. Without giving me a clue as to when he'd return, he handed me a large chain of house keys and charged me to take care of the place. It's been an adventure discovering which key fits which lock. I have no accountings, no records. I do not even know whether Mr. Woodcox's claims are false or whether my claims would hold up against his."

"But a masquerade, Nathaniel? Could you not simply wait and see what happens?"

"Certainly, I could, but I need to do something."

The desperation in his voice reminded Kelsey of herself. Hadn't she been just as eager to grasp hold of any plan, even a ridiculous one, that could possibly help? Of course, she had. She knew exactly how he felt, but what good had her scheming accomplished?

"Then write to all the solicitors in London if you must. Surely, someone will know something."

"I don't know how I could do that without word getting back to Mr. Woodcox. If his solicitor caught wind of my panic . . . No, no. I know a masquerade will be a great deal of trouble." He rubbed his face, shook his head, then smiled at Kelsey, softening her to whatever he would say next. "But I really do want to dance with you."

Chapter 25

She began now to comprehend that he was exactly the man
who, in disposition and talents, would most suit her.

Jane Austen, *Pride and Prejudice*

*K*elsey sat across from her mother and next to Nathaniel as the carriage rambled back to Barley Cottage. The night had passed smoothly, surprising even Kelsey with how well she had slept under Thistledown's roof. Though they agreed to return to the cottage to collect enough of their belongings for an extended stay, Kelsey couldn't help but wonder whether it would be more proper to appeal to their relatives at Pemberley for a safe refuge.

"Mother, the Darcys have invited us to dine with them tonight. Now that they've returned, we must let them know about the possibility of an intruder."

"I suppose we must, but I'll do it when I'm ready. I don't think you've spent enough time at Thistledown Hall yet." Her mother gave an obvious wink.

Now that the intruder had a face and a name and Kelsey knew how close he was, she wouldn't risk staying in the cottage again. The

211

only trouble with staying at Thistledown Hall was that Nathaniel was a greater puzzle to her than ever before.

The carriage unexpectedly veered to the right, pushing Kelsey into him with the force of the momentum. She promptly righted herself and let out an exasperated huff.

"Are you all right, Lady Kelsey?" he asked softly, glancing at Mrs. Wickham who was fumbling with something in her reticule.

The carriage hit a large bump in the road, making Kelsey bounce into him again. "Of course. Why wouldn't I be all right? I'm once again homeless, and no matter what I do, life keeps pushing me into you."

She bit her lips, knowing she'd said too much, but he merely leaned his head closer and whispered, "Then why fight it?"

She tried to meet his eyes, but he had already turned to face the window with a smile upon lips that, not long ago, had enticed hers. He had wanted to kiss her. She knew it now as she knew it then, but he had chosen to wait for her.

Had her father ever shown such restraint? Before they were married, how often had her father tempted her mother with a kiss she should not return? Did he ever invite and wait? Or had he simply taken what he wanted?

Flickers of light skipped across Nathaniel's face as if vying with the shade for a chance to touch him. His lips rested in their perpetual upward tilt, and his eyes sparkled with their usual specks of light. Kelsey could see his confidence as clearly as she ever did, but this time, she became aware of a light in his countenance that she finally knew how to describe. She couldn't call it innocence. She was certain he had seen too much of the world to ever be naive, but there was a deep goodness inside him, a choice to meet troubles with laughter and hope.

He was nothing like her father.

As the carriage moved with its usual mix of sail and bounce, Kelsey felt the air around her split in half, leaving her falling in the space between. There was nothing to hold to but the thought of Nathaniel.

Never had she been more certain that she didn't want to lose him, but if she imagined more between them, something permanent, fear gripped her heart. If she tried to care . . . If she allowed herself a chance . . . She was still a Wickham. He was nothing like her father, but she was more like her mother than she ever wanted to be. Kelsey was certain her mother had clung to George Wickham, luring him into scandal as often as he had lured her.

Kelsey had drawn Nathaniel into her schemes too. She had used him for his kindness and convinced him her deceptions were justified. Would she know how to care about him without eventually causing him pain? Hadn't she already caused him pain? How would she learn to fight her selfishness and pride? She had no answers, no confidence in her abilities. Even when her intentions were sincere, her actions had been poorly chosen.

But if she tried to accept Nathaniel, if he was patient with her, was there a chance she could learn to truly love him as he deserved to be loved? The carriage stopped at the bottom of the path, and Kelsey knew she would need his help once more. Only this time, she didn't know how to ask for it.

As they climbed out of the carriage, they could tell something was wrong. The cottage door and one of the windows were swinging open. Cobbled stones had been pushed askew while jagged, wild ones had been tossed in their path. Inside was no better. Drawers and tables were overturned on the floor. Clothing and linens were tossed about, and every bit of food in the kitchen had been discarded on the table and floor where dishes laid cracked or shattered.

When Kelsey found a broken comb she had borrowed from Cissy, her hands began to shake. The danger had been close and very real. Kelsey found herself checking under things and looking suspiciously in the corners as if the culprit might be waiting for the right moment to strike. Her only consolation was that Cissy had been spared the trauma. Seeing their belongings spread and discarded by a stranger's hand tore viciously at Kelsey's confidence. Each new discovery of damage left her naked.

"Why would anyone bother with this old cottage?" Mrs. Wickham's voice was no louder than a hush.

With her breakfast quivering in her stomach Kelsey looked at the stairs and didn't think she could bring herself to face whatever the intruder had done above.

Nathaniel came to her side. "Would you like me to look upstairs for you?"

Before she could answer, a high-pitched creak sounded in the floorboards above. All eyes darted up. Footsteps. Someone was upstairs.

Nathaniel raised a finger to his lips and poised his hand above his pocket. Was he carrying a pistol? "Who's there?"

Kelsey shuddered to imagine what might come next. She looked around, wondering how she might defend herself this time. The fire iron was nowhere in sight.

"Oh dear!" cried a female's voice from upstairs. "Please! I mean no harm!" A familiar young lady ran down and stared at everyone with large, unblinking eyes.

"Lucia!" Kelsey gasped. "Oh, Lucia!"

"Kelsey!"

The girls ran and embraced one another.

"Oh, Lucia isn't it awful?" Kelsey pulled back and looked around, wiping the moisture out of her eyes.

"It's unthinkable! But you are safe?" Lucia gave Kelsey another hug before embracing Mrs. Wickham. "Oh, Aunt Lydia! I'm so relieved you are all right. Have you any idea what happened here?" Lucia then noticed Nathaniel.

"An intruder, apparently. Our friend, Nath— Mr. Worth," Kelsey gestured at Nathaniel as he dipped his head, "suspected the danger and invited us to stay at Thistledown Hall last night. It was a precaution, but obviously a wise one."

"We are very much obliged to Mr. Worth," Mrs. Wickham said. "He has protected us better than if we were his own family."

Kelsey cringed at the pointed look her mother gave Lucia, but Lucia either didn't notice or chose not to take offense, probably the latter.

"Come, Kelsey," Lucia said, taking her hand and leading her to the stairs. "I'll help you collect your belongings. You and your mother must come to Pemberley with me."

Pemberley, a word synonymous with perfection in these parts. It was exactly what Kelsey should have wanted, the chance to spend time with her dearest cousin and friend, but as she caught Nathaniel's eye on her way up, she was certain half her heart curled up at his feet and refused to budge. She had no right to intrude on his generosity any further, not after rejecting him, but to be pulled away right when she was hoping to mend her mistakes left her feeling robbed anew. Would circumstances always conspire against her?

She nearly tripped on linens discarded on the floor as she stepped into her room. Every drawer had been pulled out. The bed lay covered in feathers as if torn by a flock of angry geese. What would she have done if she had been in that bed when the intruder attacked? She would never be able to thank Nathaniel sufficiently for providing her and her mother a refuge.

"Kelsey," Lucia said gently, "I walked here this morning to see how you were faring after yesterday's visit. You seemed so unsettled, not only with Mr. Woodcox but with my father and I as well."

Kelsey considered telling Lucia everything she knew about Mr. Woodcox, but now that they had a moment to talk, there was only one thing she immediately wanted to say. "Lucia, when I first arrived here only to learn that you had just left... I can't tell you how disappointed I was." Her chin began to tremble. "Was it my fault? My family's, I mean? What with my mother's reputation and old grudges between our parents, I couldn't help but wonder."

"Oh, Kelsey! I didn't know you worried about that." Was Lucia's brow bending with guilt?

"Then why did you have to leave? What is it you aren't telling me?" She reached out and took Lucia's hand.

"Kelsey, I'm not sure what to say." Her voice grew smaller with each word. "I can no longer trust myself to discern . . ."

As more questions shouldered their way to the front of Kelsey's thoughts, her mother's voice broke through the floorboards.

"Kelsey! Lucia! I finished collecting my things ages ago!"

"One more minute, and we'll be right down!" Kelsey called, though a minute in silence passed rather quickly. "Lucia, no matter what you are afraid to say, you are still my dearest friend."

Wanting to restore their closeness, Kelsey resolved to tell her about Mr. Woodcox and her own fears, but Lucia spoke first.

"Then I must tell you. Yes, I must." Lucia's face crimsoned down to her neck. "We've never kept secrets from one another before, have we?" Still, she hesitated. "The reason for my leaving . . ." Emotions battled across her face until she appeared to come to a decision. "When Mr. Chatham and his sister arrived to stay with the Salaways, I invited them to Pemberley often, and I . . ." Her voice grew shaky. "I'm embarrassed to say I became fond of Mr. Chatham. At first, he was kind and attentive. His attentions were very flattering and I . . . Well, never mind. It soon became apparent he was not sincere. When my father understood his disposition and learned for himself how Mr. Chatham was attempting to get me alone with him, my father decided it was best if I went away for a time, especially since he and my mother were going to London."

"Mr. Chatham was trying to ensnare you? Motivated by your fortune, perhaps?"

Lucia's cheeks flared. "I believe he must have been, though I was too blind to see it at the time."

"I'm so sorry." Knowing Lucia's sweet disposition, it was not surprising to learn she had fallen prey to the scoundrel's charms. "Why did your parents leave for London? Could they not have waited a little while longer? At least, until my mother and sister and I were settled?"

"I don't know. My parents have been reluctant to discuss their reasons for going. I believe it was to help a friend, but they have not felt at liberty to say more. Kelsey, I'm so sorry."

Much to her embarrassment, a small laugh escaped Kelsey's lips. "Forgive me. It's not amusing at all, but I did think . . . So, the cause of your leaving had nothing to do with me or my mother? It wasn't to escape your wicked Wickham relatives?"

Lucia shook her head. "Of course not."

"Girls!" Mrs. Wickham called again. "I shall send Mr. Worth upstairs to fetch you both if you don't come down within the minute this time."

The girls hugged and laughed. Kelsey hurried to fill her trunk with anything worth keeping and looked around her tiny room one last time. "I'm sad to leave this little cottage. I really thought I could turn it into a home."

Lucia put her arm through Kelsey's. "There shall be no more fretting. We shall have a marvelous time together at Pemberley."

Chapter 26

*She had never seen a place for which nature had
done more, or where natural beauty had been
so little counteracted by an awkward taste.*

Jane Austen, *Pride and Prejudice*

*P*emberley.

Backed by a ridge of deep green forest and heralded by a swelling stream, it rose from the ground as if Nature herself approved of its existence. But in the shade of its trees along the path the carriage followed, it was only a word that rolled in Kelsey's stomach like a loose pebble.

Pemberley.

It was the fairy-tale castle of her childhood where she, like Cinderella, on rare visits had dreamed of a happily ever after. Now, several years later, she felt more like a mouse who didn't deserve to partake of the grandness within.

As the carriage carried her ever closer, the golden light from the setting sun set the house's stones aglow. Pemberley was still a fairy-tale, but it wasn't hers. Nathaniel would never call on her there. She felt certain he would never march through the trees on foot just to see if she was using the gloves he had given her. There would be no need for the rough work gloves at Pemberley, anyway, no need to pull weeds or perform any chore when there was an army of servants flocking about. Pemberley and Thistledown Hall might as well have been on different continents.

Kelsey recalled the look of betrayal in Nathaniel's eyes when she had told him she would no longer need to stay at Thistledown Hall and would be going with Lucia.

"It is natural you should want to be with your cousin," he said, but the disappointment in his voice was unmistakable.

"I wish we had more time today," was her pitiful attempt to express her feelings.

"And what would you do with that time, my lady?"

"I would start by helping you compile a guest list for your masquerade, but then I should very much like to explore Thistledown Hall for secret passageways and other convenient places to listen in on conversations."

After he gave her a short-lived laugh, they made all the arrangements to travel back to Thistledown Hall to collect their things while Lucia returned to Pemberley to inform the Darcys of what had happened. Lucia then rode back to Thistledown Hall for Kelsey and her mother. When they climbed into the sleek carriage marked with Pemberley's insignia and waved farewell, Kelsey felt Nathaniel's gaze holding onto her for as long as possible.

Strange, she thought, how drastically her feelings could shift over the course of a few days. Yet, now that she wanted to talk to Nathaniel about those feelings, the moment never came. Perhaps she had been right from the beginning. The Wickham inside her would always find a way to twist any love she could offer into something false and unsteady.

When the carriage reached Pemberley, Kelsey stared at the stone arched doorways, the columns, the raised terraces, and wished the ride had been longer. Did the Darcy's have to own such a smooth, efficient carriage on top of all they already possessed?

"There are my mother and father. Oh, and my brothers as well!" Lucia gestured out the window.

Kelsey could see her aunt and uncle standing ready to greet them along with their younger sons, Edward and Alexander. Mrs. Reynolds stood next to Aunt Elizabeth with her hands folded neatly in front of her.

"The great Darcys." Mrs. Wickham leaned close to Kelsey and whispered, "At least they have the decency to receive us properly this time. I'd forgotten how large Pemberley is." Her mother's eyes wandered up to the topmost windows and chimneys.

With the help of a footman, Mrs. Wickham stepped out first, followed by Lucia and Kelsey. To her surprise, there were no bows or curtsies, nothing that spoke of formality, only eager smiles, hurried embraces, and the general complaint that the time between visits had been much too long.

After Aunt Elizabeth kissed Mrs. Wickham's cheek, Uncle Darcy took Mrs. Wickham's hand and patted it just as a loving brother might do. Aunt Elizabeth took Kelsey's hand next and pulled her into a hug before placing a kiss on her cheek.

"My goodness, Kelsey, what a beauty you are! Why, it makes me feel rather old to think of my toddling niece all grown up."

"Thank you." Kelsey couldn't hide the surprise in her voice and doubted she hid it from her face when her uncle took her hand and welcomed her as well.

After Lucia hugged her parents and brothers, who shifted on their feet as if eager to run off, Mr. Darcy took his wife's hand. "Before we go inside, I believe Elizabeth has a surprise for you all."

They waited as Aunt Elizabeth hurried through the two large doors that had been left ajar. A few seconds passed, and a tall, dark-haired girl with jaunty curls ran outside and threw her arms around Kelsey.

"Cissy!" Kelsey hugged her as tightly as she could.

"My darling Cecilia!" their mother exclaimed, wrapping her arms around them both.

"Did we surprise you?" Cissy laughed through smiles and glistening eyes.

"Of course, you did!"

"On her way home from London, Aunt Lizzy went to collect the boys and then decided to spend a few days with Aunt Kitty as well. Since I've been missing you all terribly, we decided I would come home with her."

Mrs. Wickham took Cissy's face in her hands. "You've grown! Oh, and you're rosier than ever! I can't wait to hear all about your stay in Warlingham."

As Mrs. Wickham gushed over Cissy, and Lucia took her turn to greet her, Kelsey quietly thanked her aunt and uncle.

"After all that has happened, this is simply wonderful. Thank you."

"My wife and I were pleased to help." Mr. Darcy's smile shifted into a more serious expression. "Lucia told us about the awful scene at the cottage. I must say, I'm terribly shocked. My conscience never would have let me forget if you or your mother had been injured."

"Thank you, Uncle." Kelsey's voice sounded small compared to his. "I am relieved to say we are quite unharmed."

"Yes, I see. Well, I'm pleased to finally be able to receive you."

"It's an honor to be here." Kelsey didn't know what to make of him, and truthfully, he was looking at her as if he didn't know what to make of her, but her aunt saved her the trouble of finding more to say.

Aunt Elizabeth placed a hand on her shoulder. "You must be tired. Lucia and I can show you to your rooms, and I'll have some tea brought up."

Mrs. Wickham's eyes lit up. "How delightful that sounds! Why, I already feel as if I'm on holiday."

Kelsey was certain her uncle frowned at this declaration, but otherwise, the ease with which he escorted them inside and made plans to meet later for dinner helped Pemberley feel a touch more hospitable.

On their way to their rooms, Mrs. Reynolds recited mealtimes and other household routines as clearly as if she had rehearsed them. Kelsey tried to listen, but somehow, her attention always strayed toward the ceilings, which were framed with ornately carved moldings and painted with cherubs and scenes from mythology.

A slender hand reached hers and gave it a squeeze. "I was in awe the first time I came here too. Sometimes, I still stare at the ceilings and forget I live here."

Aunt Elizabeth's gaze was fixed upward just as Kelsey's had been. As they walked along, she could see the similarities between her aunt and Lucia, the same kind, discerning eyes, the same natural grace, and when she looked even closer, she was startled to see the same playful lift of brow that her mother always wore.

"I do hope you'll feel at home here, Kelsey."

Home. At the mere thought of the word, her throat tightened like a drying prune, and she was grateful her aunt didn't press her to speak. Barley Cottage had held the promise of home, but home was still a fairy tale Kelsey wished could be real. She had been uprooted and dragged from house to house so often over the years that she couldn't remember the last time she had ever felt like she was home. Besides the cottage, the closest she had yet felt to it had been at Thistledown Hall.

⁊⁊

Several days passed at Pemberley as comfortably as any Kelsey had ever passed before. With a room to herself and a maid who regularly came to stoke the fire and help her dress, Kelsey hadn't the slightest thing to complain about, except that Lucia was too generous with gowns and jewelry for which Kelsey had no use. And Nathaniel never visited.

She sometimes sensed a secret hiding beneath Lucia's conversation, something that kept her reserved and quiet, but since Kelsey guarded secrets of her own, she never pressed Lucia for answers. Even if she wanted to, there was hardly an ideal moment to talk openly. Lucia's music lessons, tutoring sessions, callers, and daily horseback rides took her away for most mornings and afternoons. Evenings were spent together with all the Darcys and Wickhams.

At least, Kelsey had Cissy again. With no need to perform her usual household chores and no excuse to escape to Thistledown Hall, Kelsey spent a great deal of time wandering the extensive galleries and gardens with Cissy.

"I wish you had joined us on our ride today, Kelsey." Cissy had forgotten to write about the riding lessons she had received in Warlingham. Kelsey wasn't at all surprised to learn that riding horses came naturally to Cissy. Nearly as tall as Kelsey now, Cissy still wore the riding habit Lucia had lent her that morning. They walked arm in arm along a shaded lane close to the woods behind the estate and let the balmy, rain-scented air fill their lungs. "There was a whole family of foxes by the stream."

"I'm glad you enjoyed yourself, but I prefer to walk."

"Kelsey?" Cissy frowned as she plucked a small dandelion. Even Pemberley, it would seem, was susceptible to the occasional weed. "Did you know Mr. Baxter called on Mother yesterday?"

"Of course, I knew. Why do you think I hid in the library all morning?"

Cissy bumped Kelsey with her shoulder and laughed. "Why didn't I follow you? I chose to endure his entire visit to avoid Edward and Alexander's constant teasing. I don't remember those two being quite so tiresome. Well, Mr. Baxter acted very upset to learn about the intruder." She plucked a few petals off the dandelion and let the breeze carry them away. "The more I hear him speak, the more certain I am that he has a terrible gambling habit."

"Yes, I've suspected as much." Kelsey regarded Cissy, whose eyes were as open and innocent as ever before, but there was a keenness about them that was new.

"And I don't think he really loves her, nor she him."

"I dare say you're right, but what makes you say so?"

Cissy dropped the stem of the flower. "Neither seem particularly comfortable in one another's company. I wonder whether they are simply enchanted with the idea of finding someone." Of all the things Cissy had said since returning home, Kelsey thought this was the most perceptive. "I wish Mother would stop encouraging him, especially when she still hopes to meet Captain Styles. Oh yes, I've heard all about *the letters*. I suppose she wants to preserve her options."

The clouds drifted silently above, oblivious to the many troubles below. The confession of Kelsey's folly sat on her tongue, but she swallowed it back, concluding it better to keep Cissy separated from the mess Kelsey had created.

"And have you noticed how much time Mother spends on making up old bonnets? Has she always done that? I don't recall her ever being so intent on them before."

Kelsey nodded. "It is a bit odd, isn't it? I didn't think she would continue to fuss over them at Pemberley, but at least it is time she isn't spending with Mr. Baxter."

"True." Cissy laughed again. "Oh, I've missed you, Kelsey. Mother has told me quite a few things about you and Mr. Worth." She bumped Kelsey's side with her hip.

"I've missed you too." Kelsey stretched her arm around Cissy's shoulder and bumped her back. "But I have nothing to say about Mr. Worth."

"Of course, you don't." The newly cultivated keenness flashed in Cissy's eyes. "I know you, Kelsey."

And Kelsey readily believed her. When Kelsey and Cissy returned to the house, Lucia had just finished her music lessons and had come outside looking for Kelsey. As Cissy wandered inside, Lucia took Kelsey by the arm.

"Kelsey! Just the person I wanted to talk with. Would you join me on a walk? Oh, but I see you are returning."

Kelsey hugged Lucia's arm. "Cissy was ready to go inside, but I was just thinking how refreshing it would be to have a little more time outside."

"Well, then." A rare, mischievous smile stole over Lucia's face. "Do you remember our secret hiding place?"

Though it had been years, Kelsey recognized the challenge in Lucia's question. "I certainly do."

And like that, both girls went racing across the green, lifting their hems as they flew down to the arched stone bridge by the stream where they ducked under, each trying to be the first to sit on the cement steps that led into the water.

"I've won," Kelsey laughed, barely sitting before Lucia. "This place looks just as it always did. We used to come here whenever we had a secret to share."

"Yes." Lucia paused to catch her breath. "Exactly. Which is why we're here." Lucia took out a handkerchief and began twisting it. "There is something I've been wanting to tell you. Oh, I'm so naive!"

"Tell me what, Lucia?" Whatever she was afraid to confess, it couldn't have been as terrible as the secrets Kelsey was keeping.

"I didn't tell you everything at the cottage the other day. I should have, but after Mr. Chatham . . . Oh, I'm so stupid!"

Kelsey gave her a stern look. "Come now. I'll have no such talk. You're not stupid. I'll not tolerate anyone talking badly about you, including you!"

"Very well." Lucia gave her a half-hearted smile. "Ever since seeing you with Mr. Woodcox, with his hand on your arm, I've been thinking about how to tell you." She took a shaky breath. "He tried to court me. When I was staying with the Bingleys. Just as I had fallen for Mr. Chatham, I fell for Mr. Woodcox. I believed he cared, but then I noticed how upset he was about losing Thistledown Hall. You see, it was his brother who sold it to Captain Styles. Mr. Woodcox didn't know until his brother's recent death. The house would have gone to him if it hadn't been sold. I began to see signs of his true motivations. If he could not have Thistledown Hall, he'd try for my fortune. So, I began to rebuff him. I told him I didn't want him to call on me anymore. He grew very angry and left for Lambton, swearing to claim what was rightfully his. I . . . I thought you should know."

Kelsey listened to the rippling murmurs of the water passing over the rocks that silently urged her to confide in Lucia as Lucia was confiding in her. She let her hand dip in the stream and watched how the water curved around her fingers. Finally, in a single hurried breath, she told Lucia that she suspected Mr. Woodcox to be the intruder.

"Heaven forbid! I've learned not to trust him, but what makes you suspect him of such a crime?"

"Well, he knew about . . ." Despite her good intentions, Kelsey could not yet bring herself to confess that Nathaniel had spent the night, and Mr. Woodcox knew. "He knew certain things he should not have known otherwise."

The water continued to ripple around her fingers. Could Lucia see past this oversimplified explanation and into Kelsey's thoughts? Lucia reached for a handful of pebbles and tossed them one by one in the water.

"Kelsey, I feel like such a dolt. I'm no judge of character at all. I don't know how I shall ever tell the difference between true love and the false sort."

Kelsey's ears tingled. Where had she heard those words before? "Come, now, Lucia. You'll find love. Your only flaw is that you see it everywhere, which isn't surprising considering your upbringing. You are surrounded by people who love you."

"Apparently, I'm susceptible to anyone who shows me an ounce of attention."

"A little patience is all you need, and perhaps a bit of experience, which I dare say these two men have given you, even if it wasn't at your choosing."

"You're right, but I shall never trust myself again." She reached out and took Kelsey's hand. "I shall follow your example. I shall never trust men again."

Kelsey stared at Lucia, stunned. Was that the example she was showing?

❧

The next morning, Kelsey did her best to remain out of sight. The seams of her mind were bursting with secrets and confessions, and she didn't think she could face anyone without revealing too much of her own burdens or hearing someone else's. All she wanted was an uneventful day wandering through the galleries. However, the dauntless Mrs. Reynolds easily discovered her.

"You have a visitor, Miss Wickham."

A visitor? *Nathaniel. Could it be Nathaniel?* Had he tromped through those trees to Pemberley after all? Perhaps he still wanted her help with the masquerade. Or perhaps he would renew his proposal. As she followed Mrs. Reynolds, she prepared the speech she would offer him, begging for his patience and help as she tried to love.

"Miss Clarice Wimpleton," Mrs. Reynolds announced as Kelsey entered the sitting room.

Clarice Wimpleton? Kelsey's mind sputtered as Miss Wimpleton glided toward her as smoothly as silk. Already, Clarice appeared more at home in the splendor of Pemberley than Kelsey did.

"Miss Wimpleton—"

"Clarice." She smiled warmly and kissed Kelsey on the cheek.

"Clarice. What a pleasure it is to see you again." Both ladies sat, and Kelsey laid her hands in her lap to keep from fidgeting. "I didn't realize you had returned."

"Neither did Nathaniel," she said with relish. "Until a few hours ago. I took him quite by surprise, and as you can see, I'm not the least bit sorry. A sister should be able to visit her brother whenever she likes, don't you agree? I arrived in West Yorkshire just in time to greet my friends and settle in, but it didn't feel right. I knew I needed to be here, so I told them so. I told them I needed to return to my brother and help him through one of life's dilemmas. Shame to waste the time and expense travelling, but when one realizes what needs to be done, one must get back on course, no matter how long it takes. Don't you agree?"

"Yes of course. So, you heard about Mr. Woodcox, then?"

"Yes, I did. He sounds like a giant oaf to me, but that isn't why I returned."

"It isn't?"

"Certainly not. I came to help Nathaniel and *you.*" She sat perfectly straight as her eyes pinned Kelsey.

"Me?" Her suspicions were instantly raised. "That is kind of you, but did you know about—"

"Yes. I always know, Kelsey dear." Clarice reached out and placed her hand on Kelsey's. "I know your charming cottage was ransacked. I know you are not engaged to my brother, and I know he is heartbroken over it."

Kelsey's lower lip trembled.

"I see you are at a loss for words, so I will be frank, as I always am. You are in love with my brother and have unnecessarily complicated things. What a goose you are!" She gave Kelsey's leg a light swat with the back of her hand.

Kelsey's cheeks flared until the warmth spread throughout her whole face, down her neck, and into her stomach. Hot tears began to spill down her face.

"You don't need to say anything to me, but you will have to tell him how you feel. Otherwise, your heart will grow ill." Clarice rubbed Kelsey's back and offered her a lacy handkerchief.

"I don't know what to do." Kelsey accepted the handkerchief and blotted her eyes.

Clarice lifted Kelsey's chin and smiled. "I know. That's why I'm here. If you follow my counsel, we'll have everything sorted at the masquerade."

Chapter 27

By you, I was properly humbled.

Jane Austen, *Pride and Prejudice*

The misty air swept through the grounds of Thistledown Hall and around Kelsey like whispered secrets as she stepped off the carriage and onto the gravel path lined with waving torches. Pebbles pressed and shifted against her thin dance slippers as if deciding where they fit. The main doors of the manor were spread like beckoning arms, and even from the distance of the carriages, Kelsey could hear violins streaming on the breeze.

She patted her hair and the ribbon that held her mask in place. Nothing was loose, but she was more accustomed to her own hasty efforts to pin her curls than the skill of Lucia's maid. The pale, sea-green gown she wore, borrowed from Lucia's hoard, shimmered in the torchlight and flowed around her hips like water as she walked. Kelsey would have been too embarrassed to select such a fine gown for herself, but Lucia had insisted.

Lucia stepped down from the carriage next, in a blushing peach gown. "How enchanting!" She took Kelsey's arm. "I've never seen this old manor look so lively, but don't worry. I will be on my guard tonight. No matter which gentleman shows interest in me, I shan't believe him."

Kelsey frowned. A few months ago, she would have heartily agreed with this tactic, but now she wasn't certain Lucia's promise would serve her very well.

"Cissy will miss this," Kelsey whispered to herself, thinking how much Warlingham had benefited her.

As windows winked coquettishly from lights within, Kelsey laughed to think of Clarice arriving unannounced and taking charge of all the preparations for the ball. Kelsey had come that night fully intending to follow Clarice's advice to declare her feelings to Nathaniel, but now that she stood at the doors, her resolve weakened into a question of whether she would even mention them. If Clarice kept her promise, she would succeed in convincing Nathaniel to broach the subject first.

Mrs. Wickham alighted from the carriage next, looked at the manor, and clapped her hands together. "Finally." Taking Kelsey's arm, she leaned close. "You must alert me the moment you learn anything about the captain. I don't know how I shall recognize him, but I intend to take full advantage of the night." Even through masks, Kelsey was certain her mother winked.

"If the captain is, indeed, your devoted admirer, could we not simply wait and see what happens?"

"Wait and see? I'm not waiting for anything. The captain's notice is worth keeping. Mark my words, Kelsey, I shall find him. I'm not going to sit idly by while another lady steals his attentions away."

Kelsey bit her lip. She should have known her mother would feel that way. It wasn't enough to simply be admired. Her mother had her heart set on marriage, nothing less. Now that the captain was her target, there would be no stopping her. Humiliation was inevitable.

Unless Kelsey did something to prevent it. She tugged at her gloves and fidgeted with her fan. Was it time to confess the true nature of the letters? Of course, it was. The time for truth had come ages ago, and Kelsey knew she was late. She took full responsibility for allowing her mother to harbor baseless hopes for the captain, but if Kelsey hadn't done what she had, her mother would already be planning her wedding with Mr. Baxter.

A chill raced across her neck. Would her mother accept Mr. Baxter once she realized there was no admirer?

The Darcys' second carriage pulled up next. Her aunt and uncle would be there this time to witness whatever scenes her mother made. What would her uncle do if he did not approve of her behavior? If only Kelsey hadn't waited until now to decide what to do. Something had to be done that very night. She would have to break her mother's heart, gently, if such a thing were possible.

Mr. Darcy stepped out of the carriage first, then took his wife's hand, gazing at her as if they were the only two people in the world. Mr. Darcy had refused to wear a mask, but that only ensured that guests would know he had honored Nathaniel with his presence.

With her mother before her, Lucia at her side, and her aunt and uncle behind her, Kelsey walked into the ballroom, already asway with music and dancing. Gowns sparkled like gems in the candlelight while laughter thrived under the anonymity of the masks. Would Nathaniel recognize her among so many? If he still cared for her as deeply as he had a few weeks ago, surely, he would find her. At least, she hoped he would.

Lucia was asked to dance almost instantly, and moments later, Mrs. Wickham as well. Left with her aunt and uncle, Kelsey watched the dancing couples and wondered what to say.

Aunt Elizabeth smiled at Kelsey and playfully nudged her husband. "Well, husband, you ought to remark on the size of the room or the number of couples."

"I'm happy to oblige." His lips rose into a smile. "Which would you like me to comment on first?"

He took his time bringing his wife's hand to his lips. Their smiles spoke of an understanding that went beyond words. Then they looked at Kelsey.

"Perhaps we should ask our niece what she would most like to discuss. Kelsey, what do you think? Is it not lovely?" Her aunt gestured to the scene before them.

Kelsey did not have the chance to answer.

"I think Miss Wickham will be better able to form an opinion once she has danced." A tall gentleman with a silvery grey mask stood before her and offered his hand. "May I?"

Kelsey curtsied and excused herself from her aunt and uncle before taking the man's hand. As he led her to the dance floor, she glanced back and saw that her aunt and uncle continued to whisper and smile at each other. Kelsey's mother had often hinted that Aunt Elizabeth had married Mr. Darcy out of jealousy or a need to establish her superiority among her sisters, but after seeing so many tender moments between them, Kelsey could no longer believe it. She felt certain they had married for love.

"Are you enjoying yourself tonight, Miss Wickham?"

"Yes, thank you."

"You don't recognize me, do you?" he chuckled.

All she knew was he was not Nathaniel. The music began, and their steps fell into rhythm.

"You would not have recognized me had you not seen me with my aunt and uncle." She searched his masked face for a hint of recognition, but nothing came to her. Until he smirked. "Ah, I do believe I know you now, Mr. Chatham."

"I see there is no fooling you."

"Were you trying to fool me?" Kelsey bit her tongue for having answered so quickly, not meaning to encourage his banter.

He laughed again. "Not at all. There are much more interesting things I could do than try to fool you."

He stepped too close, and the music languished.

"What is that supposed to mean?"

"It means . . ." He paused as they spun around the other couples in the set. "Let's you and I take advantage of the anonymity of our masks and take a stroll through the trees." He lowered his voice. "Where we shan't be disturbed."

"I'll remain where I am, sir." She hoped he could see her scowl through her mask.

"No need to play coy with me. We're wearing masks, remember? You'll be lost in the crowd even to your scrupulous old uncle."

"Sir, let me be clear. Mask or no, I have no intentions of strolling through the trees with you."

He tsked. "You're not living up to the name of Wickham, you know."

"I don't think that is a bad thing." Kelsey considered leaving him in the middle of the dance.

Pulling her in for the next spin, he lowered his voice again. "I know very well there is more basis to the rumors than you let on."

Kelsey breathed through her nose and counted the beats of music as they dragged on.

Mr. Chatham pressed her hand firmly. "What's the point in bearing gossip if you don't have your share of amusement? Come. Come with me." He gestured with his head toward the gardens. "I'll make it worth your time."

"Mr. Chatham, no—"

He was no longer following the steps but was now pulling her away from the couples. "People will talk regardless, so why not? I'll teach you just how enjoyable rumors can be."

Kelsey stomped on his toe as forcefully as she could, and Mr. Chatham dropped her hand, grunting. The dancing couples momentarily stared and stumbled to keep rhythm.

"Oh, dear, was that your foot?" Kelsey put her hand to her mouth. Then for good measure, she stomped on his foot again. "That is the only answer you will receive from me tonight."

Mr. Chatham grimaced and cursed under his breath.

Just before the music ceased, Kelsey slipped into the thickness of the crowd. Much to her benefit, the green dress she had borrowed from Lucia was a popular choice of color among the ladies that evening. If she had been able to wear her pearlescent gown, she would have been much too easy for Mr. Chatham to find again.

Still hoping to recognize Nathaniel, she searched the masked faces, certain she would know him if she saw him, but she couldn't find him or Clarice.

At a light tap on her shoulder, she turned to face a tall gentleman with broad shoulders and a steel grey mask. His black coat was of a fine make but rather plain compared to the other gentlemen in attendance. The lines around his mouth were firm but not unkind, and the few streaks of grey in his dark blonde, nearly brown hair gave him a dignified air.

"May I have the next dance, miss?"

A glance over her shoulder showed Mr. Chatham scowling while pushing his way through the crowds to draw closer.

"Certainly." She took the gentleman's arm and joined the couples who were already lining up.

"I apologize for my impertinence," he said with a bow. "Even at a private ball, I wouldn't have approached you without an introduction, but I couldn't help but overhear what that man was saying to you."

Kelsey stiffened as she guessed his meaning. She should have been used to it by now, the gossip, the assumptions, but dealing with presumptuous men was always difficult.

"As I told that man, I have no interest—"

"No, no. Please don't misunderstand me. I asked you to dance to prevent him from harassing you further."

"Oh." Kelsey relaxed a tiny bit. "Thank you. May I have your name, sir?"

This time, he stiffened. "Perhaps at a later time, if you will forgive me once again."

"Very well."

He led her to the floor, and after exchanging common pleasantries, they danced without speaking. "Tell me," he eventually asked, "what do you make of the rumors? Do you believe the captain to be alive or dead?"

Kelsey cleared her throat and considered how to answer. "What is this masquerade for if not to welcome the captain?"

"Why, indeed?" he said more to himself. "Are you well acquainted with Mr. Worth?"

"Yes," Kelsey answered, suddenly wary of the man. Two possibilities ran through her mind. Either he was a friend of Mr. Woodcox, trying to glean information, or he was the captain himself.

"What do people generally think of him? Does he conduct himself well?"

"Yes, very well. I believe he is well respected." Kelsey tried to discern the look of the man behind the steel grey mask. Was he friend or foe? The man gave nothing away and spoke little for the rest of the dance.

When the music ended, instead of parting ways, the gentleman remained at her side.

"May I return you to your party?"

"That's not necessary. I—"

"Kelsey! There you are!" Her mother approached and linked arms with her. "I have the most exciting news." Noticing Kelsey's dance partner, she stopped herself. "Forgive me. Was I interrupting?"

"Not at all, madam," the gentleman replied. "I was about to escort this young lady to her party, but I see that is no longer necessary." For the first time, Kelsey saw his mouth hint at a smile.

"How kind of you, sir." Mrs. Wickham blushed beneath her mask.

"You look rather familiar, madam."

"Familiar?" she lilted. "Even with a mask?"

"I believe so." He only regarded her, never asking for a name, never giving his. With a bow he said, "I must excuse myself, but if I see you again, and you are willing to risk my acquaintance, I should like a dance with you."

"Of course." Mrs. Wickham curtsied with the lightness of the music, then watched him walk off, weaving his way through the crowds. "My, what luck we're having tonight." Tugging on Kelsey's arm, she said, "I've found him, Kelsey. I found him!"

A knot twisted deep in Kelsey's stomach. "Who did you find, Mother? Mr. Baxter?"

"No. Well, yes actually. I did just speak with him. I told him once and for all that I couldn't accept his offer."

"Really?" Kelsey's excitement came unbidden. It was the best news she had heard in ages.

"You could pretend to be a little disappointed." Her mother waited, but Kelsey could do no such thing. "Regardless, the real news is that I have found Captain Styles."

Even behind the mask, her mother's youth shone with an excitement for life and love that had never been hampered by the setbacks of life. How Kelsey wanted, for once, to allow her own spirits that same freedom to shine and burst from within, the freedom to flow through her entire being with nothing to hinder her joy. What would that feel like? All she knew was how to flatten those feelings to keep them under her thumb, and unfortunately, it was her responsibility now to flatten those feelings in her mother.

"Show me," Kelsey said, needing to see for herself who her mother had found.

Mrs. Wickham pulled Kelsey along, maneuvering through the crowds to a corner near a grand fireplace. The warmth emanating from the fire amidst all the people was too much for her, and she pulled out her fan.

"Do you see those two gentlemen over there?" Her mother tilted her head in their direction.

By the fireplace were two finely dressed men, one wearing a black mask lined with gold trim and the other a silky blue mask lined in silver. They were of a similar build and height. She knew Nathaniel right away to be the man in the blue mask, but she didn't know who the other was, though they did share similarities.

"How do you know he's the captain?"

Even with the mask, her mother managed a look that told Kelsey she was being very tiresome. "Those two men have been directing all the servants. It is obviously our friend, Mr. Worth, and who else but the captain?"

Who, indeed? Kelsey knew why the masquerade had been thrown, and it was not because the captain had arrived. Or was it? Was it possible he had recently arrived, conveniently in time for the ball?

"I need you to speak to them, Kelsey."

"What?"

"Oh, don't look so shocked. Mr. Worth is a friend, is he not? It won't be at all improper to approach him in a ballroom." Mrs. Wickham took Kelsey by the arms and pointed her toward the men. "I want you to greet Mr. Worth and naturally weave into the conversation the fact that I am here. After a few minutes, I'll walk over."

Her mother's mounting anticipation was painful to witness. "What if he's not the captain?"

"Go on, Kelsey. Cissy would do it if she were here."

"Cissy had the good sense to stay home this time because she is too young."

"Stop acting like a child. Go!"

Mrs. Wickham gave Kelsey a push toward the men. Her mind raced as she thought of what to say. Was this the moment for truth?

"Lady Kelsey." Nathaniel smiled and dipped his head.

"Good evening, Miss Wickham," said the other gentleman, bowing low. "Isn't this a magnificent sight? In all my years, I've never seen the likes of it. Worth, here, certainly knows how to entertain, doesn't he?"

Kelsey blinked. "Joseph?" Until she'd heard his voice, she never would have recognized him as the man in the black and gold mask. His clothes were sleek and modern, his hair fashionably combed and curled. His previously thin form had filled out since that day she had seen him begging in the market. Whether it was the clothes or not, Kelsey didn't know, but he stood straighter than before. Working for Nathaniel was serving him well.

"Not so loud, Kelsey," said Nathaniel. "Joseph is playing the role of my special guest tonight." He looked at her meaningfully, but she already understood. "You look stunning, by the way. How are you this evening?"

Kelsey was more timid to receive his open compliment than she would have expected. "I am well. And I agree with . . . your friend. Everything is breathtaking."

"Don't forget," Nathaniel said in his deep, waltzing voice, "that one of my main objectives tonight is to dance with you. Will you do me the honor of accepting my hand . . ." He smiled and let the words hang before adding, "For the next dance?"

Kelsey nearly lost all sense of thought. Nathaniel knew what he was doing, phrasing his request in just those words, but she forced her focus back to her present purpose.

"Listen." She addressed them both. "My mother over there, in the gold mask, thinks that you," she pointed to Joseph, "are the captain. She will be approaching us any second. There's no time to explain, but you must play the part. She believes the captain has been writing her letters with the intent to court her. I've encouraged her in this belief, I'm afraid, but since she has now rejected Mr. Baxter, there is no need for her admirer to keep up his attentions."

Nathaniel's jaw dropped. "What happens when Captain Styles does return?"

"I suppose I must face that fact when he comes."

"No, Kelsey, you must face it now. Tell your mother the truth."

"I . . . I want to, but I need time to think." What kind of scene would it create if she told her mother the truth right then? Images of tears and insults and tantrum-like yelling flashed through her mind. No, Kelsey wasn't ready. She couldn't do it. Not yet. "This is a disaster! But please, Joseph. Don't break her heart. Simply tell her that you fear you will never be free to marry. Say that a part of you will always admire her, but you would not be a gentleman if you kept her waiting for you when your duty lies elsewhere."

"Wait!" cried Joseph. "Are you asking me to pretend to be courting your mother? Then end it all the very next moment?" He sounded absolutely appalled.

"I certainly am." Kelsey would be firm on this point. "Please, it must be—"

"Kelsey, there you are, darling." Her mother was already at her side.

Kelsey looked each man in the eye, pleading but daring them to object. "Mother, you already know Mr. Worth, so allow me to introduce you to . . ." With a great inhale of air, Kelsey decided she would speak the truth after all, at least on this one point. She would introduce the man as Mr. Allen Joseph. Her mother would have to accept her mistake.

Unfortunately, Kelsey was too slow.

"Captain Styles," Mrs. Wickham lilted.

All eyes were riveted on her hand, which she held out in greeting, not to Joseph, but to Nathaniel. Kelsey realized that, in the low light of flickering candles, it would have been easy to confuse the two without knowing their differences as well as she did. Had they dressed so similarly on purpose?

Nathaniel awkwardly took her hand and bowed over it but spoke not a word.

"How wonderful it is to meet you at last." Mrs. Wickham lowered into a graceful curtsey. "There is much to say to one another, is there not?"

"Ahem," Joseph coughed, though Kelsey suspected it was to cover a laugh while Nathaniel stood dumbstruck.

"Mr. Worth," said Mrs. Wickham turning to Joseph, "thank you so much for the invitation tonight. I am enjoying myself immensely."

Kelsey couldn't think of a single social engagement her mother hadn't claimed to enjoy immensely, Mr. Baxter's disastrous dinner included.

Lowering her lashes, Mrs. Wickham turned to Nathaniel. "Shall we, Captain?"

Kelsey nodded, silently urging him to comply.

"Of course." His words came out raspy, but he offered his arm to Mrs. Wickham. As he led her away, he glanced at Kelsey and Joseph over his shoulder.

Kelsey clasped hands in prayer-like fashion and mouthed, *please*, to Nathaniel. His mouth was set in a firm line, his shoulders stiff and squared. Her mother whispered something to him, and he whispered back. The two then exited through the open terrace doors.

From where she stood, Kelsey could see them heading toward the edge of the fountain. The shrubbery behind it was dark and thick, a perfect place for eavesdropping. She knew exactly how she could position herself there without being noticed.

Off she ran.

ᏋᎿᏋ

Kelsey crouched low, grateful Nathaniel hadn't pruned the tree-like bushes that now gave her cover. A few branches snagged at her hair and gown, and the ground beneath her squished with each step. Hopefully, Lucia would forgive her for getting her dress and slippers dirty.

The stream that fed the fountain burbled softly and blended with the faded violins. Bending the branches ever so slightly, Kelsey was able to see Nathaniel and her mother. They walked slowly and didn't speak. A leaf brushed Kelsey's nose, and for a moment, the worst of her fears was that she might sneeze and give away her hiding place. Not even Nathaniel knew she had followed him and her mother out to the gardens. She leaned in close to make sure he accomplished the dreaded task.

"What an exquisite night," Mrs. Wickham sighed. With the golden mask covering the few creases around her eyes, she could have easily passed for a girl not yet twenty. She could have passed for Kelsey.

"It is an exquisite night indeed, Mrs. . . ."

"Lydia."

"Lydia." Nathaniel choked on the name.

"I can't tell you how marvelous it is to finally have this moment with you, Captain Styles."

Kelsey rolled her eyes at her mother's coyness and watched closely for Nathaniel's reaction.

Finally, he spoke. "There is something I must tell you."

Mrs. Wickham smiled demurely. "There is, indeed, much to say."

A light tickle moved up Kelsey's arm. It was too dark to see what it was, but she brushed it away as quietly as she could and tried not to imagine what kind of spider it might have been.

"As you are aware . . ." Nathaniel cleared his throat, looking anywhere but at Mrs. Wickham. "I have been writing letters to you." Which wasn't a complete lie.

"They have meant so much to me," she sniffled.

Oh no. Kelsey held her breath. Her mother was crying, and judging by the way Nathaniel's lips pressed together, he had noticed.

"Forgive me," Mrs. Wickham waved her fan. "I hardly ever cry. It's only that your letters . . ." She pulled out a lacy handkerchief and lifted her mask to blot her eyes. "You see, they, or rather, *you* have made me so happy."

Even from a short distance behind the trees, Kelsey could see Nathaniel's jaw tremble.

"I . . . I have?"

"Yes," Mrs. Wickham spoke softly, straightening her mask back in place. "I know it's silly of me to place so much significance on a few notes, but . . . Oh, you need not look so worried," she laughed lightly. "I don't expect a proposal tonight."

Kelsey pinched her eyes shut. Did her mother expect a proposal later?

"I know it was only a few rushed lines, but they gave me hope at a time when I didn't think I had anything left to hope for."

"They did?" Nathaniel's voice wavered.

Kelsey had never heard her mother admit to losing hope. She had always seemed so cheerful.

"They certainly did. I don't wish to bore you with details, but I've experienced such loss and hardship these past several years. I'm sure you've heard the rumors. I've made so many mistakes."

Kelsey covered her mouth to stifle a groan. Not only was her mother making this conversation difficult, but she had just stepped right in front of Kelsey, blocking her view. She thought Nathaniel might have mumbled something, but she hadn't heard clearly enough. Slowly, she edged her way to another overgrown shrub, one closer to Nathaniel which offered a better view.

"Did you hear something?" Her mother looked at the bush Kelsey had just been hiding in.

Kelsey instinctively shrunk back and held her breath. Nathaniel peered into the shrubs and trees, and for a moment, she was certain he could see through them to where she crouched in the darkness.

"A cat, perhaps? I imagine you must be feeling quite the chill out here. We should return to the ballroom before the other guests miss us."

No! Kelsey needed him to end the charade with her mother. He couldn't leave yet! He hadn't said half the things she needed him to say.

"Wasn't there something you wanted to discuss with me?"

Bless her mother for remembering!

"Yes, indeed." Nathaniel looked around again. Kelsey could hear him take a deep breath. Keeping to the cover of the bushes, she edged closer to the fountain to hear him more clearly. "You see," he began, "writing those letters . . . Forgive me. I'm not sure how to go on."

Kelsey hung on his words, clasping the branches in front of her and flexing her toes within her dampened slippers.

"How did those letters make you feel?" Mrs. Wickham gently pressed.

"How did they make me feel?" Nathaniel's voice grew pensive. "Until recently, I'd been so caught up in my duties with hardly a soul I could turn to. Then coming here and seeing that lovely, innocent face . . . When I think of the lady I was addressing at the time . . ." As his voice trailed, Kelsey saw him smile to himself, and an uncomfortable intuition wiggled in her gut. "I couldn't help but feel hopeful myself."

Oh, no, Kelsey thought. *He's forgetting himself! He's forgetting who he's with!*

Nathaniel reached for a fallen leaf on the edge of the fountain and spun it between his fingers. "I hadn't even realized my hope was suffering until I found it again in those moments. They were simple moments, really, but those eyes, that cinnamon-honey hair, and . . ."

Kelsey's hair could be described that way. It was lighter than her mother's, which was a deep, rich brown.

"That smile," Nathaniel sighed as he gazed at nothing in particular. "Those glimpses of possibility, of imagining what might be between us . . ."

Her mother took the smallest step closer to him. "They gave you hope."

"Yes, hope," he said, more to himself. "I don't know what will happen between us." Nathaniel looked at the sky, swirling with stars and moonlight. "But I know my feelings are strong."

Kelsey broke out in a cold sweat. He wasn't talking about her mother at all, and he was no longer playing the role she had asked him to play. Oh, what was he doing? If she didn't do something soon, he would ruin everything.

"In fact . . ."

Oh, please, no!

"If I am being true to my feelings, I would have to say . . ."

Nathaniel, please! Kelsey screamed in her thoughts. She had to do something. She had to act quickly.

"That I lo—"

At the risk of being detected, Kelsey reached out, just past the bushes, took hold of Nathaniel's coat tails, and yanked on them as hard as she could. He lurched back with a jerk, swaying as his hands searched for something to hold to, and fell sideways into the fountain. Water leapt around his tall form with a splash that sent several birds flapping frantically and squawking into the night. Kelsey stepped far back into the shrubs, hoping Nathaniel hadn't been injured.

"Captain Styles!" Mrs. Wickham exclaimed. "Are you all right?"

Forgetting to move slowly, Kelsey drew close enough to see Nathaniel pulling himself from the fountain and rising to his feet. He was completely drenched but otherwise appeared unharmed. "I'm all right. Quite all right. Forgive me, Mrs. Wickham. It seems our time together has come to an end." He raised his arms up to demonstrate the water dripping from him. "I was forgetting myself as I spoke, and I beg your forgiveness. As you can see, I'm in need of dry clothes. I must retreat inside."

"Oh, Captain!" cried Mrs. Wickham. "Must you run off so quickly?" The dismay in her voice washed over Kelsey in wintry waves. "I feel there is a great deal more to say to one another."

"You're right, but I . . . I'm not . . . I . . ." He shook his head. "I do apologize, Mrs. Wickham. I'll accompany you back to the doors, but I'm afraid I mustn't stay out here dripping, and I can't go into the ballroom like this."

The view from the bushes did not allow Kelsey to see them walk back to the terrace doors, but she assumed Nathaniel would then go around to the side of the house to enter through the servants' door. If she was right, she might be able to catch him there.

She sprinted through the trees, making all the leaves shuffle in her wake as she navigated the darkened paths to the side of the house. Before long, she heard Nathaniel's wet footsteps squishing in the grass and saw his shadowed form striding toward the small side door. Kelsey was grateful they were out of view from any guests that might also be walking on the terrace or arriving at the front in their carriages.

"Nathaniel!" she called out, running toward him.

He paused, ripped off his mask to reveal a dark glower, then continued walking.

"Nathaniel," she cried, struggling for breath. "I'm so sorry about the fountain, but I had to do it. You were about to ruin everything."

He turned to face her with eyes more heavily laden with sadness than she had ever seen before. "I'm sorry, Kelsey. Your mother . . . I didn't want to hurt her or humiliate her. I should have known this was all a mistake. I've been such a fool! Did you hear the things she was saying?"

"I heard all of it!" Her frustration rose to the surface, impossible to ignore. "Do you realize how much worse you almost made things? Why, it sounded as if you were about to declare your love for her!"

He reached out and took her hand, though he hardly stepped closer.

"I don't know what happened. Wearing that mask, you two look so similar. I was thinking of the first time I helped you write a letter. In fact, every time I wrote a letter, I thought of you. When I said those things just now, I was still thinking of you."

A stillness quieted everything around them. His hand was timid with hers, yet she could feel its strength. She gave him a reassuring squeeze, knowing the moment had come to confess her feelings. It was time to let him know she was ready to make amends and demonstrate how much she cared, but before the words could take shape, he pulled away and turned his back to her.

"Nathaniel?" A chill crept over her skin, through her muscles, and down to her very bones, shaking her insides like a leaf.

"The truth is, Kelsey, this charade has gone too far. I wanted to help you, to be your friend, but my hope was that you would be a friend to me as well if not something dearer. I believe you tried, but I can see you don't put your heart in it. What you put me through tonight . . . Kelsey, that was unbearable. When you rejected my proposal, I refused to believe you didn't care, no matter how much your words hurt, but now . . ." His voice became as rough as tree bark. "I now see that you were right. You and I would never have suited one another." He glanced at her over his shoulder and steeled his eyes. "If you cared for me at all, you would release me from this ridiculous scheme and tell your mother the truth."

He walked through the door and let it close behind him, leaving Kelsey gasping for breath.

A frosty breeze shuffled around her ankles and up her arms, chilling her heart to the core. Kelsey's toe hit a rock as she strained to see the steps before her, making it throb with an ache that was nothing compared to the searing pain in her chest. The sounds of violins had completely faded, and the half-moon cast a pitiful, sullen glow, barely enough to keep her from straying off the road entirely.

All Kelsey could do was walk and walk as she waited for the pain to lift, but no matter how far she travelled or how long she waited, the pain only worsened. She was no longer sure whether she was still on the path to Pemberley or had wandered into stranger realms where regret and hurt would plague her forever.

When the steady clacks of carriage wheels approached from behind, she shook herself from her morbid musings and scurried behind a tree to avoid being seen.

Let them pass quickly.

The carriage wheels slowed, and she held her breath. If someone from the masquerade saw her walking alone in the darkness, there was no telling what tales would be spinning about her the next day. *The way of the Wickham,* she cried as she wiped her nose on her handkerchief.

"Kelsey Wickham!"

Like a springing reflex, Kelsey flattened herself behind the tree, closed her eyes, and told herself she had only imagined hearing her name.

"Kelsey! How dare you try to hide! I see you as clearly as I see my own hand!"

Knowing exactly whose voice it was, Kelsey peeked out. Clarice Wimpleton's head protruded from the carriage window, the feathers in her hair fluttering in the wind like a bird of prey ready to swoop. With a fierce scowl, she pointed at Kelsey. "You come here and climb into this carriage this instant. I'll have no arguing!"

Kelsey finally understood why Nathaniel cowered at his sister. Every word she spoke conveyed the firm surety of an angered sovereign. It would not do to resist. Kelsey wiped her eyes and ran to the carriage and stepped in with the help of one of the towering footmen.

Tears spilled down Kelsey's cheeks, but what did it matter when she couldn't meet Clarice's eye?

"Kelsey, I am not one to lose my temper no matter what Nathaniel has told you, but I am not one to trifle with at the moment. What were you thinking? Running off by yourself in the middle of the night! Do you realize the danger that could have come upon you had I not found you in time? What if the intruder who broke into your cottage found you? Or some other man lacking in morals? You have nothing to defend yourself with except that soggy handkerchief." She yanked Kelsey's handkerchief out of her hand, threw it on the carriage floor, then fumbled in her reticule for a fresh one. "Here. Take this."

Kelsey did her best to dry her eyes. Clarice had very good reason to be upset if she knew about the scene in the garden, but was it true she also cared about Kelsey's safety? Even in her tempest of emotions, Kelsey was softened by Clarice's thought for her.

"I didn't mean to upset you, Clarice. I've never had the luxury to worry about my safety, but truly, I'm grateful you found me."

Clarice's glower didn't lighten in the slightest. "I have half a mind to march you right back to Thistledown Hall to apologize to my brother, but I suppose it won't do tonight. Why, I thought the plan was for you to declare your feelings for him, not . . . not . . . create a new debacle!"

"So, you know about—"

"Yes. I always know. Haven't I already explained that?"

"I had no time to think, Clarice! If you knew my mother . . . if you knew how I've deceived her . . ."

"Deception," Clarice bit down on the word, "is a plague on the soul. We must rid you of it immediately. Now, go on."

Kelsey hardly knew what she was saying. It was only in the middle of her story that she realized she was completely confiding in Clarice, giving her a history of her mother moving their family about to avoid men and search out new ones. She described Mr. Baxter and how desperate she was to help her mother see his flaws by providing her a comparison. She explained the letters she had convinced Nathaniel to help her write, then finished her story with the scene between Nathaniel and her mother who thought he was the captain.

Kelsey sat very still when her story ended, thinking they must be nearing Pemberley, when Clarice leaned forward and laughed.

Unleashing her fan, she waved it at her face and continued to laugh. "Oh, forgive me, Kelsey. That's the most remarkable, horribly entertaining story I've heard in ages. You and Nathaniel both deserve a sound lashing!" She laughed a minute more, then straightened her back. "Ahem, yes. Well, enough of that. I'm quite myself again." The carriage pulled up to the entrance of Pemberley as Clarice's commanding countenance uncharacteristically drooped with her shoulders. "I suppose it's my fault my brother is so compliant. I threw countless fits as a child until he obeyed my commands. He's always been eager to please the ones he loves. How he must hate that I've returned."

"Oh, Clarice!" Kelsey took her hand. "Don't spare another thought on that. I'm sure he loves you. You're the only family he has."

"I know," she whispered. "I've always known."

Kelsey stared at the house dimly flickering with lights within. She really would love having Clarice for a sister. "Thank you for conveying me here. Please let my mother know where I am when you return."

"Yes, of course."

"And please let Nathaniel know I'm dreadfully sorry." She ended on a hiccup, but just before she stepped out, Clarice took her arm.

"That I shall not do, Kelsey. You must tell him yourself."

"But I'm sure he despises me right now."

"Whether or not he does is irrelevant. You shall tell the man you love the truth. Along with everyone else."

Chapter 28

I hoped to obtain your forgiveness, to lessen your ill opinion,
by letting you see that your reproofs had been attended to.

Jane Austen, *Pride and Prejudice*

$\mathcal{K}$elsey hardly left her room in the south wing of Pemberley over the next several days. The truth, though cleansing in principle, cut deeply into her heart, and the fear of what she had to do, of what she had to confess, prowled through her thoughts like a cat on the hunt.

It was no help to suddenly have every lady in the house knocking on her door to inquire after her health, but Kelsey couldn't bring herself to speak more than a few words to anyone. She kept thinking of two things, the awful moment Nathaniel's face filled with utter disappointment in her and, for some reason she couldn't explain, the horrid painting of her parents, which her mother had brought to Pemberley.

Kelsey imagined their distorted smirks and felt that even they, the notorious Wickhams, did not approve of her recent mistakes. Such thoughts only made her sink deeper into her bed. What did it mean for her to be a disappointment in such a family?

A knock on the door pounded at her thoughts.

"Kelsey!" It was Cissy. "Do you want to come to the stream with us? Lucia says she knows a spot where the deer like to drink, and the boys are bringing a picnic for us. Doesn't that sound perfect today?"

"No, thank you," Kelsey called through the door.

"Please come, Kelsey!"

"Let me be!"

Another fierce, more insistent knock answered her this time.

"Kelsey!" Her mother's voice was surprisingly stern. "This moping has gone on long enough, don't you think?" A key rattled in the lock, and her mother opened the door. "You go ahead, Cissy. I'll join you later." Her mother came to the edge of the bed and laid a hand on Kelsey's shoulder. "Come now, Kelsey, what is bothering you? You haven't spoken hardly a word to me since the ball. Are you upset with me?"

"No." Kelsey's voice could barely be heard from her pillow.

"Did something happen between you and Mr. Worth?" Her mother waited. "I can tell something happened. I'm your mother."

Kelsey raised her head and caught sight of her splotchy face in the looking glass across the room. "I want to leave."

"Yes, I'm glad to hear it. Get up. Let's fix your hair, and we'll leave your room at once."

"No, I want to leave this place. I want to leave Pemberley and Barley Cottage, all of it. I want to relocate somewhere far away and never return."

"You don't mean that."

"Yes, I do!"

Her mother released a long sigh. "Oh, Kelsey. It's not that simple. I'm afraid our funds, being what they are—"

"Do not pretend to take an interest in our funds. If you had been jilted by Mr. Baxter, we would already be packing our things in crates and preparing to catch the next stagecoach. We've moved our family whenever you've had the slightest whim. Now I beg you to consider my feelings. I can't tolerate this place any longer. The people here are ridiculous. We've lost our last semblance of a home, and I yearn for new society."

Kelsey felt her mother reading the lines of her face as closely as she might read a book. "I see. Something did happen with Mr. Worth." A large tear slipped down Kelsey's cheek as her mother rubbed her back in a slow, gentle rhythm. "Kelsey I've wondered sometimes whether Pemberley is right for us. I know it's awkward what with our relations here being strained, but I want to stay and see what happens with the captain and—"

Kelsey groaned and flopped onto her stomach, silencing her mother. The truth was too large to contain any longer. "I have to tell you something, Mother, something dreadful."

Her mother's hand slowed on her back. "It can't be that bad."

"It's worse than bad." Kelsey spoke into her pillow, hoping to smother her guilt. "It's positively shameful."

"Then it's best to say it as soon as you can. Delaying only makes it worse."

Kelsey looked up, afraid her mother would see the lie before Kelsey could explain herself. "I don't know how to say this. You're going to hate me."

"I could never hate my own daughter."

Kelsey's eyes stung like nettles. Her mother's attempts to console her only burned her shame more deeply inside. "When we first arrived at Barley Cottage, I was so tired and worried and . . . The way we've survived these past years... I didn't know whether I could keep living like that. So, I . . . I devised a plan, and... Your admirer, the one who has been writing . . ."

"Yes?"

Kelsey took a bracing breath and let the words race down her tongue. "It was me."

"What?"

"I made him up."

"I beg your pardon?"

"I . . ." Kelsey took a shaky breath. "It was never the captain. The bouquet and the letters, it was me all along."

Her mother removed her hand from Kelsey's back, making the hairs on her neck stand as she waited for her mother to speak.

"But . . . the masquerade..."

"That was Mr. Worth, but please don't blame him. He was acting on my behalf. I caught him unaware when you mistook him for the captain. He didn't have time to think. He wanted me to tell you the truth that night, but I couldn't. He was trying to help me." Her stomach twisted as tightly as her knot of lies.

"Kelsey Wickham!"

Never had Kelsey hated the sound of her name so much.

"How could you?"

"I'm so sorry." Kelsey choked back a sob, and the words burst from her tongue like shattering glass. "I saw you rushing into a relationship with Mr. Baxter, and I was so afraid you wouldn't see his flaws. I didn't want you to marry him simply because he paid you attention, and I didn't want to see you get hurt again. I wanted you to be happy."

"It would seem my happiness had very little to do with it." Mrs. Wickham rose with her hand clenching her stomach. She stared at Kelsey with open disgust and spoke in a strained whisper. "I think you are right. We must leave this place as soon as possible." She let the door slam on her way out, making Kelsey and the frames on the walls jump.

Kelsey was stunned by how much it all hurt. How was it even possible to feel worse than she had moments earlier? She would have taken it all back if she could, the bouquet, the letters, the masquerade. She would have left her mother and Mr. Baxter alone.

She would have left Nathaniel alone too.

It would have been simpler if she had. Her heart would never break each time she thought of precious hours spent with him. Her chest would never crack with remorse for not appreciating how often he listened to her worries. She thought of their walks, their jests, and the time he had pulled her into a ditch to save her from the speeding carriage, and never would she look at a dandelion or thistle without recalling their time together in the garden surrounded by weeds.

She would never forget the kiss they had almost shared, that blissfully confusing moment when she had almost let her heart have its way. And she would always remember the moment they stood outside together, testing a temporary engagement that could have extended to forever if she had only had the courage to say yes.

Was happiness always so elusive? Merely an inch away, or a word, or an apology? Or was it across a large divide full of heartaches and disappointments that she couldn't even cross within herself? The divide was a great chasm of misunderstandings, and rather than bridge the distance, all she knew how to do was turn around and run away.

Chapter 29

It is sometimes a disadvantage to be so very guarded. If a woman conceals her affection with the same skill from the object of it, she may lose the opportunity of fixing him.

Jane Austen, *Pride and Prejudice*

❦

Careful to avoid stepping on anything, Kelsey wandered through Barley Cottage, knowing this would be her last hour ever spent there. The place was still in disarray with toppled furniture and rubbish on the floor, and the front door still swung open on its hinge. It was enough to make her wonder whether the place had been ransacked again. Mr. Darcy had commissioned laborers from town to make repairs and add new locks on the doors, but they were not scheduled to come until the following week. By then, Kelsey, Cissy, and their mother would be gone.

Cissy had stayed at Pemberley that morning while Mrs. Wickham and Kelsey sorted through the cottage for any last items that needed to be packed into crates and straw. Her mother worked upstairs while Kelsey worked below. They still had nowhere to live, but Aunt Mary and her new husband in Allendale were willing to help them until they found a suitable place of their own. Kelsey didn't look forward to Aunt Mary's tendency to sermonize, but she was grateful to have a place to go.

Regardless of whether her mother reverted to her usual ways in Allendale, Kelsey was determined not to interfere again. She was simply happy for a new beginning and a chance to leave behind her blunders. Next time would be different. Next time, Kelsey would talk to her mother more, ask her opinion more frequently, and listen with the intent to show more love.

She reached for an old straw bonnet discarded on the floor and laughed. She could even learn why her mother took such pleasure in refashioning those old things. *That would be a start*, she thought. She would learn to know her mother as a person rather than the infamous Lydia Wickham.

The idea was a cool salve to her aching heart, but deeper wounds needed time to heal and time to believe in new ideas.

She tossed the bonnet into the closest crate and continued to make her way through the cottage. There wasn't anything of much value left. The kitchen held broken saucers, a few plates, and a teapot that still needed to be wrapped in cloth before going in a crate. In her room, the only things worth keeping were a worn pair of half-boots and an old shawl. In the sitting room, she found *The Tempest* discarded under the sofa. It had come with the cottage, so she smoothed its creased pages and returned it to the shelf for the next occupant.

With everything else in crates, there was only one last thing Kelsey thought to look for. She went to the tiny space between the wall and windowsill and saw the edges of the captain's note, just visible in the familiar crack. It was a treasure the intruder hadn't discovered.

Two swift knocks sounded on the open door. "Ahem."

Kelsey straightened herself and spun toward the open doorway, feeling caught. Nathaniel stood in the frame with his hat in his hands and his head slightly bowed. His usual grin was absent.

"Nathaniel."

"Forgive me for startling you. I didn't expect to see you here."

She stepped toward him but stopped short. "Why did you come, then?"

He scratched his cheek and looked to the side. "Truthfully, I don't know. I've been walking and thinking a great deal today. I thought coming here might give me some clarity, but . . ." He looked at Kelsey with muted eyes. "I don't think I'll find it."

A lump formed in her throat, making her struggle for words. "Nathaniel, I . . . I don't know what to say. I'm so sorry for what happened at the masquerade. I've wanted to apologize ever since that moment outside. I took advantage of your kindness. I put you in a terrible position, and I . . ." She put a hand on the back of the nearest chair to steady herself. "I hope you can forgive me. For the letters as well. It was all a mistake."

He nodded, never contradicting her. "I suppose it is fortunate I found you today. It saves me the trouble of telling you the news later."

"News?" Why did the word sound foreboding before she knew what he meant?

The floorboards groaned under the weight of his boots as he stepped further in. "Mr. Woodcox persists in his claims on Thistledown Hall. He has involved an entire crew of solicitors, and they have warned me that, given my lack of documentation, my prospects are poor. It is likely I will be forced to leave by the end of the month."

Kelsey counted in her head. Six days.

"Where will you go?"

"What choice do I have but to reenlist? I've done my best to appear confident before Mr. Woodcox, but I'm defeated. I've written to the captain one last time to explain my actions. I don't expect the letter to reach him, but if it ever does, it will be too late to do anything."

His words held a finality that left Kelsey feeling like the trampled straw bonnet she had tossed in the crate.

"Could you not stay with your sister somewhere? In London or West Yorkshire? At least, until something more of the captain is known?"

He shook his head. "I have no desire to subject myself to her meddling, and my stepfather, as I've said before, wants nothing to do with me."

Kelsey wiped the moisture from her eyes before it had the chance to reveal itself on her cheek. Nathaniel now noticed the crates on the floor.

"What's all this?"

Was it foolish of Kelsey to hope the dismay in his voice meant he still cared? "We're leaving too. At the end of the week."

"I see," he breathed out. "It's the fate we had once planned against."

The lump in Kelsey's throat shook against a pathetic laugh. "Ironic, isn't it?"

"So often, we get in our own way. I'm sorry I was not more useful to you."

His words stung bitterly. She had never meant to hurt him or use him, but he was right. She had become the enemy to her own happiness. How could she vanquish such an enemy without getting gravely injured in the process?

As he turned to leave, Kelsey felt a rip inside her that threatened to split her in two. No longer caring to hide her tears, she submitted to the pull of her heart and seized his hand. "I know I've lost your good opinion, but I promise, Nathaniel, if there is anything I can do to regain your affection or at least your friendship, I'll do it."

She watched his face and waited, hoping for some indication her words had meant something to him.

A glance. A nod. He didn't believe her. "Goodbye, Miss Wickham." He pulled his hand from hers and left.

Kelsey watched his figure grow smaller and smaller until he was no longer in view. Not once did he pause. Not once did he look back. The tears flowed hot and swiftly down her face.

"After witnessing such a scene, I don't know what gave you the notion you knew more about love than I did."

Kelsey wiped her cheeks as quickly as she could. She had forgotten about her mother, who was now standing behind her with a hand on her hip, glaring.

"Let me be. I already feel wretched."

"I should say so. It's no wonder you've made a mess of both our lives."

"How can you say that at a time like this?"

"I can say it because I am your mother, and it's time you let me act like it."

"I've never stopped you from acting like a mother." Kelsey would not accept such a burden of blame.

"Perhaps not, and that is my fault, but since you do not disagree that you've made a mess of things, I think it's time you let me take matters into my own hands."

"I don't wish to discuss this with you."

"Perhaps not, but there are things we need to discuss nonetheless."

Kelsey dropped herself onto the sofa and pulled a cushion onto her lap. Her mother lowered herself next to Kelsey and placed a hand on her arm.

"I've spent a great deal of time contemplating why you would lead me to believe I had an admirer writing me letters. As angry as I was to learn the truth, I'll admit it opened my eyes."

"Mother, I—"

"Please. Let me finish."

Kelsey wiped another tear and waited.

"I still don't completely understand your reasons for the charade, but I've decided it's time to make changes. For one thing, I want to be more involved with keeping the books. I'm sorry you've carried that responsibility alone for so long. I took a thorough look at them yesterday while you were walking with Lucia. I have a few questions, but I want to be more aware of what we have and what our expenses are."

"Very well." Kelsey was tempted to argue, but if her mother truly meant it, sharing the financial responsibilities would be a great relief.

"You may not have noticed . . ." Her mother reached for the old bonnet Kelsey had tossed in the crate earlier. "But I've been rather preoccupied with fixing up old bonnets as of late."

"Yes, I have noticed." Kelsey listened, curious what her mother had to say about the bonnets.

"You always were an observant child." She smiled and patted Kelsey's hand. "Well, other people took notice too. I suppose I've been a bit secretive about it because I didn't know what would come of it. You see, a few ladies in Lambton have been bringing me their old bonnets to trim up. Apparently, Mrs. Reynolds has been spreading word that I am rather skilled with them."

"Oh." Kelsey still didn't understand what this had to do with anything.

"The ladies pay me for each bonnet I make over, and they often return with another. Or with a friend who wants improvements made to her hat. I've managed to pay for a few things without having to bother you about them, and I've saved a few pounds for us. So, I might not be a complete failure at keeping the books."

Kelsey sniffled and, in a very unladylike manner, wiped the wetness off her face with her sleeve. Her mother had actually earned income? Through her own innovation? That was news. "Mother. I'm . . . surprised."

The corners of her mother's lips rose. "I don't blame you. Quite uncharacteristic of me, isn't it? Since this is something I can do to help support us, I thought it was time you knew."

Kelsey nodded, realizing what that could mean for their family, even if the extra pounds were a small amount.

"And now to tell you about a decision I have only just come to."

Oh, no. Kelsey braced herself for the announcement that her mother had decided to accept Mr. Baxter's proposal. Her mother's eyes begged for understanding.

"I have decided we are staying here."

Kelsey bolted up, unsure whether the news was better or worse than what she had expected. "What? Why?"

"I think it's for the best."

"But the cottage!" Kelsey tried to pace but had to step over pieces of a broken picture frame. Couldn't her mother see they were practically homeless, nothing but a burden on their relatives?

"Mr. Darcy is going to have everything repaired and we can stay at Pemberley until then."

"What about the gossip? Or Mr. Baxter? Don't you want to remove yourself from his society? He'll be invited to several of the same gatherings if we stay."

Mrs. Wickham sighed and nodded. "I know, but yes. Even at the risk of being gossiped about and seeing Mr. Baxter everywhere we go, I've decided we are staying. It's time I stop running away each time I'm uncomfortable."

How could she? Why was her mother choosing such an inconvenient time to grow up? "What of my say in the matter? I've already told you. I can't tolerate it here any longer."

"What about Mr. Worth?"

Kelsey turned away and caught a glimpse through the window of the path he had just walked down. "What has he to do with anything?" Kelsey instantly regretted her question. She knew her mother had just witnessed her horrible display of emotion and heartache with him.

"He has everything to do with this, Kelsey. You are afraid of him."

"Afraid of him? Nonsense. Besides, he's leaving."

"If he knew how much you loved him, I'm sure he would find a way to make a living here. No, I mean it." She took hold of Kelsey's arm and stood by her side. "I know something has happened between you, but I see the way you look at him when your guard is down. I see what you feel when you're not busy being angry with me."

Kelsey swallowed several times before speaking again. "I've disappointed him, but whatever I feel toward Mr. Worth has nothing to do with you."

"I wish that were true, but I know better. I know what you feel for him, and I know what you feel for me. Your disdain for me, and I dare say for your father, steels your heart against ever admitting that you love anybody. But it's wrong Kelsey. Even if I've made a mistake. Even if I've made a hundred mistakes. Please don't destroy your chance at happiness because of me."

Kelsey wanted to cry out but suddenly couldn't. Her mother's words cut painfully deep, but if Kelsey was going to truly believe them, as she wanted to in that moment, she knew she needed to ask the questions she had always wondered but had never been brave enough to ask. She had spent years piecing together information from gossips and rumors about what had happened between her mother and father those many years ago, but all she had ever formed was an imperfect image with holes and doubt. Going against years of habit, she would have to ask.

At first, she didn't even look at her mother. She only stared at the empty fireplace and tried to prepare her heart to finally hear the details of the shameful history that had led to her birth.

When her mother returned to the sofa, wiping the corner of her eyes, Kelsey sat next to her and spoke softly. "I don't disdain you,

Mother. Or Father, but I do want to know what happened between you. I've known for some time that our family was formed through scandal, but I want to know just how bad it was. Why all the rumors? Why are we always met with such scorn?"

"Oh, Kelsey," her mother sighed. "I'm not sure I can answer that for you." She took a long, heavy breath. "Though, there is much I have never talked about."

Kelsey waited, not daring to speak.

"You deserve to know." Her mother wiped her eyes again and nodded. "Very well. You know your father and I eloped, but you must first understand what I felt as the youngest of five daughters. My mother never had enough time for me, always raving about Jane's beauty. So, I taught myself to capture my mother's attention by being amusing and lighthearted. I learned to focus on my appearance, and I became utterly frivolous.

"I had only recently come out in society when my mother started hoping Jane would marry Mr. Bingley. My competitive nature flared at this. I wanted to prove that I was just as capable as any of my sisters to catch a husband, no matter my age. That's when I met George Wickham. My dear, dear Wickham. My heart was lost to him before he knew he had captured it. There was a great while when I was certain he preferred Lizzy, and for all that time, I hated her."

"Is that why you and Aunt Elizabeth do not always get on well together?"

Her mother lifted a shoulder. "Perhaps initially, but the reasons are always changing. When your father's regiment left Meryton, I was disappointed, but I secretly rejoiced. If I should not have him, at least Lizzy would not either. Imagine my excitement when I met him in Brighton."

Kelsey managed a weak smile. She didn't mind seeing her mother recount those young girlhood memories of falling in love.

"Kelsey, I was set on fire. I was determined that time. I threw myself at him with a vengeance, and I'm afraid he could see it all too clearly. I was ready to agree to anything and everything, and I did. I ran away with him, thinking all the time of how envious my sisters would be. I spent several days sequestered with him in town, humoring myself all the while that we were practically engaged, though the words had never been spoken. I sometimes imagined we were a newly wedded couple, and I looked forward desperately to the time when we would be. I tried broaching the subject with him, but when I saw him avoid it, I began to doubt his intentions. It nearly broke my heart, but he hadn't reckoned on my determination."

Kelsey could easily imagine the events just as her mother described them. "I have always observed that once the decision is made, you do have a talent for getting your way."

Her mother laughed. "Don't I though? Well, George started acting strangely, making excuses and spending more time to himself. One night, I caught him placing his things in a trunk as if he thought to travel. I assailed him with every charm I possessed to make him stay. Say what you will about him, but I think he was rather captivated by me."

Kelsey wasn't sure whether the rosiness in her mother's cheeks was due to embarrassment or pride.

"When Mr. Darcy discovered us, I was secretly thrilled. Our pretend honeymoon was over, and I knew George would have to marry me. Mr. Darcy is also a determined man. It's the one thing we have in common. Just like me, when he sets his mind on something, he gets what he wants. With his help, I became Mrs. Wickham. I triumphed over my sisters. I was raised in my mother's estimation, and I had my dear Wickham all to myself."

"It sounds like you obtained everything you wanted," Kelsey observed. "Were you and Father ever truly happy afterward?"

Mrs. Wickham looked down at her lap. "Some of the time, yes, but I don't know that I ever truly had him all to myself. I don't know how faithful he was to me. I never inquired. Always too afraid of the truth, but I loved him through it all, Kelsey. I promise, I was true to him. We had many trying, tumultuous times, but whatever escapades he may have had, whatever debts we incurred, whenever anything drew him away, I could always draw him back. And you! My goodness, Kelsey, I never saw him dote on anyone as much as he doted on you. Cissy as well once she came along. Sometimes, I think the reason he loved me at all was because of you girls. You belonged to both of us. You connected us."

"Oh, Mother!" The lump in Kelsey's throat finally cleared, and she sobbed. "You never told me!"

"Whatever his faults, Kelsey, there was much to admire about him. I've never seen anyone make friends so easily. As for me, running away with him remains to this day the most scandalous thing I've ever done. I've done many stupid things since then, but none so terrible. I loved your father so recklessly, but I did love him."

"Did you ever regret your actions?"

Tears silently slid down her mother's cheeks.

"How can I answer that? It's an impossible question. If I were to do it all over again with the knowledge I have now, I would do things differently. Of course, I would. I didn't see at the time how great my folly was. Over the years, I learned what I risked, what I did to my family, and what I gave up. I've had to endure snubs and insults. Coming here where the name of Wickham is so well known has been especially difficult. I see how my past puts you and Cissy at a terrible disadvantage. It was part of the reason I was happy to let Cissy visit your Aunt Kitty, to remove her from the talk. I wish I could change the disadvantages and somehow make amends, but if I had made different choices, I would have led a different life. I wouldn't have had you or Cissy, and you girls, my darlings, are the one part of my life I can never regret."

Mrs. Wickham wrapped her arms around Kelsey, and like stepping from the snow into a warm room, her mother's love encircled her and filled her more deeply than she had ever before experienced.

"So, you see, Kelsey," her mother said, kissing her on the forehead, "I can't let you ruin your happiness because of my mistakes. You are so brave, so clever, and so beautiful. I can't let you waste your talents trying to solve my problems. I want you to solve yours."

Kelsey blinked hard, pushing out several more tears. "Mother, I fear it is too late."

"Kelsey, if there is one thing I learned being married to your father, it's that it is never too late."

Chapter 30

*Oh! how heartily did she grieve over every ungracious
sensation she had ever encouraged, every saucy
speech she had ever directed towards him.*

Jane Austen, *Pride and Prejudice*

Kelsey had been walking toward Thistledown Hall for the
past hour. Heedless of the time, she failed to see the colors
fading from the sleepy sky. She was deaf to the sounds of forest chirps
or even her own footsteps. Thoughts in her head drowned out everything else. Though she carried a new reassurance of her mother's love,
she needed time to reconcile herself to defeated hopes and the loss of
Nathaniel who had doubted her apology and was heading toward a
life that would take him away from her. Soon, he would be carried out
to sea by duties that could hurl him through storms or fold him up in
ocean waves.

Pausing for breath, she put a hand to her chest and tried to slow
her rushing heart. Kelsey had spent years retreating behind walls she
had steadily built herself, but no one had warned her that tearing
down her heart's barriers would hurt so keenly. The sharpness of loss

and regret sliced away the pride and deception and a host of other vices that had found a place inside over the years, but the uncertainty of where this raw, fleshy heart would take her left her terrified. She wanted time to cry and mourn until her thoughts found their place among other weary memories. The ruins at the edge of Thistledown Hall was the only place that beckoned her.

Kelsey walked along wondering why she hadn't declared her love for Nathaniel when she'd had the chance. Would it have made a difference if she had? Would he have stayed? Even alone, with no one to judge her or disappoint her, she once again doubted her ability to love.

When the ruins were in sight, she ran. More walls to hide behind. Reaching the stone archway, she leaned against the threshold and let the stone ease the flush in her cheek. She lingered only a moment, lest anyone see her, and ventured to the shady corner of the roofless room where the cherry tree grew.

Slits between the stones allowed the wind to blow in and caress her brow in an almost motherly gesture. As twilight descended, tiny stars winked at Kelsey as playfully as the lights that shined in Nathaniel's eyes. She gazed back, losing herself in the pattern while she imagined all her problems lifting with the wind to be swept away. Yet, the heaviness in her heart anchored her to the stone.

How she had failed Nathaniel! How she had hurt him! She had ruined everything. In her efforts to solve her mother's problems, she had lost control of her own choices until she resembled a rock careening down the side of a cliff.

Unable to bear the hurt, she hugged her knees and sobbed until every last tear had fallen. Minutes or hours might have passed. She couldn't tell, but when her eyes ran dry, she wiped her face with her skirts and finally noticed the red hanging from the cherry tree. Deep red fruit speckled the branches like rubies. Did Nathaniel know the cherries were ripe? Who would eat them after he left?

The sky was darkening, and the breeze continued to stroke her cheeks. She had no choice but to accept her circumstances, no choice but to face the truth. After brushing away hairs that tickled her face, her arms lowered with a growing weariness that urged her to submit. Without realizing it, her lids were lowering . . .

The next thing Kelsey became aware of were voices. Words slithered between dreams and wakefulness until the firmness of stone and the sweet night air roused her senses and pulled her fully awake.

"Beatrice! What are you doing here?"

Kelsey held very still. It was Mr. Woodcox, and he sounded upset. Through the cherry tree leaves, Kelsey saw a black sky dusted with stars. How long had she been asleep?

"I could ask the same thing of you, Edgar."

She recognized the coquettish lilt of Miss Chatham's voice even in a whisper.

"How did you know I would be here? This isn't the time—"

Miss Chatham giggled. "Did I surprise you? Did you think I would be too afraid of a little darkness to find you? I heard you and that carriage driver whispering plans the other night. It was terribly rude of you to exclude me. So, I came to find out for myself what you're doing. Well, Edgar?"

Kelsey hugged her knees to her chest and listened to their low whispers.

"You shouldn't be here."

"Why not? Because it's improper? Because my sister will object? We've rendezvoused like this before, haven't we?"

"Stop, Beatrice. This is different."

"Different? How so?"

Kelsey noticed a tinge of impatience in Miss Chatham's voice.

"You should trust me to take care of things."

"Oh, really? Has Mr. Worth removed himself from Thistledown Hall, then?"

"Not yet. Don't look at me like that. I'm doing everything within my power. He knows he's at a disadvantage. It's only a matter of time before all this is ours."

Kelsey blinked in the darkness and tried to fill the holes their words left behind.

"Oh, Edgar, are you certain this time? I used to play there as a child, you know. Thistledown Hall means a great deal to me."

"Do you think I could forget such an important detail? Success, my dear, is very close."

The puckering sounds of a kiss mixed with the far-off hoot of an owl.

"I want to believe you, but how can success be close when you are prowling around like a thief in the night?"

"Aren't you a curious one tonight. Let me handle the plans. You just keep being lovely." Another smack of lips squelched against Kelsey's ears. "And manage that brother of yours. You know how much I detest the way he meddles in our affairs."

"I've encouraged him to lure Miss Wickham into his charms to keep him distracted, but she isn't cooperating. With a reputation like hers, you'd think it would be a simple matter. Perhaps we'll have more luck with the younger sister now that she's returned."

Kelsey's fists clenched. She was tempted to march before them and order them to keep their distance from Cissy, but she knew she must not be discovered.

"I suppose it hardly matters at this point. They're both of little consequence. Everything is nearly in order."

"*Nearly*," Miss Chatham scoffed. "Everything was *nearly* in order last time. I'm tired of promises. This was to be our place all along, before your reckless brother ever gave it up to Captain Styles. I don't need to remind you that things don't always work according to your plans."

"If Robert had ever breathed a word to me about selling the estate, I might have killed him myself. I would have made him regret the very thought of selling, I assure you. I suffer more than you do from his treachery. Imagine the humiliation of learning the news after his death from his solicitor."

As the anger in his voice rose, the hairs on Kelsey's neck stood, sending waves of shivers throughout her body. Answers to questions she hadn't realized she had were falling into place.

"But I assure you, Thistledown Hall is rightfully mine."

Kelsey wondered how well Miss Chatham understood the depths of Mr. Woodcox's deceit as her voice grew soothingly sweet. "You've been unjustly dealt with, to be sure, which is why I want to know that you have a better reason to promise me the estate this time. I'm tired of living on the charity of my sister. I want to be married, and I want a place of my own, but if I can't rely on you . . ." Her voice grew aloof. "Well, perhaps I should put more effort into tempting Mr. Worth to court me."

"Worth? You would bother with that lout?" Mr. Woodcox's voice grew louder.

Miss Chatham giggled. "Of course not, but I like to see you jealous."

The sounds of a particularly squeaky carriage blended with the smacks of kisses until it grew louder and stopped right outside the ruins.

A new, somewhat familiar voice joined the conversation. "Ho, there, Ed. What's all this? Not mixing business with pleasure tonight, are you? You know we can't bring her along."

"I am aware, Oliver," Mr. Woodcox grumbled. "I didn't know she would be here."

"Well, what now?"

Kelsey risked a small peek through a crack between the stones and saw that the newcomer with the carriage was Mr. Baxter's carriage driver, Oliver Billows. After some minutes of arguing, Miss Chatham, with a triumphant grin, stepped into the carriage. Mr. Woodcox remained outside and closed the door, looked around, then leaned close to the driver. Kelsey slunk back down as quietly as she could and focused on hearing the rest of their conversation.

"We'll take her home, then head straight to Barley Cottage."

"You're certain it's there? Didn't exactly have luck the first time you ransacked the place, did you?" The carriage driver had a louder, gruffer voice.

Mr. Woodcox raised his voice. "Quiet, you dolt!" Then he lowered it again. "Do you think I want Beatrice to know that was me? Just tell me, did you fulfill your task?"

Mr. Billows gave an amused grunt. "If Worth tries to use that fancy carriage of his sister's tonight, he'll soon discover two broken axles."

"Excellent. It's probably an unnecessary precaution, but I don't want to underestimate Worth again. Let him remain on foot if he comes venturing out tonight. Now, let's go in case he sees us out here."

"Right. Best not to get cocky, but I'll admit, I'm losing faith in this plan."

"You already agreed to it, Oliver. Besides, I have more information now. I spoke with the captain's former maid. She once saw him hide something under the hearthstones. Says he was always leaving notes for his lost wife in case she ever returned. Could be the bundle of deeds or a hint that will lead me to it."

"That's well and good, but what about the captain?"

"Once I find the deeds, I won't worry about the captain." Mr. Woodcox seemed to forget his concern to speak softly. "I'll simply destroy the most recent deed written in his name and keep the others. When I demonstrate that I have the collection of deeds passed down through the years, including the one with Robert's name on it, I'll argue that the captain never finished his business with Robert. I'll have all the evidence I need to be rid of Mr. Worth and the captain."

The driver made a low hum. "I hope you're right. I'm not risking my neck for a half-baked plan."

"I don't have time to explain it all again." Mr. Woodcox's voice carried more edge. "You'll get your compensation for keeping quiet."

"Don't forget you also owe me for losing on those horse races in Ashby."

"Do you think I need all your reminders? I've regretted that race ever since. Now, let's go. We've lingered long enough. I don't want Worth or his idiot servant to come out and hear us."

"Fine, fine." The carriage driver sounded amused. "I just figure it's my right to know if I'm driving you." A few seconds passed, and it sounded like the carriage door opened again. "Do you really believe the captain's dead?" the driver hollered.

"Shush! Not so loud. Does it matter? If he ever comes to these parts again, it will be too late."

Miss Chatham called out, "Edgar, what's all the fuss? Come inside before someone comes along." The horses whinnied, and she added,

"But I heard several people say they saw the captain at the ball with their own eyes."

Mr. Woodcox sneered. "Lies, fabricated by Mr. Worth himself, no doubt. Else why have we not seen Captain Styles anywhere else?"

"How clever you are," she said.

"Yes, yes. Now drive on!"

Kelsey risked another look. Mr. Woodcox had climbed inside, and the carriage began to roll.

Chapter 31

*There is a stubbornness about me that never can bear
to be frightened at the will of others. My courage
always rises at every attempt to intimidate me.*

Jane Austen, *Pride and Prejudice*

Once Kelsey had the good sense to start breathing again, she came
to some painful realizations. One, her heart was rioting in her
chest, and she had best do something to calm herself, and two, Mr.
Woodcox thought the deeds to Thistledown Hall or the means to
find them were hidden in her little cottage. Kelsey's mind went to all
the guineas she had found along with the note beneath the windowsill. Would the captain ever leave something as valuable as the deeds
within the cottage? Mr. Woodcox had sounded certain.

So certain, in fact, that he was planning to return right away. Had
she heard him correctly? She reviewed each foul word she could remember him speaking.

She thought of Clarice declaring that deception was a plague on
the soul. Never had she felt the truth of it so keenly. Her heart continued to pound despite her efforts to breathe evenly. She couldn't

risk the deeds falling into Mr. Woodcox's hands, but what to do? Pemberley was too far away to run for help. Mr. Woodcox would be finished and gone by the time she had informed her uncle and spurred him to action. Thistledown Hall was close, but Clarice's carriage had been sabotaged. Kelsey didn't think Nathaniel was accustomed to riding a horse. Would he be able to reach Mr. Woodcox in time on foot? She feared too much time would be wasted going to Thistledown Hall to explain what she'd overheard.

Her thoughts were fuzzy, and the pressure to do something was spinning inside her like a boiling kettle. She needed to act. Might she be able to run ahead and find the deeds before Mr. Woodcox? She would be on foot while they had the advantage of the carriage, but if she started right away and if Mr. Woodcox was taking Miss Chatham home first, Kelsey might barely have time.

She thought of the hurt and disappointment in Nathaniel's face, hurt and disappointment she had caused, and her conviction to do something grew. Maybe it would be folly to run to the cottage, but a hungry yearning inside Kelsey rumbled awake. She needed to prove to herself just as much as to Nathaniel that she was willing to do anything for him, even risk herself. He had already done so much for her. This was her chance to help him and, hope against hope, redeem herself.

Once the carriage creaks faded, Kelsey crept to the open doorway of the ruins. At first, her steps on the shadowed road were hesitant, but she soon set off in a steady sprint. Having travelled the way several times in the past few months, she knew exactly how the road curved through the trees. Before she reached halfway, her lungs were burning, but she couldn't stop. Imagining how thrilled Nathaniel would be if she succeeded kept her moving, but the thought of his forgiveness and love gave her wings.

By the time she reached the cottage, her skin was clammy, her feet stung, and her legs wobbled like pudding, but there was no time to rest. The door to the cottage swung on its broken hinge and urged her inside. The wind whispered a warning to hurry.

She set to work by searching for a tool to help her lift the hearthstones. A broken knife found on the kitchen floor would have to do.

Kelsey immediately went to the fireplace and examined the stones. All looked equally old and solidly laid in the ground. With the blunt end of the broken knife, she tested each one. At first, nothing budged, so Kelsey struck the knife more forcefully between the stones, pressing the tip of the blade in and pushing down to see if she could leverage her weight. The noise she was making would alert any passerby to her presence, but it couldn't be helped.

When not a single stone moved, she began frantically jabbing and trying new angles. Abandoning her purpose was not an option. Finally, one on the far left shuddered as she applied the knife. The dirt and cement surrounding it were looser than she had previously realized. Testing more angles, she found a thin space where her knife wedged in and gained just enough leverage to lift the stone. It was heavier than she had expected, but she managed to slide it over, making a terrible grinding sound.

The smell of damp earth and stale air rushed up at her, making her cough. Beneath the stone was a hollowed-out space about eight or nine inches deep, and at the bottom was a cylindrical metal tube, the kind that might have held a map or a small telescope. Kelsey snatched a torn piece of curtain to protect her hand while reaching in. Even with the cover of the cloth, the dank chill crawled up her arm like tiny insects. Once she had the cylinder, she shook her hand and wiped away the dust and dirt that had accumulated on the metal.

She brought the cylinder close to her face and examined it as best she could in the dim light. Should she open it now or take it straight to Nathaniel? A tiny spider crawled from the capsule onto her hand, making her yelp and drop the capsule as she brushed the spider away.

Nathaniel had better appreciate my sacrifice.

She reached for the capsule and looked around. What now? Her aching toes were swelling in her boots. She didn't think she could survive running back to Thistledown Hall, but Pemberley was even further away. Thistledown Hall would have to do.

Finally. I have the means to help Nathaniel.

Unfortunately, she heard footsteps just outside.

Chapter 32

Are the shades of Pemberley to be thus polluted?

Jane Austen, *Pride and Prejudice*

*B*efore Kelsey had time to think, she dropped to her knees to replace the hearthstone before Mr. Woodcox and the carriage driver discovered her. In her fumbling hands, the weight of the stone seemed to have increased as it repeatedly slipped out of her grip. She was making too much noise.

Footsteps were growing louder.

She would have to leave it. Abandoning the hearth, she snatched up the capsule and raced across the sitting room, leaping into the kitchen with no seconds to spare. The floorboards in the sitting room creaked as they always did when someone stepped inside.

"I'm just saying, you had better find it this time, Ed. We can't keep coming back here like this. Someone's bound to catch us."

"Don't you think I realize that?"

Kelsey's mind raced, but it wasn't nearly as quick as her hammering heart. It was too late to question whether coming had been a mistake. She would have to leave immediately and hope she would be able to make her way without being seen.

"What's that? The stone's been moved. Someone's already been! Who else would have known?"

"You don't suppose the captain returned?"

Kelsey didn't hear what they said after that. She dashed for the back door that led to the garden. With her last step, her foot landed on something long and rounded, and she slipped firmly onto the stone floor. The broken handle of a broom rolled out behind her.

"Who's there?" the men hollered from the sitting room.

Kelsey realized they were coming before her mind fully awakened to the fact that there was a sharp pain in her right wrist. The door to the kitchen flew open, and there stood Mr. Woodcox with the carriage driver behind him. Their faces twisted with what she suspected were very ugly thoughts.

She had to get up, but where was the capsule? She must have dropped it. Her eyes roved the floor.

"Miss Wickham?" Mr. Woodcox's voice was chillingly calm as he inched closer. "Whatever are you doing here?"

The carriage driver looked between the two of them with a derisive smile on his lips.

The capsule was just a few feet to her right. The pain in her wrist was now shooting up her forearm.

"I . . . I live here . . . Or I did, before . . ." She glanced around and couldn't think of anything to say.

Mr. Woodcox advanced another step. "All alone in the middle of the night? It's fortunate we found you. A young girl with your reputation shouldn't be out alone with strange men. Imagine if someone less honorable came along."

The carriage driver snickered.

Kelsey's mouth grew dry. "You're right, I shouldn't . . . My mother will be worried... I'll just get out of your way." Knowing no subtle way to do what she had to do, she reached down and grabbed a cylindrical object at her feet, hoping the darkness would disguise the grains of wood on the broken handle of the broom in order to fool Mr. Woodcox.

When she arose, their eyes met, and she could tell he thought he knew what she held. He lunged for it, but Kelsey held tight. The back door was so close. If she could just get out of his reach, she might be able to reach for the real capsule and lose him in the trees beyond.

The pain in her wrist flared like flames as his fingers clamped around it.

"Uh, what should I do, Ed?" The carriage driver shifted his weight from foot to foot as he stood by the kitchen door.

"Stay where you are. Don't let her through that door. We'll ensure someone finds her here alone with you. Then no one will believe her, whatever she says."

Mr. Woodcox wrenched her fingers and broke her grip. The fear of what he had said shook her last ounces of strength.

"Take it!" she screamed, trying to focus despite her wrist. "And let me go!" As Mr. Woodcox reached for what he thought was the capsule, Kelsey hopped around him to where the real capsule lay. She scooped it up and kicked him from behind, sending him to his knees grunting. She then stumbled through the back door and sprinted into the welcome cover of night.

A smattering of grey clouds outlined by moonlight drifted above as calm as a whisper, but it was a false idea of safety. Each step she took felt as if her feet were landing on prickling ice, and for a moment, as her blood raced through her, she struggled to maintain her balance. But she had to run. If she could just make it to the trees by the road . . .

"Come back here!" Mr. Woodcox and the carriage driver were already on her heels.

"Kelsey! Kelsey!"

At first, she thought she had only imagined it. The faint call of her name, not the angry calls of Mr. Woodcox or the driver, but of someone looking for her. Unable to tell which direction the sound was coming from, she slowed and dared to look around. She saw no one, but her senses were spinning wildly.

A cold, dry hand wrapped around her upper arm. Mr. Woodcox had caught her. The carriage driver had her other arm seconds later. They were now grappling at the far end of the garden near the shed.

"Help! I'm here!" Would anyone come to her aid? Or had she only imagined the kinder voice?

"Kelsey!" The voice grew louder. A male voice, familiar. Had Nathaniel come for her? Did he still care? "Kelsey!" A pair of heavy boots shook the gravel. "Release my niece at once!"

"Uncle!"

"Mr. Darcy!" Mr. Woodcox's voice was laced with fear. "What the devil are you doing here in the middle of the night?"

Mr. Darcy stepped steadily forward. "What am I doing here? Have you forgotten I own the land you're standing on?"

Never had Kelsey been so happy to see the great Fitzwilliam Darcy of Pemberley, who, even in the faintest light, commanded respect with his tall form and radiated strength and dignity with his arched brow and dauntless stance.

The carriage driver relinquished his hold on Kelsey immediately, but Mr. Woodcox reached for Kelsey's free hand and laced his fingers with hers. She froze to the spot.

"I suppose you've caught us," Mr. Woodcox sneered. "We didn't think anyone would disturb us here at this hour, but I suppose there's no hiding now. Is there, my sweet?" He ran a finger slowly down her jaw.

Kelsey's stomach heaved as she leaned away. What a horrific lie, especially in front of her uncle whose scowl continued to deepen.

Mr. Woodcox narrowed his eyes. "Naturally, I want to do the honorable thing, but I won't be persuaded into matrimony without sufficient compensation."

The seconds that passed as Mr. Darcy stepped deliberately closer were torture to Kelsey. What would he say? What would he do? She couldn't be forced into marriage with Mr. Woodcox no matter how compromising her situation appeared. She would rather live out her days as an outcast completely disgraced, which wasn't a far cry from how she already felt.

Her uncle, now very close, stared into Mr. Woodcox's eyes, and for a moment, Kelsey thought her uncle would overcome him merely with a look. Without a word, he broke Mr. Woodcox's chilling hold on her hand. Mr. Woodcox said nothing. Kelsey heaved a deep sigh as her uncle wrapped her hand in the security of his much warmer arm.

"You have the audacity, Mr. Woodcox, to claim my niece's affections when she has just called for help?" Her uncle appeared stronger by the minute. "I can assure you, you have no bargaining power whatsoever. You're going to be disappointed tonight."

She wondered how he could imbue each calm word with such authority, but she didn't question it.

"Uncle, I promise I didn't come to be with him."

"I know, Kelsey."

"You can't possibly believe her word over mine." Mr. Woodcox pointed at her. "She's ruined. We've been caught together in the middle of the night."

"All I see is a lady trying to free herself from two men of questionable repute."

"I'm only the driver!" The carriage driver threw his hands in the air and stepped back. "I haven't done a thing."

"You're at least a witness and at most an accomplice. I'm afraid we're not finished with you."

"No, no. I'm no help. Just the driver. Never meant to stay anyway." He took off at a run.

"Where are you going?" Mr. Woodcox called after him.

"Back to me mum!"

Her uncle didn't seem the least bit concerned that the carriage driver was getting away. The sounds of creaking wheels and horses interrupted the night, which Kelsey assumed was the driver leaving with the carriage.

"Mr. Darcy." Mr. Woodcox still had the gall to speak. "Listen to me. You've never been able to escape the stain George Wickham left on Pemberley. I understand. Naturally, you're upset your niece has fallen into similar trouble."

"The only stain I see is the one you've made, but I intend to purge us of it immediately."

"Right. I knew you were reasonable. I knew you would want to repair the girl's reputation and yours before—"

"Darcy!" Another man's voice called out and footsteps shook the gravel path.

"Good evening, Captain Styles."

Her uncle's gaze never left Mr. Woodcox, but Kelsey looked back with a gasp.

"Captain Styles?" Panic rose in Mr. Woodcox's voice.

"Yes," said Mr. Darcy, "and he's brought a friend of ours with him. I believe you know Mr. Salaway, the constable."

Mr. Salaway was just a few feet away holding the carriage driver's hands behind his back. Kelsey hadn't even heard a scuffle. Mr. Woodcox's every feature filled with fear. He started to step back, away from Kelsey, away from Mr. Darcy.

"I . . . you can't . . . I haven't . . ."

"You've been caught trespassing on my property. The damage you've caused is visible at a glance, and I am aware of the offenses you are attempting against the captain. I have witnesses who will vouch for your guilt, and I'm certain my niece will have other interesting details to add to their accounts."

A touch of her usual courage returned, and Kelsey tightened her grip on her uncle's arm. "I certainly do."

"Constable, Captain, if you would? Come along, Kelsey."

The captain advanced on Mr. Woodcox while her uncle led her away as smoothly as if he were leading her across a ballroom. Kelsey drew upon his composure and held her head high, unwilling to look back to see what was happening behind her.

"How did you know?" she whispered as they approached three carriages waiting at the end of the path, the one belonging to Mr. Woodcox, one marked with the Pemberley insignia, and one that she assumed belonged to Mr. Salaway. One of the Pemberley footmen appeared to be preparing to drive Mr. Woodcox's carriage to, Kelsey assumed, wherever the constable instructed.

After assisting her inside the Pemberley carriage, her uncle settled himself across from her. "When Captain Styles arrived at Pemberley this evening, he told me his suspicions of Mr. Woodcox. We didn't know exactly what he was planning, but when midnight passed and you had not returned, I set out to search for you. The captain went to fetch Mr. Salaway and joined in the search."

"I'm so grateful." Her words sounded small compared to the trouble she had caused.

"Your mother is in hysterics right now, so we had best prepare ourselves for her reaction when she sees you safely returned." His mouth lifted into a slight smile but soon returned to its usual state. "What is that?" He gestured at her hand.

She'd forgotten she was still clutching the capsule. "Oh. I found this in the cottage."

When she held it up, she thought he might take it, but instead, he took her arm and gently looked it over.

"Your wrist is hurt. Are you injured anywhere else?"

"I don't think so. I hurt it when I fell." He looked at her as if trying to discern whether she was telling the truth. "I promise I'm all right. The men didn't have the chance to do anything beyond what you saw."

Kelsey hadn't noticed until now that her wrist was visibly swollen and scratched and lightly smeared with blood. She pulled it back instinctively, still holding the capsule, and didn't say anything further. The pain in her wrist was nothing compared to the heartache in her chest.

Her uncle ran his hand down his face, tugging at lines of worry. "Kelsey, I'm immensely glad we found you in time."

The relief in his eyes and the sincerity in his voice opened a floodgate of emotion. "Uncle, I'm so sorry," she hiccupped. "I went walking in the ruins near Thistledown Hall, and I fell asleep. I never should have ventured to the cottage tonight, but I wanted to help Mr. Worth. I wanted to help Nathaniel!" She blurted his name, no longer caring to pretend propriety. "But I ruined everything, including the last shreds of my reputation. I've been so improper. It simply seems to happen. I'm just as wicked a Wickham as my parents were."

For a good while, all she did was cry. Just as her uncle opened his mouth, the carriage door swung open, and in stepped the captain.

Her uncle cleared his throat and handed her a fresh handkerchief. "Kelsey, allow me to introduce Captain Randolph Styles. Captain, my niece, Miss Kelsey Wickham."

"Captain." She looked up from the handkerchief and the tears stopped.

Captain Styles settled into the seat next to her uncle. "I'm sorry to meet you under such unfortunate circumstances, Miss Wickham." His voice was kind and, to Kelsey's surprise, not unfamiliar. "Did those men hurt you?"

"No . . . perhaps a little. I'm more shaken than anything else, but I . . . I'm sorry, I don't understand. Captain Styles? Does Nathaniel know you are here?"

Was it Kelsey's imagination, or did the captain's eyes droop with guilt?

"No, he does not."

"But . . ." She didn't know whether to be relieved he was sitting across from her or upset he had not returned sooner. "Did you know? Did you realize . . ."

He rubbed his forehead before meeting her eyes again. "I'm not accustomed to confiding in people I've only just met, but considering the ordeal you've been through tonight, I feel I owe you an explanation." His took a shuddering breath. "Did I know that Mr. Woodcox had his eye on Thistledown Hall? Yes. Did I realize he was an outright criminal? No."

She didn't understand. Was that his explanation? Was he going to help Nathaniel or not?

He regarded Kelsey as if deciding how much more to say until his gaze landed on the capsule in her hand. His voice faltered. "How did you come across that?"

She remembered that the capsule, dull and grey and slightly rusted, was his, but her instinct was still to protect it. "I found this in the cottage under the hearthstones."

"Yes, under the . . . but why do you have it? How did you know it was there?"

"I overheard Mr. Woodcox talking." She looked down, not ready to say more.

"You mean to say that capsule had something to do with the trouble you were in with those men tonight?"

"It has everything to do with it." Something happened then, a flicker in the captain's eye, a snippet of moonlight, and she recognized him. "Have we met before, Captain Styles? With masks on?"

He gave one slight nod. "We have."

"Why didn't you reveal yourself at the masquerade? At least to Nathaniel?" Her fear was focusing into an anger that sat in her stomach like a hot coal.

"I had my reasons. Everyone was saying I was dead. What was I to think? Was Nathaniel trying to undermine me? After all my generosity? Was he trying to claim Thistledown Hall as his own before I had yet bequeathed it to him? It was only luck that brought me to Lambton that day to discuss a few matters with Darcy. I wasn't planning on staying, but when I heard the rumors, I had to find out for myself what was transpiring."

"And did you not realize how greatly Nathaniel needed you? That he held the masquerade to counter the rumors claiming you dead?" The coal in Kelsey sparked. She would not let the captain think ill of Nathaniel.

He scratched his cheek and looked as if he wished to be anywhere else but there. "No, I didn't. I didn't know what I was doing. I only wanted to observe Nathaniel and find out whether he's as trustworthy a gentleman as he is a sailor."

"Is that all? Of course, Nathaniel is trustworthy!" The words flew from her lips with the force of truth she had fought so stubbornly to ignore but would never deny again. She trusted no one as well as she trusted Nathaniel.

Her uncle looked between them. "Given the ordeals you have both just experienced, I wonder whether we should postpone this discussion for later."

Kelsey sensed some kind of silent conversation and a decision being made between him and the captain.

"Thank you, Darcy, but as I look at this young lady, harassed by those men because she found my treasure, I can't help but feel our stories are connected." He looked solemnly at her. "They are, aren't they?"

"Yes." She answered, staring at the capsule.

"Very well. I'll tell you my story if you tell me yours."

The coal inside still smoldered, but she loosened her hold on the capsule and offered it to the captain. Moonlight played with shadow as the carriage swayed ever forward. The time to tell the truth had come once again.

As her uncle sat across from her in all his state, with all his principle and pride, the gravity of her situation pressed so suddenly upon her that she thought she might sink. For a moment, that's all she wanted to do rather than explain how and why she knew what she did. All her indiscretions! All her time alone with Nathaniel! Her uncle, who had come to her rescue, and the captain, who was practically a stranger, would hear how she had behaved like a true Wickham. They would want nothing to do with her after hearing her confession.

But it had to be made. The words had to be spoken.

For Nathaniel, she would do it.

Chapter 33

This is an evening of wonders, indeed!

Jane Austen, *Pride and Prejudice*

The last of Kelsey's terrible confession hovered between them like a fading lantern as the carriage pulled its way up the final stretch of road that led to the grand doors of Pemberley. For the first time since Kelsey could remember, she felt free. Miserable, but free. There was strength in knowing that regardless of what happened next, she had nothing to hide.

The captain hadn't yet told his story, but they were already stepping down from the carriage and walking through the doors. Her uncle kept her arm through his, and for a moment, holding to his sustaining strength, she knew what having a father was supposed to feel like.

"Kelsey, my child! I was so worried!"

She had hardly taken more than two steps inside when her mother, still fully dressed, came running, her footsteps echoing with her cries in the cavernous entry hall. There, before the painted cherubs, her mother took her in her arms and swayed from side to side, wetting Kelsey's cheeks with her tears.

"How dare you abuse my nerves tonight! Have you no compassion at all for a mother's heart? If you weren't just delivered safely to my arms, I'd lock you in your room for all eternity!"

Just when Kelsey thought herself completely spent, she choked out a sob.

"I'm so sorry, Mother. I was walking late, and I fell asleep. I..." She glanced at her uncle and wasn't certain how to finish.

To her right, Aunt Elizabeth rushed in and engulfed her husband in a similar embrace. Uncle Darcy delicately brushed the loose hairs from his wife's face and gazed at her as if he wanted nothing more than to kiss her.

Kelsey's mother let her go, then gasped when she saw the captain. "Captain Styles?"

"Miss Bennet? Or rather, Mrs. Wickham."

Though recognition lit his features, he showed no surprise. A clock chimed in the hall, confirming the late hour, while questions thickened by the second.

Mrs. Wickham smiled and dipped into a curtsey. "Wonderful to see you again after all these years." She took Kelsey's arm but kept her eyes on the captain. "You see, Kelsey, I met Captain Styles in Brighton many years ago. I was already determined to catch your father, and I knew Captain Styles was married, but we were friends. The Forsters saw to it that we were all friends, didn't they?"

"They certainly did." He looked like he wanted to say more.

Mrs. Wickham continued in her animated way. "I recognized your name as soon as I'd heard it, but I wasn't certain until just now. Perhaps you'll understand now, Kelsey, why I so readily believed— But, never mind."

Kelsey had to admit, it was a small comfort knowing her mother was more familiar with Captain Styles than she had let on.

The captain turned a friendly eye to Kelsey. "I knew your father as well."

"I'm sorry," Kelsey muttered before she could stop herself.

"Kelsey!" Her mother's jaw dropped.

"Forgive me. I spoke without thinking."

"Never mind," said the captain. "I've learned that tongues become looser after midnight, and that relentless clock in the hall has long passed that hour."

Kelsey wanted to ask him about her father. How well had Captain Styles known him? Had her father ever cheated him? Did he have any stories that might add to her small collection of redeemable moments from her father's life?

"Kelsey!" Cissy and Lucia came running down the stairs in their nightdresses and threw their arms around her.

Mrs. Reynolds entered, looking prim and collected in a plain beige robe that covered her nightdress. "I've laid out tea in the sitting room, if you would all like to follow me." No one needed further prompting. They all followed.

"Your wrist is swollen." Cissy delicately lifted Kelsey's hand.

Kelsey had forgotten about her wrist in the commotion. The pain was settling into a dull ache that only pulled on her muscles when she moved a certain way. Mrs. Reynolds, having heard this exchange, returned some minutes later with a small bundle of ice for Kelsey.

"From the icehouse. For your wrist." She patted Kelsey's arm and took a seat in an out of the way corner where a basket of needlework sat.

Kelsey settled herself into a sofa between her cousin and sister and across from her mother. Captain Styles still held the capsule. As he took his seat, he looked directly at Kelsey and slowly nodded as if he understood her thoughts and questions. Without a word, he twisted off the cap and removed several papers. He offered no explanation, gave no preamble. With his hand trembling, he lifted one of the papers and read.

"To my beloved Lottie. *The course of true love never did run smooth.* Shakespeare." He glanced at everyone's curious faces. "Forgive me. I don't need to read the rest to know what it says. In this note, I explained to Charlotte, my late wife, that if she ever returned to Barley Cottage, she needed only come to Mr. Darcy, who has been guarding the bundle of deeds to Thistledown Hall for me, and he would help her settle herself there."

"Mr. Darcy?" Kelsey leaned forward. "My uncle has the deeds, has had them this entire time?" She thought she might be sick. Once again, she'd chosen a ridiculous path and risked too much. How had such a simple truth been within her reach?

"Indeed," Captain Styles said. "I was here on leave nearly four years ago. I had just made the final payment for Thistledown Hall to Mr. Robert Woodcox. Though I had long since accepted that my wife was lost to me, I still wanted to know what had happened to her. In law, I was still her husband. So, when the purchase was complete, I entered the cottage when it was vacant and deposited this note in the capsule for her. I wanted her to know that I had a secure home for us, if ever she returned. I hoped she would somehow learn of my success."

"But how would she have found your note?" Lucia asked. Kelsey wondered the same thing.

"Because we buried this capsule together when she was expecting our child. It was a time capsule, a symbol of our love. We laid it under the hearthstones the night before I returned to sea. It was the last time I ever saw her." He took a sip from his teacup and took a long breath. "I received word that she gave birth to a healthy baby boy. A few months later, she . . . she ran off with another man and was never seen in these parts again."

No one asked him to continue, but no one stirred from their seats. No one even blinked. The fire crackled on the grate, and Kelsey recognized in the captain's face a desire she had felt less than half an hour ago in the carriage. It was a desire to finish his story, regardless of whether others needed him to. He needed to finish for his own peace of mind.

"Shortly after I acquired Thistledown Hall, Nathaniel Worth came into my service. He caught my attention for many reasons, and after three years serving together and learning about his upbringing, I decided to make him my heir. I thought I was ready to bury the past, but whenever I looked Nathaniel in the eye . . ." The captain shook his head. "I couldn't do it without wondering about my own son. Where was he? Did he know anything about me? I couldn't rest until I knew what had become of him and my wife. A few months ago, I retired from the Royal Navy and came to Darcy."

Mrs. Darcy took her husband's hand and gave him a smile full of unmistakable confidence.

"I asked Darcy to go to London with me and use his connections to see if we might search for information. I kept the whole affair secret. I had no idea whether anything would come of it, but I had to try."

Kelsey realized the captain's search through London must have been the reason why Nathaniel's letters hadn't reached him. No one had known where he was. It finally made sense, but there was another revelation Kelsey made through this discovery. She hiccupped loudly, and all eyes turned to her.

"I'm sorry," she said, "but just to be clear. Uncle Darcy, Aunt Elizabeth, you left for London to help the captain? It wasn't to avoid us? Because we're Wickhams?"

Aunt Elizabeth covered her mouth. "Gracious, no!"

Her uncle's brows knit together. "Were you under that impression? If so, I must apologize. We regretted not being here to welcome you."

"I did worry, but oh, what a relief it is to learn the truth!" Kelsey's wrist began to throb anew, but she felt lighter than she had in months. "Please go on, Captain. I didn't mean to interrupt. Did you find what you were looking for in London?"

He stared at the fire for several seconds. "Yes."

The clock eerily chimed the hour, warning Kelsey that the captain's next words would be the most important he had uttered yet.

"I confirmed what I had suspected all along. Nathaniel Worth is my son."

All breathing stopped. Several hands flew to their mouths, including Kelsey's.

"Worth was my wife's name before we married. After years of wondering and suspecting, I finally have enough evidence to confirm it, but I haven't a clue how I'm going to tell him."

Aunt Elizabeth leaned forward. "After all that effort, I would think you'd be eager to tell him."

"You're right, Mrs. Darcy. I can't tell you how much I appreciated your good sense while your husband and I combed through London, but I'm afraid I cannot face this without trepidation. Once I share the news with Nathaniel, I'll have no choice but to tell him about his mother." The fire snapped suddenly as if reacting to the captain's pain. "I imagine she panicked when I had to leave. She was without family and gave birth alone, and she always hated goodbyes. At least, Mr. Wimpleton took care of her. Though, I don't think they ever married. I suspect they only presented themselves as husband and wife."

Darcy hummed his agreement. "Indeed. The lack of evidence for the marriage was too large to ignore."

"Even after we found Mr. Wimpleton, he wouldn't admit to the scandal, but he didn't deny it either. I suppose he wants to protect his daughter. I don't blame him. It matters little to us anyhow."

"Yes, but you still gained the confidence only truth can bestow," Mr. Darcy said. "That is what matters."

The news settled over the room like a heavy snow drift, hushing out all other thought. The flames above the logs grew short, and eyes began to droop.

Aunt Elizabeth rose. "I hate to end things when we're all so cozy, but I don't think any of us will rise before noon if we don't sleep soon."

The captain was the first to bid everyone good night. Others soon followed his example. Mrs. Reynolds took Kelsey's dripping cloth full of ice and left her to linger under the weight of all she had learned that night.

"Kelsey, one moment." Her uncle took his wife's hand before meeting Kelsey's eyes again.

"Yes, Uncle?" Her wrist throbbed without the ice, and her skin broke out in gooseflesh as she wondered what more there could be to say.

"You should know that Mr. Woodcox was mistaken."

"Yes, I know." Of course, she knew. How could he think she didn't? Mr. Woodcox had spoken nothing but lies.

"I'm referring to what he said about your father leaving a stain on Pemberley. It isn't true."

Kelsey merely stared. Not a single response came to mind.

"Your father," he said, "was my childhood friend. I cared for him like a brother. As we grew, he made many choices that disappointed and pained me as well as those I loved. I carried a grudge for many years. I needed time, but I learned that after the pain comes healing." He looked pointedly at her. "I've learned that no one is stained by another's mistakes no matter what society says. Pemberley is free from that. As are you, if you'll allow yourself to believe it."

Unable to find her voice, she nodded and blinked back several tears. Kelsey bid her aunt and uncle good night and left to ascend the stairs to her room. Did her uncle really believe what he had said? Was he truly able to look at her without seeing her parents' mark upon her? After several steps, she heard the soft hum of her aunt's voice echoing in the great hall.

Though Kelsey hadn't made out the words, she glanced back and saw her aunt and uncle standing with their foreheads pressed together and their arms wrapped lovingly around each other's waists. A wave of truth rushed over Kelsey, and the hall no longer felt like a chilled cavern. The love between her aunt and uncle filled the space and whispered of hope.

Kelsey had already concluded that her aunt and uncle truly loved each other, but it struck her as clearly as the clock chiming the hour that their love had lasted through the years. The way they always reached for one another, the kindness and respect they always showed to each other, and the way they smiled and laughed at jests only they understood were all evidence that those pulls to love and be loved could be permanent.

Though the sight of them embracing in the dim entrance hall wasn't meant for Kelsey, it was that sight, that wave of truth, that finally broke down the last of the defensive rubble around her heart. Love, real love, could be found and could last.

Tomorrow, she could tell Nathaniel the good news.

Chapter 34

In vain have I struggled. It will not do. My feelings
will not be repressed. You must allow me to tell
you how ardently I admire and love you.

Jane Austen, *Pride and Prejudice*

The velvety grey clouds in the distance promised rain, but for all Kelsey saw, the earth was bursting with light and blooming with the colors of life and newness. Never mind that the tailwind that blew her along was shaking newly rusted leaves from trees as autumn drew nearer. She skipped to Thistledown Hall with a springtime song of love and faithfulness buzzing on her lips, and when the urge to sing grew stronger than her voice, she took to the road in sprinting spurts until her lungs ached. Her uncle had offered to send her in one of his carriages, but Kelsey would go to Nathaniel as she always had, simply as herself.

The ruins ahead made her sigh like she was home, and though she was tempted to venture in and pick an armful of cherries, she was more tempted by the thought of returning for the fruit with Nathaniel.

Before leaving Pemberley, Kelsey and the captain had agreed that she was to have the honor of telling Nathaniel that Thistledown Hall was saved. *Of course, I will tell him much more than that,* she sang to herself. The captain would tell Nathaniel everything else after.

The main doors, now sanded and polished, reeled Kelsey in like a fish on the line. There was no hesitation, no wondering whether she should be anywhere else. She pounded the knocker with all the confidence her love had given her.

And waited.

Seconds turned to minutes.

"Nathaniel!" she called. "Nathaniel!" *He must be home. He must!* "Clarice! Joseph! Hannah? Mrs. Smitt! Anyone, please!"

Her rising nerves spread through her like an icy rain. Was she too late? Had Nathaniel left to reenlist? What would she do if he was already on his way to join the crew of a new ship under the authority of a new captain?

Please, no. Please be here, Nathaniel.

But there was no answer.

With her last knock echoing in her chest, she plodded to the side of the house where Nathaniel had broken her heart on the night of the masquerade. His words from that night throbbed in her brain. *I can see you don't put your heart in it.* How could she let him leave holding such a belief? She trudged through the trees and past the softly trickling fountain. A browning leaf drifted from the branches above and fell spinning into the water. Kelsey plucked it out and tossed it on the stone pavement.

"Oh, Nathaniel," she sighed as it sunk to her feet.

"Kelsey?"

She stood so quickly. She nearly fell into the fountain, which she thought would have been a fitting fate for her. "Nathaniel!"

He stood as tall and handsome as ever with his smoky eyes and hair tussled in the wind, but lines of disquiet traced his features. How long had he been there observing her?

"Nathaniel, I'm so glad to see you. I came to find you, but no one answered when I knocked."

He shrugged. "The others are gone, and I went walking."

"I see," Kelsey looked down, suddenly aware of the way several of her hairs were blowing recklessly across her face. She must look a mess after all the running she had done to get there. "For a moment, I wondered whether you had left to reenlist."

He nodded. "I was planning on leaving this morning, but then I received your letter." With those last words, the lines around his mouth lifted into the idea of a smile, hesitant to reveal itself in full.

"My letter?" Kelsey hadn't sent Nathaniel any letter.

"Last night. I was surprised it was delivered so late." He reached into his waistcoat and pulled out a crumpled sheet of paper, which she took and read.

Dearest Nathaniel,

There is something I must confess. I have been a fool. Purely and truly a fool. I've been too scared to admit to you or even to myself that I have fallen completely in love with you. I know you are planning to leave, but please, let it not be on my account. I know you are upset with me, but I beg your forgiveness again and again. I've been too upset with my mother and too afraid to love to let myself see the truth that was before me all along. All I hope for is some way we might still be together.

Yours,
Kelsey Wickham

Nathaniel reached for her, his fingers softly tracing her arm, letting her know he was ready to embrace her if she would allow it. "Your note gave me reason to hope."

Kelsey had to read the letter twice. Then she laughed. "Nathaniel, can't you see? This isn't my handwriting. It's my mother's."

What a trick to play! Was this her mother's revenge? She had called Kelsey a fool twice, but as tempted as Kelsey was to be angry with her mother, she could not regret that the letter had found its way into Nathaniel's hands and made him stay. She felt the success of it keenly.

Nathaniel tightened his jaw and snatched back the paper, scouring the lines with his eyes. "Curse my stupidity for wanting it to be true!" He turned his back to her.

Oh, how Kelsey's stomach plummeted! How the air turned frigid when he removed the warmth of his affection.

"But every word she writes is true, Nathaniel! Even the part about me being a fool."

One glance over his shoulder, and his face softened, but his voice was unyielding. "My feelings cannot bear any more trifling. If I am to believe it still, I must hear it from your own lips."

"Yes. Yes, of course. I was a fool! An utter fool!" She waited for him to face her fully. "And just as she says, I want to be with you."

He stepped closer and let his breath carry his words. "Truly, Kelsey?"

"If you still doubt it, allow me to show you this." Her heart shook like a hummingbird ready to escape as she pulled from her sleeve the metal capsule entrusted to her for this very moment. "This belongs to Captain Styles. I learned of its existence last night and went to the cottage to find it, thinking it might contain the deeds to Thistledown Hall. I worried Mr. Woodcox might find it if I didn't."

"What?" Nathaniel stared at the capsule and wrapped his hand around hers. "Mr. Woodcox? Did he threaten you again?"

Kelsey's skin pleasantly prickled at his touch. "I'm afraid so, but the deeds are safe in my uncle's hands, and Captain Styles has much to tell you himself."

"Captain Styles? Here? You've seen him?"

"Yes. He's at Pemberley." Kelsey thought she could see a small shadow lift from his brow. "Mr. Woodcox was apprehended last night. His claims no longer carry any weight." She placed the capsule on the fountain and laced her fingers with his. "Isn't it wonderful, Nathaniel? You won't have to leave. Thistledown Hall is saved, and you can stay."

He looked at their hands knit together. She waited breathlessly for his smile, for his arms to encircle her and his lips to fall upon hers, but instead, his eyes clouded with confusion and his brows grew heavy like rain clouds.

"Why did you do it, Kelsey?"

"What?" The hummingbird in her chest slammed against her ribs. Did he misunderstand her? Was something else the matter, something she did not comprehend? "I wanted to help you. I did it because I care." She pressed his hand, willing him to finally see she was ready to accept him.

"I . . . I can hardly believe it." He looked at her with all his previous pain and more. "It is, indeed, wonderful news, and I thank you profoundly. But Kelsey, don't you understand? Thistledown Hall is a pile of stone. You are invaluable. Your worth to me can never be measured by grand gestures. All I've wanted is you. All this time, I've wanted you to return my love, but it can't be half-hearted. You say you care and that you want to be with me, but what does that mean? As your neighbor? As your friend? I can give you forgiveness and kindness, but I can't go on as I did before, not when I've grown to be tormented by these walls."

"Nathaniel, what are you saying?" Kelsey's voice shrunk, its strength stolen by the fear of what he might say next, but she clung to his hand, unwilling to let him go.

"I've realized I can't walk the halls of Thistledown Hall or enter its rooms without thinking of you, without seeing you in them. I don't want to pluck the weeds that are growing out here because they remind me of the time we spent pulling them. I even ordered Joseph not to touch them." He chuckled at his own foolishness. "I hear your laughter echoing through the ballroom, and I imagine you sitting at the dining table with me. I can't stay here unless you're by my side, sharing my life as I want to give it." His tone softened. "I can't stay unless you say yes."

"Yes!" she exclaimed with a desperate need to fix what she had broken and a love she could finally declare. "Yes! This time, I say yes!" Her heartbeat thrummed in her chest and reverberated from her fingertips to her toes. "I knew I was falling in love with you ages ago, but I wanted the security of knowing I could love you without hurting you again. I was afraid of myself." She inhaled deeply, reviving her strength. "But I'm not afraid anymore."

"Kelsey." He remained motionless, his hands now returning the pressure of hers. "Did I really just hear you say yes?"

"Yes."

He closed the distance between them and fervently raised her hands to his lips. "Yes, you accept my hand?"

The stars returned to his eyes, and her heart no longer fought the confines of her chest but, instead, settled into the expanding freedom found in its desire at last coming true. "I will do more than accept your hand, Nathaniel." Her breath shook when he guided her hands around his neck, then let his fingers find her curls. "I will marry you, and I'll cherish you. I'll give my whole heart to you and count my blessings every day. And I'll kiss you—"

He leaned in at the invitation, but she placed a quick finger on his lips. She hated the confusion that filled his eyes just then, but there was still one thing she had to say. She took his face in her hands and rubbed her thumbs along his stubble. "Before anything else, you must let me say this. I love you, Nathaniel Worth, completely. I'm not afraid to say it anymore, so I'm going to say it again, and again, and—"

All patience was lost. His lips met hers with all the fervor and warmth of a love finally returned, and she could feel him smile. He might have mumbled something upon her lips about how he loved her too, but Kelsey already knew that. What she didn't know was how his kisses would make the world around them disappear.

Chapter 35

I am the happiest creature in the world.

Jane Austen, *Pride and Prejudice*

When the sun's first rays settled on Kelsey's eyelids that morning, she woke with the restlessness of knowing she was about to be married to the man she loved. After slipping into a heavy, cotton gown, she laced up her half-boots and wrapped two thickly woven shawls over her shoulders. She was halfway down the stairs when her mother poked her head out of her room.

"Kelsey?" she whispered. "Where are you off to so early? Surely, you haven't forgotten what day it is."

"Of course, I haven't." The glow that hadn't left Kelsey's cheeks since becoming engaged to Nathaniel only brightened with the reminder. "Forgive me for waking you. I'm going for a walk. Just a short one before I prepare for the ceremony."

Her mother came down with trembling lips and pulled Kelsey into a hug. "I can't believe my daughter will be married today!" Tears strayed from Mrs. Wickham's cheek to Kelsey's neck. "Before you go, there is something I'm eager to show you."

Treading lightly so as not to wake Cissy, Kelsey followed her mother into her room, wondering what the surprise could be. She already felt like the most fortunate of women just for having Nathaniel, but her uncle had also gifted her with a dowry both generous and unexpected, and Clarice had gifted them two horses and a carriage. Anything else, and Kelsey thought she might burst.

But her mother's gift was much simpler. As soon as Kelsey saw the pearlescent gown on the bed, still reminiscent of a sleeping angel, she sucked in a breath. The fabric gleamed without a single stain.

"Oh, Mother! How?" Kelsey gingerly lifted it and held it against herself, spinning around just as she had when she'd first received it.

"I finished it just last night. The stains were only on the outer skirts. Lucia had extra fabric, so I fashioned a new skirt and added more layers. Cissy helped with the lace." Mrs. Wickham's smile grew hesitant. "I know you wanted to keep things simple with your pink muslin, but I thought you might like to be married in this gown. Do you . . . do you like it? Do you think it will do?"

Kelsey laid the dress down and pulled her mother into another hug. She couldn't imagine a better gift. "Oh, yes. Thank you, Mother. It's perfect."

༄

As damp autumn air brushed her cheeks with the sweet zest of pine and coming frosts, she pulled her shawls close, grateful she had thought to add the extra layer. The sight of the ruins rose beyond the trees, and once again, the feeling of home settled in Kelsey with a sigh. The closer she drew, the more distinctly she felt herself on the threshold of a new life. It was a threshold she once thought she would never cross, but the past months had transformed her and opened her eyes to the possibilities of real love, to her worthiness to love and be loved. Now, she stood eagerly ready to fulfill her newest dreams and discover many more with Nathaniel by her side.

A few steps closer, and she saw him leaning against the stone archway where a door once stood. The sight of him sent her insides fluttering as strongly as ever, but since becoming engaged, Kelsey found those thrilling sensations expanding into something deeper, like roots seeping into the earth, nourishing her whole being with life.

When he saw her, he smiled as if he had been waiting for her, though they had made no such plans. In an instant, she was in his arms.

"Good morning, my bride." He nestled his head onto her shoulder and held her close, his breath setting the tiny hairs on her neck in motion as he spoke. "You couldn't stand to sleep any longer?"

"Exactly," Kelsey sighed in content agreement. "But some say it is bad luck to see the bride before the wedding."

"Fools," Nathaniel happily quipped. "All of them." Without any hesitation, he kissed her as earnestly and tenderly as he had when their lips first met. "I say meeting you here proves you and I are designed for one another."

He took her hand and walked to the roofless room where the cherry tree grew, now with a ring of newly fallen leaves around its trunk. Most cherries were gone, having been either picked and preserved by Mrs. Smitt or eaten on previous visits, but the occasional red still gleamed against the green.

"Are you nervous?" he whispered.

She leaned against his arm and held it tight. "A little. Marriage will be such a change."

"You're absolutely right. Instead of leaving you each night to return to a lonely house, I shall be allowed to stay by your side. And instead of having to worry all the time about whether I'm being proper enough, I'll be able to wrap you in my arms and kiss you as often as you'll let me."

"Which will be all the time." She pulled him into a kiss and savored the warmth of his lips against the cool, morning air.

"And instead of—"

"You've made your point." She traced his knuckles with her fingers and kissed him again. "But are you not at all nervous?"

They strolled through the large stone room and around the tree, searching for any remaining cherries.

"The only thing I'm nervous about," he answered, plucking two cherries joined at the stem, "is whether I will be a good husband. I haven't had any examples to look to."

Each took a cherry and enjoyed the sweetness of the ripened fruit.

"But you have the captain, or rather—"

"My father," he finished. "I'm still reeling from the news."

Kelsey knew. She had not been present when Captain Styles had explained to Nathaniel what had happened and all he had done to confirm the truth, but she knew Nathaniel had been shocked by the revelation.

"It's strange to think I've looked to Captain Styles as a father, but now that I know he is my father, I'm no longer sure how to approach him."

"It will take time to grow accustomed to the idea."

"I know, but do you think it strange that this news makes me more intimidated to be a husband myself? And one day a father?"

Kelsey turned to face him. "Nathaniel Worth, you have nothing to fear." When he didn't look convinced, she placed her hands on his cheeks. "I mean it. Even when I was ungrateful and selfish, you were patient and kind. If anyone's to worry, it's me. I'm the one who doesn't have any talent for—"

His lips were on hers before she could finish. "I may not be a perfect husband, but I will not fail to let my wife know she is the most enchanting, most adored, beloved . . ." He transitioned once more from words to kisses.

"I am not your wife yet," Kelsey reminded him.

His smile turned eager as he led her back the way they had come. "Then I suppose we had best hurry back so we can make it official. I don't want to be late to our own wedding."

She hugged his arm as they walked, still in awe of her happy fortune. "They won't begin without us."

When they stepped into the full sun with the road open before them, he caressed her cheek and admired her with all the brilliance of love finally requited. "True, but I don't want to wait a minute longer than necessary to make you Mrs. Worth."

Mrs. Worth. Though Kelsey couldn't imagine owning a lovelier name, she would never again doubt that worth and love ran deeper than words and outlasted misunderstandings.

"Regardless of my name, Nathaniel, you've already made me feel like a lady of great worth."

"And so you are, my dearest Lady Kelsey."

Acknowledgments

*I*n some ways, this book was very difficult for me to write. I loved the idea early on but worried whether I could write something that would live up to my vision. Then a pandemic hit, and somewhere in the middle of things, I became pregnant with twins. The fact that this book exists is a testament to my love of writing and the amazing people I have in my life who helped me persevere through the self-doubt, fatigue, and various challenges that arose. My husband is still the most amazing support I could ask for, not to mention the best beta-reader and editor ever. He has been patient as I dealt with morning sickness and general pregnancy discomfort, and I'm just so grateful for the countless times he did the dishes and took care of the kids. Even though my kids were not directly involved in the process of writing, they inspire me all the time. I have to again thank my mom and mother-in-law for reading early versions and sharing feedback. My writing group gives me such encouragement and support (thank you, Marjorie, Jenny, Kathleen, and Rachel)! I also really appreciate other authors and friends who took time to read early drafts and give feedback (thank you Julie, Mary-Celeste, Whitney, and Celeste!). I'm also grateful for the help and support of Angela Johnson and the crew at Cedar Fort. I appreciate so much that they were flexible, pleasant to work with, and offered me another opportunity to publish with them. Of course, thank you, my reader friend, for being interested enough in my work to make it this far! Your support and encouragement make a huge difference!

About the Author

As soon as Shelly Powell was old enough to write, she was crafting stories to share with family and friends. Her earliest works featured princesses and mermaids, which she willingly portrayed on the makeshift stages of home and school.

Although Shelly's interests have expanded since then, she still finds writing to be a thrilling process and a unique way to connect with others. She loves happy endings but also believes in happy beginnings. At this time, she is also the author of *Dear Clara* and *Swords and Slippers* and hopes to write many more stories in the years to come.

Shelly enjoys running, yoga, drawing, and spending time with her sweet husband and amazing kids.